CROSSROADS OF THE MEDITERRANEAN

THE SICILY CHRONICLES, PART II

DICK ROSANO

Illustrated by
KARI GILLMAN

To Linda, for her patience and encouragement.

To Maria, Vincenzo, Petronilla, Pietro, Angela, Antonina, and all the other Sicilians from whom I am descended...

...to my father, Vito, from whom I inherited the Sicilian blood...

... and to my daughter, Kristen, to whom I pass on the blood of this ancient people.

HOW TO READ THIS BOOK
NOTES AND ASSISTS:

This book is a work of historical fiction. The events chronicled here are derived from archeological evidence and historical records, but some of the names, characters, places, and specific incidents are the product of the author's imagination and are used with actual people and places in Sicily to illustrate the history of the island and bring it to life. Any resemblance of these characters to actual events, locales, or persons, living or dead, is purely coincidental.

The time frame for *Crossroads of the Mediterranean: The Sicily Chronicles, Part II* begins in the era referred to as B.C.E. or "Before the Common Era," which is the generally accepted scientific reference to the time before the birth of Christ (formerly written as B.C.). In later parts of the book, the reader will note the use of the term C.E., or "Common Era," to refer to the time since the birth of Christ (formerly written as A.D., for Anno Domini). The use of B.C.E. and C.E. is a religion-free nod to today's world of science; however, Vito Trovato, the old man in the story who is mentoring Luca, hasn't accepted the modernization of the term yet and, so, in his quoted passages the reader will still see B.C. and A.D.

The Ancient Place Names list attached at the end of the story describes the names of islands, villages, towns, and cities as they evolved over the millennia. The Vocabulary is an aid in deciphering the words used in antiquity, along with the modern meaning. The List of Characters includes those individuals, both historical and fictional, for each era and portion of the story in which they appear.

This volume, *Crossroads of the Mediterannean: The Sicily Chronicles, Part II*, is preceded by *Islands of Fire: The Sicily Chronicles, Part I*.

LIST OF ILLUSTRATIONS

To have seen Italy without having seen Sicily is to not have seen Italy at all, for Sicily is the clue to everything.

JOHANN WOLFGANG VON GOETHE

AUGUST 2018

CAFÉ AMADEO

Leaving my sociology students behind, I booked a flight to the island of my forefathers. I was cheered by them, envied by some, and I have to admit that I experienced a pre-trip sense of glee and anticipation as the day for departure arrived.

The plan was to rent a car and circumnavigate the island, mostly sticking to the coastline cities that I had read about in the guidebooks. One side of my father's family was from western Sicily, so I decided to begin my sabbatical there.

And "sabbatical" it was. The trip was set for summer so I wouldn't miss any classes, but to explain my extended absence to the university administration, I wrote an essay about roots and how I planned to combine research in my genealogy with a cultural study of the people of the land. I figured I could go back to the late-19th Century, when the movement by the *Fasci Siciliani* rose to counter the influence of the government. The fact that our family tree only went back this far was additional reason for me to begin there.

Arriving in July in Palermo, I did as my plan called for. I rented a car and drove around the coast to Trapani, a city that shared my family's roots with a place on the eastern shore, Siracusa, spelled Siracuse on many American maps. I assumed that since our surname was Siragusa –

a rough transliteration of the city's name – that might be an important place for me to go and pour through church records and official files to unearth more details on the generations of my family before their emigration to the United States.

Since I intended a return to Trapani, I didn't hang there very long and continued the drive around the coastline, arriving at Mazara del Vallo on the southern coast at about the right time to stop for the night. I settled into Hotel Grecu, a little hotel just off the main square and enjoyed a light supper at a nondescript café in the piazza before turning in for the night.

In the morning, I went for a walk and found that I liked the little seaside city. It was large enough to have businesses, shops, schools, and lots of cafés and restaurants. I even walked by a public library that was large enough to exceed my expectations. But then, I thought, what expectations did I have?

I decided to stay in Mazara del Vallo another night, take advantage of what the city offered and use it as the starting point for my sojourn on Sicily. I also figured that the library would be an asset, one that I would spend some time in throughout the afternoon and get my scholarly "feet wet" as they say.

The walk did me good so, upon returning to the hotel, I retrieved my notebook and began scribbling thoughts. I had a laptop computer and knew that it would be better for collecting data, but I also knew that I could carry my notebook in my backpack and always be ready to capture some item of interest.

In the morning, I was anxiouis to begin. Walking around the streets of the city to take in what it offered, I made small notes of government buildings, shrines to the Catholic saints, and churches that I intended to return to. Noon approached and the coffee and fruit of the morning breakfast left me hungry, so I ventured out and found a seat at the same café where I had supper the night before. The food was excellent, far better than the informal appearance of the establishment. I ordered *frutta di mare,* fruit of the sea, since Mazara – in fact all of Sicily – was known for seafood. The assortment of little fried fish arrived on a plate inscribed with "Café Tramonte" printed on its edge. Along with a glass of wine, some fresh bread, and olive oil for dipping, the meal was the perfect remedy for my hunger.

I spent that first afternoon at the library that I had discovered on my morning walk. It was a beautiful old building that housed tens of thousands of books, most of them in Italian. More specifically, I must say that they were Florentine Italian, the official language of the country. I knew from my family stories that Sicilian was a bit different from mainland Italian. More than a dialect, but not quite a different language. I had learned the official Italian language but picked up numerous words and phrases in Sicilian from family gatherings. I was thankful that this library's contents were not written in the local language, although there were some volumes that were clearly that, including a local version of the internationally famous *Il Leopardo* by Giuseppe Tomasi di Lampedusa.

The time spent in the library was very productive. I knew I wouldn't uncover anything about my family there – unless by some wild chance someone in my genealogy had a claim to historical events – but I also knew that the books on these shelves would undoubtedly offer a broad and deep understanding of Sicilian history and culture. I relied on the librarian's advice in finding the right books with which to begin, a tall, kindly gentlemen whose pale complexion suggested that he spent most of the sunny days indoors at his "high court" of learning. He pointed to two shelves with books that were written in English, but I soon discovered that these were mainly novels, and I was in search of history.

When I explained this to him more carefully, spicing my request with what Sicilian jargon that I possessed, it was as if a light went on for him. Brightening up and raising his right index finger as if he was pointing to the light that had suddenly illuminated, he took my hand and guided me to another row of shelves. Pointing very deliberately, he said that these books were just what I was looking for.

He was right. The shelves he had led me to were about Sicilian history and were written in Florentine Italian. Just what I had hoped for. I spent several hours piecing together a chronology of the island working backward from the present time to the 1800s. Upon completing my afternoon work, I stacked up the five books that I had pulled from the shelf. But when I stood to return them to their place, the librarian appeared at my elbow, smiling, and took the books from my hands.

"I will do," he said in accented English.

I smiled back, thanked him, and left the library. It had been a fruitful day, with intermittent visits by my new patron who guided me toward books that fit the research I was doing. I had mentioned to him only that I was delving into Sicilian history – not my own family – and that my aim was to present the findings to my students back in America when the fall semester began. He smiled and seemed to understand most of what I was saying, and I concluded that his English was better than my Sicilian.

That evening I found another place to eat, perched on the edge of the main piazza, and I enjoyed another wonderful meal. I wasn't actually in the town of Marsala but I ventured to order the *Vitello alla Marsala*, assuming that this – one of my favorite dishes back home – should be an unmatched pleasure here in Sicily. I was right. It was an intensely flavorful dish, but not what I had come to expect when that recipe is made by an Italian-American in the States. The veal was very tender and the sauce was richer, a little sweeter than the American version. Wine came with the meal and although I didn't immediately recognize the style, the owner of the little trattoria proudly showed me the bottle and proclaimed that Nero d'Avola was Sicily's own hidden gem.

After dinner and a walk around the piazza that seemed to draw dozens of locals for the evening *passeggiata* – meaning a walk around with friends and family – I retired to the hotel and fell fast asleep.

By morning, I was refreshed and ready to go again, still considering my schedule and itinerary, and how long I should spend in Mazara del Vallo. I packed my notebook, pens, and water bottle and headed out.

I hadn't had any breakfast before leaving the hotel, which sported a nice little dining area with coffee, hard rolls, and fruit. I was regretting having passed up the breakfast, meager though it was, and then I spied a glass-walled café on the corner, Café Amadeo, and slipped inside to supply the nourishment that I had forsaken at the hotel.

Here, I met Vito Trovato, a man of indecipherable age although clearly into his eighties or nineties. He walked with slightly stooped shoulders but without the aid of a cane. He had a full head of gray hair, deeply wrinkled cheeks, and hands veined and curved a bit, seemingly by arthritis. But his eyes shown brightly with a liveliness that was out of sync with the age of his body.

Vito knew immediately who I was although I was certain that we had never met. He slipped into a corner table as if he owned it, signaled once for the barista to bring coffee, and then crooked his finger at me, inviting me to join him at his table.

"You are Luca Siragusa," he said as I approached, although I couldn't understand how he knew that. He proceeded to question me, my plans for research, and my present knowledge of his "country," Sicily. And then he launched into a long discussion of the history of the island, going much farther back than my departure point, into the thousands of years that passed and the changes that occurred on the island.

He said that the librarian was a friend of his and that the two men had shared a dinner the night before, the librarian telling Vito of the stranger from the United States who was here, in Mazara del Vallo, to study the Sicilian people.

It will take all the pages of an entire book to describe Vito Trovato with fairness. His depth of knowledge and intensity of feeling for the island of Sicily made an indelible impression on me. Over our many meetings, I became convined that he is the greatest historian and culturist of Sicily, and I spent several weeks in his company learning about the island, the people, the culture, and how the dozens of countries had invaded it, leveraged it for their own purposes, and subjugated the people and their industries to foreign purposes. The earliest times – from tens of thousands of years ago – Vito described almost as if he had lived them. I captured his comments, anecdotes, and explanations in my journal, but then had to buy extra copies of blank books to continue to absorb all that he was telling me. From ancient geologic eras that defined the Mediterranean basin by tectonic shifts, droughts, floods, and migration, to the political uprisings that refined and defined the Sicilian culture, Vito kept me rapt with his stories.

My earliest conversations with him dealt with the thousands of years before the common era, from the Zanclean Flood in the Pliocene Era and the millennia of volcanic eruptions that built and then sculpted the collection of islands around Sicily, to the invasions of developing cultures who claimed the island as the way station and battleground for exploration of the region. These notes filled three volumes of my writing and I planned to explore those times in a separate volume about Sicily, treating the events and passage of time as the birth of the island.

But I couldn't tear myself from Vito and remained in Mazara del Vallo for the weeks that I had planned to spend touring the island. Instead of seeing Siracusa, Agrigento, Enna, and Cefalù, among the cities on my itinerary, I remained in Mazara del Vallo at this Café Amadeo, sipping espresso with Vito every morning and at times enjoying some wine with him at Trattoria Bettina, recording all that he was telling me about his island.

When the time allotted for my trip was expiring, I pleaded that I should go back to the States but, by that time, my mentor had only reached the time of the Roman invasion of Sicily in the first century before Christ. I knew that my studies were only just beginning, and I knew that I would have to remain in Mazara del Vallo even longer. I calculated the beginning of the fall semester and decided that I could squeeze in another two to three weeks here.

And, so, with Vito's patient – and may I say, eager – acceptance, I stayed in Mazara del Vallo studying with him to learn about the Sicilian people from the time of the Romans to the present day.

71 B.C.E. – 350 C.E.

ROMANS

71 B.C.E.

SIRACUSA

"THEY CAN'T EAT," CAME THE SHOUT. IT CAME FROM THE outskirts of an angry crowd gathered in the piazza, but the words soon turned into a chant.

The Siracusans were talking about the Romans, and what was left out of the chant was the ending: "...without our grain." The city, like most of their island, had been conquered and exploited by the Roman legions, but the citizens weren't without leverage. They knew that Rome possessed little farmland and it coveted the wide grassy plains of the island which produced thousands of ships full of grain each year.

Rome had been expanding its territory for many years, mostly to supply natural resources through taxation. The people of Trinacrium, as Rome called the island, knew this and fought among themselves over whether they should accept the situation, or rebel.

"If we don't send grain, they can't eat," was one side.

"But if we don't send grain, they'll crucify us like they did the slaves who rebelled."

"And," another added, for emphasis, "it's not so bad. They want our grain and they make their bread. But it's only a bit of what we produce. Certainly, we can share it."

For those who resisted, Rome had a response. They would declare their farmland *ager publicus*, public land, and confiscate it. It would then be redistributed among the cooperative farmers – for a price – and farming would resume.

"I said 'no,'" muttered Livaius, a farmer whose land had been taken.

"He's from Lilybaeum," said another, referring to Livaius's village in western Trinacrium. "They lost everything." The speaker didn't mention that everyone in Lilybaeum lost everything. Rome didn't like the city's resistance through the years of war on the island, and so the conquerors set the city up for the harshest punishment.

"We need to eat too," shouted Fenestra. She worked alongside her husband in the fields, often bringing her children out to help, and she hated the taxes levied by Rome.

"Sell it!" came the shout.

The crowd had grown so large and unruly that a bark could come from any corner without the throng knowing its source. But the retort to this suggestion was swift.

"We have nothing left to sell!"

Rome took the first ten per cent of the harvest in taxes and then invited the farmers to sell another ten per cent of their grain for profit. But the second portion was sold at prices set by Rome. The amount of the annual harvest varied with the climate and weather, so the tax and margin for profit would also vary. Roman administrators came each summer to assess the harvest and determine the quantities to be submitted under taxation, leaving room for dishonest appraisals of quantity and quality. If the farmer couldn't meet Rome's demand, or had to give the best crop for the tax, they were often forced to go into debt to the publicans – the Roman tax collectors – to make up the difference.

And Rome only credited the grain that was received by them after transport. Shipping costs would be charged to the farmers, costs which were distributed – sometimes liberally – to the ship captains that Rome sent to collect the grain. The ten per cent levy plus the shipping cost would be taken out of the farmers' purses before the money ever made it back to Trinacrium.

Then there were the pirates who trolled the waters in the sea between Trinacrium and Rome. The farmers were only paid for product that survived the voyage to Ostia, Rome's port, so the farmers were forced to pay for armed ships to accompany the grain shipments.

It was obvious to these farmers that the assessment of the harvest and the shipping costs could be manipulated. The system was ripe for corruption, and the angry mood of this crowd was proof of it.

Rome had declared Trinacrium a province and treated it roughly ever since taking control of the island after the wars with the Punics and the slave rebellions that had erupted twice. In retribution, Rome allowed land in Trinacrium to be parceled out to rich Romans, further alienating the people who had lived for centuries on the island. The rich families who took land required the sharecroppers to supply the grain to cover the usurpers' taxes, and then took their own cut from the remainder as payment for their ownership of the fields.

Many of the Trinacrians were reduced to a status not much better than slaves; in fact, the Roman provincial conquests and victories over the rebellious slave revolts caused the enslaved masses to grow. Between farmers crippled by debt and taxation and restless slaves lamenting their failed revolt, Trinacrium became a tense environment pitting Roman power and money against the citizens of the island.

A squad of Roman soldiers entered the square, forming two lines on either side of governor Gaius Verres who walked through the crowd as if he owned them. Which, in a sense, he did.

"Kill him."

It was barely audible, a plea that was on everyone's mind but no one dared to voice it. Until Timeus spoke out.

But on this occasion, the guards escorting the governor were walking past Timeus when he said it. The soldier in the middle of the guard, one with a red plumed helmet and armored plates covering his legs and chest, swung his head around toward the protester.

"Captain!" he shouted to the squad leader, Antipias Quadras. "Here is a man who would kill our governor."

Timeus tried to slip backward into the crowd and away from the Roman soldiers but he was unsuccessful. They grabbed him and tossed him limp at the feet of the governor. Verres looked down at the frightened man but showed little mercy.

"Fix him to the post and give him one hundred lashes. If that doesn't kill him, hang him by his ankles from the same post until the blood drains from his body."

Then, turning around to survey the crowd around him, Verres said calmly, "The man is a fool. No one can kill the governor."

At Quadras's signal, the soldiers dragged Timeus off to the post in the middle of the square and were tying his hands to it and stripping his cloak as the governor and his escort exited the piazza.

Verres was well known to the people in Siracusa and to those around the island. He had become governor two years ago and was supposed to depart after the first twelve months. But his replacement was caught up in another uprising on the peninsula, so Verres remained as governor for another one-year term, and then another. As the son of a Roman senator, the governor seemed immune from oversight or punishment, and as his time in Trinacrium kept being extended, he assumed that he could do what he wanted.

Which included raising taxes on the island, even for cities that had favored Rome in earlier wars and should have been considered exempt. Verres also confiscated gold and jewels and was even known to impound rare antiquities from his friends. His greed knew no limits, and the people of Trinacrium were his immediate victims.

It's no wonder that the locals harbored fantasies of killing him. But they knew these thoughts were mere fantasies.

At the sound of the cracking of the whip, the crowd began to disperse, just as Verres knew it would. He had enslaved sons of wealthy families on trumped up charges, forced others to pay for their sons' freedom with their money – and sometimes with their daughters – and committed an increasing array of selfish crimes against the entire population of Trinacrium. His reputation was well known and he was despised, but his connections in Rome were enough to protect the governor from reprimand.

"We can find some way, can't we?" There was a small gathering in Fenestra's home and she appealed to them for a solution. "Verres is taking everything we have, and each harvest it is worse. We will all be slaves soon."

"We already are slaves," replied Lilia sullenly. She was Livaius's wife and already familiar with the suffering of the farmers around Siracusa and the rest of the island.

"Verres does what he wants," Livaius chimed in. "There's no power higher than his."

"Not in our country," said Fenestra, "but does Rome care?"

Livaius scoffed at this.

"Of course not. They put him here. And the Romans are getting their grain. Why would they care how he collects it?"

One man had been listening from a darkened corner of the room. At Livaius's comment, he stepped forward and joined the conversation.

"Rome may care," Pilio began, "if they knew."

"How do you mean?" came the reply. "Do you think there are honorable souls in Rome who might despair at Verres's treatment of us? Or is there someone in the Senate who would confront Verres's own father, their colleague, with criticism?"

Pilio shrugged his shoulders at this.

"I believe that Rome wants to continue to get its grain, but it has also fought the slaves and the Punics and is now fighting other tribes around the world. I don't think the powerful ones in Rome want to risk another rebellion here in Trinacrium. They might be warned that Verres poses that potential, and that they should step in and correct the problems that he has caused."

"And, if they do," Fenestra added, "do you think Rome will remake Verres into a virtuous person?"

A gentle chuckle swept the room.

"Of course not," Pilio concluded, "but they could remove him."

———

Despite Verres public show of confidence, he worried that the circle of people he could trust was growing smaller. His habit of leaving no one exempt from his pillaging was alienating those he might need to count on to continue his practices, not to mention to survive.

He had fashioned a powerful career in his youth in Rome, siding with Gaius Marius, a successful and popular Roman general, even when pretenders to Marius's consul position repeated efforts to overthrow him. The general didn't reward Verres particularly well, or publicly, taking the obeisance of the young sycophant for what it was – self-serving praise.

But by manipulating his position and his name, Verres managed to move up the ranks, first as *praetor* of Rome, then – with the help of his father – as the governor of the new province of Trinacrium. In the beginning his path to power showed no outward signs of abating, but Verres still decided to maximize his profits from any position that he assumed.

Now, however, it was different. Verres walked the streets of Siracusa only under guard, less for the pomp and ceremony and more for protection. And when he laid his head down for sleep at night, he insisted on having two armed soldiers outside his door. When, in the early days, he had only one, he became paranoid that this single soldier could betray him and kill him in his sleep. He assumed – or perhaps only hoped – that no two soldiers would dare to act on the same traitorous thoughts simultaneously.

The public tension throughout Siracusa grew worse with each passing month. Verres had been the governor for three years and he believed that he could transform his power into another position in leadership – far from this island. When he gave honest thought to his tenuous situation, he had made so many enemies in Trinacrium that escape was advisable.

"We will arrange a journey to Bruttium," he told Quadras one morning. The captain knew this as the land area at the point of the peninsula, across the strait from Messana.

"I want to meet the new governor there," Verres continued.

Quadras knew that a governor had recently been posted to Bruttium by Rome, but Verres had never shown any interest in another man's position. And the governor certainly wasn't interested in a proposal concerning power sharing.

Verres plan was more complicated. It involved removing himself from Trinacrium under supposedly peaceful purposes, then moving farther up the peninsula and returning to Rome. Quadras had been in the governor's employ for the entire three-year term and was often by his side. It was not difficult for the captain to assess Verres's intent. But the soldier in him compelled him to comply. Besides, Quadras concluded that getting Verres off the island might have additional benefits for him. If Quadras remained on Trinacrium while Verres was traveling toward Rome – and before a new governor could be appointed – he would become the *de facto* ruler, even if only temporarily. And when a new governor took up his post, Quadras would be there to introduce him to the people and practices of the land. An enviable opportunity for a military man with no obvious access to political power.

Verres suggested that the voyage remain "simple," a word he used when he meant to not publicize it. Quadras understood Verres's signals, and this one convinced him even more that the governor had no intention of returning to Trinacrium.

Quietly, over the following few weeks, Quadras made arrangements for three ships to take himself and Verres to Bruttium. The crews were not told who was going nor their destination, but they were instructed to prepare for a few days' journey. The governor had made a point of shipping his pilfered goods off the island over the course of his tenure, so the small convoy would not have to bear a great cargo. Only the gold statues, gilded paintings, elaborate vases, and silver servings that Verres required for his daily enjoyment. Quadras knew that it would be best to leave some common furnishings in place to disguise the intent of governor's departure a bit longer, but he also knew that Verres would not consider leaving any of his treasures behind.

On the appointed morning, the governor rose early while the mist still clung to the harbor in Siracusa. He had his men load five old farm wagons with his remaining personal items and plundered riches, then cover the wagons with woven burlap and a layer of field hay. Departing his quarters under guard, as if he was merely going for a stroll, Verres boarded the largest of the three ships and immediately gave orders to push off.

He was on the sea and out of the harbor at the same hour the farmers were trudging out to their fields for the day's labor.

The departure of the three ships didn't raise any questions, but the arrival on the following day of Marcus Tullius Cicero did. He was not known yet to the people of Trinacrium, but his sudden appearance was cause for much discussion. By then, Verres absence had been noticed and, although he tried to keep his enquiry casual, Cicero's questions indicated that he was pursuing some allegations against the now-departed governor.

Some citizens of Siracusa dared to approach Quadras.

"Is his honor Governor Verres on a journey to procure funds for Trinacrium?" asked one man. He didn't expect an honest answer but wanted to open a dialogue and then judge the manner of the captain's answer.

Quadras did not answer the man at all, but his steely countenance, and Cicero's continuing investigation, led the people to conclude that a change was about to take place.

———

"And you, sir," began Cicero when he questioned a farmer the next afternoon, "how was your harvest? Last year, I mean."

The Roman inquisitor was sitting on one side of a broad desk in the governor's quarters. The thin, dark-haired man across from him had been brought in as part of Cicero's investigation into the activities of the governor who, by that time, had been absent from Siracusa for over a week.

"I mean you no harm," Cicero said to the man. "We are merely following up on some questions that have been raised in Rome."

"About how much we pay in taxes, and whether it is enough?" the man replied. He didn't know yet whether Cicero was on the side of governor Verres but dared to ask a leading question that might incriminate himself and other farmers.

"Quite the opposite," responded Cicero. "We are asking whether you have paid too much."

The farmer leaned back against the chair, wishing to believe the words he had heard, but suspicious of the intent of anyone from Rome, the powerful conqueror that had taken so much from Trinacrium already.

"I have paid the ten per cent," was the first reply, but the man continued. "And I sold another ten per cent to Rome. But that was allowed, as you know." The farmer's defensiveness showed through his thin layer of bravado.

"Yes, of course. But what else?"

The farmer paused, trying to decipher what Cicero was asking. The people of Trinacrium had surrendered much to Verres, including their harvest and their personal possessions, usually at prices far below the true value. And the people had often been forced to surrender their daughters, particularly when Verres toured their country in search of temple adornments to confiscate. The young women were presented to him by his soldiers as companionship for the nights that the governor spent in the rural towns across the island.

The man sighed and stared directly into Cicero's eyes. He believed the interrogator from Rome was looking for the truth, but was he willing to risk his life on that belief? A fleeting image of his wife and young son flashed before him as he opened his mouth to speak.

"The governor buys all the grain we harvest, but I wish he paid more for it."

"What do you mean?"

"If he leaves us no grain for our own families, we need money from the sale to buy food. But he – and his soldiers – buy for such a low price that we can't afford to eat."

"Can you say no?"

The farmer just looked at Cicero without replying.

"Then can you insist on a higher price?"

"No. The governor says that this is the true price. He says the harvest was very small anyway, and it is of poor quality. So, he won't pay any more."

"And was the harvest small? The grain of poor quality?"

"Every year, your honor?" the man replied.

Cicero looked at the farmer for a moment before dismissing him and signaling for his attendants to bring in another Siracusan for questioning. After another two weeks spent investigating the allegations against Verres, Cicero returned to Rome to report his findings.

———

Cicero's journey was kept quiet, given his assignment to investigate poor judgment, at the least, and embezzlement at the most. Verres's crimes were against the people of Trinacium but they were also against Rome.

"Verres was cheating the farmers," Cicero said at Verres's trial. "And his policies or, more precisely, his thievery, is fomenting rebellion."

Cicero paused theatrically in his speech, turned slightly to his right and addressed a new quarter of the Roman Senate before continuing.

"Our republic has already fought wars against the Punics to take Trinacrium, and two more wars to put down the slaves and keep the island. Now we have a new war against the criminal Spartacus."

Turning around to face another portion of the assembly, he added this.

"Rome cannot let the brigand Verres start another avoidable conflict just to fill his own purse. As the Senate knows, I have traveled to Trinacrium and spoken to the people. They have filed specific charges against the governor."

Cicero paused again, lifting his chin and looking up as if he was carefully considering his next words.

"There is an ancient law called *Lex Calpurnia*."

Some of the senators nodded as if they understood what he was referring to. More likely, they only feigned cognizance to impress the men sitting next to and behind them.

"It refers to Lucius Calpurnius Piso, a tribune in my father's day. *Lex Calpurnia* recognizes that not all men chosen by Rome to rule its provinces can be trusted. The law was put in place to control the impulses of particularly evil governors."

There was a stirring among the assembly as the senators took the speaker's inflammatory words – thievery, brigand, evil – and they recognized that the Senate would be forced to take action against Verres.

The governor himself was not in attendance on that day. He had arrived in time for the proceedings and sat through the preliminaries, but as Cicero reported his interviews with the farmers and listed the grievances they filed, Verres grew uneasy. By the third day, as Cicero warmed up to his subject and littered his speech with caustic remarks and vile insults, the governor took his leave.

The prosecution of the former Sicilian governor was so successful that it could not be disputed. After failing twice to subvert the process, Verres' lawyer, Quintus Hortensius faced a determined Cicero whose opening remarks are recorded to have been sufficient in themselves to convict Verres.

Seeing that Verres' prospects of acquittal had grown slim in the face of Cicero's magnificent presentation, the lawyer told Verres that his best option was to flee the country, which he did, going to Massalia on the northern coast of the Mediterranean in exile.

36 B.C.E.

TYRRHENIAN SEA

MANTIUS BENT LOW OVER HIS OAR AND PEERED OUT OF THE SMALL slit in the hull of the ship at the dark, choppy waters beyond. It was quiet belowdecks at this time, in the middle of the night. Beside him slept his benchmate Samson. Mantius was Greek but the snoring man who was slumped over his oar next to him was from Africa. His sweat-glistened skin was as dark as the moonless night that Mantius saw through the oar hole.

Mantius elbowed Samson to push him back away, then returned his attention to the night sky outside his tiny window. Some stars were visible; the night was as cloudless as it was moonless. But the gentle rocking of the ship made it hard for Mantius to concentrate on the star clusters as he had always done in his home in Thera, back in Greece. Now, after having fought and lost a battle between Octavian and Sextus Pompei on these very waves, Mantius was destined to spend all his remaining days chained to the bench of Octavian's ship.

Before his capture, he had been a middle-level sailor in the Greek navy that protected the cities on the eastern half of the island of Trinacrium. He was high enough in the command that he was privy to some of the news that drove events in his life and the lives of all the others who fought these wars. In his ten years of naval service, Mantius had come to know of the assassination of Julius Caesar some years back, and of the rise of Caesar's heir, Octavian, to a position of power. That whole family had dreams of empire and their individual control of Rome and its provinces, exactly why Julius Caesar had himself proclaimed dictator for life. It was a self-serving advancement that led directly to him being attacked by a knife-wielding crowd of other Roman statesmen, and to his death.

Mantius was a proud Greek citizen and he prized the democratic rule of his country. He had come to Sicania – what the Romans called Trinacrium – just as his countrymen had come, to settle in the new land and extend the Greek culture throughout the Middle Sea. So, he was opposed to the rise of Julius Caesar and his followers, particularly Octavian, who most people agreed would rule with less tolerance than his predecessor if allowed to follow Caesar's rise to singular power.

Mantius also knew of Sextus Pompei, a Roman commander who had been successful in battle, successful enough for him to dream of political advancement in the provinces. Pompei wanted a more republican system, with shared power and elected leaders. Mantius thought this followed his native country's example and should be fought for.

A sudden thud on the hull of the ship brought Mantius back from his thoughts, but after a moment of calm, he returned to his reverie. He peered outside again, stooping low enough to look upward toward the stars. He knew that a certain cluster was toward the east, in the direction of Greece, and he hoped to catch a site of it so that he would know that he faced his ancient land. But the gentle rocking of the boat made a blur of the constellations and prevented him from finding the cluster he was seeking.

Pompei's fleet had sailed the Tyrrhenian Sea for weeks, occasionally coming into contact with Octavian's warships. Battles were waged, some won and some lost, and the contest continued. The cities on the eastern side of Sikania favored Pompei, so the boat that Mantius was on would occasionally dock and pick up rations for more sea-faring battles, places like Mylae and Tyndaris, but the slaves chained to their oars were not permitted beyond the deck of the ship. On the open seas, where there was little fear that the slaves would jump ship, Mantius and Samson and the others could come up to breathe the fresh sea air. For once, they were allowed to shit and piss over the side of the boat rather than in their place on the bench below decks. But that was the limit of their freedom.

In the solemn darkness of the hold that night, Mantius dreamed of those sunlit afternoons in the clean air of the sea. He dreamed of his home, and how he got to this awful place in life.

It was a terrible irony that a Greek, like Mantius, who made eastern Sicily his home and who supported the political vision of his captor, Sextus Pompei, would be a slave sentenced to a lifetime of hard labor. He would have willingly fought Octavian above decks and he had experience as a fighter in his earlier life. But Mantius was captured in a battle off the shores of Sikania three years before and he was labeled as an instigator against Roman rule.

He peered once more out of the little porthole made for his oar. The sea was a bit calmer now and the boat rocked a little less. With just a bit of blurring, the constellations began to come into view. Mantius pressed his face up against the porthole and shifted his head so that one eye was positioned directly through the opening. Despite the loss of his paired vision, he thought he could make out some of the star clusters that he was seeking. And, there, yes – there it was. A tiny, closely bundled star group that he knew hung over his original home in Greece.

Mantius stared at this tiny, far-off favor from his homeland for as long as he could, but the shifting of the boat and the waves that tugged on its anchor pulled the star cluster out of view after a few minutes.

———

"Stop it," Mantius said as he elbowed Samson again. "Move!"

It was morning and although the area below decks remained gloomily dark, sunlight peeked in through the portholes and made the horrid conditions of the slaves more apparent. The stench from human waste and sweat, the rough-cut boards used for both bed and seat, and the lonely sighing of pained men long-chained to their billboards made the torture of enslavement as mentally tormenting as the work of an oarsman.

"Sit up. I'm tired of you using me as your pillow," Mantius said, again pushing his elbow into Samson's ribcage. His rough treatment belied a fellowship that all slaves felt for each other. Survival was a primary virtue, but when ships were seized or threatened with capsizing, slaves often worked together to free each other from their chains, or went down to a watery death in their attempt.

The fresh air that was outside the hull couldn't be fully appreciated inside these slave quarters, but Samson pushed his mouth up against the hole near Mantius shoulder and dragged in deep breaths of what air he could capture.

"It is early," Samson said, as if his assessment of time mattered to anyone aboard, these men whose lives would be kept or ended by the whim of the gods.

"Yes, it is," replied Mantius softly. He was still a human, a man in captivity yes, but still a human. And he could appreciate the air, the sky, and his wish for freedom even while all around him seemed devoid of hope.

"So, what would you like for breakfast today, my good sir?" asked Samson. His benchmate's humor always made Mantius smile, in spite of their surroundings.

"A loaf of fresh-baked bread, and some apricots to cut into it. A pitcher of clear water to quench my thirst, and then another of wine to make me smile."

"Oh, well," said Samson with rolling eyes. "That is a tall order, I'm sure!"

"All port!" The cry came from the ladder leading from their deck to above. The voice was loud and insistent, and the legs of the man crying out were appearing on the rungs of the ladder as the oarsmen reached to grip the handles.

"All port!" The command came again as the bearded, armored soldier jumped down from the last steps of the ladder into the oarsmen's deck. "It is time to beat them solidly, or it is time to sink into the sea where the demons will molest you and eat your flesh."

Mantius knew that "beat them" meant the navy commanded by Octavian. His attention went to his oar and he ignored the other threat of eating flesh.

Port was considered the left side of the vessel, and oars were put in from that side to push the boat to the right. Mantius had not pulled an oar in his earlier position in the Greek navy, but had come to know it better from his years in slavery. The Roman design for a boat had no rudder, so steering was accomplished by emphasizing the strength of pull on one side or the other of the vessel. By the time of the Pompei-Octavian naval battles though, a 'steerboard' or 'steorboard' had been developed and deployed on the right side of the boat. By pulling on the steerboard, or by holding it and the steorboard oars in the water and plying backward, ships could make sharper turns rather than simply relying on the over-pull of one side or the other.

Mantius and Samson sat on the steorboard side of this ship, so they held their oars out of the water until commanded to do otherwise. This allowed Mantius a moment to look out the porthole. If they were putting portside oars "all in," the ship would be turning around so that Mantius, on the steorboard side, could see the array of enemy ships that they faced.

What he saw shocked him. Mantius took in a deep breath and Samson cocked his head to see what his oarsmate had spotted.

They were turning the bow of the boat toward the right and, in the sea on that side, Samson and Mantius saw a flotilla of dozens of ships under Octavian's flag. Their ship was turning toward and into the battle.

Just as the maneuver was being completed, and just before the bow had swung full 'round, another cry went up.

"All in!"

That meant port and steorboard oars in the water at once. The smooth arc of the boat as it shifted its weight and direction corrected into a straight line as the vessel came about.

"Pull on!" came another command, reminding the oarsmen of their duty to put their strength into it. The soldier held a rough wooden club that he used to beat a rhythm on the wooden beams that held up the ceiling of this deck. Every two steps, as he spanned the distance from beam to beam, he would strike the heavy column with his stick and the thud would serve as a metronome for the oarsmen to complete another cycle.

"Pull on!" he said again. The water was beginning to quicken at the sides of the boat as the vessel sped forward.

"Pull on!" as he beat the club against the next beam.

"Pull on!" His commands – like his steps – were coming with greater frequency now. Mantius could hear waves breaking on the hull outside the ship. He couldn't take time to look, but he knew that some of the waves were made by enemy ships that threw up a wake as they passed. The sunlight came and went as the looming shapes of warships passed within a man's length from their boat.

"Pull on!" again. The boat began to rock and it became harder for this deck of oarsmen to keep their strokes in the water. The trireme they were on had three decks of oarsmen, and Mantius and Samson were on the highest deck. That mean that their oars were longer and required more effort for the power of their arms to reach the water below.

Soon, the ship began to bob fore and aft as the waves of the battle grew. Shouts and the thunderous clap of ramming could be heard, and the acrid smell of burning wood sifted through the porthole to the slaves chained to their benches. The scattered screams of dying men were now becoming more frequent, and Mantius knew that boarding was taking place on many of the ships – because boarding meant slaying warriors with lances and swords and the screams attested to this.

A crunching sound on the port side shook the boat, but it also caused the hull to suddenly shift sideways. There appeared to be no damage from the collision, and the force of it had driven their boat away from the charging vessel. Another jolt and a similar reaction of their ship happened almost immediately.

"All out!" shouted the Roman soldier. The oarsmen pulled their oars up from the waves and Mantius knew this meant they were going to be still in the water. Oars are used only to move into a contest or to flee it, sometimes to push off against a rushing enemy vessel. Pulling the oars "all out" meant the captain intended to stay put and fight it out.

With a thunderous crash, the pointed bow of a ship rammed into the portside of theirs, right at eye-level across from Mantius. The boards of the hull splintered in a thunderous crash and Mantius could see several of the slaves impaled on the boards and beams of the marauder. Another shove from the ramming ship drove its bow deeper into the oarsmen's deck, unsettling the planks of their quarters and splitting beams that held up the deck above them.

As the bow of the enemy ship retreated and pulled from the hole in Mantius's vessel, it snared the links of chains that held some of the slaves. Those freed by the damage were dragged out of their boat and flung into the sea; those whose chains were only partly severed by the impact but caught by the retreating ship were torn to pieces as some links bound their ankles to their bench while other links were wrenched out by the painted bow of the enemy vessel.

The battle was waged for most of the day, but slowly sounds of battle began moving away from them, still intensely fought, but not upon the deck of their ship. Either it was thought damaged by the enemy and out of service by Octavian's forces, or left to sink. Either way, it seemed hopeless.

A quiet fell over his ship as it drifted beyond the fiery tumult of the center of battle as Mantius dreamed of his home and the family he had left behind. He had not planned to be a warrior, and certainly had not planned to be a slave. But his mother would probably never see him again, no matter what his fate on this day or the next.

"And what would you like for supper, my good sir?"

It was the first time Mantius thought of Samson during the struggles of that afternoon. The terror of the battle and the nearness of death had occupied his every thought. Now, he turned toward his oarsmate who was slumped over slightly. Samson was not asleep, that was obvious; something more cruel had doubled him over.

There was a jagged, blood-stained, splinter the thickness of a man's arm protruding from the man's stomach. It was either a beam from the ceiling of their captive space or a ragged edge ripped from the hull itself with the impact. The smile on the black slave's face hid the horrible pain he must have been in. Mantius wasn't sure what to do, but he was certain that Samson's injury would be his last. Deciding whether to pull the wooden shard out of his friend or drive it fully in to end the man's life seemed to be his only choices. And neither was welcome.

As the boat listed to steorboard, the smell of fire and smoke began filling this third deck. It was the first time that Mantius thought about the silence he had taken some comfort in. There would be no silence if there were still Roman soldiers on the vessel. Instead, it was quiet, which now he realized was because the Romans had abandoned the ship. And the tilting into the water meant they were all doomed.

Mantius refocused on his mate. He resolved to push the wooden spear into the man's body and save him the pain of drowning as the ship went down.

"I wish I had a wooden beam sticking out of my belly, too," he muttered before the final thrust.

Mantius was caught up in the sounds of dying boat, the creaking of splintered wood, the occasional thud of a rail or beam that fell to the deck above his head, the eerie whistling of the wind that blew through the holes in the ship that he was chained to. A rocking motion that went side to side gave courage that the vessel would remain on the surface, although an occasional jolt as the hull tipped sideways dispelled any brief hopes of survival.

The deck and benches they were chained to tilted sideways and water splashed upon the floorboards. With an unearthly shrieks of metal and wood, the hull boards themselves began to give way, sliding surface upon surface, the iron nails intended to fasten the craft together instead ripping the wood apart. There was another jolt as a wave from a passing ship flooded the deck where Mantius and Samson sat, shackled to their bench.

Once again, quiet, a rocking of the boat, with sounds of battle growing more distant.

"The others down below," Mantius murmured to his oarsmate, "are already drinking sea water." He meant the slaves chained to the two decks below on this trireme, clearly already submerged by the waves. He wondered what it would feel like to gasp for breath, to savor an occasional respite in a receding wave to gulp once more of heaven's air. And he wondered how long he could hold his breath when he knew the ship was headed for the sea gods' bottom.

As the water that now swirled around his feet and legs became deeper, Mantius sat cradling Samson in his arms. Leaning into his friend, he put his right hand on the butt of the wood that impaled Samson and shoved it cleanly through the black man's chest. A heave from Samson, and a smile of satisfaction, and Mantius knew he had saved the man chained next to him from the horror of drowning.

Mantius didn't get to enjoy the same reprieve.

AUGUST 2018

CAFÉ AMADEO

"Octavian ruled Rome, though," I began. The slowness of my comment disguised my attempt to find the right page in the book I had borrowed from the library.

"Yes, here it is," I said, with the little triumph caught in my throat. "Octavian, the first Emperor of Rome."

"Yes, certainly," said Vito between sips of his espresso. "But you can't be an emperor without an empire."

The point seemed obvious, so I waited for more. Besides, I wanted to know why this mattered to Sicily.

"Octavian wanted to rule Rome as a dictator," he began, "much like his mentor, Julius Caesar. It had been a republic until that time, but Julius was trying to take ultimate control so that he could be sole master of Rome and its provinces. It was his desire to become *dictator perpetuus,* a plan that threatened the power structure and led to his downfall."

"Pompei wanted it to remain a republic, right?" I asked.

"Precisely. And Octavian, Caesar's chosen successor wanted an empire."

"So I assume that Octavian won the struggle, or else Rome wouldn't have become an empire, and he wouldn't have become its first emperor."

Vito's smile was a sufficient congratulation for me.

"But that still doesn't explain what Octavian's victory over Sextus Pompei meant for Sicily."

The barista brought another round of espressos and a plate of orange slices, which Vito immediately turned his attention to. After a few moments watching – and listening to – him suck on the orange rinds, I pulled his attention back to the subject.

"Caesar intended to make the people of Sicily into Roman citizens," he began once he had wiped his lips with the thin paper napkin next to his plate. "That would require that their cities be recognized beyond the simple status as urban aggregations into a province that Rome considered their granary. In fact, these cities – Panormus, Siracusa, Katane, Thermae, and Tyndaris – were classed as colonies of Rome, a higher status than before and, consequently, a number of rights were bestowed on their citizens."

"Like?"

"They could vote, work for the Roman government, and hold office in a Roman administration. But there was a catch."

"What was that?"

"Rome, and Octavian who now ruled the empire, still didn't trust the Greeks and Carthaginians who populated the island. After the wars were over..."

"Wait. The wars never really ended, did they?" I asked.

Vito smiled and tipped his cup in my direction.

"I'm sure you would be safe in concluding that wars, particularly those fought on Sicily, never ended. But, back to my point: Rome decided to replace the citizens of these honored colonies with their own people."

"Replace? What did Rome do with the original Siracusans, Panormians, and so on?"

"They were deported or shoved aside into minor roles in the region. The point is, though, that Rome was bringing in new people in such great numbers that they could effectively replace the sitting population and assume positions of citizenship with control of the offices, laws, and courts of these new colonies."

"So, in a way, Rome declaring these cities as new colonies was a matter of sleight of hand."

"I don't know that phrase," begged Vito.

"It means to substitute something in place of what the observer thinks is real."

"*Perfettu*," replied Vito, raising his cup in salute. "This was precisely right. I'll have to remember that American phrase. Anyway, Octavian ordered control of Sicily in a new way. The best and most important cities were transformed into Roman colonies, the cities like Gela and Selinunte that clung to their Greekness were eliminated, and Sicily-as-granary resumed production of its supply of essential farming produce, with a plan that most or all of it would go to Rome.

"As Rome's power expanded and as its territories increased, grain, fruit, oil, and other products could be sourced from elsewhere. Over the years, Sicily lost its spot as the sole provider of these important things. The Romans showed renewed interest in the eastern portion of the Mediterranean Sea and in North Africa, so the reliance on Sicilian grain was relaxed. It could have been that this reduced dependence on the island's farming contributed to the declining interest in Sicily at the time, and the slow slippage of the island's culture during the latter part of the Roman Empire, coinciding with the onset of the Middle Ages."

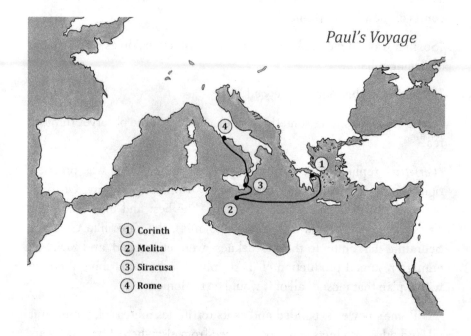

Paul's Voyage

1 Corinth
2 Melita
3 Siracusa
4 Rome

59 C.E.

SIRACUSA

THE SEAS WERE HIGH AS THE BOAT NEARED THE PORT OF SIRACUSA. It was not fit for a long voyage, too small for many nights on the water, but Balfornus, the captain, assured his passengers that the voyage would make port in Rome as planned.

They disembarked from Corinth, in the islands of Greece, a few weeks before and proceeded on their circuitous route to the island of Melita just south of Trinacrium. There they made port and planned to bring on some supplies before proceeding to Siracusa. Saul stood beside the captain on the deck, looking toward the spit of land ahead.

"It is a good night," Balfornus said to Saul, who couldn't understand his captain's confidence.

"Yes, it is," Saul replied, to be gracious. Balfornus nodded in his direction and smiled, then returned to his duties as captain of the ship. Saul returned to his position on the rail. The idle time allowed him to think, and the gentle undulation of the waves relaxed him.

Saul was born into a Jewish family in Tarsus but spent many of his early years in Shalem, an Israelite holy city in the Kingdom of Judah. His father was a Roman citizen which allowed Saul to enjoy the rights of any other Roman. And, like many Jews of that era with Roman connections, he had two names: Saul and Paul.

His Roman lineage made him skeptical of a new cult that followed the teachings of a dead mystic named Jesus. With his upbringing, his father's status, and a strong association with the Empire, Saul soon found himself pursuing these people called Christians and bringing them before the legal powers in the region.

It was on a journey to Damascus to arrest some of the new cultists that Saul was thrown from his horse and left dazed and groggy. His men helped him to recover, and he told them of visions he had had.

"You were knocked unconscious by the fall," said one attendant. "I would be seeing stars myself!"

"No, you don't understand me. I saw..." but his voiced drifted off. He knew he had experienced visions and was confident that they were of the mystic himself. But Saul knew the man had been crucified – he was dead – and he wouldn't be encountered on this road to Damascus. As his senses returned to him, he thought at first that his story would make the others believe he had gone mad. So, he kept his thoughts to himself for a time.

By the next morning though, as his headache and pain had subsided, Saul still had a clear vision of Jesus from the encounter. The spirit of the dead man had come to Saul and challenged him to cease persecution of his followers. Saul chose to believe that this was a true revelation and decided that he would share it with the men accompanying him on this mission.

"Paul," said a Roman soldier when he heard the story, "this can only be the deranged thoughts of a madman. Don't share it. We have far to go and many things to do. If you create confusion in the minds of the men, this mission will dissolve. And you will probably be thrown into a jail cell."

"Saul," added the wizened old Jewish man who sat by his bedside. "He is right. You were thrown from your horse, you fell on your head, and then you had visions. Everyone would think these 'visions' were the result of the pain in your head. Besides," he added, with a crooked finger pointing to the sky, "he is dead. This Jesus fellow was crucified."

The mission continued but by then Saul was convinced that he would not arrest any of the Jesus's followers. In fact, as day came after day, Saul began to think of himself as a follower of the holy man, and he began asking questions of those around him. The old Jewish man told him what he knew of the history of Jesus, having come from the same city of Jerusalem, but he continued to remind Saul that the man was dead.

Saul adopted the teachings of Jesus and preached his mission throughout the region. It was in Corinth, after being hounded by the authorities for a few years that Saul was arrested himself and threatened with trial. Using his Roman citizenship as a shield, he requested that he be tried in Rome, which brought him to be on Balfornus's ship on its way from Corinth to Rome, via Siracusa.

Gentle waves rocked the boat as it approached the dock and Saul continued with his musings. It was almost as if the undulating movement of the boat was a signal to him of peace and calm ahead. Saul believed in Jesus and his teachings and had proclaimed his divinity in his teachings throughout the world. When the boat was roped to the dock in Siracusa, Saul approached Balfornus.

"I would like to go ashore," he told the captain.

"That would be quite unusual, Paul," came the reply, although the captain smiled as if to say he didn't intend to deny the request.

"I would like to see for myself what everyone says about Siracusa," Saul continued, "and judge on my own if it is as beautiful a city as the Greeks and Romans have claimed."

This was almost a challenge for Balfornus, proud as he was of the provinces that his Rome had captured. He treated Saul with a light hand, not convinced that a man who preached love and sacrifice could be a threat to the Empire. So, he was quite ready to let the bearded prophet disembark and wander the streets of Siracusa. Under guard, of course.

Saul disembarked and walked up the wooden planks of the dock, followed closely by a single Roman soldier armed with a *pugio*, a small dagger intended more to ward off any threats rather than actually carry out a fight. The pair walked together toward the center of the city, through the marketplace and into the piazza where an orator was holding the attention of the crowd. He spoke in Greek, which was the common language in this part of Trinacrium, even though the island had long been a Roman province. Saul understood both Latin and Greek, so he stood for a moment listening to the man's spirited sermon about the threats from beyond their city. Saul was not sure of the identity of the people the speaker was calling out, as Trinacrium had already developed a long list of enemies and invaders, but he enjoyed the man's emotional rendition.

The armed Roman soldier by his side knew very little Greek.

"Why should I learn the language of the heathen?" he asked Saul.

Saul smiled at the soldier, twenty years younger than he himself, too young to respect the history of the Greek culture and the impact of the Greek adventurers who had settled in this land.

The two men returned to their ship before nightfall, according to Balfornus's orders, and Saul recounted for him the beautiful Siracusan architecture, the wide streets, and the towering fortress at its peak.

"Of course," responded Balfornus with a condescending smile. He was a few years younger than Saul but had traveled more than the preacher, and he had seen Siracusa close up many times already.

"I would like to go ashore once again. Tomorrow, if I may."

Balfornus had allowed Saul to walk into Siracusa that day, not fearing the possibility of trouble, but the preacher's request for an additional visit made the captain uneasy. Saul's curiosity about the city should already be satisfied, 'what would be his purpose in returning?' the captain wondered.

Despite his misgivings, Balfornus decided to let the man go ashore again. He liked Saul and had many fine debates with him while on the waves of *Mare Nostrum*, the Roman name for "our sea," a clear indication to all that the Empire had claimed the entire region. So, with only some reservations, Balfornus agreed to let Saul return to Siracusa on the following morning.

"But Taritius will be there once more," the captain said, speaking of the soldier who accompanied Saul.

"I want to be sure that you won't stir up trouble and make me add to your charges," Balfornus added. And, yet, he smiled at his captive, revealing his kindness and respect for the man.

The next morning Saul and Taritius went ashore and walked directly into the center of the city. Saul had a specific destination in mind, so instead of wandering the streets and squares as they did the day before, Saul went straight to the piazza where the orator stood on the previous afternoon. Taritius followed closely but didn't immediately suspect anything. The captain treated this man like a friend, the soldier reminded himself. 'What could he do?' he thought.

When they made it to the piazza, Saul went straight to the raised stone platform in the center and mounted it with ease, despite his advanced age. Taritius quickly knew that something was not good about this, but Saul's speech was made in Greek, so the soldier couldn't piece together what was being said. His eyes darted left and right, trying to extract from the crowd's reaction what Saul was saying, but he gained little from this strategy.

After allowing his charge to speak for many minutes, Taritius approached the back of the platform and shook Saul's robes.

"We must go," he pleaded. "This is not why we came here."

Saul looked down at the young man with kindness and sympathy, then he turned back to the crowd and completed his sermon in short order. Stepping down from the platform, he faced Taritius.

"What were you saying?" asked the soldier.

"I was telling them that Jesus of Nazareth was their savior, and that his followers, like me, are bringing the word of the Lord to them."

Taritius was beginning to panic at Saul's telling.

"I told them that they would find peace and eternal life if they followed his teachings. And I said that I would return from my journey to Rome and tell them more about Jesus and his mission."

Taritius put his hand lightly on Saul's elbow and swung him around toward the edge of the crowd. The speech had been well received, although most of the people in the crowd were questioning each other about the words he spoke instead of approaching Saul. So, it was easy for the soldier to get his charge out of the piazza and back to the ship.

On their return, as they walked along the docks, Taritius asked Saul not to talk of this with the captain.

"He will be displeased," the young man said. "I doubt he will take out his displeasure on you...but then there is also me."

Saul assured his escort that he would say nothing to Balfornus unless asked. But, if asked, he would not lie.

Fortunately for Taritius, the only question the captain had for Saul was about the riches of the city. Balfornus, too, suspected that some problem could result from letting Saul go into the city, and he didn't want to know anything if it had turned out that way.

The next morning, when the wind was up, they set sail for Rhegium on the tip of the mainland, and nothing more was said between Balfornus and Saul about their brief stay in Siracusa.

350 C.E.

VILLA ROMANA DEL CASALE

Nomitius stood on the low wall of stone that was laid to surround the villa taking shape within the enclosure. His eyes traced the outline of the stone wall that ran off for a hundred cubits before turning a sharp corner and disappearing behind the tall stone walls of the villa itself. He had overseen the construction of several of these grand villas, but they were usually on mountaintops and difficult to reach. Huge building blocks and all the instruments of construction had to be drawn up steep inclines, rocky slopes and hills chosen by the rich owner as security against attack.

This villa was located on a low hill, in a valley between larger hills. The choice of such a low spot indicated that the owner, Proculus Populonius, governor of Trinacrium, did not fear attack. Nomitius laughed at the thought. The island had enjoyed many years of relative peace, but the builder knew that the people of this land could only hope to avoid a new war for a little while, no more than a single man's lifetime, and perhaps less. His master, the governor, was calm about his choice, but Nomitius wondered how long it would be before a marauding force took the villa by storm and desecrated it.

"Hopefully, not before I complete the work," he muttered to himself.

The footprint of the structure had been stepped out by Nomitius three years earlier when construction began. He understood right away why this plot of land was chosen. It was as flat as a tabletop and allowed him to design a grand structure of massive size without having to tailor the foundation to the dips, slopes, and crevices of a hilltop location.

Most of the building materials would come from the fields around Enna, just a half day's ride away, and most of the labor would be supplied by the slaves taken in earlier Roman conquests. Nomitius took the free labor for granted; in fact, he never even considered a situation in which labor would have to be sought out and paid for. Slavery was an institution throughout the history of the known world, and slaves were as ubiquitous as wild animals, and worth only a little more.

The builder's concerns focused on design, layout, and supplies – not labor.

A dark spot moved slowly across the valley in the distance, tracing the rough outline of the dirt road that had been worn down by the three years of construction activity. Nomitius couldn't see much of it from afar but noticed the small cloud of dust that trailed the spot as it grew in size on the approach. After about an hour, he could make out the outlines of three horse-drawn wagons moving slowly toward him and, when they were closer still, he could hear the horses snorting as they struggled to pull the weight of the wagons laden with stone and marble.

By noon, the wagoneers had pulled their cargo up to the work shed on the fringe of Nomitius's project. They unhitched the horses and led them to water and shade, then a short man among the trio of drivers approached the builder.

"Hallo," he said with right hand raised to head level. "How is the work?"

"It is coming along very well, Cantone," replied Nomitius.

The man may have been short, but his broad shoulders and muscled arms warned even taller men to avoid trouble with him. Cantone was also a builder, but he preferred to work supplying the materials rather than be stuck at the site all year long. Especially on this project. He wanted to return to Enna for a good night's sleep and a whore and jug of wine. He knew that Nomitius kept a slave woman here at the Villa Casale, 'but why have just one to choose from,' thought Cantone.

The two men consulted their inventory sheets to compare written records of the supplies and carved stone. The wagons could only bring the smaller stones by that road; Nomitius and Cantone were working with quarrymen in the nearby valley to cut and transport the larger stones for the villa so less travel was required.

Cantone's wagons also brought more mosaic tile for decorating the villa. The entire structure had made much progress in just the last few months under Nomitius's direction, so it was time to begin stockpiling the tiny painted chips of glass and marble for the artisans to use in laying the floor of the villa.

The governor had grand plans for this house. He chose the widest plateau to allow the longest and widest mosaics to be constructed. He cared little about the rooms within his villa. It was being built primarily as proof of his wealth and power, and he ordered Nomitius to oversee the laying out of massive mosaic works showing hunting and fishing scenes. Proculus Populonius was going to prove to everyone who visited his Villa Casale in the plains of central Trinacrium that he was the richest and most accomplished governor that the island had ever seen.

A dark-skinned female slave approached the two men as they stood in the shade of the trees around the villa. She was a young beauty, with high cheeks, a high forehead, and lush lips. Her slender physique suggested that she was not kept for hard labor, unless one would consider sleeping with Nomitius to be hard labor.

"Thank you, Daphne," said Nomitius, as the slave handed them a jug of water. The smooth condensation on its outer surface made it clear that Daphne had drawn the water from a deep well, perfect refreshment to drive the road dust from Cantone's parched throat.

"So, this is it," said Cantone after taking a deep gulp of the cold water. He was looking at the high walls of the villa and the surrounding walls. His nodding smile suggested his approval of the progress.

"We have done much since you were here last, my friend," commented Nomitius. "Look over here," he said, inclining his head toward the western façade of the estate. He raised his arm and pointed toward where a massive stone arch was being assembled by the workers. Cantone was familiar with this strategy of building in which a wooden arch is built as a scaffold, then beveled stones are set in series around the arch, reaching upward from the left and right sides simultaneously. The two builders were there at just the right moment as they were able to witness the tapered keystone being hammered into the narrow opening between the two rising stone curves. When that top stone was set in place, it put pressure on the sides of the arch and forced the assembled stones to hold their position, after which the laborers could kick out the wooden scaffold and open the arched doorway.

"It leads to the main entrance?" he asked.

"No, to the baths," Nomitius replied, drawing a hungry sigh from his visitor. The water quenched his thirst but Cantone wished he could wash the dirt from his skin out here on the plains. Sensing his desire, Nomitius called Europa over to join them. She, too, was a slave, but one taken from a Greek conquest. Her skin was lighter than Daphne's, and she had shiny brown hair held up by a clip and a low-slung toga covering her chest and mid-section.

Cantone didn't recall this one from his earlier visit but looked at her with approval.

"She will show me to the baths?" he said, with some further expectation in his voice.

Nomitius laughed.

"No, of course not. We have no baths here yet. But there is a stream in the vineyard down the hill. She will take you to that place and help you get comfortable after your long journey."

"It was a long one," Nomitius could hear Cantone telling Europa as she led him away. "A very long and arduous journey."

Laughing again, Nomitius wondered why Cantone felt the need to woo the little slave, as if she required any convincing of her role in this encounter.

"Sire," came a call from behind him. Turning around, the builder saw Dintare, the stonemason.

"The arch is completed and we are going to move the stones for construction of the basilica. Would you like to survey the plan while the men assemble the materials?"

"Yes, I would," Nomitius added nonchalantly, his attention still drawn by the view of Europa's hips as she departed. After one more glance, which Dintare also enjoyed, the two men walked off toward the northeastern segment of the building, for the basilica, the most impressive feature of the villa.

The walls of the basilica were now at a height of three men, with openings left in the stone to allow light to enter. The floor was just dirt, although cement had been poured in some sections in preparation for the mosaics that would be arranged to showcase the artist's geometrics as well as scenes that depicted life in a Roman province. The beginnings of a wood frame for the cathedral dome stood at the far end of the room, held firmly upright by the many cross pieces and long iron nails that pinioned the joints of the structure.

Nomitius had spent many years in heavy lifting of the building process itself, serving both as a laborer and a stonemason before moving up to supervisor of such constructions. He swept his eyes from left to right, taking in the solidity of the stone walls and the brilliance of sunlight that peered in through the windows on either side. He smiled at what was being accomplished and was anxious to see what the finished product would look like.

Nomitius and Dintare exited the basilica through an unfinished doorway and set off to inspect the shelter where the mosaic stones were being kept. There were more than a dozen men there, more than half of them slaves working alongside some freemen. All were concentrating on their tasks when Nomitius and Dintare entered; none bothered to look up at the two men even when they were noticed.

Linaeus was the master artisan. At the moment Nomitius and Dintare entered, Linaeus was drawing an intricate design with white chalk onto a rough paper spread across the table. It was a preliminary drawing of one of the mosaics and would only tell the artist the arrangement of figures. Later, he would use this drawing to develop a new version of the same mosaic on the floor where the final piece was intended, switching from the white chalk on the paper to use a tapered finger of charcoal of the floor.

Nomitius stood behind him and watched as he drew. Linaeus was so focused on his work that any activity around him went unnoticed, so the presence of the two visitors would be overlooked by the artist until he stood back to observe the result.

Walking back outside, Nomitius discussed the process of mosaic building to Dintare.

"Here, in Rome, you know that mosaics are almost as important as marble. Some places, even more important. So, the governor wants to show off his estate with the finest mosaics ever created."

"Why not show off with marble?" Dintare asked.

"Well, he will have marble also," commented Nomitius, "but nothing made of marble can rival some of the great temples built by the Greeks and already standing on Trinacrium. Populonius thinks to use the slaves on this island, the ships bringing fine stone and glass, and the manageable weather of this region together. His mosaics will be finer than anything seen in Rome."

"But won't that put him in trouble?" asked Dintare. "Roman leaders don't like to be outdone by their governors."

"Perhaps," Nomitius. "But that is not my concern. I am a builder, and I am very pleased to be building something so magnificent."

"Where did you find Linaeus? Has he been an artist in Rome, too? He seems to have the great pictures in his head already."

Nomitius laughed at that.

"Linaeus has seen some of the finest art throughout the world, but not as an artisan."

"What then?" asked Dintare.

"Linaeus is a slave, and he has worked for rich Romans all over the empire. He has seen the greatest artwork everywhere from Shalem to Gadir, from Massalia to Melita. And he has the best memory that I have ever known, and the most exacting hands any god every created."

"But he is a slave. And he is trusted to accomplish this great project?"

"All he cares about is his art. We have treated him with respect, given him a good home, and even some *denarii* for his expertise. We even let him keep his own wife with him, so he wouldn't have to bother the other slave women."

At this Nomitius paused and regarded the slave artisan once more.

"He does not spend the Roman money we've paid him," Nomitius added. "Says he will use it to buy his freedom. But the governor already promised him his freedom if he completes these mosaics on schedule."

Dintare and Nomitius looked over the drawings that Linaeus was crafting on the paper. The artist still had not noticed their presence, so they departed to oversee the unloading of the wagons.

AUGUST 2018

CAFÉ AMADEO

"Is it still there?" I asked.

"The Villa Casale? Oh, yes, and much of it has been restored. It was rediscovered a long time ago, but excavation and recovery didn't begin in earnest until the early Twentieth Century. It had been known as the Villa Casale, but if you go looking for it at this point, you should search for the Villa Romana del Casale, the name attached to it by the archeologists."

I added that to my journal for later research.

"Ancient Rome is known for many things," Vito continued, "including conquests and building, the aqueducts and the legal system, but the mosaics tell us about the people who designed them, the culture they cherished, and the craft that preserved them. In Sicily, along with the wonderful Greek temples, there are mosaics as fine as those found in Italy itself.

"The extent of the influence of Rome on life in Sicily goes far beyond the mosaics, though. As Rome's 'granary' obviously we know that the island supplied Rome with grain, at least until the latter stages of the Empire when other conquered territories contributed their share. But Sicily had been heavily wooded for centuries, so when Rome demanded more and more grain from the people of the province, the farmers were forced to clear more fields and plant more crops.

"Wheat became a staple of Roman import, and farming it became a staple of the Sicilian economy. This directly affected the rural communities, but the taxes were levied on a region-by-region basis. So even the people who lived in the cities like Agrigentum and Siracusa and Panormus would have to manage the grain crop and ensure its success.

"But Rome's pressure on Sicily for grain imposed additional burdens on the people of the island. Once the tax system was in place, it was easier for corrupt leaders – especially with the power of governors – to exploit. Intentional undercounting of the harvest, price fixing, and threats to other freedoms were all attached to the farming economy.

"But beyond the Roman influence – mostly commercial at this point – Sicily already enjoyed its Greek culture and heritage. The architecture of the island resembled that of the Greek isles..." and here he paused and smiled.

"It's ironic in a way," Vito said thoughfully.

"What?" I asked.

"It's ironic that Rome overpowered the Greek settlements in Sicily, but the Greek language remained the language of the Roman intelligentsia here."

Vito huffed at this, reached for his espresso cup, and was still smiling as the cup touched his lips.

"But there is another, very important difference in the life and culture of the island under Roman rule," he added.

I waited for Vito to continue, or add the missing noun to his sentence, but he didn't, so I took the bait.

"And what was that?"

"Peace."

"You mean the peace that comes from military might and subjugation?"

"Yes, there was that, but by and large the Roman rulers didn't make use of terror very often to control the masses. Other than crucifying rebellious slaves – a terrible blot on their history – and putting down the occasional Jewish revolt with armed force, Rome preferred to manage and control their provinces with a...let's say...a light touch. No, I don't mean they wouldn't use force, but the threat of force was more useful than force itself to quell insubordination. In fact, one interesting thing separated the time of Greek hegemony in Sicily and that of Rome."

Again, the pause, as if he was waiting for me to guess at his answer. I had none.

"Yes, of course, it's not that obvious, is it?" Vito asked reading my pause. "Most of the centuries when Greek migration and settlement defined the culture of Sicily – the time from 800 B.C. to about year zero – were full of wars. There were the so-called Sicilian Wars between Greece and Carthage, the Athenian invasion of Siracusa, the Pyrrhic War, all three Punic Wars, and the Slave Wars that took up most of the last two centuries B.C. By the time Rome took over the island, peace reigned, and it reigned for hundreds of years.

"What about culture?" I asked.

"Oh, that's a different story. The Greeks, in their homeland and in Sicily, thought of culture as plays, grand orations, and art. The Romans were a bit rougher than that. They considered culture to be gladiatorial contests and ribald bacchanalia. Fortunately for us Siciliani, we still have much of the Greek influence to be proud of."

440 C.E. – 660 C.E.

BARBARIANS

AUGUST 2018

TRATTORIA BETTINA, MAZARA DEL VALLO

"Barbarians," Vito began, as I slid into a chair across from him that evening at the bar in Trattoria Bettina. It was a sultry night, with little wind but a clear sky above. The tiny white lights that were strung across the edge of the bar gave it a festive appearance, and the lively chatter coming from the rows of patrons crowding the barstools contributed to the feeling.

"What about them?" I asked, waving to the waiter to bring another glass. Even on a warm, humid evening, Vito had his bottle of Nero d'Avola, a well-regarded red wine from the region, on the table. I might have ordered a chilly glass of white wine, or a sparkling Prosecco to beat the heat. But I didn't expect my vintage mentor to change his ways.

"People use the modern meaning of the word, 'barbarian,' to think of these people as uncultured, rootless wanderers, with little culture and less virtue."

"Is that not true?"

"Well," Vito replied with a chuckle, "actually it is true." He raised his glass almost as a vote of concurrence with the comment, or was it to salute these long-ago disrespected hordes?

"They came from the area north of the Roman Empire in the first few centuries A.D. It was long called Germania by the Romans, but the various tribes of barbarians came from a diverse geography. For example, the record is pretty sure that the Vandals came from as far away as Scandinavia, passing through the European continent to raid some cities and villages, take on supplies, stay a while perhaps, and then move on."

"They were a migratory people?"

"Yes, but not in the marauding sense that they're thought of today. They hadn't developed agriculture, at least not like the Mediterranean peoples had – remember, the growth of agriculture was the single greatest reason for people to give up their nomadic ways and settle down. The Vandals also hadn't developed a ritual of art yet."

"What do you mean by a ritual of art?"

"Art is anything you draw or paint or sculpt. Maybe more than that, for example when you design buildings, construct dolmens, pluck out sonorous notes on a stringed instrument, or build bridges. We're not saying the Vandals didn't know how to draw or paint, sculpt little human-like dolls, or string beads. But the 'ritual of art' means more than that, it means the inclusion of artisanal creations in the ritual of life, in religion or belief systems, in the use of artistic expression to capture these beliefs in buildings, great sculptures, and megaliths to the gods. Carved land features from funereal mounds to Stonehenge are part of the ritual of art."

"So what did the Vandals do?" I asked.

"We know very little about what art they did possess. We have found trinkets and small objects in gravesites, but we have few examples of Vandal gravesites. And they left no real great sculptures or megalithic constructions because they didn't stay put very long. In fact, the absence of art, and the ritual of art in their culture, is precisely why we have trouble pinning down the essence of their culture and belief systems."

"What about the Goths? The Ostrogoths and Visigoths?" I asked. "Aren't they considered in the historical record of barbarians?"

"Sì, *certamentu*," Vito replied. "But not all barbarians were the same. Remember that the Vandals came from Scandinavia, but the Ostrogoths came from the Baltic Sea, while the Visigoths came from an area farther west."

"The common perception is that these...I'll call them 'hordes' of barbarians..." I added, with some reluctance, "were descending on the remnants of the Roman Empire when it was crumbling," I added, referring to notes in my journal.

"Very good, Luca!"

"So, tell me about Sicily."

"That's what we've been talking about for weeks," Vito replied slyly. He lifted his tumbler of wine and drew in a gulp, then reached for an olive from the bowl on the table.

"Yes, and you know what I mean," I said, joining in on his jest. "What did the barbarians have to do with Sicily?"

Vito leaned forward, put his elbows on the table, and looked directly at me with a serious face.

"Let's go back to what you just said about them. You said the barbarians descended on Rome when the empire was losing its vigor, when corruption and violence had loosened its social fabric, when the immorality of the leaders was destroying the empire from within."

"Well, I didn't say it quite so elegantly," I smiled, and took a sip from my own wine glass. "But I concur with your description. Tell me more."

"Let's begin with the Vandals. As you know, they came from the area now known as Scandinavia, and they migrated south. They went south and then east for a while, through areas we know as Germany, Austria, the Baltic region, and Switzerland. But they continued moving and then swung west again."

"Why?"

"It's hard to tell," Vito replied. "As I said, the barbarians left very little evidence of their culture, so we can't extract much information about why they did what they did. Anyway, the Vandals went west through the areas of modern France and Spain, where they crossed the gap at Gibraltar into Tingis, what is now Tangiers. From there, they ventured east along the North African coast…"

"Just like the Sicanians did," I interjected.

"*Esattumentu*," Vito said approvingly. "Just like the Sicanians five thousand years before. So, the Vandals moved toward the same place the Sicanians had reached, by then it was called Carthago, but we know it as Carthage, or today's Tunis."

"How did they get to Sicily?"

"A better question might be, why did they go to Sicily?"

"I give up." I didn't really, but I needed to prod Vito to continue.

"Genseric, the Vandal leader, had long plotted to defeat Rome. Remember, this was a time when the Roman Empire was collapsing and outside forces thought it would be ripe for the harvest. So, Genseric devised a plan, not unlike a siege, in which he would begin by cutting off the Empire's access to grain, starve its citizens, and loosen them up for his invasion. To do this, he had to bring his forces – some say there were tens of thousands of men, although I think there were many fewer fighters among them – he had to bring his forces across the African coast and up into Sicily.

"He led his men to great success in capturing the cities that they invaded as they moved eastward. In the year 432, they defeated the forces of the Roman general Bonifacius to capture Hippo Regius in the area that is now Algeria. There was a slight pause in the action, and Genseric even gave the impression of reaching a treaty with Rome. But I suspect he was merely gathering his forces, so in 439, Genseric drove them even farther east where they took Carthage. From there, they continued to the southern shores of Sicily, the scene of many battles yet to be waged."

"Between whom?"

"Rome was still angry that the Vandals had broken their treaty," Vito continued, "but the Empire was now divided into two parts, east and west."

"And..."

"And so this complicated the response to the Vandal advance into Sicily. Who would act, and when? Rome's Western Empire was fighting tribes to their north, so they couldn't spare anyone to expel the Vandals from Sicily. The Byzantine Empire, what you call the Eastern Roman Empire, sent forces to drive the Vandals back into Africa – and hopefully beyond that and out of the region – but by 441, the Byzantines were still stuck in Sicily.

"By the following year, the leaders of the Western Roman Empire began to sense the threat that the Vandals posed and decided to swing their attention from the north to the south of their territory. So, they made peace with the invading Vandals, offering them much of the African theatre to complete the bargain, but using Sicily as a new border to protect Rome's southern flank."

"Did it work out?"

Vito paused for some wine, first sipping then swirling the liquid around in his glass as he pondered my question.

"For a while. But it seems this Genseric fellow was difficult to please. After the treaty was arranged, he began raiding and looting all over the Mediterranean, especially while Rome's attention was redirected north once again. This was a primary factor that led to the Vandal sack of Rome in 455."

"And Sicily?"

"As always, our country was caught between the warring forces, the Vandals and the two halves of the Roman Empire, a battleground upon which our people died in greater numbers than the armies on either side of us who waged the conflict.

"Finally, Genseric sold most of the island to Odoacer, a Germanic general sent by the Byzantine powers in Constantinople, but he kept Marsala – Lilybaeum at the time – for himself. With that, Genseric, a Vandal, occupied a small portion of western Sicily, surrounded by Byzantine forces everywhere else. The Christians who survived on the island were now outnumbered by Vandals and Byzantines.

"Looking back with the telescope of history, however, we now see how the Vandal invasion settled in over Sicily, which was a bad thing for us. The Romans didn't quite give up the mission of driving back the barbarians though, in fact, it would all come to a head some years later."

"In Agrigentum," I offered.

"*Bravu*, Luca." Vito sounded greatly impressed with my minor factotum. But I couldn't tell if he cared more that I recalled the battle fought in the year 456 or in my pronouncing the name of Agrigento in the Roman form that it would have had at the time.

"So, what happened in 536?" I asked. It wasn't a test, but Vito was up to it anyway.

MARCH 536 C.E.

SIRACUSAE

"They are coming," said Clio as she looked out of her home toward the harbor below.

"Who?" her husband Theodes asked.

"More ships. The same as those that landed over the last few days, but more now."

The harbor in Siracusae was now becoming crowded with these three-masted ships. The Ostrogoths had been driven from the city – and the entire country – easily by the Byzantine forces the previous season, and now the Siracusans were host to another invading force.

These new ships posed no direct threat to the native people, since Siracusae had maintained its identification with the Eastern Roman Empire – called Byzantine by the leaders of the new invasion – throughout the period of Ostrogothic rule. But the new style of warship did draw their attention.

Ostrogoth warships had a horizontal beam-and-sail design with sails that stood crosswise against the width of the deck. Similar ships had been used in the Middle Sea for centuries and depended on a tailwind to drive the ship forward.

Byzantine vessels put their sails diagonally across the deck, using headwinds blowing past the fabric to reduce the air pressure and pull the boat forward. They were faster than earlier designs and more agile in changing winds. Unlike the bireme and trireme, which boasted two and three levels of oarsmen, these new vessels had only one level of rowers, and the addition of a rudder gave the captain more control over direction. The use of metal in the hull design also offered additional protection against ramming.

On this bright spring day, the Siracusans had no single-masted Ostrogothic vessels within view, only the sleek three-masts of the Byzantine warships.

The fleet was led by Belisarius, the Byzantine commander, who had taken three *banda* of soldiers – about five hundred armed men – to Africa to put down a rebellion by locals who threatened his empire's control of the continent. The mission was quickly completed and, on this day, his expeditionary force returned to Siracusae, adding to the crowd of vessels in the harbor and becoming the morning parade of naval power spotted by Clio from her kitchen.

Belisarius was already famous before landing in Sicily. Born in an area to the north, he grew quickly into a military man. He entered the service of Justin I, Emperor of the Eastern Roman Empire, where he came to know the emperor's nephew, Justinian. For that young man, Belisarius volunteered to form a regiment of bodyguards, called *bucellarii*, a private army employed solely for the benefit of the key person; in this case, the man who would become the next emperor. From that position of influence, it took little to be promoted along with his patron, the Emperor Justinian I, to be the most powerful military leader of Byzantium.

"His advance ship arrived late yesterday evening," said Theodes, "and reported that the barbarians in Africa were easily defeated. In fact," he added with laughter, "they ran before the Byzantines' ships had landed."

"But why do we need so many here, in our city?" she asked. The edge in her temper was obvious in her tone of voice.

"We don't need them here. I overheard a soldier saying they would be moving on to Rhegium."

"Where did you hear that? We're supposed to stay away from the soldiers."

"He came into the *Calic' Bellu*. I was there already."

"What? You said old man Salidus only serves pig piss in his taverna."

"He owes me for the table I built for him, so at least that 'pig piss' is free."

Clio came over to sit next to Theodes and couldn't suppress a smile. She appreciated her husband, even if he seemed to drink too much. But he had been a good and loving father, had kept her and the children safe during the recent wars with the Ostrogoths, and knew how to make just enough *denarii* to take care of them.

"What did he say?"

"Who? Salidus?"

"No," Clio said, slapping his arm playfully. "What did the soldier say?"

Theodes grabbed the heavy cup of wine and dragged it across the table as he sat back to relax against the wall.

"The Byzantine commander, what's his name? Belisari?"

"Belisarius."

"Okay, Belisarius. He is not interested in Siracusae, or anything on the island of Trinacria. He has come here for provisions, and a place to rest his soldiers, before marching north."

"Where north?"

"Into Italia, and as far north as he can chase the Ostrogoths."

"But he has rid Trinacria of the barbarians, what does he care about Italia?"

Theodes smiled at Clio's concern only for local issues.

"The barbarian tribes have been troubling the Roman Empire for two hundred years. I have heard that they were attacked by Roman provinces in the north even longer. Now, Belisarius thinks he can defeat them once and for all. He can drive them from Trinacria..."

"He has already rid our country of them," Clio interjected.

"...yes, and he can push them out of Italia and back where they came from."

"And where is that, pray?" she asked. "Where did they come from?"

"I don't know," smirked Theodes while bringing the cup to his lips. "I'm just a poor carpenter. What do I know about the things that go on in the world?"

Theodes understood the things of the world quite well, though. At least at this moment.

Belisarius was bringing a flotilla of ships to Trinacria to stage a massive assault on the peninsula to the north. His vessels would carry seasoned sailors but also had to make room for the *moirai* – divisions of about two thousand soldiers – composed of *lochaghiai* (infantry), *allaghia* (cavalry), and *skutatoi* (archers). Never had a military force of this size been brought to their country, not in recent memory and not in the stories that the elders told of past invasions.

Fortunately for the people of Siracusae, it didn't seem that the Byzantine army meant them any harm. They paid for quarters when sleeping in the city, paid for their wine, and behaved better than the Ostrogoths who had controlled Siracusae for many years. Soldiers are soldiers, though, and some of their behavior around women and girls was not appreciated, but the Siracusans knew how to deal with them. There was seldom any reason to make complaints to the Byzantine officers about their men's behavior, and nearly no incidents of grave danger to the population.

Still, the people of Siracusae felt like they were an occupied city with little control or say over how their affairs would be managed. The sooner the Byzantine force left to wage war on Rhegium and greater Italia, the sooner the people would be able to regain some order for themselves.

Clio returned to the hearth and stone oven she used to prepare their meals. The small square wood block table was used for both preparing the meal and serving. It was only big enough for four people, and close enough that anyone could reach across to fork a bite off of someone else's plate.

This kitchen was in a darker corner of the room than the one where Theodes sat. With only one window in their home, he had arranged two chairs in front of it, the spare furniture in the setting made of wooden frame and well-worn leather slings for seats. Theodes stared out the window to the rhythm of cutting and chopping that Clio made preparing the meal for the night. But Theodes also kept a flagon of wine on the floor at his feet. He filled a carved wooden cup with the ruby colored liquid, sipped slowly and looked out the window.

"We have hare tonight, and carrots and celery. I'll have some broth left from boiling the meat and we can use it to dip the bread in."

Clio's words were meant for Theodes but he paid only slight attention to them. She didn't focus either on the message, although it came from her own lips.

It was in quiet times like this that the couple considered their life in Siracusae, the Greeks who the stories say built it and gave the people their language, the Goths who took over control and fought battle after battle to retain it, and the Byzantines who now have sailed in to claim it.

After another sip of wine, Theodes's thoughts went to Hermedes and Calentus, their daughter and son. Hermedes married a young man in Siracusae, someone with a future – Theodes hoped – a man who was favored by the ruling class that had survived the Goths and now was favored by the Byzantine leaders. Marriages within cities were more common now than in centuries past, since the populations had grown and there were many young uncommitted men and girls to choose from. The city culture had also become more insular and inward-looking, so as children grew into adulthood they spent most of their time around fellow citizens and were more likely to remain there rather than travel abroad.

Clio didn't whistle when she worked and didn't talk to Theodes. While her husband stared out the window and drank wine, she fell into a quiet rhythm of work, but her thoughts were on their children also, and the years when the two youngsters used to live there and crowd that little square table that she leaned on for a moment of rest.

Theodes was not as happy with his son. Calentus hated the Goths and was drawn into gangs of men who resisted the control that the invaders placed on them. Calentus had been jailed several times for his behavior, and Theodes had to pay fines to get his release. But it would happen again.

One morning when Theodes rose to go to the mill for some wood to make furniture for a man's new home, he saw his son already up and dressed, and standing outside their home talking to some of his tough young friends.

"Get to the house," Theodes told him, but Calentus stood firm.

"They are killing us," he told his father, "they're killing you. Why don't you do something?"

"Calentus, the Goths are just like everyone who came before. They want our country, they take our cities..."

"And they take our daughters," Calentus huffed.

Theodes slapped his son hard across the face with the back of his hand. It's true that he feared every day that one of the soldiers garrisoned in their town would take Hermedes, and the thought kept him awake most nights, even now that she has found her own man. Soldiers sometimes care about another man's property, but they usually care only about their own hunger.

Calentus left that day, going off with his compatriots to form an organized resistance. And Clio and Theodes had not seen him since. That was a year ago, before the Byzantines came to drive the Goths out of Siracusae. Theodes wished he could reach his son and tell him the news, but Calentus probably already knew. If he was still alive.

"How long will they stay?" Clio's question brought Theodes back from his thoughts.

"Who?"

"The new sailing ships, and their soldiers?"

"I don't know."

"Why don't you go down to the *Calic' Bellu* and ask your friend?"

"Salidus? He's says he's paid up and doesn't owe me anything anymore. You would have to give me some *denarii* for drink."

Clio eyed her husband keenly and smiled lightly.

"I meant your friend, the soldier. Ask him."

"I would still need some *denarii*," Theodes replied, putting his hand out, palm up.

AUGUST 2018

CAFÉ AMADEO

I NEARLY RUSHED INTO THE CAFÉ THE FOLLOWING MORNING, anxious to nail down what I knew about the barbarians or didn't know. I tried to slow down to a deliberate pace as I stepped through the door, but my eagerness got the best of me.

"So, the barbarians, all of them, the Vandals, the Ostrogoths, the Visigoths..."

"No, not the Visigoths," Vito corrected, an arthritic finger pointed upward to reinforce his statement. "Remember, they didn't get to Sicily."

"Yes, I know. That isn't where I was going. But, okay, the Vandals and the Ostrogoths. They were only in Sicily for a very short time, right?"

"Yes, if you're speaking in geologic time," he replied with a smirk and a sip of his espresso.

"Come again?"

"The barbarians were here for just about two hundred years, from the mid-Fifth Century to the mid-Seventh Century. In geologic time, that's a single heartbeat. But what do you think the Sicilian people were feeling? Did it seem so fleeting to them?"

"Well, no, I suppose," I replied. "Two hundred years is two hundred years. Considering the average life span of people at the time, that would have been about five generations. Some folktales last that long, but five generations of telling is enough time for the story to change. Enough time for the facts of the story to be rearranged."

"Sì," responded Vito, "long by a single human's standards, but only a moment in the whole history of Sicily. So, you are right, and wrong, at the same time. Still, we shouldn't underestimate the importance of the barbarian invasion of our country. They didn't leave very many of their own artifacts, any more than they left along the trail they cut prior to coming to Sicily. But they brought some paganism in their religions, and one more thing."

Vito paused again, for emphasis.

"And that was?" I prodded.

"Blond hair and blue eyes." He was close to laughing and could barely get the punchline out.

I laughed too. He was right. The Vandals who came from as far away as Scandinavia would have brought some of their Arian features, the blond hair and blue eyes that would crop up sporadically in the people of Sicily. Suddenly, I thought back to the barista's blue eyes and Antonio's green eyes. I had come across some people with light brown hair and even some with blond hair. I realized just then that they were all, probably, descended from the Vandals.

As a friend once said to me: "To assume that there are any pure races is to assume that invading armies didn't get off their horses."

"They were driven from the shores of Sicily, but not from the gene pool, I guess," I concluded.

"Too late," Vito said, sipping again from his espresso.

"But didn't it begin to change after Belisarius conquered them and staked the Byzantine flag in Sicily?"

"Of course. Then our country became more like the Eastern Roman Empire and its church, and we assumed the Byzantine way of life. As it turns out, the Greek language that had persisted here through the years, since the invasions in the Ninth Century B.C., was the language of the Byzantines, so we had no problem adjusting to them. You would be surprised at how comforting a common language is to a people who experience waves of change over time."

Actually, I wouldn't be very surprised. I recalled how, in my travels around the world, whenever I entered a society with a language I shared, my nerves immediately settled down. I slept better, ate better, and generally felt more at ease, even if it was a country I had never been to before.

"Even being driven from our country, though, the Goths weren't done yet."

"How so?"

"Totila. Ever heard of him?"

I shook my head.

"Totila was king of the Ostrogoths and he waged a new war against Belisarius and the Byzantines. These two bigger-than-life heroes fought it out on Sicily, on the mainland of Italy, and all the way north to Rome. They took turns winning, and then losing cities and territories. Totila actually conquered Rome twice on his way to retaking Sicily."

"How long did this go on?"

"Totila took over the Ostrogothic kingdom in 541, just a few years after Belisarius defeated the Goths in Sicily. And he reigned until 552."

"Did he give up, or die?" I asked.

"Kings with that much power don't give up. No, Justinian I of the Byzantine Empire was getting pretty tired of this Goth and planned to drive him from the region. Unfortunately, a number of factors – including a bubonic plague that swept through Byzantium in 541 – prevented immediate action. But when Totila invaded Sicily again, Justinian was ready to deal with him. He built a massive army in 552, put a new guy Narses in charge, and set out to defeat Totila once and for all. The Goth had already plowed up through the peninsula and reached north central Italy, where he took on the challenge from Narses at Taginae.

"It was a famous battle waged near the Adriatic coast, Narses ultimately prevailed, and Totila was killed in battle. And with that, the barbarian hordes in Italy – and therefore in Sicily – were vanquished."

"Never to return? I mean, the barbarians?"

"Oh, that would be too easy, but let's talk about that. I believe that the most significant historical achievement of the barbarians was the destruction of the Roman Empire."

"Seriously? The direct, or even indirect causes of the collapse of Rome have been debated for centuries. Is the answer as simple as you suggest?"

"No, not simple, but possibly clear. And it wasn't just the barbarians. Rome in the Third and Fourth Centuries A.D. was already weakened because of its overextended the empire. This over-stressed the command structure – try to control a governor in a province that is three months march away – and the supply lines. It's not only in war that supply lines matter; direct and easy connection with the heart of empire is required throughout its life to ensure that imported and exported goods arrive properly. There was also the matter of the people."

"How do you mean?" I asked.

"Rome was relatively forgiving when it came to the cultural practices of the areas they conquered. That tolerance kept resistance in check, but it also allowed the Roman Empire itself to become a polyglot of ideologies, religions, and legal principles. Confusion began to creep in and unsettle the foundations of Roman society. So, in its weakened state, Rome couldn't withstand outright attacks on its borders. Like the Visigoths from the north, and the Vandals and Ostrogoths from the south. These barbarian tribes constantly pestered Rome and nibbled away at its perimeter."

"Well," I suggested with doubt in my voice, "I wouldn't exactly call the sack of Rome 'nibbling.'"

"Of course," Vito continued, "and that's how serious the constant pressure from the barbarians became for Rome. It was also victim to other forces, including corruption from within – both political and genetic – and it was bound to come tumbling down. But while this internal cancer was eating away at the structure of the Roman body politic, our friends, the barbarians, just helped pull it apart from the edges."

"And, again, back to Sicily."

"*Sì*, of course," Vito continued. "Sicily was a province of the Roman Empire, but not just any province. Sicily was the granary or 'bread basket' of the Empire. It was also geographically closer to mainland Italy than some of the far-flung provinces and, therefore, easier for Rome to oversee and interfere with. But the emperors continued to send corrupt men to govern the island..."

"Like Verres?" I asked.

"*Esattumentu*," he replied. As governor of an island province, Verres immediately assumed that he could pillage at will. He shipped much of the stolen material to other lands, for example, Sardinia and Marseille, to protect them from recovery. He wasn't the only governor to take advantage of Sicily, but his involvement took place directly during the time that Rome was beginning to come apart."

"So Rome's corruption filtered down to Sicily and brought the island down to the level of the Empire," I offered.

"*Sì*, but a bit different. Rome's decadence and corruption brought down the government but not the infrastructure. The Roman buildings, roadways, aqueducts – even its legal and criminal codes – survived beyond the slow crumbling of the Empire, even to this day. In Sicily, the buildings remained, and many of the ancient Greek temples, but Sicily was not as robust a society yet to survive the dissolution of Rome. The Dark Ages set in when the Empire collapsed and most of Rome's provinces, including Sicily, suffered from the effects of this time. Your 'wild west' in America is nothing compared to life in Europe during the Dark Ages."

"Is it Middle Ages, or Dark Ages?"

"They're not the same thing. The medieval time is thought to be from 500 to 1500 A.D., a time when societal change, population movement, and cultural reconstruction dominated. It started with about four centuries of spectacular migration, in and around Europe and the Mediterranean region, from roughly 400 to 800 A.D. We've already talked about that, with the Vandals' invasions across the known world. In the second part of the Middle Ages, from about 700 A.D. to about 1300 A.D., things settled down a bit. A significant factor during this time was the rise of power of the Church."

"The Christian Church, I assume."

"Of course. There were many other theologies at the time, and polytheism was on the wane. Judaism was still practiced in small communities, but Mohammed established Islam during this period. Anyway, going back to the Christian Church...there was money tied up in the power that the pope and his clergy commanded. This money was taken from the people the same way taxes had always been taken. But there was a difference now. In the past – and maybe today also – taxes are drawn from the population on threat of legal measures, including imprisonment. The Church demanded tithes on threat of eternal damnation. This part of the Dark Ages we understand.

"Education was closely guarded and limited usually to nobles and the clergy. In fact, even some of those donning robes weren't very educated, but clearly the peasantry was not. So the Church could convince the people of nearly anything, including paying for the right to heaven."

"Buying graces?" I asked.

"Yes, one of the fundamental causes for the Protestant Revolution. So, with this control of education and – therefore knowledge – the Church could cudgel its people into blind obedience. And the church had the most money, using much of it to build amazing cathedrals and commission religious art."

"How does this affect Sicily?"

"We're getting there. You asked if the Dark Ages and the Middle Ages were the same. Well, I described the Dark Ages as the early and middle part of the millennium between 500 and 1500 A.D. Although the

Middle Ages is often used to refer chronologically to that entire period, most people think of the advances during this time, including the Renaissance and, later, the Age of Enlightenment, as being the progeny of the Middle Ages and the direct descendants of the Dark Ages.

"Remember, the Church controlled the money, and the Church commissioned the cathedrals, stained glass windows, sculptures, and paintings. Of course, most of this had a religious theme, as you will see from the massive artistic output of that period, but the Church also served as a patron of the arts and was largely responsible for the birth of the Renaissance.

"But, we're getting a bit ahead of ourselves. Let's go back to the invaders from Byzantium."

535 C.E. – 827 C.E.

BYZANTINES

AUGUST 2018

CAFÉ AMADEO

"*Corpus Juris*," Vito said, looking up at me as I entered the door of the café. Perhaps he was especially anxious to begin on that morning, because I was still ten feet from the table when he addressed me.

"I give up," I replied with a smile. There were times that I was so clueless that I had resolved to be honest and stop flipping through pages of my journal as if I had a clue what he was talking about. I didn't, and he knew it, so I saved myself the embarrassment.

"*Corpus Juris* translates to..."

"A body of law," I said, redeeming myself a bit with a quick translation from Latin.

"*Certamentu*," Vito replied. "It's sometimes called Justinian's Code. Justinian I, the Eastern Roman Emperor during the Sixth Century A.D. compiled it. It had three parts, the first – and most important of which, at the time – was the codification of Roman law up that point."

"How does that impact Sicily?" I asked.

"Directly, and indirectly," Vito replied. "As emperor, Justinian's method of ruling was critical to all territories within his power, including Sicily.

Up until that period, the legal system was governed by natural law, precedent, and written – sometimes unwritten – decrees by a long line of kings and emperors. Justinian wanted to bring order to this tangle of records, a good step for the common person who wanted to know what types of behavior would be expected, and which ones sanctioned. In 528, he created a council to research extant texts and decisions and compile and sort the results."

"Natural law...wait," I begged. "Is that the same as common law?"

"That's the closest corollary. Yes, natural, or common law, means everything that we would expect to be proscribed. Murder, theft..."

"Rape," I added declaratively.

"No, sadly, we can't say rape was proscribed all through history," Vito responded with his chin and eyes cast down.

"What? That seems like a natural, or should I say, common law."

"Not in all places. In fact, rape was not illegal throughout medieval times and it was not specifically called out in the body of law in Italy until many centuries later."

I wasn't sure how to explore this terrible oversight in the law, so I paused in asking Vito about it.

"Rape was too often considered an act of opportunity," he commented.

"You didn't say a 'crime' of opportunity," I chided.

"No, because that's precisely the point. The men of a society were expected to guard their women, especially the young women and girls, or else they might fall victim to an 'act of opportunity.'

"You know how early Sicilian societies require that the women remain indoors, out of sight?" he asked.

"Yes, and, well, if I can say it, not only the *early* Sicilian societies. I have noticed even today, in Mazara del Vallo."

"Sì," Vito allowed, and continued. "Girls are not supposed to look out the windows, or appear on the doorstep of the home unless they are escorted."

"But this can't be a universal custom. It sounds too antiquated," I objected.

"And, of course, it is. But that doesn't mean it is not still followed. In Sicily, many of the old ways are still new. And the men of the families are still considered responsible for the women, and for ensuring that they do not fall victim to 'acts of opportunity.' But, let's go back to Justinian and common law. His council organized the known laws, precedents, and judgments and compiled them in a way that would sort out discrepancies."

"Did it?" I asked.

"Mostly, but the council and, to some extent Justinian himself, were reluctant to throw out judgments that seemed fine on their face, even if they conflicted with a parallel body of decisions. Anyway, this *corpus juris* was an historical achievement and paved the way for many other compilations of law in the Roman theatre and, therefore, throughout Europe."

"And, so, to get back to Sicily, this mattered how?" I asked.

"Remember Narses?"

"He was the general appointed by Justinian to rid the region of the Goths."

"In 552. *Correttu.* Narses's victory over Totila and the Goths established rule by the Eastern Roman Empire over Sicily and southern Italy, and Justinian's system of justice suddenly became the law in Sicily in that period. Luckily for our people at the time, Justinian's approach was a thoughtful, long-considered melding of tradition and justice, not just some new tyrant's rantings."

Vito paused, shifted in his seat, and sipped at his espresso.

"All through the Byzantine period, there were sporadic – and mounting – threats from the Arab world. Mohammad, who was born in 570 A.D., just after Byzantium took control of the eastern Mediterranean, established a new religion, Islam. His following grew and although they didn't begin their migration and conversion of Europe until long after his death in 632, Islam presented a constant challenge to the Eastern

Roman Empire from the very beginning. Battles in Damascus, Jerusalem, and Alexandria left these areas in Muslim control, but the Byzantine Empire held onto southern Italy and Sicily. By around 650, that would change.

"However, we should postpone talks of the Muslims and their invasion of Sicily until later, but never let them out of your sight or mind while we talk about the Byzantines."

Then Vito chuckled.

"Surely, the Byzantines could never let them out of their sight either," he added.

"Constans II, the Byzantine emperor in the mid-Seventh Century, was worried enough though, that he came to Sicily himself. In fact, he moved the capital of the Byzantine capital to Siracusa, a dramatic move for history because that would make Sicily the capital of the Eastern Roman Empire, on an island at the center of thousands of years of conflict. Constans's concerns were not unfounded, since Islam was beginning to surround the Byzantine territories. Between his arrival in Sicily and about 667 A.D., Islam would stage so many attacks on Sicily – carrying off plundered treasures and enslaving Sicilians – that Constans himself was threatened. Ultimately, he was murdered in Siracusa by his own troops in 668 A.D. Still, the importance of the Byzantine Empire residing in Siracusa was not without historical significance."

He paused again to nibble on the cantucci on his plate.

"Do you know about Pope Leo II?"

I shook my head.

"Pope Leo was born in Sicily during the Byzantine period and was elevated to the papacy in 682."

"So, a pope came from here?"

Vito nodded.

"Did his proximity to the center of Byzantine power help in his ascendancy?" I asked. "Of his Sicilian heritage?"

"Doubtful. There were many priests and bishops from Sicily who went to Rome during this period to escape the continued threat of Islam perhaps. Our little boy from Sicily only lasted a short period in St. Peter's chair."

"How's that?"

"He died with a year of his selection. In that short period though, he accomplished much, mostly working out the complicated relationship between Byzantium and Rome. Perhaps as a Sicilian living during the Byzantine period, he was the perfect character for that role."

655 C.E.

ORTYGIA

ANATOLE HAD WALKED THE SAME DISTANCE EVERY DAY FOR THREE months. From his home in the Hebrew quarter of Ortygia to the flat plain near the edge of the little island. Ortygia had served many roles for Siracusa over the centuries, from trading outpost to military compound, from humble camps for the slave trade to its current status as neighborhood for laborers. There were many nationalities represented there, with a lineage that could trace its history back to the slaves, and there was a cluster in the center where Anatole lived with the other Jews of the island, called *Giudecca*.

Access to water for ritual cleansing was a central part of Jewish practice. Running water from streams and rivers was used, as was the standing water of lakes and pools. The Jews of Sicily had access to the water of the Mediterranean, not to mention the rivers of the island, but the people of Siracusa wanted to build a temple. The first step for that design was to build a *mikveh*, or ritual bath, on the grounds that the temple would occupy.

Anatole was one of the laborers bringing stone and block to the site for the *mikveh*, and he was trained in laying the stone in the design that had been already been lined out. It would be larger than any ritual bath he had ever seen and it would form the central part of the plan for the temple, a sacred building that would be erected around the *mikveh* after the bath was completed.

"It's about time," said Azriel, hailing Anatole with a laugh. "I thought we began at dawn."

"It's still dark out," complained Anatole, pointing to the sun that had barely risen over the water to the east of the island.

"That sun has been up for a long time, and so have I," but Azriel was not arguing. He knew his young friend had trouble getting out of bed in the morning.

———

It had taken the Hebrew community several months to decide on the location for the temple and, therefore, the *mikveh*. The bath used for this purpose must be connected to a natural spring that would not dry up and which would produce enough water to fill a pool so that a grown person could be immersed completely within it. The rabbis of Ortygia discussed this at length while walking across the little island.

"I would feel better if we could use the stream that runs through Siracusa itself," said Rabbi Tzadok.

"That will never work," countered Yosef, another rabbi who was younger than the elder Tzadok, and who accepted the Christian control of the city. "Our *Giudecca* is here, on this little island just off Siracusa. The Romans would never allow us to take up space in their city."

"We are welcome in Siracusa," was Tzadok's rebuttal. "They want our goods and will buy our linens."

"Yes, and we hope that this will continue. But our *Giudecca* is here, as I said," repeated Yosef. "It is a beautiful island, surrounded by the pristine waters of *Mare Nostrum*, and we can find a spring here in our area. Besides, what if we could get the Romans to let us build a *mikveh* in the center of Siracusa. Would you want to walk every day from here to there for temple?"

Tzadok waved his hand as if he was shooing away a pesky insect.

They slipped through an orchard of pear trees and grapevines and approached the broad flat space where Anatole and Azriel were working. The ground had already been leveled and the footprint of the *mikveh* was laid out with a series of small rounded stones. The rabbis stepped up the edge of the foundation and paused to watch the men at their work.

"Lift!" urged Azriel, coaching his young apprentice in moving a block into place. The older man was the stonecutter and he had just completed smoothing the block before Anatole's arrival that morning. The cavities for the baths had been excavated carefully over the preceding weeks, a process that could only be accomplished during the dry season to avoid rain-washed collapse of the walls. Now that the dig had been made, it was time to begin to set the blocks in place around the perimeter of the bath, as low walls and columns, forming a permanent enclosure that could endure the seasons.

The entire *mikveh* was below ground, which required an enormous effort to excavate, involving all the men of the community for many months. Once that was done, digging out the holes for each bath had required additional cutting into the limestone bed itself, but this was more exacting work and left to specialists like Azriel. Together the overall dig and the carving out of the baths took nearly a year, with picks and shovels at times and Azriel's pick at other times to shape the contours of the cavity whenever the rock could be used in place. But two sides of the excavated *mikveh* required fresh stone to be cut and placed, since the limestone bed had threads and seams on two flanks that would not have served well as side walls for the bath.

"Is it deep enough?" asked Tzadok. He was the first to doubt projects such as these, always questioning the appropriateness or adequacy of their efforts.

"*Tevilah* requires full immersion, you know," he said to Yosef, as if the younger rabbi didn't already know the ritual.

Yosef only smiled. He knew his elder would critique every movement and every placement of block and challenge the site they had chosen even after the last stone of the Temple was laid.

Azriel overheard the elder rabbi and smiled a bit at his words. The stonecutter had lived in the *Giudecca* his entire life, as had Anatole and nearly everyone they knew, and he had listened to Tzadok's interpretation of the Torah during their evenings on Shabat. The old man was known to be wise and correct in his reading of the old texts, but with age he was beginning to sound too much like an old woman who worried about everything. He sneaked a look in Yosef's direction and saw the two rabbis engaged in a whispered conversation.

'Probably about me,' thought Azriel, and he smiled again as he continued to fit the block into place. In fact, the rabbis weren't talking about the *mikveh* or the men working it. Yosef's eyes strayed in Azriel's direction and he nodded at the man.

With his calloused hands, Azriel could muscle a large block into place with the same precision that he cut the stone to fit the opening.

"Just so," he said to Anatole and the other man operating the pulley. The rectangular stone was nearly identical in size to the stack of building blocks Azriel had already completed, but each piece of this construction would have some individual differences – veins that cut a furrow in the side, notches made by a random chisel hit – so that each one would require personal attention. That was why Azriel stood in the pit of the *mikveh* while Anatole and the man on the pulley stood above.

"A bit," the stonecutter said, with one hand on the side of the block and the other above his head, using hand gestures to indicate the direction of movement and the speed of the stone's descent.

"Yes," Azriel said as the block nestled into the gap left between two other stones. It had to go down perfectly aligned with the others on their face; the rough planes of the sides of the block would never allow it to be slid back into place. Working together and following hand directions, the three men had lowered the new stone into place with Azriel's own words, "Just so."

Now freed up from the precision work, the stonecutter turned back toward the rabbis, but saw them walking away from the construction site in the direction of *Giudecca*. In their place, Azriel saw some men from the city. They were not Jews; that community was small enough that he would recognize every one of them. These men spoke in Greek, which Azriel and Anatole understood, although in their small conclave the Jews had still maintained their common use of Aramaic, another of the polyglot of languages heard around the city of Siracusa.

Azriel climbed out of the bath cavity and then up the ladder that brought him out of the entire subterranean *mikveh* itself to the level ground. There awaited him a neatly arranged line of stones that would need to be lowered into the *mikveh* over the course of the day. Anatole knew his duties, as did the other men, so Azriel gave few commands and just moved on to his other tasks. All was arranged beforehand, all workers understood their roles, and everyone knew the importance of keeping the pace up until the sunlight faded and they would return to their homes.

By midday, as the sun was overhead and light streamed directly into the *mikveh*, two women approached carrying baskets and tall jars. Azriel smiled at the sight of his wife, Dina, and her younger sister Rebecca, strolling in their direction with a meal and cool water for them. It took a moment longer before Anatole appeared from behind a wall of limestone, but when he did his smile went broader than Azriel's as he laid eyes on the young sister in tow. He had long had an interest in Rebecca and she returned the favor, but he had not been around her in private. Their meetings had taken place until this time in situations such as this, when Dina was delivering food for the men.

Dina also smiled, and nodded in a friendly way in Anatole's direction. She knew that the apprentice's awkward behavior was caused by her pretty sister.

The women set down their sacks, platters, and jugs on the work table and the full crew of eight men crowded around. Dina was young and pretty, not yet a mother, and she wore a soft, blue robe that exposed her right shoulder and draped loosely across her breasts, customary attire for a woman of the period and in this place. She didn't have to make an effort to be comely and attractive; she just was.

And her eyes were glued on Azriel, the strong man and leader of this project whom she had just married the year before. They were inseparable, except for when he was required to work and when they attended services at the temple where the men and women were kept apart. Dina was anxious to have a baby with Azriel, but she was enjoying their easy childless life together too.

Unlike Dina who kept a demure smile on her lips and reserved her looks for Azriel, Rebecca played the part of an eligible unwed girl. She had clear intentions for Anatole, but she also wanted him to know that she had options.

As the women unfolded the baskets and poured the water for the men, Anatole worked his way through the little crowd to stand beside Rebecca.

"Hey, wait your turn," came a good-natured gibe from another worker. The man knew that Anatole cared less for food than he did for another hunger, but Shemule wasn't going to let him get through without some harassment. "There's plenty here for all of us," and the double entendre made Rebecca blush.

And so did Anatole. He stepped back from the throng, deciding to wait for his food and, hopefully, less competition for Rebecca's attention once the other men had gone off with their meal. His strategy worked, and the young girl turned toward him after the workers had walked away.

"May I help you with some food? You look like you have been working hard."

Anatole appreciated her words, and it sounded like a compliment, but in his nervous mind he suddenly wondered whether Rebecca meant that he looked disheveled. He darted a look at his feet, then the short tunic he wore from his shoulders to his knees, and then the color of his dust-covered hands. Before he could mount a defense – if one was needed – Dina came to his rescue.

"Be nice to Anatole, Rebecca. One day he may be a relative."

Both the young man and girl looked stunned and tried to unravel her words. Did she mean as a brother-in-law to Dina through Rebecca, or a relative as husband to the girl?

Dina didn't give them any time to consider her enigmatic statement. She walked away and left the two to themselves.

"Thank you," Anatole said belatedly to Rebecca's offer of assistance.

She reached for grilled artichokes, lima beans, and fresh pears and put a portion on a plate for him. Then she stabbed some lamb that had been grilled earlier and cut before bringing it to the worksite. She poured a thin, brown liquid over it that, when Anatole smelled it, reminded him of a salted meat broth. Rebecca handed the plate to him and then turned to pour him a cup of water from the jug she had carried.

With the plate in one hand and the cup in another, Anatole looked around for a spot to sit. He didn't want to rest near the other men and he wanted to find a bench wide enough for Rebecca to join him. If she would.

He spied one just around the edge of the pit, a long bench purposely left empty by Shemule and the other workers as a kindness to the man they knew was wooing this beautiful young lady.

Anatole started in the direction of the bench then turned back to Rebecca. She was standing alone with her hands held together in front of her, and she was looking directly at him.

"Would you eat, too, and sit with me?" he asked.

Rebecca smiled, relieved a bit that this man of her attentions was able to understand her motive.

"Yes, I will sit with you, but Dina and I already ate."

And with that, they moved toward the bench and sat together.

Dina and Azriel watched this youthful courting with amusement. They were young too – well, Dina was about ten years younger than the more mature Azriel – but their romance had begun in much the same way. They watched Dina's sister and Anatole who seemed so careful and confident when he was moving stone, but so clumsy when he was in Rebecca's presence.

Rebecca sat in silence out of courtesy, and Anatole ate in silence out of fear. He had a full head of dark, curly hair and when he bent over his food, the locks would tumble down over his forehead. At one point, Rebecca reached up and brushed the curls away with her fingers.

Touching was not forbidden, but public displays of intimacy were not common either. To touch someone unbidden was a suggestion that carried meaning, and an unspoken question that required an answer. Anatole looked at her and tried to conjure up an answer, but he was speechless. After an uncomfortable moment, he dove back into his food to busy himself with chewing on a bite of lamb.

"She's trying," said Dina of her sister.

"So is he," replied her husband, "she's just better at it than he is."

"And how do you think I caught you?" replied Dina with a jab to Azriel's ribs.

"What? You didn't catch me. I stopped running and you ran into me."

"Yes, sure you did," Dina said with a dismissive look.

By the time the men had completed their midday meal and climbed back down into the pit, Yosef and Tzadok had returned, with the older man still shaking his head.

"It won't hold it," he said.

"Hold what?" asked Yosef.

"Enough water. The *mikveh* must be deep and wide, and it must hold enough water for a man to go completely into the bath and be under the water."

"Not exactly under the water," was Yosef's retort. The younger rabbi was also well schooled in the teachings and, while he agreed in general with the elder rabbi's point, he knew his lessons.

"The man must only be able to sit in the bath up to his chin."

"It won't hold it," repeated Tzadok.

The two men debated the volume of water in the *mikveh*, the number of *seah* it would hold – which they knew meant that the bath must have a volume of forty *seah*. While their debate waged, the two Romans returned and stood watching the men in the pit carving out the contours of the baths below.

"Why are you in there so deep?" asked one of the men. He had the plain clothes of a worker from Siracusa, but the Jews on the site knew him to be a Roman and, therefore, he must be treated with deference.

"This is our land," Azriel said without apology. "We are preparing our *mikveh* for the temple."

"What is a *mikveh*, and why does it have to be under the ground?" asked the other Roman.

The questioning was becoming a bit of an annoyance, and the workers, the rabbis, and Dina and Rebecca were watching carefully to see how this would turn out.

"The *mikveh* must be fed by fresh water, by a stream," said Anatole. It was risky for him to step into the conversation best handled by his foreman, Azriel, or the rabbis. But with Rebecca as a witness, he wanted to show that he was not cowed by the Romans.

"So we dig here," Anatole pointed to the ground at his feet, "to find water. When the spring was discovered below the ground, we sought out the source of the water to fill our bath and keep the water pure, without drying up."

The Romans stood at the lip of the excavation looking on with some interest, but their presence made the Jews who worked and attended the site nervous.

"Is it a problem?" asked Yosef. "Is it a problem that we have dug this well for our *mikveh*?"

The Romans shrugged and walked away. It didn't seem like censure, but the inquisition left the Jews assembled there uneasy.

The work continued and the women remained. They had little to do in the late hours of the day and, with the Romans causing some concern, they decided to wait at the site until the men were done with their work. When the day's work came to a close, Azriel climbed out of the pit with a hand from Shemule, and Anatole collected his tools and prepared to leave.

"Would you join us for supper?" came a soft voice.

Anatole didn't realize someone was speaking to him, but turned around to see Rebecca's glowing face. She had just asked him to join the family for dinner, and he was not about to refuse.

"I'm glad you explained our practice to the Roman," she said. "It was a strong statement."

Anatole brightened at the compliment and nodded quickly to accept her invitation. He knew that she lived at home with her parents, and that Dina and Azriel lived in a home very nearby. Anatole didn't know which home Rebecca had just invited him to for supper, but he also didn't care.

674 C.E.

CATHEDRAL OF SIRACUSA

THE BISHOP WALKED SLOWLY AROUND THE PERIMETER OF THE OLD Greek temple. It was a magnificent beginning, he thought, but a Christian architect could do so much better.

"We would use these pillars," Bishop Zosimo said, pointing the rows of stone columns that were set in a rectangle around the Temple of Athena, called the Athenaion by the Greek locals in Siracusa.

"This is a strong structure that will..." he continued before being interrupted.

"Your lordship," said Penarius, "this is a pagan site. It was built to honor a Greek goddess."

Zosimo looked at his guide turned interrogator and laughed at his comment.

"It is what I say it is," Zosimo declared. With a dismissive wave of the hand and his head tossed to the side, the bishop said that since pagan gods did not really exist, the temples built to praise them were worthless husks that needed to be reclaimed and used for prayerful homage to the true God.

Zosimo continued his tour of the temple, making sweeping gestures to describe how he wanted to revise what was there, and make it a consecrated church. He wanted the building to represent him and to represent his reign, so he began by converting ancient buildings such as this to his purpose. The Temple of Athena had held a prominent spot on the island of Ortygia, just off the coast of the city of Siracusa itself, a short walk from another religious site, what the Romans and Christians called *Bagno Ebraico*, which meant the Jewish – or Hebrew – bath which also resided on this tiny barrier island off the southeastern coast of Siracusa.

The Temple of Athena had long fascinated Zosimo. Its architectural components were impressive, and the precision by which the temple was laid out suggested careful attention to detail. Unlike many older European monuments and temples, the Athenaion had no ancient history that would tie it to polytheism or sacrifice, but Zosimo was still intrigued with the evidence his men had found of an ancient altar below the surface of the temple itself. He considered it a sign that this place had mystical powers and he wanted to make its powers his own. And, of course for the Catholic Church, he often reminded listeners – if there were any powers left over.

"We will build strong walls of stone here," he said, drawing a line between the pillars of the Athenaion, "and replace the floor with marble."

The architect walking with him was making mental notes of the bishop's desires and nodding affirmation to every one of his design ideas.

"Yes, of course. As you say, your holiness," were the obsequious replies from the man.

Penarius had worked for the bishop since the holy man's ascension to the highest seat of the Church in Sicily some years before. He was skilled at numbers and pictures, which meant that he could understand building concepts and render them into drawings. His ability at mathematics allowed him to compute distances, weights of building blocks, and stresses on structural members designed to hold up the building once it was erected.

Penarius also knew how to nod and say 'yes' and be agreeable. He was more knowledgeable than the bishop – more knowledgeable he thought than Pope Adeodatus, a follower of Benedict who had preached throughout the Eastern Empire during his useful lifetime. Penarius studied the Church leaders and the popes because he knew that Zosimo and others who held the purse strings here in Siracusa could be convinced to be generous if the supplicant paid attention to the pecking order of the religious hierarchy.

When Zosimo drew designs in the air, Penarius knew to remember them, at least enough to make his bishop think he was paying attention. Like most projects imagined by Zosimo, this one would require a little management, the word Penarius used when he had to revise the design to fit the model, and sometimes to fit natural laws.

Just about then, Martha, a young beauty who was already known to have captured the bishop's fancy, strode by. Zosimo stopped in his monologue to watch her and Penarius respectfully stood by until the holy man's ogling had been completed.

Martha noticed the attention and did nothing to discourage it. She had been the bishop's consort for nearly a year, enjoying his company but, more importantly, his money and power, and she had to show herself now and again when he was in public. It was important to her own selfish mission that the Siracusans – even these poor souls who lived on Ortygia – knew that she held some power over their destinies.

But in passing by, Martha also threw a beckoning look at Penarius. He was married, so she heard, but if she played her cards right, she knew that she could win his favor while still sharing the bishop's bed.

After Martha passed from the scene, Zosimo redirected his attention to the project at hand.

"Let's put new columns here," as he indicated with his hands. He wanted to enlarge the simple rectangle of the Athenaion to add a portico, common in Roman design, and with several new columns carved in the fashion of the day. This portico would include a staircase of five steps, and the ground in front of the former temple would have to be excavated to allow space for a stepped rise of this nature.

A temple could sit on the ground, Zosimo thought, but a church must be raised above it.

After another circuit around the footprint of the aging temple, the two men were ready to retire for the day and seek other entertainment. For the bishop, that meant music, food, and plenty of wine – perhaps a friendly visit from Martha. For Penarius, the evening would be spent with his wife and two sons, full of good food made possible by his profitable employment with the bishop. Wine would be enjoyed also, and Penarius's wife and young boys would be allowed to partake. He liked it when his wife supped with him, and even more when she lingered after the meal – after the boys had gone to their beds – to drink from the last of the jug of red wine for the night.

———

The following morning, Zosimo was slow to rise. The previous evening, Martha decided that her suggestive look at Penarius might have been detected by the bishop and misunderstood – well, her plan was easy to understand, but she wanted to dispel it. So, she made a point of coming to the bishop's home after he had had his final meal of the day. His housekeeper would have prepared it and, if she served him enough wine, the cleric would also have made suggestive comments to the middle-aged woman tending his table. Martha knew that after Zosimo had exhausted his fantasies and his energy on the housekeeper, she could sail in and propose an amorous evening without having to actually carry it out.

So, she awoke in his bed to the sound his drunken snoring. Zosimo was, by then, an ample man. The rights and privileges of the Church had led him into a life of pleasure and his waistline showed it. Martha was not put off by this; she worked for a living and could not always choose the height and weight of her customers. But on this particular morning, she wanted to rise and dress, then get out of the bishop's home before he was roused – or aroused, as it were.

Out on the street in Siracusa, Martha encountered Julia, wife of Penarius. They knew each other and had shared some childhood friends, but their lives had taken different paths. Julia was a good Christian and had married Penarius when she was only fifteen years old.

Martha, however, wanted the kind of power that women of the day seldom possessed. The men in Siracusa – as far as she knew – held all the power, but the women knew that they could control the men with sex or other favors. Martha knew that no man could resist her body, and so instead of marrying and settling for only one man's power – like Julia had done with Penarius – Martha decided to share herself with many men and have each of them yield to her and empower her to carry on her life like no other woman could.

"And you are well, today, I trust?" she asked Julia when they passed in the square.

"Yes, very well, thank you," replied Julia. They were both playing a game. Each knew the other's chosen role in Siracusan society, each regarded the other with mild disdain, but each also recognized the strength that was required to choose the paths they were on. Martha seldom envied Julia, but she did long for a life when she only had to please one man. And a man as simple as Penarius, at that.

Julia regarded Martha as a whore, plain and simple. But she had to admire the power that this young beauty possessed, throughout the city and beyond.

"Your husband will be winning a major project from his holiness, I hear," Martha said to Julia. Despite their equal status in the city, normally the Siracusans didn't refer to the husbands of other women by their given names. It was considered improperly casual.

"Your husband is very lucky," Martha said, an offhand remark that cast Penarius's accomplishment as more fate than talent.

"But, then," Julia countered, "a man is lucky who is good. I'm sure you agree."

Martha didn't want to wage a battle of wits with this woman. The prostitute was proud and would engage anyone in the city who challenged her, but she knew that Julia's ability to twist the language could embarrass Martha in the verbal combat, if their words were overheard. She looked around to see if anyone was listening to her conversation with Julia before responding.

"A lucky man is good, but a good man might not be lucky," she said, before moving away from the discussion.

———

Penarius returned to the temple site that morning. He had consigned the bishop's thoughts to his memory, revised them as necessary – without telling the holy man – and intended to give the laborers his first plans for reconstruction of the temple.

"It will be a magnificent church, a cathedral, to rival those in Rome or Byzantium," he declared with confidence.

The men standing in a circle around him had been to neither of these cities but had heard about their grandeur. Without trying to envision the plans that Zosimo or Penarius made for the Cathedral of Siracusa, they had to assume that it would be a place that the gods themselves would visit.

"We will build walls of stone that span the gaps between these pillars," he said, indicating how the rows of blocks would be assembled to reach across the floor from one column of the Athenaion to the next one, "but the columns should show on the outside and the inside. The thickness of the walls must be less than the diameter of the columns, so that the curved surface of the pillars will stand out on the inside and outside."

The laborers understood some of what Penarius was saying but they lacked his ability to visualize the structure, so most of them nodded blankly or shrugged their shoulders. To accomplish this plan, the walls would have to be noticeably thinner than the columns to allow the curved surface of each pillar to be displayed. The workmen mumbled among themselves but did not have the skill to calculate the strength of a wall proportional to its thickness and height.

"Will these walls be strong enough to hold up the roof?" one of the men asked.

Penarius had already considered that problem but replied with nonchalance: "Of course."

This did not concern the workers around him. If Penarius and the bishop wanted to waste their funds building a cathedral that would fall down, these men didn't care. As long as they were not standing below the roof when it collapsed.

Construction began swiftly, according to Zosimo's orders. The bishop himself visited nearly every day but when he saw that progress would be slow, he lost interest. Penarius was on the site every day and guided his workers to move the block and complete the design according to his measure. Such an undertaking would require years of arduous building, which Penarius knew; yet he was patient. Long projects meant long paychecks, and Julia and their sons would appreciate the money that he made.

———

"The bishop tends to his own affairs and you tend to his church," Julia said one morning when Penarius entered the room. Their servant had picked some fruit from the trees in their courtyard, including peaches, pears, and apples, and Julia was cutting them up and adding the small aromatic leaves from the tops of the basil bushes growing in the sunny platform outside their home.

"Yes, the bishop's own affairs are all consuming," the builder replied, but he had a slight smile as he said it, as if he doubted that Zosimo's activities were anything more important than affairs of the flesh.

"He pays you well," Julia said, with a slight uptick at the end of her sentence, almost sounding like a question instead of an answer. "Yes?"

"Of course. You know that he does. And we enjoy the status and importance of his position in our society."

"You enjoy the status," she reminded her husband, but he scoffed at that.

"I enjoy watching the crowd part at the market to let you through," she added.

Julia's eyes remained fixed on the rough wooden surface of the table on which she was cutting the fruit. The strands of light brown hair that hung past her cheeks nearly hid her face from Penarius, but not enough to keep him from noticing the wry smile on her face.

He sat down on a chair next to the table and reached out to touch her right hand, the hand that brandished the knife.

"We have much to be thankful for. We have a fine home, two strong sons..."

"And respect," she interjected.

"Yes, and respect."

Then her hand stopped its motion and she laid the knife down. Looking kindly at her husband, Julia sat down too.

"The new church. Will it be beautiful?"

"It will stand for many lifetimes as a tribute to the greatness of bishop Zosimo."

"But not to you? Not to the people of Siracusa?"

Penarius thought for a moment before responding, looking down at his hands as if the answer might be written there.

"The Greeks built the temple. It was a glorious homage to their goddess Athena. And I've heard the stories of the ancients who said that there was something else there before the Greeks built their temple."

He paused, still looking down at his hands, but turning them over to inspect their rough texture and the calluses that covered his skin.

"And now the people come from Byzantium and build their church." He looked up and brushed the silky locks of hair back from Julia's face. The sunlight coming in through the window highlighted the faint blond streaks that appeared randomly through her hair.

"Our people have been here before, we are still here now, and we will be here later when another great church or temple is built upon this one. Time seems to change and go on for the people who come here, the armies who fight to take our land from us, or the governors who simply come and buy it, taking our estate with taxes or new laws, or whatever.

"For us, time does not seem to change or move on. There will always be our people, and there will always be a new people coming to build their church upon ours, and then another church to replace that one. What does it matter if it is built as a tribute to us?"

———

Later that morning, Penarius was on the site of the temple, looking over the parchment designs of the new church. His apprentice, Ottimo, came around the stack of cut stones that had been brought to the site, and waved as he saw the builder bent over the drawings.

"It is a fine day, my friend," he said to Penarius. "We should build a great cathedral today!" he added, clapping the man on the back.

Penarius put down the wooden calipers and smiled at his assistant. He enjoyed the young man's lightheartedness. Most of the laborers on the site were slaves, probably from the provinces of Regio Tripolitana or Carthago, and for them the dawn signalled the beginning of another back-breaking day of hard work. Ottimo's jests gave Penarius a break from that and reminded him of the privilege he enjoyed as an artisan favored by the ruling Byzantines.

"We will begin moving the wagons of block today," he said, turning their attention to the project at hand. "First," he said, pointing with the caliper in his right hand to the broad-beamed wagons that were loaded with pre-cut stones, each about half the size of a man. "First, we move these to the edge," slowly drawing his hand toward the periphery of the foundation of the church.

The deck of the Temple of Athena would be used for the floor of the cathedral, and these wagonloads of blocks would be brought to the edge where the stonecutters would finish the surfaces and then stack them up to create the walls. These walls would, in turn, close the gap between the Athenaion's columns to enclose the new structure.

Ottimo stepped in between two wagons and signaled for the foreman of the slaves to bring his squad over to him. Little instruction had to be given; both the slaves and their foreman – a slave also, but one who had earned a position of power above the lowly ones – had performed similar tasks many times before and knew what steps were required.

Oxen had been used to bring the wagons to the site, but the brute animals could not be easily controlled so close to the temple, so the slaves would be used as the animals for this assignment.

The foreman, Acctual, pointed to the wagon that would be pulled first, and six men came to it. Four took hold of the ropes that had bound the wagon to the oxen, and the other two went to the back of the craft. On Acctual's orders, all the four ropemen pulled while the two at the back put their shoulders into the effort, sweat joining with the dirt caked on the wagon from its time in the quarry.

After moving the wagon to the proper position near the construction site, these six slaves were replaced by stonecutters who would finish the styling of the blocks and ensure a tight fit. In the meantime, the crew of slaves returned to bring up another wagon and position each at alternative places around the perimeter of the building. On this day, the stones could be laid in place by the men while standing on the ground. In the months that would follow, when wagonloads of stone would continue to be dragged to the site, sturdy wooden scaffolds would be required so that the men could continue to raise the walls to the great height required of a cathedral. Tripods of pulleys with heavy wooden block and tackle devices would be perched above the scaffolding and stretch far into the air above the top of the columns themselves.

At the end of each day, when the sun fell and darkness came over the structure, Penarius would remain after the labor was completed. The slaves would have been herded back to their quarters and Ottimo would retire to the tavern nearby. Without a wife, his meals were always taken in the company of other men, with plenty of wine and some local women whose plans included sharing the workers' pay.

"It is for the glory of us all," Penarius muttered.

He was a Christian, having converted to that faith as the power of Byzantine rule grew. The people of Siracusa didn't consider beliefs and religion to be united in any way. Each of them could entertain their own beliefs; some still clung to polytheistic ways, much like the Romans and

Greeks before them. Choosing a religion, on the other hand, was more of a political decision. And choosing the dominant religion of the time, Christianity, seemed to make sense. Aligning oneself with a religion was a practical decision; choosing one's beliefs was another matter altogether.

"My sons will be pleased with the money I make," he said aloud to himself.

When darkness made it hard to pick out the seams between the blocks, Penarius knew it was time to return home. Julia would prepare some food and he would consume enough wine to drift off to sleep, then he would awake the next morning and begin again.

———

A few weeks later, Zosimo appeared on the site. His visits had become infrequent and unpredictable. Penarius assumed that a bishop would have other important responsibilities, at least this bishop pretended to. Besides, the builder didn't need the holy man to bother him at the cathedral. The work was proceeding well, Penarius had enough materials and men to continue, and he was being paid regularly to continue the project.

"I see," the bishop said in a serious tone. He was circling the footprint of the cathedral as the activity continued, repeating "I see" at intervals and nodding approvingly at the walls that were being erected.

On this particular morning, Martha was with him. She had been born free but was considered *infama* – a member of the lowest class just above slaves. Still, her association with Zosimo and other wealthy men rewarded her with privileges above that status.

Penarius assumed that her presence at the new cathedral on this day was primarily to publicize that she remained the bishop's attendant. Her power over the people in Siracusa was limited to her perceived power over the cleric. So, she periodically paraded through the city with him to remind everyone and make sure the connection was not lost.

"I will name it after Theotokos," the bishop told her, loud enough that everyone would know he had made a pronouncement. It was the Byzantine title for the Mother of God and, just as the Greeks had erected their temple on this spot to Athena, the goddess of fertility, Zosimo intended to build his cathedral to honor Theotokos, the mother of Jesus.

"It is perfect," cooed Martha. She was always more flirtatious when they were out in public. Her physical closeness to the bishop and her coy comments were a theatrical move to remind onlookers of the bond the two shared. In private, she was more contrived and not always as subservient to the holy man.

"When will it be done?" the bishop asked Penarius.

"In your lifetime."

"Is that a question or a commitment," Zosimo said in retort, but his builder did not reply. Although Penarius was employed by the bishop, he had established a relationship that allowed him some small freedoms. But he also knew not to press it in the presence of others. Like all leaders, Zosimo had to maintain his power through persuasion and by convincing the people around him that he possessed some unspoken power over them.

"The great church will honor you, my lord. And the holiest of holies, the Mother of God."

The bishop seemed sufficiently satisfied with this and walked away. Martha trailed behind him and gave Penarius a knowing look. Perhaps the *infama's* look was a little too expressive, because Julia had appeared with her husband's midday meal and took a little offense.

"Is she planning to have you too?" she asked derisively.

"No," he replied. "I can't afford her."

To which Julia swiped at her husband playfully.

827 C.E. - 965 C.E.

MUSLIMS

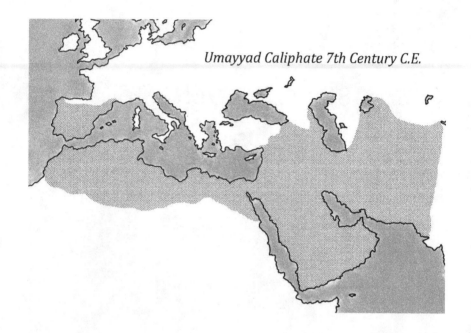

Umayyad Caliphate 7th Century C.E.

AUGUST 2018

CAFÉ AMADEO

VITO WAS AT THE CAFÉ WHEN I ARRIVED THE NEXT MORNING. HE sat in the corner facing the doorway and raised his leathery hand to me and smiled.

"Athena," Vito said.

"Yes," I replied, but was unsure where the Greek goddess would take us.

"The Temple of Athena. You remember it, no?" asked Vito.

"Yes, no...wait," I begged as I flipped back through my journal.

"Himera...480 B.C..." Vito offered kindly.

"No. What am I saying? Of course, yes," but I was stalling. While I paged backward, Vito returned to tell me the story again.

"Gelon, tyrant of Siracusa, defeated the Carthaginians in a great battle near Himera in 480 B.C. He celebrated the victory by building a massive Temple to Athena outside his city. Well, it was upon this foundation that Zosimo built the Cathedral of Syracuse."

I thought I knew that but by now my notes were as confused as my memory.

"Zosimo. He's new. Did we talk about him already?"

"No, Luca," said Vito with a pat on my hand. I think he realized that his mastery of the historical facts exceeded even my ability to write them down, much less integrate them all.

"He was not a terribly important figure, all things considered. From most accounts, Zosimo rose through the ranks of the clergy simply by being in the right place at the right time. It doesn't mean that he was impotent," at this he chuckled, but continued, "but his knowledge and training were not important in determining where he would go in the church hierarchy."

"Tell me more about the cathedral," I asked.

"Well, it was – and is – quite a sight. The elements of the Athenaion – that's what it was called – especially the columns and the floor itself, are pretty impressive. The Romans tended to enclose their temples of worship, whereas the Greeks wanted to keep theirs open to the world. So, whereas the Temple of Athena was an open-space design with only widely spaced columns and a roof, the church that Zosimo built from it was closed in. This was before openings for windows were common, so there was little natural light in the thing that the bishop of Siracusa built. But it was solid, permanent...in fact, the cathedral is so imposing that it stood as is for centuries untouched by new construction.

"The Muslims converted the building to a mosque later, around the year 878, then the Normans took it back when they came here, returning it to its Christian purpose. About two hundred years later."

"I assume it's still standing?" I asked. When the question slipped from my tongue, I was suddenly – and unexpectedly – embarrassed. I had come to Sicily to drive around the country and learn the culture. With all that had happened in Siracusa over the millennia, it was hard for me to accept that I hadn't been there yet, but had spent my entire sabbatical here in Mazara del Vallo.

"Si, it still stands," Vito replied. "There have been earthquakes, of course, and Mt. Etna is not far away. But the Cathedral of Siracusa still stands. I think, maybe..." but then he paused. The barista came over with another espresso and a plate of orange slices, and Vito shifted his attention for a moment. I wonder if I will be as resilient as this man when I am...then I realized that I didn't even know his age.

"Vito, I'm sorry, can I ask?"

"Ask what?" was his response.

"How old are you?"

He thought for a brief moment.

"Not as old as the temples, but much older than the memories," as he slipped an orange slice between his teeth.

I guess it served me right. What did it matter to me – or to him – how old he was?

"Anyway," he said, trying to recapture the thread of our conversation, but then he paused again.

"What was I saying?"

"About the Cathedral of Siracusa," I suggested. "It still stands, but you were about to say something more about it."

"Of course. It has been damaged by earthquakes, you know, and some pillaging over the centuries. But it was partially rebuilt in the late-Eleventh Century by Roger I, the first Norman count to rule Sicily. He liked a more elaborate design, so the Cathedral of Siracusa took on a Baroque appearance. You'll see that when you go."

I noted that Vito did not say "if you go." As much as I wanted my time to be spent with him, I think my mentor had assigned me a bigger task. He wanted me to learn all that he had to offer, but then also continue on my original quest to travel the roads of Sicily. I was becoming increasingly eager to fulfill that assignment.

"Tell me more about Mazara del Vallo," I asked. Vito was from here and claimed that his family had always been from this area. Back many conversations ago, I recalled that Vito claimed some of the original settlers on the island of Sicily arrived right here, in Mazara, although it wasn't called that originally. Each one of his stories brought my heritage to life, and I wanted to know more about his.

"A few weeks ago," I began slowly, fumbling through my journal to recover the right notes, "you said that the people from Iberia settled Mazara. But then, later," again pulling pages back and forth, "you said the Punics. The Phoenicians settled it. Clarify this for me."

"I think the earliest people to come to our country were from Europe and they established a colony here on the southern coast of Sicily," he said. "They probably came from Iberia, modern-day Spain, across the gap at Gibraltar and across the northern coast of Africa before landing here. But just as the Greeks took over earlier settlements on the eastern edge of the island, like Nassina, Myla, and Katane, the Phoenicians settled on the west coast by moving into some of the existing settlements there."

"Did they establish some new cities of their own? I mean, not by overrunning an existing city?"

"Yes," Vito replied. "The most important of these was Zis, the Phoenician settlement that was to become Palermo. The Muslims called it Bal'harm."

"So, these cities, settlements, whatever," I interjected. "The names kept changing over time? Why?"

"Each new tribe, or by now I suppose we should say 'each country,' that invaded brought their own language and their own culture here." He paused for a moment as his eyes swept the room, taking in the artifacts of the Arabs, Normans, Romans, and Byzantines who had populated this area and now decorated this café.

The barista came to our table with another round of espresso and a plate of roasted almonds. Vito nodded, I said *grazie* – then realized that I had pronounced in the Italian way, not the Sicilian *graziu* – and we returned to the subject.

"So, yes, Bal'harm it became; some records show it as Balerm. But you asked about Mazara.

"When the Arabs first came here, they sailed from Kairouan and established this as a trading post. They came and went many times from Kairouan. Have you heard of it?"

I shook my head 'no.'

"The Umayyads – they were members of the caliphate that took over most of northern Africa and the Persian Gulf area in the Seventh Century – they spread as far west as today's Tunisia and Morocco. They established Kairouan as the first great Islamic center in that part of Africa. It is a masterpiece, both the city and the mosque that stands as one of the Arab world's greatest architectural achievements."

Vito looked at me keenly, tapped his finger on the back of my hand and said earnestly, "You should go see it." Then he sipped from his cup and returned to his story.

"As their empire grew, they absorbed other areas already populated by earlier settlers, including Carthaginians, Romans, and Goths, and all those people who fought over the land for centuries. The blood of these victors – not to mention of those conquered by them – ran through the people now subject to the Umayyads.

"Around the year 800, some Arab trading ships began making more frequent trips to Sicily, landing here in Mazara primarily. They didn't stay, but I think trading in goods from Kairouan and greater Tunisia was just one purpose they had in mind. I think they were scouting the land. When they saw Mazara – remember, we had already been here for many centuries, since the Phoenician period – the Arabs decided that this island to their north should also become part of their empire. However, at the time, they were still loosely bound to the Byzantine Empire by treaty."

Vito reached for a few almonds, popped them into his mouth, and chewed for a moment. I took advantage of the break to scribble some more notes. After a sip of his coffee, followed by a gulp of the water that sat nearby, he resumed.

"While this was going on, the Byzantine generals controlled much of the island. Emperor Michael II allowed a general named Constantine to control the east, ruling from Siracusa, and a general named Euphemius to control the west from Panormus..."

"That's Palermo, right?" I asked.

"*Correttu*," he said with a nod. "The emperor was content to let a lot go, knowing that he couldn't control everything that his appointed rulers did throughout the region, but he took particular offense at Euphemius."

"Why's that?"

"It seems that the general married a woman that Michael objected to. Well, not the woman herself, but the marriage."

"What did he see that was wrong?" I asked. "If the emperor was keeping a hands-off perspective on their activities, why would he care anything about a marriage?"

Vito chuckled before taking a sip of water.

"Well, one story has it that the woman involved was a nun." And he sipped from his espresso while eyeing me for a response. I had no reply but had to laugh at the situation.

"Wait," I said between smiling lips. "If it was okay for popes and bishops to have women in their beds, why not the nuns?"

Vito raised his hand and wagged his finger.

"No, no. You're not painting a full picture yet. "There was no prohibition against sex and marriage for priests yet. That didn't come about until 1123 A.D., at the First Lateran Council. But," and again he laughed, "you're right about the uneven application of morality. Priests of whatever robe were treated like men and, like men, were assumed to have desires."

He looked at me and held up a hand to stop me from saying what would naturally come next from me. That women too have desires.

"But nuns were thought to be brides of Christ. Already. The concept was later formalized in certain Christian orders, but the women who took the vows were already considered 'off limits.'"

"So, what happened next?"

"Michael told his eastern general, Constantine, to go to western Sicily, release the woman, and cut off Euphemius's nose."

"That's ugly."

"Yes, well, the emperor wanted the man punished. I know you've read about the medieval European custom of making an adulteress wear a scarlet letter."

"Yes, like in the Nathaniel Hawthorne book."

"*Sì*. So, having your nose cut off was probably a good enough badge for all to see. Anyway, Constantine ended up losing to Euphemius after a series of battles, including losing his own capital in Siracusa before being killed himself. The victorious Euphemius wasn't satisfied yet though – or maybe he just really wanted to keep his nose – so he continued to battle the Byzantine Empire."

"How so?"

"He was afraid that Michael would mount another challenge, so Euphemius offered much of western Sicily to Ziyadat Allah I, the emir of Ifriqiya in Africa, in return for Muslim army support in defending him against the Byzantines. At first, Ziyadat Allah hesitated; there had been enough division in his emirate in North Africa and splitting his attention with the chaos in Sicily didn't seem worth it. But an advisor, Asad ibn al-Furat, convinced him of the benefits of raiding the island. Asad assembled an army of nearly ten thousand soldiers and a fleet large enough to carry them all to Sicily."

Vito paused for a moment and sipped his espresso. I tried to copy all the Arabic names into my journal but knew that I would have to research them later and correct the spelling.

"They sailed from Ifriqiya in 827 A.D., in summer, and landed a few days later here," and then he pointed down to the floor, "right here in Mazara. The Muslim assault on Sicily began here, in my city."

Vito's tone was a mixture of pride and concern, and I wasn't sure which way to characterize it. He obviously took notice of the importance of his city in the Muslim invasion, one of the most important historical events in the course of Sicilian history. But he also knew that the hoards that landed on the shores of his country a millennium ago altered the culture, religion, and legal systems of his island.

He sipped from his coffee cup, emptying it, and then breathed a long sigh. In a moment, he stood to go. I didn't know whether to comment to him about that moment, or let him drop the subject, as he seemed inclined to do. Vito was proud of everything that was true of his country, and over the days of conversations I had noticed also his pride in the art and architecture of the Arab period, so it wasn't that he resisted their inclusion in his history. I wondered what about the Muslim period affected him so.

"Euphemius met the Muslim army as it landed here," Vito added, "but he hadn't realized that they had bigger plans than just supporting him. Sensing that Asad might just take the entire island and leave him out, Euphemius devised a stalling tactic. Asad could take his army and capture the west, and Euphemius would take his army and move toward Siracusa and take the east. First on his list was Enna..."

"That's the city that the slaves rebelled in."

"Just so. But Enna has figured prominently throughout history, especially as a fortified city. Look it up. But for right now, we'll stay on the Muslims. Euphemius laid siege to the town – remember, Enna was notoriously difficult to capture – and waited through a period of time. He became convinced that the forces of Enna were prepared to surrender, so he accepted an invitation to negotiate. Pride got the better of him, though."

"How so?"

"Euphemius had always had an outsized impression of himself. When the invitation to negotiate was received, he boasted of his conquest prematurely, and approached the emissaries from Enna without sufficient protection."

"That doesn't sound wise."

Vito laughed. Now standing, but not wanting to quit without a conclusion to the story, he said, "Euphemius walked into a trap. He was stabbed to death by the men from Enna and his escort fled from the scene."

"Did his army take the city?"

"There's more to tell on that, and it didn't happen quickly. But Euphemius did accomplish one thing he set out to do."

"And what was that?"

"He kept his nose until he died." And Vito laughed at his own joke, put a finger on the brim of his hat in goodbye, and walked out of Café Amadeo.

827 C.E.

MAZARA

FOR THOUSANDS OF YEARS, THE COASTAL AREA OF NORTHERN Africa – known as the Maghreb – had been populated with a polyglot of ethnic groups. There were indigenous Berbers, themselves an ancient melting pot of Iberians, Capsians, and Algerians. There were the early Arab explorers, some Sicani who stopped short in their migration to Malta and Sicily, and many others whose small tribes drifted toward the Mediterranean Sea and the larger region over centuries.

Mazara was the closest Sicilian port to Ifriqiya and so it fate was to be converted to a Muslim military post, a staging area from which they could maintain close contact with their bases in Africa while pushing their ventures further north and east into Sicily. The proximity of Mazara to their homeland was the first attraction, guaranteeing rapid transit by water, but once there the Muslim commanders came to appreciate the geographic advantages of the city. It was at the mouth of a river that allowed the settlers to bring supplies from upland as well as deliver them to the north. And the city was surrounded by rich farmland that they could use to feed their people. In fact, the farmland once owned by the Romans for its grain stocks could now be turned to the advantage of the new lords of the island, and the Muslims wanted Mazara to fulfill the role of trade and mercantile center.

Islam spread to the region in the Umayyad era under Caliph Mu'awiyah, who governed from Bilad al-Sham – modern-day Syria. It was a logical extension of Islam as the Muslim society explored the contours of the world as they knew it. The region was still largely controlled by the Byzantine Empire when Islam grew in stature and power, and it was inevitable that the two would collide.

Mu'awiyah was the second caliph of the Umayyad dynasty, following Mohammed's disciple and founder of the Umayyads, Uthman ibn Affan. Mu'awiyah struck a memorable pose. Taller than many Muslims, he had a bald head yet sported a beard that he colored with dyes made from henna. His rise to leadership owed something to his connections with Yazid ibn Abi Sufyan, his brother, and was one of the first Muslim leaders sent from Bilad al-Sham.

Planning his expedition, Mu'awiyah staged his advance carefully, not readily engaging in situations that might be resolved to his disadvantage. When he was ready, he waged a successful battle against the Byzantine Empire with a force of Muslim soldiers, Christians, and Copts, a victory that opened up the Middle Sea to further Muslim encroachment.

When an Arab army commanded by Uqba ibn Nafi conquered the Maghreb, Islamic rule moved into near total control of the area from the Atlas Mountains north to the sea coast of the Mediterranean. Arab art, science, and culture were advanced beyond anything seen in that region, and the conquest was managed as much by a show of superior culture as by military might.

Over the years and changing caliphs in the Maghreb, relations between the Muslims and the Berbers continued in an uneasy peace. By supplanting the indigenous culture with the Islamic one, and by imposing the Muslim legal system for that practiced by the Berbers, the region assumed the nature of an occupied society.

Jewish settlements sprang up, and Christian communities appeared to dot the landscape, mostly following the itinerant disciples who preached the word of Jesus. Called *dhimmis* by the Arabs, these groups continued to live in the area as they had done for centuries, and they could thrive under Arab rule as long as they kept their religious practices to themselves and paid the yearly *jizya* – a tax on all non-Muslims that was used to underwrite the Muslims' own tax, called the *zakat* – a religious requirement in Islam to aid the needy.

It was in this time that Euphemius, a Byzantine general in Sicily at odds with his own Emperor Michael II, appealed to the Muslims in Africa for assistance in turning back the military attacks waged against him in western Sicily by another Byzantine general, Constantine.

Asad ibn al-Furat, a philosopher and *qadi* – a judge in a Shari'a court – but not a military tactician, was the one who convinced Ziyadat Allah I to come to Euphemius's aid. Ziyadat Allah appointed Asad to lead an expeditionary force to Sicily to supplement the forces of Euphemius, but he came with his own agenda.

———

She pulled her shawl across her face when she walked through the crowded marketplace. It worked to hide her face but not her identity, since the Mazarans knew this woman from the rumors.

Homoniza had been a nun until a powerful general of the Byzantine army fell in love with her. She had only vague feelings of attraction for him; her oath to Jesus Christ was strong. But Euphemius was not going to be denied. He had first spotted her in the garden at the convent where she lived. The general had access to the grounds because he insisted on a place more private than the Christian church in Mazara and the convent served his purposes well.

Some people wondered whether the old man battled other desires and enjoyed the quiet solitude of the convent garden for reasons other than meditation. But he was also a Christian, not as devout as the emperor, Michael II, and certainly not as devout as the young novitiates and nuns who wandered in twos between the mulberry bushes and olive trees that filled the courtyard outside their living quarters. But Euphemius's need for a peaceful place for prayer was his real reason for coming to the abbey. At least at first.

On a quiet spring morning, Homoniza walked through the garden alone. She was on her way to the communal kitchen to assist in preparation for the meal after prayers. Her head was bare and her youthful skin shone beneath a halo of golden hair. As she bent down at the waist to pick some herbs off a plant by the walkway, the hem of her robe rose above her ankles and exposed the skin above her leather sandals.

She didn't notice Euphemius who was standing in a corner of the garden. He had just entered through the gate and froze when he saw someone else enter the area. He watched Homoniza while she walked, head bare, hair cascading down to her shoulders, and he gaped when he saw her bend over and expose her ankles. Without making a sound, Euphemius allowed Homoniza to walk through and out of the garden without knowing that she had been watched.

He returned to the convent garden the next morning, and the one after that, but he did not see Homoniza again on these mornings. So, a few days passed and he requested a meeting with the mother superior, Sister Anita, to discuss the security of the convent.

"The men, the soldiers, you know," he began awkwardly, searching for something to say, "they cannot always be trusted. I do not want your sisters to be at risk."

"Yes, of course," Sister Anita replied, but doubted the sincerity of the general's message. The soldiers were never to be trusted, she knew, but why did Euphemius want to meet to discuss this, and why now?

As they talked, there was movement just outside Sister Anita's open door. She glanced up, nodded to the person walking past behind Euphemius, and returned to the discussion.

"I am sure that the sisters who live here, under my charge and protection," she added for emphasis, "will be safe. Especially knowing that the great general Euphemius is concerned for their welfare."

He rose to leave and turned toward the door. The person who had passed by the open portal was still there, waiting for the mother superior to be available, and Euphemius saw her as he stepped across the threshold. It was the young nun he had seen in the garden; he knew it from the strands of hair that escaped from the drape of shawl she now wore over her head. Her face was uncovered, and her blue eyes shown against her honey-colored skin.

Euphemius stopped to enjoy a longer look at her, then turned back toward Sister Anita to cover his intentions. Smiling and saluting the mother superior, he turned once again to gaze at the young nun Homoniza before departing.

Over the coming weeks, Euphemius found more reasons to visit the nunnery, and not just for prayer. He was seen often in the garden, or visiting with Sister Anita, or wandering the grounds. He always seemed in search of something, and when Homoniza would happen by, his attention spiked. Such behavior was noticed by the other nuns and especially by Sister Anita, but she was powerless a month later when Euphemius sent for Homoniza to be delivered to his quarters.

He spoke to her that afternoon in the privacy of his own home and, although he didn't touch her, his intentions were becoming clear. She had taken vows of poverty, obedience, and celibacy, but she couldn't resist the temptation of knowing a man with such great power. In time, she allowed herself to remain in his home for longer periods, even overnight. Then, one morning, Euphemius sent a note to Sister Anita that her young nun would not be returning.

"It is my pleasure to announce to you and the world that Homoniza has become my wife."

The mother superior knew that a great sin had been committed, but she also knew that the power of a Byzantine general here could not be denied.

———

Byzantine Emperor Michael II was outraged at the news. When he was informed that one of his generals in Sicily had taken a nun for a wife, he immediately commissioned general Constantine, also garrisoned on Sicily with a large army, to expel Euphemius, release the nun, and cut off the man's nose.

"Sire," the soldier said quietly, interrupting Euphemius at his midday meal. "We are told that Constantine has been sent to capture you and absorb our forces into his army."

Euphemius considered the news. It did not come as a surprise; he knew that the emperor would be angry about his recent marriage. But the general also wasn't prepared to simply surrender. In Byzantine law, actions such as his would be considered not only adultery by an abomination, and the guilty party was seldom allowed to escape unharmed. So Euphemius proceeded with the plan he had originally fashioned for the time he expected to come.

He arranged a small flotilla of boats to sail with him toward Ifriqiya, on the coast of Africa. He planned to meet with Asad ibn al-Furat, a Muslim who had been sent there by emir Ziyadat Allah over a disagreement concerning the emir's impious lifestyle. Euphemius intended to offer the Muslims control over the western part of Sicily which he, the Byzantine general, was in command of, in exchange for having the Muslim army support his conquest of the remainder of the island, including the eastern half where general Constantine resided. This would turn over western Sicily to the Muslims, but win the eastern half for Euphemius.

Asad agreed and sent Euphemius back to the island to prepare for the landing. Euphemius massed his forces in the area surrounding Mazara and awaited Asad's army.

In the hottest month of the year, a great fleet of ships from Ifriqiya loomed over the horizon and approaching the bay in Mazara. Hundreds of ships under the flag of Islam appeared, bearing thousands of Muslim soldiers, who alighted from the craft and set up camp in the outskirts of Mazara.

Euphemius was thrilled to see such a show of force and concluded that he would most certainly prevail against the smaller army held by Constantine. He donned the embroidered mantle that was the symbol of his power and, with a long staff topped with a regal ornament, he walked through the encampment of Muslim soldiers. They regarded him with forbearance but owed their allegiance solely to Asad. When Euphemius questioned any of the soldiers, he seldom received a reply, so he returned to his own quarters.

"It is not what you expected, sire?" his aide asked him the following morning.

"Not what I expected? What do you take me for?" he replied with derision. Euphemius was enjoying fruit and fresh bread for his morning meal as Homoniza sat quietly on the lounge behind him.

"The Muslims. Will they follow you?" the aide asked.

"I rule the west," Euphemius said. "Of course they will."

But he already had his doubts. There had been some small skirmishes between the armies already, and the Muslim soldiers seemed better trained and equipped than his own men. The forces co-existed uneasily in Mazara while plans were devised between Euphemius and Asad for their movements.

————

Plans progressed for the Muslim army to join Euphemius in the march eastward. They would secure the coastal cities first and, when they reached Siracusa, expel Constantine – or hang him, Euphemius thought – and then split the island between Asad and Euphemius. He didn't care what his emperor thought; this military action would defeat the Byzantines in Sicily and the land would be his.

Or some of it, at least.

The troubles between Asad's army and that of Euphemius continued, however, and the Muslims began to assume too much control. They disregarded Euphemius's commands and, when the general reported the problem to Asad, he got little in return.

For his part, Asad had come to realize that Euphemius needed him, but he didn't need Euphemius. Recalling a suggestion from Ziyadat Allah, Asad decided to ignore the treaty between the armies and proceed on his own. The Byzantine general would become expendable; the Muslim leader didn't intend to kill him, but Euphemius would not be needed to expand Arab control to engulf all of Sicily.

Asad attempted to avoid open battle with the man who had invited him to Sicily, but the events prevented him from remaining aloof for long. In time, the natural enmity between his forces and those of Euphemius, coupled with each man's desire to control the island, were bound to create irresolvable differences. Within a few weeks of their arrival in Mazara, the Muslims clashed with the Byzantine forces and forced them back from the area around the city. With a continued push, Euphemius and his army were driven from the region altogether, and forced to retreat to Enna, where he stayed to lick his wounds and consider how to defeat Constantine in the east without the Arab support that he had surrendered western Sicily for.

"It is time for us to proceed," Asad said to Galal, the captain of the Muslim forces. Asad's way of phrasing the statement was understood between them to mean a plot to control all of Sicily, a plot that had been developed far in advance of their arrival in Mazara. The Muslim conquest of the island was foreordained, and Asad intended to be the general who carried it out for Allah.

"Yes, sire," replied Galal. "I will command the men to prepare for march on the morning after, when they have slept and prepared their weapons."

"Their weapons are prepared," Asad assured his captain, "as Allah has proclaimed."

Galal only nodded. It was his command to carry out, not one to quibble with. In one day's time the thousands of Muslim soldiers would be on the march east. They would take the cities that dotted the Sicilian southern coastline, sparing the lives of non-believers if these people would swear to not support the present Byzantine empire, and garrison sufficient soldiers in each city to maintain control and exact the taxes that would continue to finance the Arabs' eastward line of conquest.

After some weeks, Asad paused his march to allow the men some respite from fighting, but he never rested from his plans to continue eastward, all the way to Siracusa, the former capital of the island. While the army rested, an emissary from the city approached with an offer for Asad. When he realized that the emissary's goal was a deception, intended to allow Siracusa time to strengthen its defenses, Asad laid siege to the city.

"Prepare to outlast them," he commanded his men. Galal made arrangements for an encampment of many months. He had participated in sieges before and could judge from the size and design of the city, and other intangible factors that he could judge from intuition, how long each siege would last.

"This will take a long time, sire," he said to Asad, who already showed signs of a weakened spirit himself. Galal noted that his commander had less energy than usual, and that his eyes seemed swollen and black.

"The siege will last as long as it takes for the infidel to surrender," Asad declared confidently. But he retired to his tent where he remained for the several weeks, under the doctor's observation.

Asad tried to summon supplies and troops from Africa, but initially had little luck. At the same time, the Siracusans called for help from their Byzantine empire. Both armies waited for reinforcements to arrive. The Arab reinforcements arrived in small lots and, although the Byzantine army came later, it was larger.

"Pull back," was the sudden command. Muhammad ibn Abu'l-Jawari had assumed command of the Muslim forces when Asad succumbed to disease. He witnessed the arrival of forces to support the Byzantine command of Siracusa and was losing confidence in the original plan. In the intervening months, the Muslims had had great success in conquering most of the island, and certainly controlled the west, north, and south of Sicily. If they could not capture and hold Siracusa, that would be set aside for another day.

"Sire, you wish to quit the siege, or stand down for the time?" asked Galal, who had survived his first commander and attended to the second.

"We will quit the siege," said Muhammad. "We have other important work," he concluded, knowing that his army could be of service to Allah in other parts of the island.

Galal was reluctant to give in. He had invested much time, lost some men, and kept Siracusa surrounded for over a year. He did not want to just give it back to Byzantines, and the new commander could sense the captain's lack of enthusiasm for the order.

"And you, Galal. What do you think?" Muhammad asked. He was not interested in this man's opinion; he was an underling and the two lacked the connection that once existed between Galal and Asad ibn al-Furat. The question was posed more as a challenge, as if the general was daring Galal to dispute the decision.

"I think that we serve Allah, and that he has given you for this enterprise." It was a carefully worded reply, a mixture of respect and obedience to Allah. But Muhammad sensed the absence of sincerity in Galal's voice, and that tone would infect their relationship going forward.

"Then make the arrangements," was all the leader had to say.

Galal returned to the encampment and walked among the stalwart soldiers at first without saying anything. There had been little direct danger during the siege, as these actions were commonly nothing more than land-bound blockades with the prey trapped inside their city and little physical contact between the armies. But life in the fields that surrounded Siracusa had its downside. The men were required to remain until the end of the siege and had no information to tell them how long that would be. Galal's earlier sense that it would be a long endeavor played out in his organization of logistics, such as building semi-permanent camps and cooking facilities, and insisting that latrines be constructed far from the camp with longer, deeper trenches. The men picked up on these signals and obediently settled into the quotidian chores of an army bivouacked in a foreign country.

Now Galal would have to tell them that the last several months would be left without a victory. That they would pull back, perhaps return to their homes. As welcome as a homecoming seemed to the soldiers, they regretted having nothing to report to the families that they had left behind. The captain kept his own counsel for hours that afternoon, visiting the soldiers and then returning to his tent to consider the situation.

"Sire," said a young man who had pulled the tent flaps apart to peer inside. "Emir Muhammad requests you come to him."

Galal stood and followed the man to Muhammad's quarters, a large, high-posted tent with wood beams at various points along the side to support the many tapestries and oil lamps hanging from above.

"So, it is time for us to go," Muhammad said. Again, more like a challenge than a question.

"Yes, sire. The men are ready," Galal replied, but he chose that wording – knowing that his soldiers were always ready – instead of explicitly saying that they had been informed.

"Then we raise the siege today. The infidels have arrived from the north. They are near the city already and will bring their *skoutatoi* – archers – and their horsemen by tomorrow."

Muhammad paused for a moment to assess Galal's reaction to this description. He had no intention of sounding like he was running away, but he had no intention to stay and fight a stronger force when the Muslim army had already been depleted by disease.

"We leave tonight."

Galal then knew that he would have to tell the soldiers immediately so that they could strike the tents and prepare to load the wagons. True to the training of the Muslim army – and to Islam itself – he was certain that the men would move swiftly and confidently. They would leave Siracusa for conquests elsewhere, and he would praise them for their courage and strength.

"*In shā'allāh,*" he said to Muhammad – "As Allah wills it" – bowing his head in praise of Allah but conspicuously not in deference to his commander.

———

As Galal expected, the men responded quickly to his orders and organized in ranks to withdraw from Siracusa. They retreated to their ships where they found out that Muhammad had ordered a complete pullback, a return to Ifriqiya itself, abandoning the island as well as Siracusa. But once they boarded their ships, the Byzantine force dispatched from the north intercepted them and threatened to destroy the Muslim navy and the men aboard.

In flight from a naval battle that they were unprepared for, Galal took control and ordered the men back onto the island. He didn't have the time – or interest – to consult with his commander Muhammad, so Galal acted on his own authority. He held some men back to set their ships on fire and prevent confiscation by the Byzantines, and then instructed them and the army assembled on the southern coast of Sicily to organize a march inland. They reached the hilltop town of Miniu, a poorly defended village in the Hyblaean Mountains west of Siracusa and reorganized there. The Mineans were ill prepared for this unexpected onslaught; theirs was a minor outpost on the island and battles between the Muslims and the Byzantines – not to mention the centuries of Greeks, Goths, and Romans – were fought in bigger cities with more treasure for the taking.

Miniu surrendered to Galal's army almost immediately.

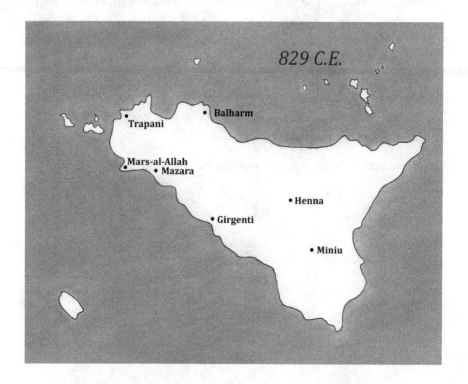

829 C.E.

HENNA

AFTER MINIU SURRENDERED TO THE MUSLIM ARMY, GALAL SET his sights on Henna where he knew that Euphemius had retreated to create a manageable space between his western Byzantine army and the Muslim invasion force that he had brought to the island. Euphemius was aware of Asad's death, and also knew that his captain, Galal, was driving the Muslim army now without the presence of the new leader, Muhammad, in the region. This, Euphemius hoped, would allow him to get the upper hand over the Arab military leader.

"We have captured Miniu," Galal told the Byzantine general when they met in the fields below Henna. He stood tall before his counterpart, posturing as a strong leader to deny Euphemius an opportunity to take command.

"Yes, so I understand. It was after that unfortunate business in Siracusa," came the reply. The Byzantine leader had been humiliated by Asad in previous encounters, and he would not let Galal enjoy the same advantage. The Muslim captain smiled back at his interrogator, more of a sneer than a smile, but he chose not to engage in a battle of words.

"And what will you do with Henna," Galal responded, hooking his finger in the direction of the hilltop fortress that had resisted attacks so easily in the past.

Euphemius's plan was to lay siege to the town, but he was reluctant to say this since the Muslim army – stronger and better equipped than his own – had just recently failed in that tactic at Siracusa.

"We will surround the city, cut off its contacts with others outside of Henna, and deliver an ultimatum."

That sounded a lot like a siege to Galal, but he didn't say so at first.

"And when they are surrounded and cut off," he began, choosing his words carefully, "they will decide that it is in the best interests of their people to join Islam?"

"Oh, no," said Euphemius with a proud smile. "They are already Christians, from Byzantium, and they will be invited to remain Christian, but under my rule."

Each man's words took on the feel of a speech, or a warning. But little more was said as the two armies encamped near one another.

———

On a morning soon afterward, two men stepped through the east gate in Henna and trudged down the winding path that took them to the fields below the town. Their movements were noticed by the Byzantine guard on duty at this early hour, and he sent a message to Euphemius. The general rose quickly and stepped out of his tent to consider the events.

He was met at the center of the Byzantine army's camp by Galal who had also been advised of the scouts from Henna. Galal went to Euphemius as a show of cooperation, since neither man knew yet which direction the scouts would head, and whether they considered the Byzantines who had arrived at Henna first, or the Muslims who reinforced Euphemius later were the commanding army.

As Galal and Euphemius watched from their camp, the two Ennaean scouts continued their long walk down the path from the city, across the open fields, and into the grove of trees where Euphemius had his command tent.

"We welcome you to Henna," began one of the men. "I am Santoro, and I have a message for the honorable general Euphemius."

"I am he," the general said, stepping forward and in front of his ally, Galal. "What is your message?"

"We are told of the great victories that you have enjoyed over the enemies of our empire," Santoro began. He carefully avoided distinguishing between the eastern and western regions of Sicily and how they were commanded by two different generals from Byzantium. He also avoided mentioning the Arab military that backed up Euphemius. Santoro was a Christian and intended to keep this negotiation between Christian peoples.

"And we are told that our Emperor Michael has appointed you to this great and honorable position to protect our people and to deliver us from evil intentions."

Santoro tried to avoid eye contact with Galal on this last comment, but his vision drifted in that direction. Galal responded wordlessly, but with great emotion in his face. He was not happy with the course of this conversation and intended to exact revenge when the time was right.

"We in Henna would like to give ourselves to you, sire," Santoro continued, while assiduously gazing solely at Euphemius. "It is our conclusion that the rule of Byzantium, under either of the generals that the most holy Michael would choose, is the correct path."

Euphemius beamed at the messenger now. He was surrendering the entire town to him, the fortress that others had failed to claim, and he was doing it without an armed battle and without even a lengthy siege. It appeared to him that the siege – possibly to be waged by both Christian and Muslim armies – would end the contest in Henna and that the citizens there would rather fall under the rule of the Byzantines.

Galal was a careful student of people's emotions, however, and he did not accept Santoro's pledge exactly as it was stated.

"We will return at dusk," Santoro continued, "and meet you at the foot of the Ennaean hill and bring our elders with us to show you into the city."

"We will bring our escort to that meeting," interrupted Galal. Euphemius turned angry and a red color rose in his cheeks. Galal's comment suggested that Euphemius's conquest of Henna would be split and shared with the Muslims and he had no intention of agreeing to that. The fortress was his; the victory would remain his alone.

"I do not need your help," he said to Galal, his words accompanied by a dismissive gesture. "We have reached an agreement," then nodding to the messenger from Henna as if they were old friends. "We will meet the city elders ourselves as described."

Galal sensed trouble in this plan, but since the danger would be faced by this arrogant Byzantine standing beside him, the Muslim captain decided to remain quiet.

Euphemius celebrated the victory with a grand midday meal. Two lambs were slaughtered and a great fire built to roast the meat and warm the broth. He enjoyed the camaraderie of his soldiers, even the company of the two women that he thought it necessary to accompany him on this mission. The sun shone brightly on this day and the general was in high spirits celebrating his victory.

Late in the afternoon, as the sun began to slip below the peaks of the mountains behind his encampment, Euphemius dressed in his most elaborate uniform. It had braided threads woven into the chestplate, a silk robe draped over his shoulders and hanging past the long white tunic he wore. When he felt that he was sufficiently dressed out, he called for the twisted cane staff that he walked with and ordered two of his tallest soldiers to accompany him to the foothills of Henna.

Galal had returned to his own camp while Euphemius celebrated but when sunset approached, he returned to watch the Byzantine general depart for the meeting.

Euphemius and his two-man escort departed the camp just as a small group was seen exiting the gate at Henna. The Ennaean party worked their way down the slope as the three Byzantines walked across the fields between the army camp and the city. When proximity allowed a better view of the Ennaeans, Galal could see that there were six or seven of them. At first, he supposed the group to include Santoro and the elders of the city, as promised. But as the team of men descended the hilltop town and became easier to see, Galal could see that not one of the men in the Ennean party looked old to him, unless the 'elders' of this city never lived longer than a young man. He watched keenly as his counterpart, Euphemius, continued his confident march toward Henna, and he wondered if the Byzantine or the two men who escorted him were aware that this might not be the meeting they were expecting.

"We welcome you to Henna," said Santoro as the two parties approached each other. He was accompanied by six other men who, although they were dressed in city clothing not armor, looked less like elders and more like soldiers.

"Who is with you?" asked the general. He was growing uneasy but couldn't retreat immediately without looking like he had been overly trusting in agreeing to this summit.

"These are my fellow Ennaeans who have come to welcome you."

"And they have names?" Euphemius persisted.

Santoro regarded him momentarily but showed little interest in answering the question. He raised his right hand as one would do in a salute, but the smile faded from his lips. As Santoro dropped his hand quickly to his side, the other Ennaean men took the signal and fell upon the three Byzantines with knives and short swords.

The scuffle lasted only a few moments before Euphemius and his escort were cut down.

———

The failed attack on Henna was a turning point for the Byzantine army and the Muslims. Galal informed Muhammad of the treachery of the Ennaeans and blamed Euphemius for falling for their trick. Muhammad instructed Galal to remain at Henna and lay siege to the town. Asked what to do about Euphemius's men who remained after the attack, Muhammad told his captain to drive the Byzantines away, defeating and destroying them if necessary, but under no circumstances to let Henna survive this moment.

Galal carried out the orders and drove the Byzantine army from the region, then reset the siege on Henna. Hearing of the conflict with the Muslims, Emperor Michael sent another force from Byzantium led by Theodotus, who sailed quickly and went directly to Henna to join the battle. By then, Galal would have nothing to do with the Byzantines. He abandoned all notion of the original invitation from Euphemius to unite in conquest of the eastern part of the island. Galal intended to win Sicily for Islam, and he would not cooperate with any Byzantine general going forward.

Theodotus arrived at Henna while the Muslim siege was still on, but he and his forces were driven up into Henna in retreat, in a strange treaty between the Christians of Henna and the Christians from Byzantine uniting against an attacking Muslim force.

The Muslim army lost Muhammad ibn Abu'l-Jawari during this period, and he was replaced by Zubayr ibn Gawth, a man with less wit than his predecessor and unable to continue the successful campaign. Theodotus took little time to appraise his new opponent and surmised that the Muslim army would fold when sufficiently threatened. He staged a downhill assault on their encampment, routed the army and send Zubayr fleeing for his life. Not content to savor his first victory, Theodotus pursued the Muslims into, and then, through their camp, driving the forces of Islam from the region in an all-out attack the likes of which Muhammad would not have allowed had he still been in command of the army in Henna.

In cold retreat, the Muslims made haste for Miniu where memories of a more successful enterprise were still fresh. They garrisoned there but were soon once again in Theodotus's sights. He brought the Byzantine army to the enemy and laid siege to Miniu, a siege much more successful than either the ones at Siracusa and Henna, forcing the army of Islam into starvation. The news from Miniu was so grave that Muslim forces as far away as Girgenti abandoned their fortress and returned to Mazara in the west. These actions and troop movements resulted in a nearly complete clearing out of Muslim soldiers from the eastern half of Sicily, returning them to their strongholds in Mazara, Balerm, Mars-al-Allah, and Trapani.

Theodotus's siege of Miniu kept the Muslims under close arrest, although they had not surrendered. The news that their leader got out the Muslim forces in Girgenti was also received as far away as the Umayyad Emirate in Iberia. A fleet of hundreds of ships commanded by Asbagh ibn Wakil arrived at the shores of Sicily soon to break the Byzantine siege and, with the assistance of more soldiers from Ifriqiya, they managed to free their brethren in Miniu.

Asbagh terrorized the fleeing Byzantines who retreated to the west, but in the hostile environment of summer, the Muslims were overwhelmed with more sickness and death in the camps. The plague that swept the Muslim army gave Theodotus another opportunity to set upon them, this time killing so many Muslim soldiers that the stragglers took flight and sailed back to safety of Ifriqiya.

859 C.E.

HENNA

Ludovico Parmentum had been the captain of the Byzantine guard at Henna for four years. He was chosen for the post by general Attilio Vergine and his name had even been mentioned by the emperor himself, so he took great pride in his assignment and his responsibilities in protecting the hilltop town.

But these were not tranquil years. The Muslims had sacked a number of Christian cities on Sicily, including a dramatic defeat of the Byzantines in Panormus, killing scores of his fellow soldiers and rebuilding the ancient town and renaming it Bal'harm. He heard that Messena had fallen to the invaders and then Modica, and after them Leontini and Ragusa. Most tragic of all was the battle at Butera, where the Muslims not only defeated the Byzantine army but butchered thousands of the men who defended it.

"Call the men," Vergine said curtly, as Parmentum entered the general's quarters. The old man was slumped over his table, staring at the crude map of the island spread out before him. He didn't even look up at the younger soldier, and didn't say anything else, so Parmentum stooped through the low door and exited.

"Call the men," Parmentum repeated the command to Philippus, the *turmarch* – leader of his infantry. The soldiers were huddled around a table playing dice, but Parmentum was adamant. "Vergine wants everyone in the courtyard."

"What for?" came a reply from one of the men. It was an impertinent question and Parmentum didn't like it. He swiped at the man's head and pushed over the table, sending the dice and the soldiers' coins onto the floor.

"I said, call the men," he repeated, to Philippus, although he was not the one who had questioned the order. Parmentum was a patient and understanding man, but he didn't like the mood that some of his army had gotten into lately. Either they were bored from long months of duty in the quiet of Henna, terrified of the possibility of a Muslim advance on the city, or just wasting away, letting their training and military duty atrophy. Parmentum could forgive many minor breaches in behavior, but he would not tolerate questions about orders.

In less than thirty minutes, the entire regiment of soldiers in Henna had gathered in the courtyard. Normally a city as important as Henna would be protected by thousands of armed soldiers, including *koursorses* – or cavalry – *skoutatoi* – the archers, and machinists to operate the pulleys and catapults. But Henna was essentially impregnable and had been for as long as there were records of its existence. So, the emperor decided to outfit the city with only several hundred men. Well-trained, certainly, but not a force to reckon with the Muslim hordes if they ever figured out how to scale the mountain.

"There is an army of the heathen approaching," general Vergine began. He paced back and forth in front of the rows of soldiers as he addressed them. He was short and stocky, but he was also considered a brilliant tactician. Perhaps he was chosen for Henna precisely so that his genius could offset the absence of more troops. But Vergine hated the assignment. He believed all the comments about his tactical abilities, but he also knew that they could only be used in open field battle. Flank movements, diversions, and fades wouldn't do him any good in a walled compound on a plateau like Henna.

"We have heard from scouts that they will likely arrive three days hence." He looked at the faces of the soldiers gathered before him trying to discern their mood and whether they would stand up and fight – or shrink from the test.

"I have also heard that Abu'l-Aghlab al-Abbas ibn al-Fadl is leading their army to us."

This announcement struck a chord, so Vergine looked more closely at his men. Al-Abbas was well known to them. He took command of the Muslim army in Sicily a few years earlier and had been on a perpetual raid of the eastern half of the island ever since. He was the commander who defeated and razed Butera and ordered the execution of the Byzantines there. He was also the one responsible for defeating many other towns and cities in the Val di Noto – a region encompassing the entire south-eastern portion of the island. This would be his first sally against Henna, and the rank and file soldiers who were lined up in front of Vergine wondered about his chances – and their own abilities.

The men were edgy, and looked down and around, avoiding Vergine's gaze. The general had seen this behavior before. He knew enough to not take it as the soldiers' only reaction; many had been startled by news of a fierce fight to come but, after consideration, had stood tall in the face of the enemy. No, Vergine was looking for more subtle signs. A soldier who showed tears in his eyes, or who rubbed his hands together, or whose eyes darted back and forth. These were the ones, Vergine knew, who would either flee or fail. He spotted a few and gave a quiet sign to Parmentum who tried to remember each of the soldiers that his commander had doubts about.

Parmentum himself had only been in a handful of battles. He survived but not all conflicts were resolved to the glory of Byzantium. In the process, though, he had developed some of the senses that he admired in Vergine. As the general inspected the troops' reactions, so did Parmentum.

"This city is impregnable," Vergine continued, still pacing back and forth. "No army can scale its heights, march up its paths, or" – and here he paused for effect – "or fly in from the sky." He completed his sentence with a hand waving toward the heavens, and then crashing down on the earth.

"We will not lose Henna," Vergine declared firmly. He may not be able to use his famed tactics here in this walled city, but Christ himself would not let the Byzantines lose Henna.

————

Diryas had doffed his armor, layers of leather tunic, and chain mail covering, and was enjoying the breeze of fresh air that his chest and arms missed when decked out in this soldier's clothing. He was a *Rashidun*, an elite Muslim soldier and, like others who were skilled and courageous enough to serve in this infantry, he was proud. But he didn't mind removing the heavy protection that he wore to battle when he didn't need it.

In fact, Diryas wondered why the infantry was required to wear this armor while on the march. Al-Abbas, his glorious and honorable commander, had ordered it. He said that the soldiers must be prepared for battle and wearing the chain mail and carrying the leather shield and sword that dangled from the leather strap called a *baldric* over his shoulder would teach them to manage the weight of their armaments.

But in camp, they could take these things off and recline near the fire with only a light tunic to cover themselves. It was true, what Al-Abbas said: Carrying the weight made the use of it easier. And when battle came, they would cripple the infidel, *in shā'a llāh*.

They had been marching for two days already since the last battle. That had gone well, with Naaqid giving orders in the field. Diryas trusted him; they had fought together for two years while Islam was conquering this island, and Diryas knew Naaqid's style well. He would drive them forward, and throw everything at the enemy to frighten then, then pull back while the *skutatoi* rained arrows on the infidel's fixed position. Then Naaqid would mount another assault, timed for the moment when the enemy rose to see why he had faded back. The back and forth movement was difficult for the Byzantines to predict, and they couldn't sally forth to inspect the battlefield for fear that they would get caught in another advance.

Diryas, for himself, had decided to relax as much as possible for a while, knowing that Al-Abbas would want them to move again and he would have to shoulder the armor once more in a march toward Henna.

Naaqid came over to the circle that Diryas was in and stood over the men. He was not an intruder; the men respected him. But his appearance after coming from the commander's tent was meaningful.

"We will stay here this night," he said, and all the men breathed a sigh of relief.

"We are within a few hours of Henna, and we would like to reach the city in the morning, not this night as the sun falls. So, we will camp here."

A few of the man collected more wood and built a bigger fire. The others prepared to eat the salted fish they had in their sacks, and the bread – now stale – that the women who trailed the army had cooked for them. These same women would deliver more food, perhaps some wild grapes and cherries, as the evening wore on. There would be very little cooked meat; the army traveled light and couldn't bring sheep and goats this far so the only meat the men had was the dried strips of flesh that had hung in tents before their departure from Siracusa.

"This is not so terrible," said another *rashidun,* Inamur, as Aqsa approached. She was veiled as was the custom for all Muslim women, which was particularly important for the women who traveled with an army, hungry for many things, including food. She was bringing the fruit that they men hoped for, plus some more beef jerky.

"And so," Naaqid challenged him, "you are ready to fight the infidel?"

"I am always ready," Inamur boasted. "They are nothing to us."

"*In shā'a llāh,*" said the man to his right.

"We will see them tomorrow," said Naaqid. At that, the boasting ended, and the men ate more slowly. Theirs was a solemn mission, to defeat the infidels and to bring Sicily under the control of Islam. But it was also a formidable task. They had endured many months of marches and battles, and lost some of their friends. Praise Allah, they said, but warfare for the soldiers on the front lines is not so noble as it is for the commanders on the back lines.

———

Philippus was awake before the sun rose. He knew that the enemy was drawing closer by now; a few days had passed since Vergine had announced that they were coming. The *tourmarch* knew his duties and knew that his men were prepared, but battles always meant casualties.

'It will probably be a siege,' he thought to himself. 'Al-Abbas will not try to march up the mountain.'

And he was right. When the Muslim army was seen coming across the plain toward Henna, the formation split into four segments. The two groups in the middle slowed their march while the groups on either side spread out and moved to positions around the mountain on which Henna stood. It was a maneuver that took several hours to complete, but the Byzantine soldiers at the towers watched as the Muslim army arranged a complete circle around the foothills of the mountain. There were so many of them that, even by stretching the army out, the Muslims still seemed to form ranks ten to twenty-deep completely around the mountain.

There were some breaks in the circle, but not large enough for an escaping army to manage to exploit. The Muslims made camp, began their fires, and spread out in highly organized detachments, strictly ordered in "tens of tens," the hundred that constituted a squadron. There were archers and machinists in every quadrant, and the officers, cooks, and supply managers were arranged at the rear of each squadron.

The army settled in with little fanfare. There were no arrows arcing over Henna's battlements, no fiery pitch thrown from catapults, and no offers to negotiate. Ibrar ibn Afsad – an ironic name since Ibrar meant 'peaceful' in Arabic – was the commander of this particular assault, and he didn't intend to negotiate a surrender. It would come on his terms.

And the siege was on.

———

"Where are we going?"

Traestum's question seemed odd, even to Philippus who knew his friend's penchant for anomalous thoughts.

"We're not going anywhere," was Philippus's simple reply. He was sitting in a circle of men he commanded, having a midday meal, and wondered what Traestum was wondering about.

"No, I mean where is this going?"

"You mean the siege?" asked a soldier to his left.

"Do we sit here, and wait for them to come?"

"The general told me what we would do, and I repeated his orders. The Muslims will encircle us, but not attack because they can't get into Henna without being stoned on their way up the mountain. We, however, have lots of fresh water from our cisterns and lots of meat from our animals. We even have..."

"Yes, I know. We have grain from the fields we've planted here within the walls. But does that mean we just sit here until those heathens give up and go away.

"Oh, they won't go away," remarked Sterios. "They want Henna and they will remain as long as it takes to get it."

"So why don't we talk to them?" asked Traestum.

"They don't want to talk," replied Philippus. "They want our town and, maybe our lives, and they don't think they have to negotiate a settlement."

Conversation lagged a bit as the men contemplated the meaning of Philippus's last comment. It sounded as though the Muslims would put them all to the sword if Henna fell. After a brief silence as the men finished their meal, Philippus offered some words of confidence.

"Henna has always survived and will always survive. We are in the most secure city in Byzantium."

———

Venatos was responsible for the farm plot that the Ennaeans had cultivated for many generations. It was particularly important during these times, because they needed to feed themselves without going outside the walls and without depending on imports of grain, fruit, and animals from the countryside. He was the best in the city and knew that they could produce enough food to keep alive, and the water would come from rainfall and be stored in the cisterns until needed. A dry season could be very difficult, though, so Venatos was careful to maintain his crops and keep them healthy enough so that a long dry spell could be weathered.

But he was less sanguine about the Islamic army that encircled his city. Venatos occasionally climbed the steps up the perch used by the soldiers, and he was awed at the thousands of soldiers camped below. They were a short distance away and he could see individuals moving about the Muslim compound, but the collective impression was of a solid hemp noose looped around the foothills. If it tightened, he would become very worried.

As it turned out Venatos was already very worried. He was not a soldier but he heard the same stories that the Byzantine army heard. The Muslims had laid siege to many other cities in Val di Noto and brought them all down. Why would Enna be any different?

One morning, Venatos slipped through the opening in the city walls that was well hidden, but which gave him access to the small herb plants that he cultivated there. Eshaal, the young woman whose name made her seem like a Moor, was already there. Venatos and Eshaal often worked side by side in the garden, he the well accepted Christian and she, the dark-skinned foreigner who still had difficulty being received as a true Ennaean.

"What do you need today?" asked Eshaal.

"I want *trichiagon,* he said, referring to a bright green plant with thin leaves that sprouted all the way down the branch. "It is for the calf that we have slain. It is for the general, Vergine."

"Here," Eshaal said. Her accent was like her skin, decidedly southern. All in Henna knew that she was from Africa, and that she probably came to their country as part of a slave exchange. Somehow, she ended up in Enna and was free.

Venatos took the branch that she had plucked from the bush but, instead of leaving with it, he stood there admiring the young woman. Her skin glistened in the sun, and her black hair was silky smooth. Venatos knew its texture because he and Eshaal had more than once met here in the garden for reasons other than plucking tarragon.

"I want to help," he said.

"With what?" asked Eshaal as she stood up. "What other herbs do you need?"

Venatos paused, not knowing how to say the next thing.

"I don't need other herbs. I want to help...I want to help save Henna."

Eshaal smiled at him. She knew Venatos to be a gentle man, certainly not a soldier, and she didn't know how he could help save Henna.

"How will you do that, Venatos?"

Again, he paused, and wasn't quite certain how to proceed. He couldn't take his eyes off of her, and if his plan worked, he wanted her to go with him.

"I want Henna to surrender without fighting," he said suddenly.

Eshaal stood up even straighter and gave him a confused look.

"I don't know what you mean," she said finally.

He knew he had to phrase his next statements carefully, so Venatos thought carefully before saying anything.

"The Muslims will win, and many of our people will die."

Eshaal's expression remained stolid, although she knew the truth of what he said. Unlike many other invading armies, though, she didn't fear rape from the soldiers of Islam. She had heard some stories, true, but the occasions were rare.

"And how will you prevent that?" she asked him.

"If the Muslims could come into Henna without fighting, if they could be here before our soldiers could resist, it would be over, yes?"

Eshaal didn't know how to respond to that. It was the first time such a thing entered her mind and it made her nervous and excited at the same time.

"How would that be?"

"You know the cistern system, yes?"

Eshaal nodded.

"There is also a runway, a long pipe carved through the rock for our..." he paused before continuing. "For our excrement to flow out of the city."

Eshaal thought for a moment, and then smiled. She had never considered how Henna remained so clean and healthy. She knew the engineers had found ways to bring water in, so there must be ways to send it out. But what did that matter to Venatos?

"It is an easy way into the city, and no one watches it."

"Do they know about this?" asked Eshaal.

"No. But..." and Venatos stalled.

"But what?" asked Eshaal.

"Will you come with me?"

The sudden change in subject startled the girl.

"Where? What do you mean 'go?'"

"I will go to the Muslims and tell them how to take Henna without having to fight the soldiers. Will you go with me?"

"Where?" she asked again.

"Not to see the Muslims. That is far too dangerous. But I will ask them to let you and me out, to leave, to go somewhere where there is no war. Will you go with me?"

"That is too much to consider, Venatos. You must give me time to think."

But he didn't. Venatos had already decided that he would use the tall sewage throughway cut in the rock to climb down to the foothills that night. He would ask to see the Muslim commander and tell him what he knew. He was going to do this, but he needed Eshaal to agree to come with him.

After dark, Venatos followed his plan. He hadn't gotten a commitment from Eshaal yet but he would tell the Muslim commander in the middle of the night. That would mean that they wouldn't arrange an infiltration until at least another night, and he would have time to talk Eshaal into joining him.

Venatos trod carefully through the tunnel that had been cut for their waste. It was a sloping pipeline that had a natural spring dripping in from overhead, enough flow to allow the excrement to be washed out naturally. It was into that opening that many Ennaeans poured their buckets of waste, not knowing where it went but pleased to have it gone.

On his excursion, Venatos was careful to step on the rocks on the side. He wasn't afraid of the things that floated along the slow river in the pipe, but he didn't want to smell of human waste when he reached the Muslim camp.

The Muslim commander Ibrar received Venatos with glee. He listened to the gardener's sometimes meandering story, but was quick to realize the importance of what the Ennaean was telling him. This pipeline, though defiled by Roman waste, was a clear opening into the city that many armies before him had never conquered. Ibrar knew that this would mean his victory and, just like Butera, he would raze it to the ground. He would use this man Venatos to find the opening and his men would pour into the city.

"This is right and just," he said to Venatos when the gardener had completed his description. "And Allah will reward you."

Venatos didn't give much thought to the fact that Allah's rewards came in the afterlife.

"You will remain with us tonight, camped with my best soldiers, and we will enter Henna tomorrow in the darkest hour," Ibrar told him.

Venatos protested that he must return to the city, but didn't reveal that his primary reason was to rescue a woman – a Berber Muslim woman in fact. He was instead swept out of Ibrar's tent by two strong men who placed him in a circle of Muslim soldiers, who were given strict instructions not to let him escape.

"He is a very valuable Ennaean," one of the soldiers said with a smile.

The following night, when even the stars failed to come out because of the dense cloud cover, Venatos led the Muslim soldiers up the side of the hill that approached the sewer tunnel hidden in a shallow cave and with an entrance disguised by abundant trees and bushes. When the infiltration began, he was standing at the outer end of the tunnel, pointing to it and saying that they would be inside Henna shortly, but they wouldn't need their swords since the Byzantine army would be asleep and not expecting them. Venatos himself turned toward the tunnel and was going in to find Eshaal when a soldier impaled him on his sword.

"We do not need you anymore," was the last thing that Venatos heard as the Muslims rushed past him. He survived long enough to feel the soldier rip the sword back out of his abdomen and watched in horror as his blood and guts poured out of the gaping wound.

When the invasion of Henna was complete, Ibrar entered through the main gate.

"This city will be Qas'r Ianni for evermore, as Allah wills it." With that, the renamed fortress became a Muslim stronghold and Ibrar ordered a constant guard on the tunnel that they had used to enter and conquer the city.

878 C.E.
SIRACUSA

BASIL WAS ANGRY. HE WAS VERY ANGRY. HE HAD SUCCEEDED IN supplanting Byzantine Emperor Michael III – not without treachery of course – and now he intended to recapture Sicily from the Muslims. They were still pestering him – a favorite phrase of his because he didn't believe that the God of Christianity would let these heathens occupy the island, much less the world.

He came to his power indirectly. The emperor, Michael III, had married Eudokia Dekapolitissa but they had produced no children, a problem which threatened the continuity of the empire and left Michael looking for solutions. Emperors were keen on progeny, and sons were of paramount necessity.

So Michael took up with another woman, Eudokia Ingerina, his mistress and despite the similarity of names was no relation to his wife. He was concerned about the the public reaction if he contrived a way to marry her so, instead, he arranged to keep Ingerina close to the court and at his disposal by marrying his chamberlain, Basil, from Macedonia. An added incentive to sanction the marriage between Basil and Ingerina was that she was pregnant with what he – Michael – believed to be his baby.

A son was born whom Basil and Ingerina decided to name Leo, and immediately a plot was hatched to arrange for the boy's eventual ascension to the throne.

Basil manipulated his situation as the apparent "father" of Leo, contriving to draw a share of power from Emperor Michael who was reluctant to allow a public debate about the question of parentage. In those uncertain circumstances, Basil assumed the role of co-emperor. When the opportunity arose, he caught Michael in a drunken stupor and, with the help of a ruthless and notorious conspirator, hacked Michael to pieces and then stabbed him in the heart. With Michael out of the way, Basil was cleared to claim title to the throne and become Basil I of Byzantium.

While this battle for power was being waged between the two men, Muslim forces were tramping across the island, capturing cities, razing some and occupying others, and when necessary executing the populations that resided there, especially the army detachments that had been brought to defend the cities. Ibrahim II had ascended to power in Islam by replacing his brother, Muhammad II ibn Ahmad and he was determined to complete the conquest of the island that his brother and others before him had begun many lifetimes ago. He appointed Ja'far ibn Muhammad to carry out the assignment.

Ja'far and his army walked through the villages around Etna and in the area north of Siracusa. They had no trouble taking control and setting up an Islamic administration. He was employing this as a long-range tactic of strangulation: capture all the populated areas around Siracusa so that the city's supply lines and support systems would be cut off, then lay siege to the city itself.

The early stages of his plan went so well that Ja'far gave command to his son, Abu Ishaq, and Ja'far retired to Bal'harm. Abu Ishaq laid siege to the city and subjected the Siracusans to a long series of attacks by soldiers using assault machines like the new *mangonel*, a type of traction trebuchet that could launch objects farther than a traditional catapult. His siege tactics were more successful than those that had been employed against other Sicilian holdouts and they resulted in the Siracusans being reduced to slow starvation. The situation reached a point that eating animal skins – even the flesh of their own deceased brethren – was not uncommon.

Abu Ishaq's siege included both land and sea, a critical part of the plan, since he knew that the Byzantine Empire was busy with other matters and might not have the resources available to send armed forces to Sicily to resist the Muslims' attack.

The siege continued for months and the supplies of food in the city continued to dwindle. When the Byzantine army let down their guard, the Muslims seized the moment and raided the city. In the ensuing melee, thousands of Siracusans were massacred, the leaders were taken prisoner and later executed, and some of their closest defenders were beaten to death with clubs. The city was pillaged and nearly destroyed along with its population, left in ruins as the Arabs removed themselves from the wreckage, satisfied that they had finally annihilated the Siracusan people.

———

Before the siege, Italo had wandered about the garden, wondering how it would fare when water became scarce and rationed only for drinking by the thirsty humans in Siracusa. He was sympathetic to his fellow citizens but also attached to the beautiful garden that he had cultivated during this era of strife. Romano had helped him, but the young boy was only an apprentice, and not learned in the difficulties of raising plants in difficult conditions.

Many times, Italo had ducked in fear as the sound of burning pitch came over. It was launched from the catapults that the Arabs had and he knew that each of these could set fire to whatever they struck. The green garden should be mostly safe, what with the spacing between the plants and the moist soils, but Italo couldn't still his heart when the fiery bombs screamed over his head.

Romano didn't seem to care. In fact, he was somewhat amused by it all. Thus far, the launches from the Arabs' catapult had not struck the garden, and Romano knew too little about the city at his age of ten years, so he was not invested in the prospect of utter devastation of Siracusa.

"Will we go?" he asked Italo.

"Go where?"

"Go from here," Romano replied.

"No. Why should we go from here?"

"People say that the invaders have taken all the cities in the country, even Enna, and now they want to take ours."

"Don't worry," answered Italo. He wasn't sure he believed that himself, but he didn't know what else to say.

The following day, the Muslim attack on the city took on greater urgency. Italo was in his garden and soldiers appeared on the rise. They came at him swiftly and he didn't have time to react. He put his hands up in the common signal of surrender, but a Muslim soldier drove a spear through Italo's chest and out the back. The gardener had a startled look on his face when the weapon pierced his body. He looked down, as if he couldn't believe that the hardened wooden shaft that showed out of the front of his body could be connected to the sharpened spear-point that protruded from his back. In a few seconds, he fell the ground and the soldier ripped the weapon out of his chest and continued on.

954 C.E.

BAL'HARM

A MIXTURE OF PEOPLE CROWDED THE STREETS IN BAL'HARM. There were Muslims in flowing robes, Christians in tunics, Berbers whose dark-colored cloaks stood out in every crowd, and Jews with curled braids hanging down from under their yarmulkes. What was once Zis, then Panormus, had become Bal'harm, center of Muslim learning on the island and capital of its wealthy leaders.

The *kasbah* was the center of the town. As the primary marketplace, it could always be counted on to draw a crowd and as the cultural center for art and government, the square would serve as a staging area for speeches and demonstrations.

But Saabih never looked at the *kasbah* in this way. He was an architect, one of the best in Islam, and he was brought to Bal'harm to introduce the city to the beautiful art and design of his culture. He looked out over the *kasbah* from the window of his room on the second floor. He absorbed the energy of the square, an essential part of delivering the kind of decorative masterpiece that was expected of him.

"Do you know what is wrong with your lofty ideas?"

The voice was none other than Nudair, another designer from Islam but not one who put the artistic ahead of the mundane. He had approached

Saabih from behind but joined him on this ledge that overlooked the market below.

"What?" asked Saabih, almost rhetorically, since he knew that his friend would focus on something truly ordinary.

"Water."

"What do you mean water?"

Nudair was silent for a moment, then looked up at his friend.

"Water is essential for life, and..."

"And we came here for water," Saabih said, finishing the sentence.

"Of course, but we think that water is endless."

"It is," replied Saabih. "We have water all around us," he said, sweeping his arms from right to left.

"But," interjected Nudair, "how do you get it?"

"I send the slave," Saabih said, smiling.

"No. I mean how does the water get here?"

It was from that conversation that Saabih and Nudair decided to combine their skills and create a permanent water source for Bal'harm, one that would not be subject to the tides of nature or the tides of war.

The friends spent the following day walking the ridges of the low mountains that defined the harbor of Bal'harm. From above, they could see the terrain and the slope of the land. With some effort, they could pick out the slow movement of natural streams that broke from the hillside and tumbled down into the watery harbor below. They could also see the spread of houses below, the footprint of a city that continued to grow.

"These," said Nudair. "These springs are the solution."

"How so? They seem to amble in a lonely fashion, until they reach the bottom."

"And that is what we need to fix," said Nudair, staring deeply into his architect friend's eyes.

They went back to their dwellings and brought maps out to compare. Saabih had one that detailed the city plan for Bal'harm; Nudair's map was devoted to natural formations, like streams, hills, caves in the hillsides, and so on.

Aqsa appeared so quietly that Nudair was surprised by her presence. Saabih wasn't. Aqsa was his wife, a beautiful girl from Persia. She was covered in a *hijab*, with a gossamer veil pulled across her mouth and nose. It was the customary mode of dress for the Muslim women, but Nudair could see beauty in her eyes. She left a platter of figs and almonds, with sliced oranges on the side. Then she turned toward the fireplace and retrieved a heavy iron two-handled pot that carried the unmistakable aroma of cloves and coffee. Not all the Arabs put cloves in their coffee, but Aqsa did, and Nudair was forever grateful.

Aqsa smiled, a facial gesture that could be seen behind the thin veil she wore, and Nudair smiled back in thanks. He raised his hands, held together, and brought his forehead down to them clasped in front of his face. Aqsa returned the gesture and stepped back, and away from the men.

"Be careful, my friend," said Saabih, "she is my wife."

At that Nudair blushed. It was not appropriate for Muslim men to show an interest in another man's wife, although they all showed a sexual desire for their own wives. Nudair was unmarried and he had to be mindful of his gestures so that he didn't suggest something to a woman that would end up sanctioned by the emir.

"Here," Saabih said, drawing Nudair's attention back to the city plan. "Here is where we could build the tunnels and the pipes – the *qanāt* – that will draw the water down from the streams to the homes in the city." He was drawing his finger across the map from the high points of the hillside behind Bal'harm to the slopes of the harbor, to the sea itself.

"It is a constant slope," mused Nudair. "But that is what the Romans did," objected Nudair. "Can we not do better than those pagans?"

"It is about the flow of the water. You know that it flows from the mountain to the sea. We want to capture it, put the water that flows from the mountain into these pipes that we will build – the *qanāt* – and send it to the city."

"But the city is crowded and already built," said Nudair, sweeping his hand across the map. "Where would we put these tunnels that you imagine?"

"Under the city."

"That's impossible. How would we get under the city?"

"Some would be channels, above the ground," explained Saabih, "some would be between the buildings that are already built, and some would be under the roads that we use, especially the roads and homes that are on the hillside."

"Those would be the hardest," replied Nudair.

"But that is essential to the project," said Saabih. "We have to tunnel under the buildings on the hillside so we can maintain a steady slope. If we rush down to the harbor and then try to snake the pipes along the ground, there will be no flow."

"And when does the water stop flowing?"

"Do you mean when we have no water?"

"No. We have mountains and springs. They will suffice. But how do we move the water so that it doesn't just stay in one place?"

"Water flows down," said Saabih, acknowledging the obvious. "So, we will build our tunnels, pipes, and channels that must always go downward from the mountains to the harbor."

Their idea was either too crazy or too smart, but they would find out later when they tried to do it. Saabih got the permission of the emir to hire workers and bring in slaves to embark on this project. There were hundreds of men employed, not counting the more than hundreds of enslaved peoples who cut and dug into the limestone bedrock of Bal'harm to establish a foothold for the system. One thing Saabih hadn't anticipated was the limestone. Not that he didn't know it was there, but he had never drilled through it before so he underestimated the time it would take to cut their troughs for the pipelines.

Above the ground at the highest elevations, the springs would be allowed to sprout from the earth but cisterns would be chiseled in the rock face of the mountain to pool the water before it entered the first pipe and its long downhill journey. From the lower edge of the cistern-pool, holes would be cut out and pipes inserted, and the hole would be closed by clay and reeds that would harden like the impermeable surface of the rock itself.

Each length of pipe would be affixed to the one above it in much the same way, using clay and reeds to seal the joints. Partway down the hill, the men would begin to dig trenches for the next lengths of pipe to sit in. Farther still, the trenches would be deepened, filled with pipes, and then covered over. Farther still, the men would dig great holes in the ground and begin the difficult task of tunneling down the slope of the hill to insert the pipes all the way down to the buildings at the bottom.

"I need only a moment," said Imtiazud. He was hired for the project as a digger above ground. It was a favorable job, better than the tunnellers who were mostly slaves. But still the labor involved in splitting the limestone and digging out the trench for the pipes was hard work in the summer sun.

"Yes, please, sire, rest your weary bones," joshed his partner in the trench, Sawrat. "It is good that you rest. Allah approves it," he continued, pointing upward to the sky first, and then down toward the sea.

Imtiazud smiled wanly but thought the joke was more like prodding to resume work. So, he stood, pretended to swing his pick at his friend, and went back to digging.

"The pay is good, and Mahira likes that about it," Imtiazud added, referring to his wife.

"The pay is good enough," said Sawrat, "but my wife, Isha, she says it barely feeds our family."

"That's because you have beautiful children, five beautiful children," replied Imtiazud between swings of the axe. "And Allah says you must feed them!"

"*In shā'a llāh*," prayed Sawrat. "And when, my friend, are you going to have children?"

Imtiazud didn't look up or stop the swinging of his axe.

"In time, my friend, in time."

Wives were not allowed to climb the hills up to where the men worked, so when it was time to break for a meal, they sat down where they were and pulled loaves of bread, dried meat sticks, and fruit from their leather pouches. The repast began with thanks to Allah, and then the men ate in silence. The time for food was treated as a reminder of what Allah had given them, so the Muslims on this hill didn't fill the air with babble. They ate, sipped from the buckets of water brought up to them by slaves, and stared off into the distance, going over silent prayers in their minds.

The slaves working far below in the tunnels were mostly non-Muslim, and their meals were not as quiet. These men of the island, and some who had come from the north, chattered throughout the meal. The break from hard labor and the opportunity to chew on the morsels of food were also revered by these men, as with the Arabs on the hill above, but their thanks was shown in reverie and friendly talk.

————

The digging and trenching and tunneling went on for many weeks and months. Imtiazud and Sawrat were favored with the right to work together, as were other Muslims employed as paid labor. The slaves who worked below were often moved from team to team, depending on where they were needed and what labor called for them to perform.

As the cooler weather came late in the year, the work went along more easily. The summer heat had faded and although the back-breaking work continued, the men could suffer the circumstances with greater ease.

"How long until this is finished, I wonder," Imtiazud pondered one day.

"How long? How long for this pipe?" asked his friend.

"No, for the whole system," replied Imtiazud.

"I was in the *kasbah* one day with Isha," said Sawrat, "and I overheard the architects describing the system to the emir's aide. It was about one line of the pipe from up here to down there," he indicated the endpoint with a finger pointing down to the lowest row of houses on the slope below them. "He said it will take about one year."

"One year for one run of pipe?" asked Imtiazud. "That is a very long time. And then we have only gotten to the first houses before even trying to get down to the harbor. Are we to cut all the lines of pipe?"

"Oh, no," laughed Sawrat. "You've seen all the men on the hills, yes?"

"Of course. Well, I don't know how many there are, but..."

"There are hundreds, maybe thousands," said Sawrat. "I don't know how many, but the *qanāt* is being laid in the ground for the entire city. I have heard that in some places, when the pipes join, there are tunnels so tall that you could stand in them."

Imtiazud stopped his work to consider his friend's fantastic ideas.

"Why would I want to stand in them?" he responded.

"Well, you wouldn't, but that is how big the water will be when it comes down from the hills and joins the other pipes. The *qanāt* is the biggest project that Allah has ever designed for Bal'harm."

———

More months went by and the summer heat returned. The Muslims working up the hills had finished their work at the peak and had moved on to other spots along the ridge of mountains that fell gently toward the harbor of their city. They knew the first opening stages of the *qanāt* and how to settle the pipes into the limestone, and so they were shipped from one ridge to another as a new line of pipes was begun.

They were also responsible for digging out the cisterns along the pipeline but learned early in the process the tricks to keep the water from flowing before they wanted it to. They cut side channels in the hillside and let the free run water from the stream dribble into these new routes, diverting it from the direction of their work. When the pipes were ready to be used, they would dam up these alternate channels and let the water flow directly into the waiting cisterns and forward down into the pipes heading for the city.

The slaves continued their work below, in the deep trenches and the tunnels. When the large rooms that Sawrat had described were cut below the ground into the rock, Muslim stone cutters were brought in to build arches and walls to keep the earth from shifting and falling in on the tunnels.

It was a long and slow process, employing thousands either as free labor or slaves, but the *qanāt* system was designed for the entire city of Bal'harm. With advance planning, sufficient funding, and dedicated oversight, the Muslim plan to provide irrigation for the city transformed the infrastructure of that settlement and modernized it like no other project before them.

AUGUST 2018

TRATTORIA BETTINA

"It took years," Vito said as we walked toward a table in Trattoria Bettina, "but the Muslims cut through the rock and laid pipes and tunnels all across Palermo, providing pathways for the water to run from the streams above the city to the homes and businesses below."

We settled into a table under the darkening sky, and Vito waved to the waiter. He didn't have to order; a bottle of his favorite Nero d'Avola would be coming.

"It was a truly amazing feat, as successful as the Roman aqueduct system but, in its way, more complicated. The aqueducts brought water from the mountains to the cities and mostly filled the cisterns and fountains. The *qanāt* brought it right into the buildings themselves, and it did so underneath an already-constructed urban environment.

"But, then – with apologies to the ancient Greeks – the Arabs were the most advanced civilization to inhabit my country by that time, most advanced in science, mathematics, even literature."

"Why literature?" I asked, as Vito poured a half-glass of red wine for me.

"The Quran is a marvelous literary achievement. Whether you subscribe to the tenets of Islam or not, you should read that book for sheer enjoyment. Pay attention to the *sūra* – the chapters – from the

Sūrat Ta-Ha that relate to the existence of God. And what about the poets of the Middle East?," he said, shifting subjects so quickly that I had trouble keeping up. "Not all were Muslim, but all were products of that culture. Like Omar Khayyam and, many years later, Kahlil Gibran. And what about Rudaki, who probably defined Persian poetry in the Tenth Century, and Sanai, and Abu al-Faraj Runi?

"You seem to have immense respect for the people from Islam," I said.

"I do," Vito replied. "And not just for their poetry, the *qanāt*, and their mathematics, art, and architecture. Their impact on the Sicilian culture was dramatic, and lasting.

"Palermo – Bal'harm – had been taken over by the Muslims in the early 900s A.D. and they made it their capital, moving the focus of civilization on Sicily from the east to the west. But the city's fate actually lay with the decline of Byzantine control of the island as much as the rise of the Muslim caliphate.

"Emperor Michael II had died during the Ninth Century battles between the Byzantines and the Muslims, and he was succeeded by his son, Theophilus. The son swore to continue his father's war against Islam throughout the Mediterranean region, and especially on Sicily which the Muslims had chosen as its staging ground for a broader assault on Europe."

I continued to write and take an occasional sip of wine, and Vito paused to give me a moment.

"To Mazara and Bal'harm, the Muslims brought their most significant import: art and education. Islam led the world – well, the Western world – in matters of art, philosophy, science, and education, and it was the Muslim respect for these things that would alter the history of Sicily forever. They insisted that education was a natural right and they provided classrooms, books, and lectures for every citizen. It was a somewhat limited concept. Like Athens long before them, 'every citizen' was defined mostly as Muslims; in fact, mostly as Muslim elite. But just as the Catholic Church had financed the growth of art for their Gothic style churches, Islam fostered the growth or fine art and education in Bal'harm, Mazara, and Mars-al-Allah – Marsala, what was Lilybaeum to the Romans – as well as Sicilian cities to the center and east of the island as Islam conquered those regions."

"And they ruled from Palermo?" I asked.

"Yes."

"And so the art of that city, and the architecture...was it the model for the country?"

"And education, don't forget," Vito added. "The emir of Bal'harm was personally devoted to the delivery of art and education to the people he now commanded. He decided that the centers of learning would be open to all, although not everyone could participate in the open process of learning. However, he exposed all people, Muslim and non-Muslim, to the beautiful architecture imported from Islam that would now define the public appearance of Sicilian cities, especially in the west."

Vito took a sip of wine and seemed prepared for a tangent in our conversation.

"While they brought their art, the Muslims also brought their food. They introduced melon, eggplant, and papyrus plants to the island, they brought saffron, lemons, and limes, and they planted groves of date trees. They cultivated sugarcane for the sweet foods they long enjoyed in their homeland, and featured lamb, fish, and beef in their dishes.

"The indigenous people of Bal'harm were already accomplished fishermen, but the Muslims introduced another practice not yet used in Sicily, called *mattanza*. Fishermen would row their boats out into the stream of fish and then create a circle with their vessels. Slowly, they would tighten the circle to entrap the fish, then club them and drag them onto the boats. This and other fishing and agricultural practices from their home region added to the complexity of life in my country, and to its delights."

Here, Vito paused and drank some wine. Smiling, he continued.

"One of the most enduring Muslim imports to Sicily was a product of water, salt, and flour called *rishta*. The ingredients were combined in a dough-like mash, then spread out to a thin layer on a wooden surface. When the mash had dried for a few hours in the open air, a knife would be drawn across it in a series of long, parallel lines, cutting the dough into thin noodles, and then cooked. This would often be served with chunks of cooked lamb steeped in a sauce made of the broth from the meat, and onions that had been grilled over a flame. This 'pasta' as it was called became common stock in Sicilian kitchens. You might think of it as lamb ragout over fettucine," at which he smiled broadly.

"A lot of people use the terms 'Muslim' and 'Arab' interchangeably," he continued, "but they're not the same thing. Islam has spread across the world, and just as the original Berbers of North Africa became Muslim – the religion – they did not become Arab – the ethnicity. But, the art and architecture, and the science and math that the people brought from the Middle East were all a product of Arab culture. So, the design flourishes you see on these walls," sweeping his hand to encompass the geometric patterns that adorned the crown molding in this room, "these are Arab influences. Islam adopted them in their places of worship and in their liturgical texts, but the Muslims were inserting artifacts of the Arabic culture of their origin."

The waiter came to the table bearing bowls of olives; a basket of bread still steaming from the oven; hunks of *caciocavallo, canestrato, maiorchino* – typical Sicilian cheeses – and sliced pomegranates. He checked the level of wine in the bottle and, seeing that only about one-quarter remained, lifted it in a gesture to Vito. The old guy simply nodded, enough of a conversation to spur the *cameriere* to bring a new bottle of wine.

"From the year that the Muslims first arrived to capture the island, in 827 A.D., until the fall of Palermo in 831, then Enna in 859, and Siracusa in 878, the Islamic caliphate carried out a lengthy and very successful campaign to take control of Sicily. It was probably the constant push forward that kept the effort going because after the conquest of the east, the Arab people on the island fell into what could only be called boredom."

"What? That sounds extreme." I had to chuckle at the thought.

"It seems that the different factions in the Muslim populace – and army – that had worked together through the period of subjugation had trouble getting along when there was no external enemy to fight. The

Aghlabids argued with the Berbers, the Fatimids argued with the Kalmids, and they all fought among themselves.

"Ja'far al-Sadiq ibn Muhammad was the first to go. His demise inspired a battle for succession between the Ismailis and the Ja'Fari. The result was that Ja'far's grandson, Muhammad ibn Ismail, succeeded him to power.

"But that didn't resolve the territorial dispute. Husayn ibn Rabah was appointed to rule Sicily and he re-ignited the fight with the Byzantines by raiding some of their remaining cities near Messina. Husayn probably thought this would re-unite the feuding Arabs but it went the other way completely. The internal dissension was, by then, so rampant that the normally well-organized Muslim army was unable to stage a successful campaign against the Byzantines. He suffered a series of disappointing defeats at the hands of his enemy and was forced to retrench and rethink his strategies."

"How long did this go on?"

"The back-and-forth between the Muslims and the Byzantines continued throughout the century, with a long string of victories and defeats on both sides until about the year 900. But Emir Ibrahim II – who still tried to rule the island from Ifriqiya, kept appointing governors whom he expected to quell the discord among his own people. The Muslims were, in effect, fighting a war on two fronts: the Byzantines in the east and their own people over the rest of the island.

"The occasional victory helped quiet the Arab discontent in their own ranks, but these happy events were too often interspersed between defeats and setbacks. Enough so that the dissension continued to fester. Ultimately, the Muslim commander, Sawada ibn Khafaia, brokered a peace with the Byzantines who saw an opportunity to continue to dig the knife deeper into the heart of the Muslim army. The treaty called for a gradual release of Muslim prisoners, so the Byzantine general chose to release groups of Ifriqiyans and Berbers separately and, by doing so, they sowed more discontent among the two groups according to whom each believed should be released first.

"Taormina fell to the Muslims in 902 A.D. which effectively represented the end of the upsurge of Muslim conquest in Sicily. Once they controlled the east, Ibrahim – who had by then been demoted from emir to merely a military commander – turned his attention away from Sicily and toward mainland Italy. As a result, most of the Tenth Century on Sicily was relatively calm, at least free from the tumult of invasion and war."

I was amused at the thought that this island, which had been the battleground for so many conflicts already, could point to a century of peace as an interlude.

"This was the period of the *qanāts,* the time of the rise of education and art, and the years when the blood of the Sicilian people truly mingled to form the mixed race that it is."

"Do you mean that this was it?" I asked. "The many people who had invaded the island over the millennia were by then the stock that makes up the Sicilian ethnicity?"

Vito laughed and drained his glass before standing to leave.

"Oh, no. There were still the Vikings, Normans, Angevins, Aragonese. Let's see...Austrian, and Bourbons...and more," he replied. He turned to go, but then turned back around.

"Have you ever heard of Jawhar al-Siqilli?"

"No," I said, shaking my head.

"He was a *ghulam,* a slave. He was a Greek Sicilian, born right here. In chains he was delivered to the emirate of North Africa."

"Why do you mention him?"

"He won his freedom through battles and he became a general under Caliph Al-Mu'izz. He conquered most of the Magreb, is credited with founding Cairo, and built the al-Azhar Mosque in that city.

"Not bad for a poor slave from Sicily, huh?" Then he tipped his hat and walked out into the dark night that had fallen as we spoke.

1030 C.E. – 1193 C.E.

NORMANS

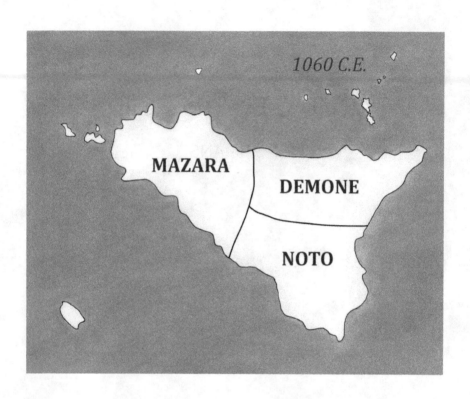

AUGUST 2018

CAFÉ AMADEO

"Vikings," Vito said. It was an unseasonably mild day in August and, for a brief moment, I considered suggesting that we sit out at the sidewalk tables. But thought better of it.

"What about them?" I asked, sliding into a chair next to him.

"They're Norsemen, *correttu*? But a subset of all the Normans who conquered Europe and the British Isles."

I wasn't going to argue. I knew enough about history to know that the Vikings were memorialized as marauders who sacked towns and pillaged regions before moving on, but I couldn't swear to it.

"There are some reports of Viking ships landing in Sicily very early, perhaps while the Muslims still ruled the island. It's more likely that they didn't come until about 1038..."

"...when the Muslims were beginning to fade in importance in Sicily," I interjected.

"Yes, quite so," he said smiling. "But while the Vikings themselves don't figure prominently in the history of my country, their allies do."

"Who was that?"

"Tancred de Hauteville, first of all. He was the sire of many generations of Hautevilles in my country. And the Hauteville family brought legions of Norman mercenaries to assist Harald Hardrada, the Norseman who was later to become the King of Norway."

"Okay," I said, holding up my hand in a sign of surrender. "What's the difference between a Norseman and a Norman?"

Vito laughed and sipped his espresso. He chewed on a *cantuccio*, then looked back at me.

"Think of it this way: A Norseman, which literally means a 'man from the north,' usually refers to people from Scandinavia. Although it is a word used loosely to refer to anyone from that clump of islands, including the Vikings, the term refers more specifically to the few centuries surrounding the end of the First Millennium A.D., roughly from about the Ninth Century to the Thirteenth or Fourteenth. On the other hand, Normans were – well, are – a subset of the Norsemen who settled in northern France and have long outlasted the brief era of the Vikings."

The barista appeared at the table, but Vito signaled that he wanted no more coffee. That was a bit strange, knowing his capacity for espresso, and my worried look elicited a response from him.

"Too much lamb ragout last night," referring to a favorite dish among Sicilians that had been introduced by the Muslim invaders. But while rubbing his stomach softly, he smiled.

"Not to worry. I had some Marsala to wash it down."

It is the local dessert wine which, apparently, the old guy uses as a digestif...or antidote.

"Where was I?" he said thoughtfully.

"Vikings," I replied, falling into Vito's habit of one-word sentences.

"It's important to clarify something," Vito added. "Many people write the Vikings into our history, but they played only a small part. They came around the year 1038 but were gone within a couple of decades. That's why the Hauteville family's role is so important. They teamed up with the Vikings and, after the Vikings left, the Hautevilles stayed. And the generations of Hautevilles on down the line dominated politics and culture in our country for nearly two centuries. The so-called Norman Period – led by that same family – was one of the most important for the island, and it happened during the deepest of the Middle Ages when culture clash and religious dogma drove much of what was happening in Europe."

"So, let me see if I can interpolate. The Hauteville regime – the Normans – was pretty much the Eleventh and Twelfth centuries, right?"

Vito nodded.

"Why do I need to know this?" I asked. It wasn't a challenge, but I knew Vito's style and I knew that if I phrased the question that way he would give me a point of reference, a focus for me to wrap the rest of the narrative around.

"Feudalism," Vito said. "Well, also eradication of the Muslims, but let's stick to feudalism for the moment. As the Hauteville descendants consolidated more power in Sicily, one of them Roger – who was made Count of Sicily by his brother Robert Guiscard – introduced feudalism. He thought it would be a natural since our country was an agricultural society.

"In feudalism, the king – or in this case the count – would distribute parcels of land, the *feudi*, to the lords. You'll notice," he added with a nod of his head and a wink, "that 'feudalism' comes from this Italian word. Anyway, the lords would then redistribute the lands in smaller parcels among their vassals who managed the estates, where the serfs – the peasants – would actually do the work.

"But in feudalism, the lords, vassals, and serfs are required to offer a pledge of loyalty to the count. Only Christians could be trusted to keep a pledge," at this, Vito scoffed, "so the Muslims, Jews – even the Greeks – in our country were omitted from the feudal distribution of land. The Christians got the most land and, therefore, stood to gain the most in a feudal system, but uneven gifting of land could also cause dissension among the tribes."

"That doesn't sound good," I said. "Sicily had had enough battles to fight against outsiders; why would Roger want a system that would introduce internal division?"

"True, true," Vito said. Then, pointing his arthritic finger up in the universal gesture, he added, "Roger had an idea. As count, and with power over all that happened in Sicily, Roger knew of a way to settle this."

Vito wagged his finger in time with the syllables of his statement.

"He would offer an exception called *alod*, which allowed anyone who already held the land before the feudal system was imposed to keep that land. In that way, he could...what do you call it?"

"Ummm," I hedged. "I'm not sure. Do you mean 'grandfather?'"

"Sì, that is it. I don't know where that particular American phrase comes from," he laughed, "but yes, that's it. Roger could prevent arguments between the various groups and preserve the peace, as it were. Or, so he hoped.

"With this solution, each group held both an advantage and a disadvantage," said Vito, "and the disadvantage is what could still cause Count Roger many problems. The Christian lords and vassals who got land through redistribution got it free, so to speak, although they had to pledge loyalty to the count and, perhaps, fight in his wars. The Jews, Muslims, and Greeks who had owned the land before Count Roger imposed the system could keep their land under *alod*, and not proclaim loyalty or fight in his wars, but their possession of the land was more precarious and they knew such a liberal allowance could be turned off quickly. They knew that the Christians would be arguing to gain control of the land held by non-Christians. Both groups disliked their situation."

"How did he resolve it?" I asked.

"Hmph," grunted Vito. "That, indeed, is the question. More on that later."

"How about the matter of the Muslims?" I asked, returning to the question Vito left hanging.

"The other thing that the Hautevilles did for Sicily – or did 'to' Sicily – depending on your perspective, was drive the Muslims from the island."

"But there is so much of their influence, still," I said. "The art, the architecture, even you have said that this was important to Sicily."

"And so it is," Vito enjoined. "I said the Hautevilles drove the Muslims from the island. I didn't say they drove out the Arabs."

I had to concur in his distinction but remained silent.

"The Arab culture brought the science and math, the art, literature, and architecture. The Muslims didn't. The followers of Mohammad brought his beliefs and the *Quran*, but the Arabs brought their culture. The Arab 'sign' – by that I mean the common geometrics of their art – remained in Sicily. We are very much Arab in that way, in the way we perceive reality, in the way we decorate our homes, and in many of the ways that we conduct our lives."

"And it is this Arab influence that has remained, even with the disappearance of the Muslim religion here?" I asked.

"Christianity is very much the theology of my country. After the Norman era, Christianity reigned and continues to this day. But it has a peculiarly Arab accent."

"How so?" I asked.

"Here, in Mazara del Vallo, our marketplace is called the *kasbah*," Vito said smiling wryly at the thought. "It has been so for centuries and will probably remain so for centuries. We have words that come from Arabic, like *gebbiu*, meaning cistern, which comes from *giebja*. Or *zagara*, meaning blossom, from *zahra*. And then there's *zibbibbu*, from *zbib*, for raisins." Here Vito smiled and paused. "Zibbibbu is also the name of one of our most celebrated wine grapes.

"Our favorite cake, *cassata*, comes from an Arab word. There are many more. And the temples, churches, call them what you like – they have evolved to many purposes over the centuries, and have been used by the Arabs to practice their religion while they were here.

"We will always have the Arab influence in our art, and in our culture. And even in our clothing."

"What do you mean?"

"Our women who lose their husbands. They wear black for the rest of their lives."

I didn't respond. Didn't know what to say.

"This is very much an Arab custom. When their women become widows, they mourn the loss of their husbands forever. We, the Sicilians, do the same."

"So," I began slowly, "the difference between Christian and Arab..."

"Yes," Vito interrupted, "but isn't it interesting that you and I are comparing a religion to a culture." Vito took a sip of his coffee and peered out at me over the rim of the cup. "Christianity is a religion; Arab is an ethnicity. Religions and cultures are frequently intermingled, but often at odds. The Arab culture is strong in Sicily, but since the Muslims were driven out in the Eleventh Century, their influence – Islam – is not strong."

"So, what I see here, in Mazara," I added, "reflects the Arab culture, but it may not..."

"Does not," said Vito, emphatically.

"...it does not reflect the Muslim culture."

He nodded.

"Tell me about the Normans," I suggested.

Vito paused, sipped again, and considered the orange slices on the plate. I watched as he scratched the stubble on his chin, and then drag his fingers through the still thick gray hair on his head. His eyes never left the table, but I could tell he wasn't looking at the table or the plates and cups on it. He was just focused on his thoughts and as his familiar smile dawned on his face, I could tell that he had come out of his reverie and was ready to engage me again.

"Normans. *Si*, after the Arabs, we were not yet ready for another invasion, but..."

He let the thought drift away without completing his sentence.

"The Normans followed the order and beauty of the Arab period with, well...order."

"You didn't say beauty," I remarked.

"No," and he grinned. "I don't mean the Normans didn't have a beautiful way of life, but there was a romance and a...a loveliness to the world of the Arabs. I think you Americans think of it as 'exotic' or some such thing. As if 'exotic' explains why you are enamored of a culture distant from your own."

I had to grin at the perfect way that Vito described the American fascination with other worlds.

"But the Arab world brought us poetry and literature, the art that is at the same time elementary and also complex. They also brought a kind of promise."

"From Allah?" I asked.

"No. Allah had nothing to do with it. But the Arab way of life, their teachings, the certainty of their rituals and customs. They were very reassuring."

"And did the Sicilians take well to that?"

"Oh, yes, certainly," he replied with a nod of his head. Then Vito fell silent again for a moment.

"Jews."

"What?" I asked. I was confused by the sudden switch in the conversation.

"The Jews are like that."

"How so?"

"They are comfortable with their beliefs; no, more than comfortable. They live their beliefs and their customs, and they are happy in that life. Just like the Arabs."

"Too bad the Jews and the Arabs can't get along better," I said, saddened at the state of affairs of the Middle East.

"Well, yes," Vito added, then he straightened up in his chair. "But that is not our affair. At least not right now. We must understand the Normans and how they changed our country."

"For the better?" I added hopefully.

But Vito only nodded and smiled.

1061 C.E.

REGGIO

THE MAN SAT UP STRAIGHT IN THE SADDLE ON THE MARE, HIS LONG gray hair and beard gently waving as the horse's pace jostled the rider side to side. With his left hand resting on his thigh and his right hand folded in a loose grip on the reins, Robert Guiscard easily conveyed power, presence, and command.

Albert Prater rode beside him but even with his mount's ornate saddle and braided halter, he was clearly the companion and not the leader in this troop of a dozen soldiers riding up to the gate of the castle. Robert, of the Hauteville family, had come to southern Italy several years earlier following his older brothers' conquest of this region in the toe of the boot of Italy. Like William and Drogo before him, he had carried the Norman banner this far south on the peninsula to extend the empire of the Hautevilles, an impressive and imposing family originally led to glory and power by Tancred de Hauteville years before.

On this day, Robert was making plans to receive his younger brother, Roger, at his fortress and military post. They had corresponded by messenger for months and were considering an invasion of Messina on the island to the west. It would further enlarge the lands claimed by their family and prove to the world the inevitability of the Hauteville dynasty.

"The Muslim people are still there," said Albert as they rode through the gate. "This is of no concern because they are a minor people. But we..."

"We will remove them," interrupted Robert. "Messina and Sicily will become ours. The Muslims are of no consequence, and we will certainly not let them interfere with our business."

In the habit of many monarchical families, Robert spoke of himself with the royal "we," a linguistic manipulation that allowed him to assume a broader base of the power that he desired.

When the tenders met the horses and took hold of the reins, the two men dismounted, followed respectfully by the dismount of the soldiers who accompanied them.

"They have been in Sicily for some time," Albert continued. "And they will not like being overpowered."

Robert laughed at the notion.

"Overpowered is the correct word, my friend. We will do just that. Whether they like it...well, that's a problem they should ask God."

"Do you mean Allah?"

Robert laughed, but in a way that suggested disgust.

"Their Allah was a preacher. He is not God. Only the Christian God of our people is the true God."

The two men walked through the courtyard, past the stables where their horses were kept, and through the phalanx of uniformed attendants awaiting them at the portal to the main building in the compound. A pair of columns framed the doorway, rising vertically then arcing toward the midpoint above the opening. A prominently sculpted pediment capped the portal and an artist who was chiseling the Hauteville family crest on the shield above it paused as Robert and Albert passed through below his ladder.

Three of the soldiers who had accompanied Robert and Albert to the castle followed close by; the others retired to the barracks.

Once inside, the attendants helped Robert out of his ceremonial armor. As the count of this region, he always wore armor when he left the castle, but he had two versions at his disposal. A suit of armor for battle was heavily made, with thicker sheets of metal hung over a tunic made of chainmail. The leggings were covered from hip to toe, while the arms were only exposed below the wrist. When the day's events merely meant riding through the countryside or attending affairs among his vassals, there was a light-weight suit that featured a breastplate and backplate and had fewer "shingles" on the arms and legs.

It was this lightweight suit that Robert wore on this day, so disrobing was done quickly. It was only after the Count was attended to that the assistants turned their attention to Albert. The three soldiers who accompanied them to this room – a large, high-ceilinged hall – milled around the periphery while the older gentlemen got settled.

"Wine," Henry said to one of the attendants. Henry Crayton was the senior officer in the threesome, and he addressed the staff with authority. It was customary that the Count's desires should be known to the staff without him having to ask. But it was also customary for someone else to speak for him. Henry assumed that role as Robert's captain.

Robert and Albert took seats at the large wooden table at one end of the hall, and Henry and the other two soldiers sat on the bench by the wall. The Count's assistants soon returned with jugs of wine and goblets for all five of the men, followed closely behind by three young women bearing platters of food.

"When does my brother arrive?" asked Robert to no one in particular.

"By nightfall, sire," responded Henry, between sips of wine.

"Well, then..." the Count continued, but he was interrupted by a presence at the door to the hall.

"Good day!" came the call from the shadow in the doorway. It was Roger who had arrived far ahead of schedule. Robert rose quickly to greet him, grasping Roger's hand in a strong handshake and wrapping his other hand around his younger brother's forearm.

"What? How so soon?" he asked.

"The horses you gave me are spry. And when I told the dumb animals there would be dry hay and wet drink at the end, they nearly galloped the whole way here."

Another goblet was quickly provided and the brothers joined with Albert, Henry, and the soldiers in a toast to the Count of Apulia and Calabria.

"To my brother's health!" said Roger. "May he soon rule the entire world."

Robert grinned at Roger but held up a hand.

"No, my young partner. It is you who will rule the world. My name will be but a small note in the Hauteville history."

———

The brothers worked on a plan to cross the water to Messina and lay siege to the Arab fortress that protected the city. Over the next several days they weighed their options concerning size of the contingent, time of day, and whether to land far from Messina and then turn back toward the city to attack with an army rather than from the sea with a navy. In the end, they kept coming back to the same idea that Roger had proposed on the first afternoon.

"At night, or in the early morning hours, and with a swift fleet..." he explained.

"Swift means small," protested Robert. "Do you mean to bring only a part of our men?"

Roger sat back from the table with the map of the Strait of Messina and eyed his brother.

"Do you remember what happened the last time we tried this?"

"Yes, I do, and it was with a small army," laughed Robert.

"No...well, yes, that's what I mean," chuckled his brother in return. "I mean the time of day and manner of approach. We took about four hundred armed men, about one hundred more on horseback, and floated nearly two hundred more ships filled with other fighters. And we landed south of Messina and marched to the battle..."

"Hoping to surprise the infidels," said Robert.

"Exactly, but we didn't. The size of the fleet was too easy to spot and in the time we had marched across the plain, the infidels had called on support from Milazzo ahead of our march and from Katane to our rear. There was no surprise, and the Arabs provisioned their fortress to endure a long siege."

"Meanwhile," Robert admitted, shaking his head, "we had no supply route since we had crossed the seas. We ran low on food and the men were sick from the swamp."

"This time," Roger indicated, "we will do it a different way. We will sail at night and arrive before dawn. We will take fewer men so that the fleet can move across the water in darkness and remain undiscovered. And we will fight a naval battle, attacking Messina from the sea rather than attempting a ground onslaught from the landside."

Plans were made to set sail on the following night. They would leave in the darkness with enough time to make the bay of Messina just before dawn, and surprise the Arabs holding the fort before they were fully awake.

———

Ayyub ibn Tamim was the son of the emir of Ifriqiya and controlled all of eastern Sicily. Even as the Muslim society was beset by internal dissension and externals attacks, Ayyub's methodical command gave the impression of absolute power.

He ruled from Siracusa but relied on his fortress at Messina to also play a significant role in his emirate. The city was located in a far northern part of the island, close enough to the mainland that it straddled both worlds. The urban center of the city had grown over the centuries to include a vast marketplace, crowded clusters of houses, and a military garrison positioned near the sea so that its guards could maintain watch over any approaching enemy.

Ayyub demanded discipline and structure among the ranks of his soldiers in Messina. He knew that this was the only way to hold onto power, and the only way to maintain his own prominence in a society composed of so many warring factions. Due to his frequent absences to tend to his affairs in Siracusa, he needed a ruthless officer to maintain order when he was away from Messina. Ahmed ibn Agha was just such a man. He was born in the outskirts of Mecca, devoted his life to the service of Allah, and had been merciless in battles against the enemy infidels.

The emir of Ifriqiya had learned of Ahmed's heroic victories and called for him to come to northern Africa. Unmarried, and not likely to ever find time for family life, Ahmed quickly accepted, traveling to the new country when he was only twenty years old to take up the sword against the enemy of Islam. The emir soon sent the young man to Siracusa to serve Ayyub, who in turn was pleased with Ahmed's single-minded approach and put him in charge of the fortress in Messina.

It was not long, however, that the emir of eastern Sicily was forced to make difficult decisions to tame the youth's aggressions.

"I need you here to protect my kingdom, which means preserving the peace," he told Ahmed. "We will not fight the infidel if they do not challenge my emirate."

Sensing Ahmed's disappointment at being directed to just supervise the peace of the region, Ayyub quickly added, "Remember, if the Christians come to Messina to fight or to take away our country, you must slay them!"

The prospect of battle excited the passions in the man, so he began drilling the men under his command, outfitting them with new uniforms and better weapons, and preparing them for the battle that he hoped would be his fortune, and the test of his devotion to Islam.

He frequently paraded across the parapet of the fortress to oversee and survey his troops. At times such as this, Ahmed wore a simple blue cotton tunic with short black trousers tied below the knee, just as his men did. His boots were black leather, and the twisted cloth headgear also matched that of his men. His sword was a few inches longer than the general issue, but one more thing was important in distinguishing his attire: Ahmed wore a bright red sash across his chest, draped from his right shoulder and tied at the waist on his left hip. He would not be mistaken for any normal soldier, even at a distance, and that was exactly the way he wanted it.

Emir Ayyub was away at Siracusa for several days in May of 1061 C.E., leaving Ahmed once again in control. The commanding officer checked the guards at the fortress late one night, then retired to his bed leaving the usual contingent of armed soldiers on watch. It was a cool, crisp night, but warm enough to pull back the heavy drapes that shut the air out from the arched opening of his home at the top of the hill inside the fort. Ahmed always slept lightly, a natural asset for any leader of armed men, and in this way he passed swiftly to sleep under a thin cotton blanket.

———

"Ah, there you are," said Robert as he approached his younger brother on the bow of the boat. They had set sail just past midnight under favorable winds and expected to make the crossing to Messina before daybreak.

Roger didn't reply but stared out at the water. In the darkness, with only the faint light of a crescent moon, he could see the coastal edge of Sicily only by sizing up the looming blackness on the horizon. They chose a night with some light to aide them but sailed while the moon was still rising so that is would be behind them in the east. In that position, they would be able to see some of the Muslim fort and the outlines of Messina, but their ships would be hidden in the darkness in between.

"Do you recall when we tried this last?" Roger asked, as Robert approached. He was dressed for battle even though his rank would have allowed him to be fitted out in the flowing robes of a ruler. Roger had made his reputation as one willing to lead his men into battle, and this attack on Messina would be no different. For this expedition, however, he chose the blackened chain mail cover that would not reflect light, even the dim light of the sliver of moon, and told his men to wear the same. The long tunic he wore beneath it was likewise made of a darker material, not the red that the Count would normally have on. He even went so far as to apply ashes to blacken the metal surface of the pointed helmet he wore, another advisory shared with his soldiers.

"Yes, I do recall," said Robert. He smiled a bit at the memory. Although there had been loss of life and the shame that attended a failed enterprise, he smiled now because he foresaw success in today's plan.

"We could have taken Messina at the time, but too many men were sickened in the field, and too many died before we could strangle the city into surrender."

"We will attack them from the front this time, and Messina will be ours," said Roger. "And then..."

"And then we will march across the country," interjected Robert, "first to take Siracusa and execute the emir, then on to al Madinah in the west, their capital."

As the darkness that was Messina loomed larger on the horizon, Robert retired to his quarters to don his armor and retrieve his weapon. Orders had been preplanned and were given discreetly among the two hundred soldiers passing through the strait on the thirteen Norman ships. All were instructed to remain quiet, and they would count on the winds drawing them near to the city so that the slap of oars on the water would not alert the Muslims of their approach.

Before the roosters were awake, the Norman fleet arrived on the shore. Secretly they crept up the flanks of the fortress and were able to mount the walls of the city before the alarm went up among the Muslims there. A soldier of Islam was dispatched to wake Ahmed but by the time he joined the fight, it was nearly over. And when he entered the courtyard of the fort, the Normans were already cutting down his soldiers emerging sleepily from their quarters.

Ahmed slashed with his sword at the helmeted attackers, but he had been unable to don his own protection and was soon set upon by a threesome of the enemy. Battling fiercely with skilled strokes of his weapon, he withstood the challenge for ten minutes that seemed like an hour, but when the three attackers spread out in a circle around the Muslim commander, one was able to spring upon him from behind, plunging his sword into the man's back and all the way through his ribcage.

Ahmed's survived the thrust and twisted about so that the Norman lost his sword, still protruding from the Muslim's back and chest, but the quick loss of blood weakened Ahmed and his fighting arm dropped to his side. Trying one more time to raise his sword, another Norman soldier came down on Ahmed's right arm with a brutal slash that severed the man's forearm from his body. Bloody hand and arm fell to the stones below and with a heave of his chest, the brave young soldier fell onto his broken limb and died.

Meanwhile, mayhem ruled the courtyard and the parapet of the fort as the Normans took advantage of the surprise attack to conquer the Muslims there. As the sun crested the horizon, the light of dawn revealed the carnage of the battle. Of the two hundred Normans called to action on that day, most lived. Of the greater number of soldiers of Islam who defended the fort, most were killed and the rest were put in chains and led to the prison cells that had until then been used for their enemies.

Messina had fallen so quickly that Roger and Robert themselves were surprised, but pleased.

"I said that one day you would rule the world, brother," said Robert to his sibling. "Today is the first day of that new reign and, with it, I consign to you the title of Count of Sicily."

1146 C.E.

PALERMO

King Roger of Sicily sat on the imposing granite throne facing the large hall of the palace that he had inherited from his father, Count Roger I. True to the customs of the Hauteville family, the king energetically pursued greatness for his country just as he pursued splendor and riches for himself. This palace, rising from the foundations of a Phoenician villa and on the walls erected by Muslims, was now the grandest feature of his kingdom.

As king of Sicily he controlled the entire island, and his province included the mainland regions of southern Italy from the "toe" of Calabria to the "heel" of Apulia. Since these regions were separated by another region, Lucania – in the instep of the boot – Roger commandeered that area too so that he controlled everything from Trapani and Palermo on Sicily's western edge across the island and stretching all the way across the lower part of the peninsula to the Adriatic coast. His kingdom had control of all lands south of Rome.

There was an important feature that distinguished him from his warfaring father, though. Count Roger conquered the lands by force, defeating the then-current reign of Muslims in Sicily, and establishing a new government of laws. But the first King Roger respected the people who inhabited the island and allowed them to maintain their religious practices, their art and culture, even their laws as long as they did not interfere with what the Hauteville tradition would expect of them.

The king respected the art, science, culture, and mathematical expertise of the Muslims in Palermo so much that he surrounded himself with them and put many of the wisest and most accomplished Muslims in charge of raising his son, who would become Roger II, the King of Sicily.

Because of the Muslim cultural influence, his son grew up with greater respect for Arab institutions than the Christian traditions that he was born into. As an adult he was known to dress in the flowing robes common for Islamic men, and he studied and discussed the teachings of Islam with his court and family. As king, Roger II invited artists, scholars, and scientists to his land, financially supported them and, in return, expected to rule over a kingdom that was the economic rival of all of Europe, and the cultural center of the world.

Now that he was approaching fifty years of age, Roger's life was a chronicle of the success and progress that he had planned. As he sat on his throne pondering what had been accomplished, his mind wandered back to his father and mother, and the Norman culture that the Hauteville family had brought to this island nation.

Adelaide was the third wife of his father, Count Roger of Sicily, of the Hauteville family of Normans. She married Count Roger the elder when he had already sired four children by Judith of Evreux and eight by Eremburga – all daughters. Adelaide delivered him male heirs, first Simon and then Roger.

When Count Roger died in June of the year 1101, Simon succeeded him to power but was only eight years old – and Roger only five – so Adelaide served as regent. Simon, himself, died in 1105 leaving the position of count to his younger brother. But once again, due to the boy's youth, his mother stepped in to fill the role of regent until Roger was old enough to rule.

After Count Roger I's death, Adelaide relied on the counsel of Chrisodulus, the Greek emir of Palermo, and she later married Baldwin I of Jerusalem. That marriage was soon abandoned by her when she discovered that her new husband was already married, so Adelaide went back to Palermo.

King Roger II, therefore, had two solid reasons for not joining the Crusades begun by Pope Urban II to take the Holy Land from the Muslims. He was offended by the treatment his mother received at the hands of Baldwin and had no interest in securing land from that region. And he had been raised in a strong Muslim tradition and didn't object to their culture as strenuously as the Latin Church of Rome did.

His kingdom was here, in Sicily and southern Italy, and he was satisfied to rule over it and use Palermo as the base for the expansion of the science, literature, and art of the world. The popes who oversaw the Roman church while Roger II sat on the throne wanted more from him, expecting his to push harder for conversion of the heathen Muslims to Christianity, but he paid them no attention.

In the year 1117, he married Elvira, daughter of Alfonso VI of Castille. Together they produced four sons and lived happily in their time together. These were among the finest in his adult life, but she died in 1135 when still a young woman.

As all these thoughts brought his family back from memory, Roger stood from his throne and wandered toward the tall carved doors that opened onto the outer promenade and overlooked the square below. *Al-Qasr*, his royal residence, was originally designed in the Arab tradition, with angular rooms, straight hallways, and no courtyard. The ornate carvings that decorated the walls and ceilings created the appearance of opulence – what first attracted his father, Count Roger, to the site – but the Hautevilles turned the rectangular edifice into a series of hallways and buildings that wrapped around an open space and raised castle battlements to create a fortress design.

It was to this promenade in the open air that King Roger went to now, with his mind filled with thoughts of family, his sons, his lost wife, and the future of the Hauteville line. He was left alone in his reverie while he mounted the stone steps that led to the guards' walkway at the top of the fortress. Once there, he leaned against the cold stone and surveyed the scene below him.

Al-Qasr was perched high on the slope and he looked down on the city and harbor that had grown over the centuries, and he considered the prospects for another wife. Roger knew that his role as sovereign was not suited to parenting, but he had to find the proper mate to fulfill the family architecture.

He strode along the walkway, saluted intermittently by the Norman guards who protected him and this castle. They were at the ready, as always, but much of this was ceremonial. There had been no conflict on the island during the Norman reign, and there would be none today. But guards were kept and Roger II returned their salute in a most formal manner as if the guards were preparing to be called upon on a moment's notice.

After circumnavigating the castle, Roger descended the stairs and made his way toward the chapel where he did his greatest thinking. The *Cappella Palatina* had been built under his command and according to his design, parts of it on top of earlier Arab constructions, and he made it a superb blend of Arab, Norman, and Byzantine styles. Mosaics covered the walls, the vault was reminiscent of a Byzantine cathedral, and the art that adorned the towered walls and arches carried the clear influence of the Norman-Christian architecture.

At the entrance to the church, Roger encountered Hanislaw, the captain of his guard, and Peter, his banker. Both men thrived on the success of their king in a symbiotic relationship that both men counted on for their success also.

"Sire," Peter said as Roger acknowledged their presence. The three men stood on the uppermost step just outside of the chapel, the late afternoon sun bright in their eyes.

"It is a matter of planning," Peter, the banker, continued. He would not mention money or finances in public and used this indirect approach to gain Roger's attention. The king would not permit talk of money inside the church and so he guided them into the vestibule only and out of the hot sun.

"What is it?" asked Roger.

He was fully informed on all matters in his kingdom, so he wasn't expecting a sudden announcement, but he let the banker choose the direction of the conversation.

"Your army has taken Tripoli," Peter began, although this was only a prologue – Roger knew of this conquest earlier in the year. "And now you must consider your next campaign."

Roger kept his attention on his banker, even while discussing military matters in the presence of his captain. Wars were won with money, he knew, because logistics and supplies made his soldiers braver and more successful.

"What do you suggest?" he asked, and addressed this question to both men, since Peter would have to finance the operation but Hanislaw would have to wage it.

"His holiness, Pope Eugene III, has decided to begin a new crusade, a campaign against the infidels in the east," said Peter.

"It is a campaign worth joining," added Hanislaw. He knew that his king had been reluctant to wage war against the east, or to join with papal decrees to do so, so Roger would have to be talked into doing this.

"Why?" was the sovereign's one-word challenge.

Roger knew the back story. Imad ad-Din Zengi, a powerful Muslim emir, had laid waste to Homs, Baarin, Baalbek, and Aleppo in Syria and was threatening to control the entire Levant. He had already fought the Byzantine emperor John II and prevailed, been granted full control of Homs by marrying Zumurrud, and then conquered Damascus. He planned an attack on Jerusalem but was turned back by an alliance between Mu'in ad-Din Unur and the people of Jerusalem.

There was only a brief time of quiet – such as it was – before Zengi went on the attack again. This time it was directed at Edessa, a seat of Crusader power but poorly protected and not up to defense against a formidable military man such as Zengi. The city fell, and Zengi's reputation rose.

Roger had first heard of Zengi in the midst of the Muslim campaign against the Christian church and the Crusaders. Over a handful of years since that early news reached him, the man became a figure of myth, and Roger realized that Zengi could be the one to topple the Christian empire. It was just two years before that the fall of Edessa proved the Muslim army's ability to threaten the heart of the Christian lands.

"It is a campaign worth joining." Hanislaw's words came back to Roger.

"His holiness the Pope calls for all kings of Europe to repulse the infidel," suggested Peter, "and you are the mightiest of all the kings."

Roger tended to believe his banker's assessment, but he also knew that the other kings might not be ready to share power or control of this new crusade. He had read the pope's pronouncement, *Quantum praedecessors*, but was unimpressed with Eugene III's rationale for the new crusade. Nevertheless, he felt that he needed to participate in this one.

"What do we need?" This question was pitched directly to his military advisor, Hanislaw.

"Two thousand men, with arms and armor. Five hundred horses, wagons to draw up the provisions behind the march, support from..."

"Women?" interrupted Roger.

Hanislaw looked back at him with a smile.

"Yes, sire, but that isn't what I was thinking. We will need support in clothing, medicine, food, and not a little from the gods."

Roger turned to Peter but did not have to ask a question.

"Yes, we have that," the banker declared. "But it will be best if we add some to the taxes that we expect of your people. So that the treasury does not run dry while this crusade is waged."

Roger nodded. It was all that was necessary in this trio of power brokers. If the sovereign had the advice and consent of his military expert and his banker, and if they all agreed, there was nothing more that was necessary to go into war in a distant country.

When Peter and Hanislaw departed, Roger continued his path into the church itself. No one used this chapel except him, and he enjoyed the quiet privacy within. It was the place where he could talk to God and hope for guidance on the next steps for the Hauteville empire.

As he walked toward the gilded altar at the transept, Pater Michael entered from the nave and intercepted him. Michael had joined Roger's court five years earlier, coming from the abbey in Cefalù, and was Roger's confessor and religious counselor. He did not dabble in the military decisions, nor advise the king on development of his kingdom; his sole responsibility was guiding the sovereign toward his expected entrance into heaven.

"Good morning, Roger." All his subjects called the king 'sire' except Michael. The priest answered first to God – a freedom allowed to him by Roger – and second to the Hauteville empire, so he would not use the honorific title when addressing this subject of the Lord.

"How is your day?" Michael asked.

"I am well, and the land is safe and calm."

"I saw you conferring with Hanislaw and Peter. Are there events afoot?"

"Yes," replied the king simply, but without further explanation. The affairs of the state were not the province of this man of God, and Roger would not engage him in a conversation on these matters.

"Are you here to confess your sins?"

It was a natural enough question for the priest to ask, without suggesting sin on the part of the king. But Roger only smiled.

"I have sin enough for all my subjects," he began with a resigned chuckle, "but none to confess today, father. What do you know of His Holiness calling for a new crusade?"

"Crusades are more about soldiers than about souls," replied Michael, evading the question.

"But your pope believes otherwise, or else he wouldn't say that the Church must reclaim the Holy Land?"

Michael looked keenly at the king, staring for a moment with his head cocked to the side in thought. He wanted a moment to organize his words carefully.

"The Holy Land is where Our Lord began his church and where he began his teaching. It is holy because it is the place where his most holy mother Mary lived and gave us the Son of God."

Roger looked back at Michael and wondered when his monologue would approach an answer to the question.

"And it is holy because there He was crucified, buried, and returned from the dead to save our souls. But grace resides within us, and not in the soil of Jerusalem, or in the waters of the river Jordan."

"So," interjected Roger, "you would not care if we recover the Holy Land."

Michael had spent his years in Palermo learning the Muslim religion and coming to understand their way of life, their beliefs, and their justification for differences with the Church of Rome. He respected his brethren from Islam more than he thought he would when he arrived in Palermo, thanks in large part to the equanimity shown to them by the man who stood before him at that moment, and he had greater tolerance for them too.

"Our Muslim friends believe that Mohammad rose to the heavens from the rock in Jerusalem, and so that place is holy to them also."

The priest paused for a thought, then continued.

"Should we have it – and they not – or should they have it and we not?"

Roger regarded the comment as more of an unanswerable riddle than a question. In reply, he only smiled lightly and turned to continue his way toward the altar where he knelt on the cool stone step and bowed his head in prayer.

AUGUST 2018

CAFÉ AMADEO

"The Hauteville era brought stability," Vito said after settling into his chair. He paused momentarily waiting for the barista to bring his coffee, which was forthcoming. I knew the routine and sat quietly until the teacher was ready.

"Roger I – actually he was not called 'the first' since that generally signifies royalty and he was – according to his brother Robert's decision, only a count – but anyway, Roger was a wise and patient man. He was in his thirties which was considered middle age by the time he conquered Messina, married to a Norman woman of high birth, Judith – his first of several wives – then proceeded to take control of the island and rule from Palermo. He realized that Christianizing the mix of Byzantine, Muslim, and Jewish populations laced through the land was going to require a deft hand.

"Pope Nicholas II expected a quick conversion of the people on Sicily, but Roger thought it best to let everyone practice the religion of their choice. Some of the houses of worship had already been converted from Greek temples to Christian churches, then to Jewish temples and later to Muslim mosques. Roger re-Christianized some of them when he took control of my country, but he left many of the structures alone so that his subjects would live peacefully together."

"Did it work?" I asked.

"Yes. In fact, it did. Roger brought order and structure. Oh, I don't mean to say it wasn't good before, but," Vito continued with a twinkle in his eye, "we had our tumultuous times too! He had to do it delicately, though. For example, although he let the Muslims remain in Sicily, he had the emirs removed. They represented a former power and a throwback to the Arab past, and their presence might conjure notions of a return to the exercise of Islamic rule."

"But, how..." I stammered to clarify my thoughts, before beginning again. "If Roger expelled the emirs and imams..."

"I didn't say he expelled the imams," Vito said, interrupting my thought and requiring another adjustment to my question.

"Okay, so he expelled the emirs because they represented power. But he allowed the imams to remain because they represented religion."

Vito nodded approvingly and sipped at his espresso.

"I assume there were also rabbis, and Christian clergy."

"All," was his reply. "In fact, he allowed each religion's community to continue in the ways of their culture."

"How does that work?" I asked skeptically. "Religion and law are separate, I know, but..."

"Spoken like a true American."

That brought a smile to my lips.

"Yeah, well, I am an American."

"Sì, Luca, you are. But most of the world, especially the old world, didn't keep the church and the state that separate."

The barista returned with two new cups of espresso and a plate of dates.

"Let's use the Arab community as an example," I began. "How would that work?"

"First of all, Roger believed in the rule of law. He did not rule on his own instincts or whim, as many monarchs had done. This allowed him to keep his emotions out of the application of the law. So, he could let the imams apply their laws, the rabbis theirs, the Byzantines theirs, and so on. As long as the religious application didn't challenge his authority or deny him – the Count of Sicily – his own prerogatives, Roger felt that such magnanimity would ensure the peace.

"His rule also paved the way for perhaps the biggest change in Sicilian cultural history. For nearly two centuries, the Arab world had ruled the island and, so, it was thought of as belonging to North Africa. Roger's time as ruler brought Sicily back into the sphere of Europe, making the island more European and – not incidentally – more Italian.

"He died in 1101 A.D. and his son, Roger II..."

"Wait," I begged, left hand raised and right hand scribbling notes. "Let me confirm something. Roger 'the first' wasn't called that."

Vito nodded.

"But his son was called Roger 'the second'?"

"Sì," he replied. "Roger II was made the King of Sicily and he adopted 'the second' to...what is the word...rewrite?"

"Do you mean revise, like revisionist history?"

Vito smiled broadly at that and nodded.

"Of course, he wouldn't have referred to it that way, but yes, he was revising history to suggest that his father had also been royalty.

"So, anyway, Roger II's wife, Elvira died after giving him four sons, including William I, who would later succeed his father to the throne as king. His second wife was Sibylla, but after giving birth to a sickly boy who died young, she herself died in childbirth the second time around."

"How long were they together?" I asked.

"Less than two years."

"Then what?"

"He soon found another, Beatrice of Rethel..."

"He. Roger II, right?"

"Sì, Roger II. He married Beatrice, a Frenchwoman of noble birth. She was only sixteen at her marriage to Roger, and he was already fifty-six years old. He died three years later but, in the meantime, produced another child, Costanza. And THAT," he said with emphasis, "is a name to remember. She had a significant role in the history of my country."

"How so?"

"Okay, it gets a little confusing, but..." he began.

"A little," I laughed. This whole chronology was a labyrinth of cultures, countries, and names.

"Her father died in February of 1154 and she was born in November of 1154." Vito paused while I wrote down the dates.

"Wait," I said. "That's nine months."

"More specifically, Roger II died on February 26 and his daughter, Constance, was born on November 2nd. Less than nine months," Vito replied, lifting his espresso cup for a sip. "Why do you ask?"

"I just wondered whether Beatrice had conceived after his death."

Vito just sipped his coffee and didn't respond. When he put the cup down, he turned toward me and passed right over the question.

"Upon his death, Roger II was succeeded to the throne by William I, his son, who died in 1166. Keep track of this," he said, tapping his finger on a page of my journal to suggest that I write this down. "At that time, the year 1166, Constance was only twelve years old. Now remember, William I and Constance were cousins. Upon his death, William I was succeeded by his son, William II who, because he was only twelve at the time..."

"The same age as Constance."

"Exactly," Vito responded. "Because of his age, his mother, Margaret of Navarre – King William I's wife and therefore the Queen of Sicily – served as regent until William II reached the age of maturity. He served for twenty years, during which time Constance also reached maturity. When William II died in 1189, he was succeeded by his cousin,

Tancred, dubiously certified as the illegitimate progeny of Roger III, Duke of Apulia."

"What does all this have to do with Constance?"

"I'm getting to that," Vito said, with a single nod of his head. "Tancred served as king until 1194 when he was succeeded by William III, a Hauteville. In fact, he was the last Hauteville and the last Norman king of Sicily."

"And Constance?"

"Impatient, aren't you?" Vito teased. "During this time, Constance married Henry VI, the Holy Roman Emperor...."

"Wow! Really?" I said. "A Sicilian woman married to the Holy Roman Emperor."

Vito smiled.

"We're not just some...what do you say, 'kids from the sticks!'" he added with a mirthful grin.

"Anyway, yes, but he was 'only' the King of Germany when they married and became the Holy Roman Emperor five years later. He was from the House of Staufer, known as the Hohenstaufen family, and here's why Constance's life mattered so much to Sicily. She was a Norman, and since the royals in Sicily would not welcome a German like Henry taking power here, Constance – a Norman – was offered as a compromise sovereign."

"That's an odd way to get around to it," I offered.

"Yes, but it worked. Over a series of years and several conflicts, including several attempted military excursions into Sicily, Henry VI and Constance secured Sicily as their own. In addition to his other titles, Henry VI could add King of Sicily. But Constance was the true first blood queen of my country. A break with centuries of male-line succession but made necessary as a way to manage the transition of the crown, a feat that kept it in the Norman-Hauteville family but also introduced the Hohenstaufen line from Germany to my country."

1194 C.E. – 1266 C.E.

SWABIANS

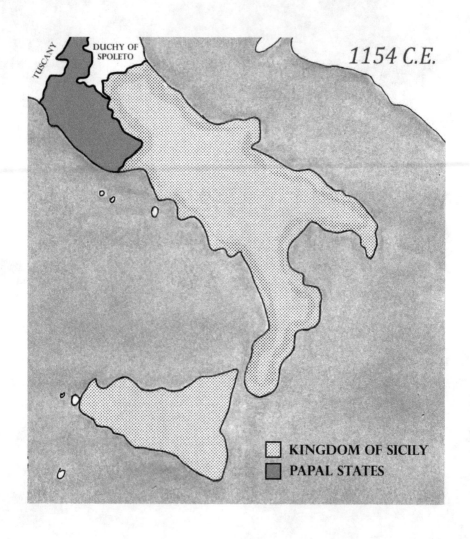

1154 C.E.

TUSCANY

DUCHY OF
SPOLETO

☐ KINGDOM OF SICILY
☐ PAPAL STATES

1204 C.E.

SIRACUSA

GASPARDO LEANED INTO THE WIND, PERCHED ON THE BOW OF THE *Carroccia* as it sailed south from Genoa and toward the Strait of Messina. It had already been a long day, and night had fallen, but with the improved rigging of this vessel, he knew that tacking from west to east and back again would be easy. In the months since he had been given command of this ship, he had come to admire her agility and speed. He knew that they would reach the north-eastern corner of Sicily by dawn.

Alamanno da Costa walked up from behind and passed by the captain, stepping up to the bowsprit of the boat. He leaned into the wind as Gaspardo did, as the counter-clockwise spin of the wind pulled across the sails. His ship tacked back and forth, zig-zagging through the waters south of Genoa, cutting across the low waves. He had his sights set for Siracusa, a city that had been first inhabited by a primitive tribe called the Siculi, had grown under the management of the Greeks from Aegea, been occupied for centuries by the Romans, and attacked by the Athenians. He knew that the city had passed into Arab hands and then been liberated by the Normans. Its position on the sea made it a prime objective for any trading expedition, so he was impressed, but not surprised, by the series of conquests.

Da Costa had been born and raised in a merchant family, but his dreams of global riches drew him from the counting house to the waters of the Mediterranean. So now he was proprietor of this powerful warship and heading toward an encounter with the *Leopardo,* a corsair from Pisa whose mere presence interfered with his command of that part of the Mediterranean. The Pisans were vying for the same trophy as he was, dominion over the eastern edge of Sicily, and had in recent years taken the city of Siracusa hostage. Da Costa planned to free that hostage; or, more specifically, to take it for his own. In doing so, the merchant-turned-adventurer intended to end the competition between his native Genoa and the people from Pisa once and for all. It would be a confrontation that he chose, when he chose it, and where.

Da Costa had followed the events in Sicily closely through the reports of his agents who plied the waters of the Mediterranean Sea, and by the merchants who plied their trade on the dozen islands that crowded around this one special jewel in the middle of the sea. He was drawn to Siracusa because it was here that the merchant ships from the east made landfall, and where the Siracusan merchants pushed off into the sea in search of markets as far west as Valencia in Iberia and Tangier, even beyond the Pillars of Hercules to the great unknown ocean beyond. Da Costa knew that Siracusa – more than Messina – was a linchpin to the trading empire of the Mediterranean, and he wanted it for himself.

Despite his merchant heritage, da Costa knew that conquests such as he desired could not be accomplished with the lumbering hulks used to ship the goods. Instead, he chose a ship worthy of battle, a vessel outfitted with the triangular-shaped lateen sail for speed and efficiency, a vessel that could cut across the winds of the sea to ply the waves and attack other vessels.

But before he could realize his dreams of conquering Siracusa, he had to vanquish the ships of the Pisan navy like those powered by the *Leopardo,* then sink them or adopt them as his own. The mission he set out on should be easy, he surmised. His crew of five hundred far exceeded the two hundred or so on the rival ship, and his *Carroccia* was considered faster than the enemy's vessel. The battle, if there was to be one, would be swift and certain.

"It is a fair wind," said Gaspardo, addressing his commander without looking at him.

Da Costa acknowledged the comment by a nod of the head, but he too didn't bother with eye contact. He had found the captain in a seedy tavern in Genoa one month before. In a dimly lit and smoky room filled with sailors drunken from their brief shore liberty, Gaspardo sat alone, drawing deeply on the wooden pipe and sipping occasionally from the heavy mug of wine on the table. Da Costa had never laid eyes on the captain, but with the name and a vague description, he knew that this was Gaspardo the moment he stepped across the threshold and ducked his head through the portal. The description included more words about the captain's presence of mind and stolid confidence than about his outward appearance, and the man da Costa saw there that night fit the description perfectly.

"I am Alamanno da Costa," he began in introduction after he had approached the captain's table. "I am...," but Gaspardo cut him off. Politely, but in a firm voice that communicated respect, but impatience.

"You are the merchant who is looking for someone to pilot your boat."

"Yes," replied da Costa, "but more. I want you to help me take Siracusa from the Pisans but, in the process, take them from the sea and end Pisa's claims to this region."

Gaspardo laughed a bit at da Costa's big plan.

"Shall I also move the islands north of Sicily that might be in your way, sire?"

"That won't be necessary," answered da Costa. "We will claim those too."

And on that evening, their bond was established.

———

Ferdinando Renata was the titular head of the commission sent by the governor of Pisa to maintain peace once they had established a sea route to Sicily and taken control of Siracusa. He was not an imposing figure;

he would not have been chosen for a military role in this arena. Renata was a politician and an administrator, a man who knew how to achieve compromise and how to coax compliance. The people of Siracusa weren't happy to see another empire such as Pisa take the reins of their city, but if the new invaders left most of their city and traditions intact, they would be tolerated. So the calm presence and light hand of someone like Renata was critical for maintaining harmony.

His title was governor, but Renata didn't bother with governing. He preferred to remain in the castle perched on the edge of the hills surrounding the Siracusan harbor and require his emissaries to oversee the activities of the city. That included the commerce as well as the behavior of the citizenry and, when the need arose, silencing and punishing disruptive behavior. Renata had appointed two judges – one from Siracusa and another that he brought with him from Pisa – to adjudicate matters and keep the peace. There was no police force; that function was performed by the armed men who had been used to capture the city in the first place.

It was on a quiet evening with the setting sun still falling behind the western wall of the city that Renata's wife, Abulafe – a child of Siracusa's dwindling Arab population – came to sit with him.

"You are to eat later this evening?" she asked him as she slid into the carved wooden chair across the table from him. She lived the life of a modern woman in most respects, but maintained elements of her Muslim upbringing, including not sitting directly next to a man, even her husband. She took the more respectful place across from him, on the other side of this table that was wide enough that their feet would not touch beneath it.

"Yes, that would be good. Perhaps *coniglio* tonight?" he asked, referring to the sweet meat of the rabbits that were raised in captivity precisely for his dining pleasure.

"If that is what you want, my husband. I will tell the servants to prepare it for soon after the sun sets," she added, then rose and left the room.

Renata turned his gaze back out of the room through the window that looked down upon the city's largest piazza, and the harbor beyond. He was not a restless man, so sitting for long periods didn't bother him. He was sent to control the activities of the city and he had surrounded himself with capable people, including soldiers, so that he could simply reside. An easy task and one his superiors in Pisa had known the man could handle. Renata was a thoughtful administrator and had the vision to see beyond the petty quarrels and selfish motives of the ranks about him. He didn't have to threaten punishment or retribution to hold onto the affairs of Siracusa. And he very much preferred the placid order of the city.

————

The *Carroccia* crested the waves and fell lightly upon the troughs between them. It was a gentle rise and fall, and both da Costa and Gaspardo felt the rhythm of the vessel in their bones and sinew. The captain was born for the sea and although his commander came to it later in life, both men knew that this was the style of life that was meant for them.

When the light fell from the sky and the *Carroccia* continued on, Gaspardo stood on the deck directing the path of the ship. He knew that they would encounter the *Leopardo* before they would see the harbor of Siracusa, and he wanted his scouts to remain alert for any sign of the Pisan vessel. He did not want to come upon the enemy in the dark, but he would not shrink from the encounter whenever it occurred. So he instructed the pilot to tack closer to the shore of the Italian peninsula where the winds were calmer that night. By remaining within sight of the land in the thrall of milder breezes, they would slow the speed of the *Carroccia* and preserve the possibility of running into the *Leopardo* in the light. And this is precisely what happened, just as Gaspardo had planned.

It was at the first hint of the sunrise off the portside that Gaspardo saw the mast and sail of a ship coming north. Like the *Carroccia*, it tacked with the wind, but veered farther from the coast, a hint that the captain quickly interpreted as a tactic to add speed rather than slow the vessel's path. Da Costa was summoned to the deck and Gaspardo pointed out the image just rising above the waves in the southerly distance.

"Is it the *Leopardo*?" he asked. The sea was huge and there would be many vessels upon it, but none need be feared – or anticipated – as much as this one, so da Costa would only care if the hulk that bounced toward them on the waves was the enemy ship.

In the brief time they had been tracking the oncoming vessel, the image had grown with proximity and Gaspardo was better able to identify the ship's profile and sail. By doing so, he was prepared to claim that it was, in fact, the *Leopardo*, by the cut of its sails and the breadth of its hull.

"Sire, yes, I do believe that this is the Pisan warship."

Gaspardo and da Costa kept a close eye on the approaching vessel, just as the captain of that ship undoubtedly kept a keen eye on them. It was only a matter of about an hour before the two vessels were close enough to make out the crew size and weapons onboard. Gaspardo knew that his commander had insisted upon a large force of men, large enough to threaten the stability of the *Carroccia*, but also large enough to overwhelm the crew of any average ship the size of the one that was approaching. He studied the enemy vessel's bearing and tip, clues as to the weight it carried, and decided that it rode the waves too lightly to be outfitted with weapons as the *Carroccia* was. And as he studied it, he was able to confirm that it was the *Leopardo*.

"We will draw upon them in a few moments, sire," he told da Costa. "And we will throw all our force at them at once."

"I want this battle to be completed quickly," said the commander, looking at Gaspardo for acknowledgment.

The captain looked back at da Costa and nodded.

———

Renata woke late the next morning. He had had a long, satisfying meal shared with Abulafe, and he had consumed too much wine. He didn't always imbibe so much, but it was a pleasant evening and the governor had little real work to do. In waking late, he was helped into his clothing by the servant and he took up his position in the great chair placed before the window. He would have a long breakfast of fresh bread, fruit from the peach and fig trees grown in his personal orchard, and a fatty slab of grilled pork flesh that he enjoyed each morning.

"You are well, this morning, sire?" asked his wife when she entered the room.

Renata only nodded.

"You will meet with Don Filippe today?" she asked, referring to the man who managed the banking affairs for the Renata merchant house.

"Yes, I will see him in the afternoon," he replied, a time that was not too distant, considering the governor's late rising that morning.

Abulafe managed her husband's schedule. He was not an ambitious man and she knew that matters would slip if he was left to his own devices. She wasn't interested in controlling him or taking anything from his estate; rather, Abulafe simply wanted them to continue a life of comfort and she knew that this could be at risk if Renata's business matters weren't managed properly.

"I will see that he is here this afternoon," she said, and then left the room.

————

On that same morning, the *Carroccia* and the *Leopardo* were locked in battle on the seas just north of the island of Sicily. Just as da Costa had requested and Garpardo had promised, the battle was waged with fury, with dozens of soldiers from the *Carroccia* sent to board the smaller enemy craft as soon as the fight began. The Pisans could not withstand the might of the Genoan ship nor the tactics of its captain, and it soon surrendered.

It was common for sailors to be conscripted into the conquering army's force. Sailors were often reluctant combatants anyway and were known to change sides according to the command of the new captain. This is what happened on that morning, as the *Leopardo's* sailors were offered continued employment by the Genoans in place of being tossed into the sea. In this way, da Costa acquired another ship – soon to be augmented by another two sailing under the flag of Genoa – and continue on course to Siracusa.

————

Renata met with Don Filippe who advised him not only of the state of the family's business, but also the news that their warship, the *Leopardo*, had been taken by the Genoan merchant Alammano da Costa. The governor took the news with skepticism at first, but then asked the banker what this news would mean to him.

"The Genoans have planned to take the city from you, from Pisa," he replied. "It has been rumored for some time and now it appears that they are on the way here."

"What do you mean 'on the way'?"

"Their ship, the *Carroccia*, was outfitted with five hundred soldiers and heavy weapons. Now they have the *Leopardo* which has been drafted into their navy. And on their course to this island, two more warships have joined them to increase the fleet and assure them that they can overpower anyone who would intercept them."

"Then we will not try to intercept them," the governor said. He had little experience with combat and knew nothing of tactics on the open sea.

"Yes, sire, that would be a wise course," continued Don Filippe. "But what is the plan for when they enter our harbor?"

Renata looked down at the table and muttered, "Call Telio del Stanno." He was asking for the captain of his guard.

When the commanding officer arrived several minutes later, Renata briefed him on the status of the Genoan fleet's approach. Del Stanno was already aware of all the actions and knew more than Renata did, if chiefly because he understood them better.

"What do you advise?" the governor asked.

"We will strengthen the guard on the harbor, make the enemy fight them first before reaching the docks, and then fight them from the heights of this castle."

"Will that be enough?"

"We will fight with what we have, sire."

———

Two days later, da Costa's ships entered the Siracusan harbor. There was some light resistance but the soldiers who guarded Siracusa were aware that they were opposing a powerful navy and many of them gave up before entering the fray. The conquest was completed in short order, and the Pisans surrendered on land just as they had done on the sea.

Renata was permitted to leave the city with his wife and closest advisors, sent back to Pisa on the single ship allowed by da Costa to depart Siracusa. Genoa now controlled the eastern coastal cities of Sicily and would soon move inland to take others, and Alamanno da Costa was recognized as the new Count of Siracusa.

1239 C.E.

PALERMO AND MAZARA DEL VALLO

KING HENRY VI, HAD ARRIVED IN SICILY IN 1194 C.E. AND, ON the road from Germany, the king's wife, the Norman lady Constance, birthed Frederick, who would follow his father into nobility and become the Holy Roman Emperor in the year 1220.

Frederick had been raised on tales of his family, how they conquered Sicily, and all the folklore that the people of the island attached to them. His mother was a Norman from the Hauteville family and his father was a German from the Hohenstaufen family, so Sicily had already been ruled by foreigners before Frederick ascended to the throne. His family had redefined Sicily, taken it from the Arabs, and he knew from an early age that they were destined for many generations of leadership on this island in the Middle Sea.

But it wasn't all that easy. In his years of growing into his responsibility, Frederick paid close attention to the things that his family had done right, and the things that they had done wrong. Tolerating the Muslim faith alongside the Christian – not to mention the Jewish theology and practice – was the right thing and maintained a level of peace in the community.

But the Muslims were showing signs of reverting to the teachings of Islam, which included the mandate to convert or enslave those who rejected their theology. The 'infidels' must be brought to heel, they thought, even the dominant Christians, but with a Christian at the head of government, pursuing the Muslim objective was difficult if not absolutely impossible.

Frederick was faced with an unenviable challenge. As a sovereign, he didn't need to ask permission from anyone, yet as a man representing a single faith in a polyglot community, he didn't want to alienate the other groups. But he had also grown fearful of the protests and outspoken manner of the Muslims who still occupied his island. Frederick felt that the time would come – if it had not already arrived – that he would have to remove the Muslims and their Islamic teachings from Sicily in order to ensure the survival of the island.

He had been named king when he was only four years old although his mother ruled in his stead for many years. That time included multiple and continuing conflicts between Constance's Sicilian roots and her husband's German lineage and included frequent disagreements with the Vatican. Frederick was brought to Sicily, then rushed back to Germany for safekeeping, only to be returned to Sicily again and again. As a youngster, he was both the pawn and the declared ruler of this vast empire. At one point, Markward of Annweiler teamed with a force from Genoa and invaded Sicily, took Frederick hostage, and claimed the land for himself.

The young king was sequestered in the royal palace in Palermo for a time, during which he grew to maturity and, once there, asserted himself and his power over the regions of Sicily that had been commandeered by a host of barons acting without a centralized power to fear. Ruling often from afar, including trips to his other kingdom in Germany and on Crusade, Frederick returned to Sicily in 1237 C.E. to survey how the land had experienced more dissent among the various religious tribes on the island.

By 1239, Frederick was on his third wife – Isabella, who was both Queen of Sicily and Holy Roman Empress according to her association with Frederick – yet he still found time to entertain Bianca Lancia, who bore him three children, and several other mistresses throughout his marriages. He was a religious skeptic, a stance that resulted in his being excommunicated not once but twice, and yet he still aligned himself with the Christian society.

Striving for peace in Sicily, Frederick considered cracking down on some of the factions and outlawing their religious practices but he wasn't ready to reverse the policies of his ancestors. He separated the religious cohorts and minimized the tolerant ways of his predecessors. He even considered dividing the island from east to west but decided that this would be impractical since ruling over an undivided Sicily was already a formidable task.

"Sire," said his counselor Mateo D'Amato, "may I have a moment?"

Frederick pointed to the cushioned chair next to him where they stood in his library. The king's passion for learning was well known and he surrounded himself with teachers and philosophers as well as a rich supply of leather-bound volumes of famous treatises that lined the walls of this great room.

"You wish to deal with the Muslims, no?" asked D'Amato.

The king nodded.

"I have an idea. Would you like to hear it?"

Just then, Isabella entered the room followed by her court of three ladies in waiting. D'Amato held his tongue and Frederick looked up and smiled at his wife. He was as passionate about her as he was about his learning, and he always enjoyed her being with him. He would not have minded talking about serious things in her presence, such as his counselor seemed ready to do, but he didn't want the young ladies in attendance to hear it.

"My lady, can you stay?" he asked Isabella, but by pointing to the only other chair in the room he made it apparent that her attendants were not welcome.

"No, my lord, I cannot. I have come only to advise you that you have visitors from Mazara del Vallo awaiting you in the throne room."

Frederick looked at D'Amato who smiled, proving that he, too, knew of the visitors and that his counsel and their visit might be connected.

"Who are they, if I may ask?"

"Baron Sirico Laurentiis of Mazara, Baron Dante Cremia of Agrigento, and Baron Adolfo Triponte of Gela."

"Did they say what is their business, their reason for coming to Palermo on this day?"

"No, my lord," Isabella replied, then smiled demurely. "They do not believe a woman should be included in talk of business..."

"But I do," said Frederick, adding a phrase that he knew his wife would think but not speak.

"Anyway, thank you Isabella. Please inform them that I am pleased that they are here and that I will see them shortly."

Isabella left the room followed closely by her young attendants. King Frederick paid particular attention to the last of them, watching as her hips swayed beneath the thin cotton of her dress. He knew her form quite well without the covering and appreciated her shapely exit from the room.

"So, what is your business today?" he asked D'Amato. "Or should I say what is their business and yours, assuming you, Mateo, have called on me for the same reason that our barons have arrived."

"The Muslim community is making more noise and seems prepared to oppose you, sire."

"Oppose me? How?"

D'Amato demurred for a moment, looking down at his hands before raising his gaze to make direct eye contact with the king.

"They could be a problem, could start protests in the streets. They could insist on more freedom for their religion."

"And what would that mean?" Frederick asked. "I already allowed them to practice Islam without interference."

"They want to build more mosques across Sicily…"

"But it is a long-standing decree, as far back as my grandfather, that they can practice Islam and even enforce their own laws in their community. But we will not have domed mosques being built in every spare space in the cities."

"They could demand that *shari'a* law be enforced."

"I have let them do that, in their own community, as long as it doesn't contradict the laws of the Holy Roman Empire or Christian teaching."

"They want to enforce *shari'a* on non-Muslims too."

Frederick stood quickly at this affront, began to speak, but then held his tongue. This suggestion was outrageous and he knew that he could not let this grow into open revolt.

"And how is this connected to the visit from my subjects from Mazara, Agrigento, and Gela?"

"Laurentiis has an idea."

"Laurentiis. From Mazara del Vallo?"

"Yes, sire."

"And have you already discovered what his idea is?"

"Laurentiis – and if I may say, the others – believe that you should ship the Muslims off the island of Sicily, out of your kingdom, and back to the East."

Frederick laughed for the first time in this discussion.

"My kingdom is vast. I don't know where I would send them if outside of my kingdom."

"Your kingdom, sire, is truly vast. It stretches from here in Palermo, east across the entire country of Sicily, across the lands south of Rome all the way to the Adriatic Sea."

Frederick nodded approvingly, acknowledging D'Amato's respectful recitation of the lands under his control.

"And you are here in Palermo."

Again, Frederick nodded, but wondered where his counselor was going with this.

"The city farthest from here is, I think, something like Lucera, in the province of Foggia, wouldn't you say?"

The king regarded D'Amato closely. He knew the man to be an astute listener with a keen ability to read people's intent.

"And is this what the men from the south want to discuss?"

D'Amato only nodded.

"Let us go see Laurentiis and his friends," said the king already striding purposefully toward the door.

———

Principe DeLoro sat in the baron's chair in Mazara del Vallo. He was entitled to do that in the baron's absence since his role as military commander in the city included assuming Laurentiis's duties when the baron was away. But the eleven men standing around the desk also knew that DeLoro enjoyed the trappings of power too much, and that his quick assumption of the baron's power might one day get him in trouble.

"We will send them away," he said directly. "The Muslims must be gathered up."

"But the baron is now pleading his case with the king," commented Gino Stefano. "We must wait to hear the result."

"We will not wait. That is my order," replied DeLoro, holding his hand up to prevent further discussion. "We begin today."

"And how will we do that?"

"Call the men together," and by that it was clear that DeLoro meant his garrison of soldiers. "We will go to the mosque during evening prayers. When the Muslim men exit the building, we will bring them to the stockade." He paused to think through the next steps. "We will only tell them that they are being relocated, and that their families are already taken care of; that will make them reluctant to resist. Then we will await word from Baron Laurentiis."

"And what if he tells us that the king refused his suggestion to relocate the Muslims?"

DeLoro considered that possibility before responding.

"Then we will do it ourselves."

———

King Frederick entered the room on the east side of the Castello Normanni, the seat of his power in Palermo. The visiting barons were already in the room, standing in the glare of the sun rising over the city and its harbor. Mateo D'Amato was close behind, as he usually was, particularly whenever the king was expected to discuss important affairs of state.

"Good day," the monarch said quickly.

"Yes, sire, good day." This was Baron Sirico Laurentiis, who spoke for the group. "You are well, we trust."

"Yes, the king is well," said Frederick, speaking in the third person as he normally did when addressing those of lower rank. The linguistic tactic helped elevate the position of king even above the man himself and demanded that the audience accept this as a truth given by God.

"What brings you to Palermo?" Frederick asked. His subjects would often follow polite protocol and carry on in small talk for a while at first meeting, but the king wanted to get on with things.

"We bring you news of the Muslim uprising in our cities," said Laurentiis.

Frederick looked from face to face, scanning the barons before him and looking for hints of intent and purpose.

"Have they already engaged in an uprising? Is it violent?"

"Well, no, sire, it is neither already begun nor is it violent," said Cremia from Agrigento. "Of course, we would never tolerate a violent protest in your kingdom."

"Then what?" This was D'Amato, who not infrequently guided the sovereign in pushing questions and demanding answers.

"There is talk that they plan to rebel against your reign," responded Laurentiis, but he addressed this to Frederick, not his counselor who had asked the question.

"What talk?" asked Frederick.

"In the streets we hear what they have said in their houses of prayer. They want their religion to be free and they have been called upon to convert us to Islam," explained Cremia.

"But, of course, that is not possible," said D'Amato. "They should appreciate that his lordship grants them the right to prayer."

"They say that Sicily was once Muslim, and they want it to return to that," explained Adolfo Triponte, but he regretted the comment as soon as he made it.

"Sicily is Christian," said Frederick emphatically, "and it will remain Christian."

"Lucera, sire," hinted D'Amato.

The king regarded his counselor thoughtfully, then turned back to his visitors.

"The king will consider your news," he told them, "and we will speak again two days hence."

———

That evening in Mazara del Vallo, the Muslim men were called to prayer. The women and children were excluded from this ritual and so they remained in their homes. When the doors to the mosque were closed, DeLoro brought his men up and formed an armed squadron surrounding each of the three doors. They waited quietly while the sound of murmured prayers filled the air. When the sounds died down and the soldiers knew that the Muslims had completed their religious duty, DeLoro instructed his men to close ranks around the doors.

One door drew open in front of DeLoro and a man stepped out. He was startled to see all the armed men standing at the ready, pikes held firmly in both hands, and he searched for a familiar face in the crowd. DeLoro stepped forward, waving aside several of his soldiers to address the supplicants exiting the mosque.

"Who are these men?" asked Kaabir, the man standing at the front of the Muslim congregation.

"They are my men," replied DeLoro.

"And what are they doing here?"

"We have come to escort you to your families."

"What? Our families are in our homes," said Kaabir. "We do not need an escort to our homes."

"They are not in your homes," said DeLoro. In fact, he was reversing the order of things. He knew that he could induce the men to go to the stockade if it was in search of their families. And when they were secured there, he could roam the streets of the Muslim neighborhood and collect all the wives and children who would rather be with their men than be left at home.

"They are in the fort on the eastern side of the city," DeLoro added.

"Why are they there?"

"It is no problem. We are only trying to make sure that you are safe and not threatened."

Kaabir looked at the commander with distrust and more than a little fear. He knew that resisting DeLoro's orders would be pointless, but he also knew that once inside the fort, escape would be nearly impossible.

DeLoro's men allowed the Muslims to exit the mosque but maintained a tight circle around them. They then marched them to the fort and locked them inside the battery of rooms within.

"Where are our families?" cried Kaabir to the soldiers as they walked away. No one answered his question, and he knew they had been betrayed.

Over the next several hours, all the Muslims in Mazara del Vallo were gathered up and put into the fort. The men were told that their wives and children were being detained but to keep the men from rebelling, they were kept separate from their families.

"How do we know that you have them this time," shouted Kaabir at DeLoro as the commander walked by.

DeLoro expected to be challenged, so he carried with him the veil from Kaabir's wife's robes and held it aloft for Kaabir to see. The Muslim was shocked that this infidel would be holding a piece of his wife's clothing, but he could do nothing about it from behind the bars of the cell.

———

Two days later, Palermo's marketplace, still called the *kasbah* from its Arab days, was abuzz with activity. King Frederick II strolled among the crowd attended by D'Amato and several others. No one had heard of the news from Mazara del Vallo yet, so there was no sign of concern among the Muslims who worked the stalls in the *kasbah*, selling vegetables, fish, and ornamental beads. As he reached the edge of the square and stepped out of the throng, Frederick was approached by the three visitors from the south.

DeLoro had dispatched riders to Palermo, Agrigento, and Gela informing them of the news that he had arrested all the Muslims in Mazara del Vallo. The riders had just arrived in Palermo that morning after a furious two-day ride and told Baron Sirico Laurentiis of the events in his hometown and how messengers had been sent to Agrigento and Gela with the same news.

"It is time to bring the Muslims into the stockade," the rider told them, repeating the words DeLoro had given him before departing Mazara del Vallo.

Laurentiis addressed Frederick first.

"Sire, may we speak with you," he said, adding in a stage whisper, "in private?"

Frederick only nodded and turned toward the castle, followed closely by d'Amato and the barons from southern Sicily.

When they arrived and were in the king's library, the doors were ordered shut and the news was delivered to the sovereign.

"They are where?" asked Frederick, too surprised by the news to formulate a more detailed question as to why.

"They are under arrest. Whole families," said Laurentiis.

"Why were they arrested?"

"They were threatening rebellion against the crown. Messengers were also sent to the other cities," he noted, pointing to his fellow barons, Cremia and Triponte. "To warn them to be on guard and to take action before the Muslims rebelled."

"But now," Frederick began with some anger, "you have forced my hand. News will get out and there will certainly be open rebellion."

"Yes, sire, but is it not best to quell the revolt before there are problems than to let the Muslims force themselves on us?" said Cremia.

Frederick stared angrily back at him and Laurentiis and Triponte without saying anything.

"Tell Verelli to come here," he said to d'Amato, referring to the captain of the Palermo army. "Tell him I need to speak with him right away."

The die was cast and no time could be wasted. If there was any threat of rebellion in the hearts of the Sicilian Muslims, this act had clearly fanned the flames. Frederick ordered the capture and imprisonment of the Muslim population in Palermo and ordered messengers to be sent with his signed proclamation that all Muslims in Sicily were to be gathered.

Just above the elegant swirls of the king's signature, D'Amato had added a single line to the conclusion of the proclamation:

"All Muslims in Sicily are to be deported and sent to Lucera, in the province of Foggia, and they will remain there until granted permission to travel elsewhere."

1266 C.E. – 1282 C.E.

ANGEVIN FRENCH

1282 C.E.

PALERMO AND ALCOY

By the year 1268, the Norman line of kings in Sicily had ended, made abundantly clear by the beheading of the last of them, young King Conradin, in the Naples marketplace. The struggle between that old line of rulers and the invading French line from Anjou – the Angevins – was won by Charles I. He enjoyed the support of his subjects throughout France and northern Italy, but more importantly by Pope Urban IV whose power often exceeded the religious realm and stretched into affairs of state.

Charles was not from Sicily, and he did not live in Sicily, but he financed his various military endeavors on the taxes that he levied on the people of the island. The Sicilians came to think of themselves as nothing more than a remote treasury to be raided by the king whenever he chose to wage a war somewhere else, without any benefit trickling down to the people of the island.

The king also extracted other money and benefits from the Sicilians, everything from trade in spices and grain, to forcing the islanders to exchange foreign currency to one that he controlled. Adding to the economic pressure on the local Sicilians, Charles exempted many French subjects in Sicily from these taxes, shifting the burden to the indigenous peoples in order to satisfy his avarice.

Pope Clement who succeeded Urban IV tired of Charles's antics and ruled against him countless times, but the uncertain relationship between the papacy and the royal families of Europe allowed kings and counts too many clear paths to ignore papal commands, just as Charles did repeatedly in Sicily.

The Kingdom of Sicily included not only the entire island but also the provinces on mainland Italy south of Rome, so Charles didn't even go to Sicily after 1271 A.D. To make his absence from the island even easier, he transferred the capital of his kingdom from Palermo to Naples, putting distance between him and his subjects and isolating him from the growing complaints about his rule.

March 30, 1282, was a quiet spring evening as crowds gathered for a festival outside the Church of the Holy Spirit in the outskirts of Palermo. Festivities in Sicily at that time combined religious homage with drinking and eating, but when the native Sicilians were joined by French soldiers working for Charles, trouble brewed. The soldiers took liberties with some of the women, at times justifying their intimate touching of the women as an important search for weapons as they fondled the women's breasts. One Sicilian man drew a knife and attacked a French sergeant, stabbing him in the back for the assault on his wife. When the French soldiers fought back, violence erupted.

"*Moranu li Francisi*," could be heard as the chant – 'death to the French' – and the Sicilians who had long harbored resentment against the forces of Charles I resorted to an orgy of disorganized violence. At that very moment, the church bells began to ring for Vespers, the evening prayer, but instead of signaling a time for prayer, the tolling of the bells sent a signal throughout the city that an uprising was afoot.

Frenchmen who bore arms were cut down first, but the anger spread unabated, and women and children of these men were also stabbed and mutilated in the frenzy. Even Sicilian women whose marital choices had put them in French households were summarily executed by the rioting hordes. Confusion reigned, separating the Sicilian from the French and putting both at risk.

How should the mobs decide who was French, who was Sicilian, and who was sympathetic to either side?

A simple test was quickly installed. The captives were forced to pronounce the Sicilian word for chickpeas – *ciciri* – a tongue-twister that the French couldn't master. Those who uttered it without proper pronunciation were dispatched with the sword.

By the morning of March 31, thousands of French men and women had been slain and the local Sicilians had taken control of Palermo.

The riot that began in this western city, called *The Vesper Uprising*, spread quickly to the other regions of Sicily. Within days, rioting hordes had killed or captured thousands of Frenchmen and looked to take control of the entire island. The prominent exception was Messina, but even that city could only last until April 28. Under the command of Alaimo da Lentini, who brought the revolt against the French to that city, Messina fell in a blaze of glory, a blaze that included setting fire to the entire French fleet of Charles in the harbor of Messina.

Charles I and his family, on the island at that time, sought refuge in Matagrifone, a fortified castle at the outskirts of Messina, and remained there until they could negotiate a safe retreat. Granted safe passage on the condition that they would never return, Charles left Sicily. Thus, began an international struggle to maintain control over the island, with Charles maintaining his claim to royal power as others whose more propitious placement geographically challenged his claim. Charles continued to issue edicts from his new home in Naples, assuming that he could still maintain his suzerainty of Sicily from exile.

———

Meanwhile, the aspirations of Peter, King of Aragon and Valencia, seemed to come to the fore. He had married Costanza of Sicily, the only daughter of King Manfred of Sicily and his first wife, Beatrice. So Peter, through his connection with Costanza, believed that they had a claim to the kingdom of Sicily which Charles seemed to be losing control of.

"Sire," began a mumbled interruption by Franken, the burgher from Palermo. He was calling upon Peter at the king's home in Alcoy, Spain, and he brought news from the once-capital of the island.

Peter was in conference with several military commanders but turned to acknowledge the intrusion by Franken.

"Sire, as you know we are struggling under great taxation and abuse at the hands of Charles."

It was telling that Franken would venture into such a direct criticism of another sovereign, telling that he believed Peter to already be on the Palermitani side of this dispute.

"We have paid his taxes, given up our granary, exchanged our money for his, even risked the safety of our women at the hands of his soldiers. But we can bear no more."

"What do you want me to do?" asked Peter, although he was already hatching plans to overthrow Charles.

"We wish to invite you and our Queen Costanza to Sicily to free us from the yoke of oppression under Charles."

Peter smiled at the mention of his wife. 'These people from Palermo,' he thought, 'still consider her to be their queen. And so, therefore, they must already consider me to be their king.'

"Why should I do that?" Again, Peter kept quiet about his intentions in order to extract favors from the burgher before committing to the enterprise.

"You are our king, sire," said Franken while lowering his eyes. "You already deserve what is ours." Taking the role of supplicant cast both Franken and Peter into a relationship that the burgher thought would appeal to the king's ego.

"Yes, I am, but if I save you from Charles, would you anoint me properly? You know that others might oppose me, perhaps even the pope." He was clear with this messenger that he needed the people of Palermo – indeed, all the people of Sicily – to come to his side of the contest quickly. In doing so, Peter hoped to win the island by unanimous decision, which would smooth the way to render new laws and taxes.

"Sire, if you come to Sicily and remove the infamous Charles from power, the people of Palermo will announce to the world that you are our king, and that our queen has finally returned."

Peter smiled, then turned to his military advisors.

"This is the right choice," declared Roger of Lauria, the admiral of Peter's fleet and not incidentally of Italian birth. Roger had served the King of Aragon for many years and held strong personal feelings about recapturing Sicily from the French king Charles.

"Charles is a stain on the Italian empire and must be removed," Roger continued while Peter listened intently. The burgher's request and grant of sovereignty plus Roger's confidence in carrying out the mission emboldened Peter and increased his resolve to follow through on his plan to invade Sicily.

"And how would we do this?" he asked Roger. By this point in the conversation, Franken had become irrelevant. The Palermitani promise of kingship was all Peter needed from him; from this point it had become a military exercise.

"Sire, you have the strongest navy in the Mediterranean. We will assemble our fleet, bring the soldiers at your service from Catalonia, and include our most elite fighters, the *almogavars*, who will dispatch the enemy quickly," at which he paused to draw a finger across his throat, "and cleanly."

Roger was a master tactician and he knew not only how to draw the enemy into a weakened fighting position, but also when and how to deploy the *almogavars*. These fighters were lightly clothed to ensure speed but carried two javelins and a dagger each. In close combat, they could harass the enemy and slay more heavily armored soldiers who were inhibited by the heavy body armor. And the *almogavars* could move from engagement to engagement, choosing their victims quickly as they wove their way through the ranks of the enemy, tearing at the fabric of the regiment and rendering organized resistance impossible.

"We should land at Trapani," continued Roger, speaking with such knowledge and confidence that even Franken figured out that this invasion had been already long in planning.

"Why Trapani?" asked Peter.

"Palermo is the jewel of the island, which is three days march from Trapani. We will land there, organize our forces..."

"And openly declare our intent to Charles," insisted Guillem Galceran de Cartellà, the Catalan commander who would drive the ground troops. "He must be told that we have arrived, and that he will soon be deposed...or hung."

"And what if he resists?" asked Peter, but he only needed reassurance. His opinion of Charles was that the man from Anjou was a coward and would shrink from a confrontation with Peter's forces.

"He will not," said Roger with finality.

Franken was excused from the room but, before he departed, Peter rested his bejeweled hand on the burgher's shoulder.

"We accept your crown," he told the shorter man, "and we will remove the stain of Charles from the island of Sicily." With a nudge on Franken's back, he ushered him out the door, and returned to his military advisors to plan the adventure.

AUGUST 2018

CAFÉ AMADEO

"Vespers," said Vito when I saw him the following morning. I knew of the term and its historical meaning, so I didn't have to prod my mentor to begin the day's lesson.

The barista had already served Vito his espresso and *cantucci* by the time I arrived, so he returned to the table to bring my breakfast also.

"What began as a quiet devotion at the Church of the Holy Spirit quickly spiraled into a slaughter of the French and the invasion of the Aragonese. I'm sure Charles didn't wake up that morning of March 30, 1282, prepared for those events."

"Well, of course, all these things didn't play out in a single day," I commented, even though I knew the clear line that connected all the dots.

"Peter was plotting to take Sicily from Charles for a long time..."

"Wait. Peter who?" I knew the answer but had to slow Vito down so I could find the page in my notebook.

"Peter of Aragon," he replied, but he smiled at my transparent ploy.

"He – just like so many other monarchs throughout Europe – saw my country as a jewel in the middle of their world and it was nearly impossible for the greedy powers that surrounded the Mediterranean to withhold their grasp, to avoid reaching out to take Sicily for their own. It has been our fate for thousands of years, and Peter was just another king in a long line of them who couldn't resist taking our land for himself."

"Do you not approve of Peter, or his actions against Charles?"

"That's not the right question. You should be asking do I approve of anyone outside of Sicily taking it for their own."

"Okay," I said, "but Costanza was one of yours..." but he held up his hand to stop me.

"How do you know Costanza? You pretended not to know Peter?"

I might have blushed a bit but only grinned back at Vito.

"Okay, back to Costanza," I said when I had recovered. "Even though she married outside of Sicily, she had a right to consider herself the heir to the throne."

"A mere convenience for Peter. He would have invaded Sicily in any case. But, yes, having Costanza as his queen gave him a rightful claim. He drove Charles from the island, forcing him to retire to Naples..."

"Charles didn't really retire, right?"

"No," chuckled Vito. "Kings don't retire. Let me just say that, once driven from our shores, Charles contented himself with claiming the mantle of King of Naples, a separate kingdom from that of Sicily."

"And how did your country fare under Peter?" I asked.

Vito paused for a moment, then sighed.

"He lived for only another three years, succumbing in 1285 and bequeathing Sicily to his second son, James, who was followed to the throne by Peter's third son, Frederick. But Peter's invasion of my country began two centuries of rule by the royal family of Aragon, transitioning easily into another three centuries of rule by the Spanish. But, most importantly, he ended the campaign of the French to rule Sicily."

"And his reign was better than rule by the French?"

At this, Vito smiled and sipped his espresso.

"Of course," he said.

———

Another day passed and I was wandering around Mazara del Vallo. The din of voices and clinking glasses at the Trattoria Bettina always made me smile. It was such a contrast from the half-sleepy quiet of the Café Amadeo. But it was Vito's favorite place at night and since I didn't see him in the morning, I sought him out this evening here, where he seemed to always be.

"I'll be out early," he had told me the night before. "I have some doctor's appointments."

It made me worry and my furrowed brow brought out a smile in him.

"Why?" I asked.

Perhaps my inquisitiveness was not welcome. Vito had become my best friend and constant companion, but he still was three lifetimes older than me and my prying might not have been appropriate.

"Oh, don't worry," he said, patting me on the arm. "I'm just going to give them a lesson in geriatrics."

So, evening came and after I had spent the day walking around Mazara – 'I still have to get to the rest of Sicily,' I thought quietly – I knew that dinner at this trattoria would work.

At Bettina, you didn't so much walk through the door as pass under the awning that stretched overhead on the sidewalk. Little white lights were strung across the cross beams of the patio and the tables and chairs crowded the space so that waiters had to turn sideways to get to their customers. As you penetrated the maze of shiny metal and noise and got closer to the bar, the density of humans increased as did the noise. There was a local soccer game on the television and the partyers were alternatively roaring their approval or dismay and waving their hands in disgust at the latest non-call by the officials.

I stood for a moment on the barest periphery of this soccer crowd and smiled at the utter Italianness of it all. Soccer. What was more Italian than that?

"Azzurri," came a voice that I immediately recognized as Vito's. "The Azzurri. They didn't play."

That was obvious to me. The Azzurri – the nickname for the Italian national team – would not be playing in this local game.

"I can't believe the Azzurri were not in the Cup," he continued, and then it dawned on me. It was August 2018 and the World Cup had just completed. The Italian team was for the first time in memory not one of the thirty-two teams to qualify. For a country so in love with the sport, a country that had won as many Cups as any country, to not even be in the tournament, was shocking and destabilizing all at once.

"Oh, well," Vito said, hand waving in dismissal. "But don't say it."

"Say what?" I asked.

"That it's only a game."

I knew better. I had grown up an Italian-American – well, Sicilian-American – and despite the blood running through my veins I didn't have the requisite passion for the sport. At least not in the eyes of these people, yet I knew enough not to disclose that fact.

Vito steered me toward the same corner table we had occupied the last time I was here with him. In the mass of people crowded into Trattoria Bettina, I marveled at how even one table would be free whenever he wanted it. But then I thought better of my surprise.

"Aragon," he said as he slipped into the chair facing the room.

"Peter," I replied, as I slipped into the Vito-like habit of one-word openings.

Vito looked up approvingly at me.

"Sì, sì. I know that you have been studying. But it was inevitable that someone would come along and run Charles out of my country. The French king was never meant to be sovereign over Sicily. All he wanted was land and power and money and...well...money. He visited now and then but always preferred to return to Naples or France or who knows where."

"You asked yesterday morning whether Peter's rule was better than that of the French, of Charles," he continued.

"And you didn't answer."

He ignored my gentle rebuke.

"As with most monarchs, Peter's goal was expansion of his empire through land acquisition. And with Costanza at his side, arguably the heir to the Sicilian throne, my country seemed like an obvious place to reach."

"But he was Spanish," I countered.

"Si, but modern people put too much stock in the political boundaries that we have drawn across the continent. Except for some island kingdoms surrounded by natural borders, do you think that tribes saw lines painted in the hills telling them where their land ended? No. Peter, Charles, all of them, they saw a great sprawling continent that belonged to the person whose army set up its own unpassable line."

"But Sicily is one of those island kingdoms, right?" I said. I was sure I had struck a winning note.

"Oh, of course it is. Picture a chessboard with powerful armies lined up on either side. To the north edge of the board are the growing populations of Europe, and to the south are the peoples of Asia and Africa with their ancient cultures. Each look upon the middle of the chessboard as a place to wage battle, the place where Sicily sits facing threats from both sides. As one pawn ventures forth and is knocked from the game, a bishop follows, and then a rook, each in turn being challenged and sometimes replaced by the forces on the other side.

"Surely, my country could be called an island kingdom with natural borders, but every other culture for thousands of years has thought of it as bounty that can be taken by the fiercest competitor. The open space in the middle of the chessboard. Peter was next in line to do so, but we had no illusions about his grace or his equanimity."

Vito spoke of King Peter of Aragon as if he knew him personally.

"But a lot did change after he took over. Perhaps it was the influence of a Sicilian wife, perhaps Peter was just wiser than Charles and those who preceded him. But, with hindsight, we can piece together a fascinating evolution of society in Sicily."

"How so?" I asked.

"During the period of the Aragonese, we can look back and see the first glimmer of a Sicilian culture emerging. Oh, it was still a grand mixture of genes, blood lines, and accents from all over the western world, but partly because of Peter and partly because of so many outside influences, a notion of 'Sicilianità' could be seen."

"How do you mean? There were still remnants of the Arabs and Greeks, still some Jews, not to mention aboriginal Sicani, Siculi, and Elymi. I know the French had been run out, but..."

"Not completely," Vito said, with a finger raised. "Think bigger."

"What do you mean?"

"Think outside of Sicily. And thing longitudinally. You talk about the early tribes, but their blood had been blended in with the invaders to the point that the Sicilian population was one big melting pot. And outside of Sicily, think about the constant threats and the vigilance of a nation protecting itself against Romans, Greeks, Punics, Muslims, and what not. Surviving these invasions would create a sense of inner strength, a sense that the true Sicilian would emerge and be the last man standing.

"It had a distinctly Spanish, or Aragonese, accent – Catalan was the language of the royal court – but

most importantly, Peter introduced a rule of law. Generally speaking, he avoided the selfish whims of prior monarchs – Charles was among the worst – who too often levied taxes or fought wars to settle their own private vendettas. Peter's reign, and the rule of his sons to follow, was more consistent and predictable, so the people of Sicily could begin to settle down into a comfortable lifestyle.

"Other external events shaped the course of Sicily, though."

"Like what?" I asked.

"The end of the Middle Ages and the first glimpse of the Age of Enlightenment. The standardization of trade and the reduction of privateering and piracy on the sea. The emergence of parliamentary structures of government. Recognition of the prerogatives of other sovereign governments. And more."

"And how did Sicily enter into this phase of history?"

"With the treaty signed in Caltabellotta."

1282 C.E. – 1492 C.E.

ARAGONESE

1302 C.E.

CALTABELLOTTA

"Why would I go there?" complained Charles II. This heir to the kingdom of Anjou was very comfortable in his surroundings in Valois in northern France. At thirty-two, he had already traveled over much of his kingdom and had little interest in seeing more of it.

"Sire," said Panguin, his agent, "it is not to see Caltabellotta, but to find a settlement with the Spanish to end the war."

"Well, it's a good thing," said the monarch, as the beads of sweat gathered on his forehead. He was on his way to the southern Sicilian town and accompanied by his counselor Panguin. Charles II was only interested in settling the matter of the war that had erupted twenty years before. Those Sicilian peasants had had the audacity to attack his soldiers when they were merely doing their duty. Charles couldn't understand how that hot, humid island would be of interest to anyone, forgetting the pride his father had put in controlling the middle of the Mediterranean trade routes.

His counterpart in Spain, Frederick II who claimed the throne of Sicily – "just because of his wife" Charles was fond of saying – spent most of his time in Barcelona but had been going to Sicily more often now, specifically Palermo, to oversee his kingdom on the island. He was already on the island in June 1302 when plans for this historic meeting were made.

"Why do we have to go to this 'Caltabellotta' anyway? Why can't they simply send me the paper to sign?"

"It is not so easy to arrange for a person as important of yourself to meet with another king of inferior status," said Panguin, deftly massaging his lordship's ego.

Charles liked that description, but despite his fussiness and reluctance to attend this meeting, he was keen on the politics of the era. He had been invited by Frederick II to discuss and, hopefully, sign a treaty ending the War of the Vespers, a conflict between regents in their two countries that began in Sicily but spread to other lands and – if it continued – threatened to engulf some monarchies who had no stake in the battle. Charles had seen the waste and carnage, he had been part of it, and he wanted a treaty that required both parties to step back from the edge and let peaceful gestures ensue.

Charles's long journey down the peninsula, across the strait of Messina, and across the southern border of Sicily to Caltabellotta was a challenge for such an impatient man. He wanted peace but didn't want to have to endure this process any longer.

Caltabellotta was about a day's ride inland from the sea, about five days journey from Messina. They would have to skirt the Monti Sicani to the north and bend a trail north from Sciacca to reach Caltabellotta. The weather was typical for this season in Sicily, but too warm for the blood of this spoiled monarch.

"We travel by carriage," said Panguin, "and his lordship may stop at any time. The affair in Caltabellotta will wait, if you wish to take a more moderate route."

Charles waved him away.

"Let us get there, sign the papers, and remove ourselves."

Panguin knew that it would not be so easy. And yet he also knew that the elevation of Caltabellotta would provide some relief from the heat.

The castle that was chosen for the meeting was built into the side of the mountain there. Charles might even like it, the agent hoped.

———

Meanwhile, Frederick had departed his residence in Palermo and was riding the relatively short distance over land to the same destination. His route took him south toward Sciacca, thankfully just west of the Monti Sicani, and he expected to arrive after a leisurely three days ride, even on horseback. He was more Sicilian than Charles and he knew the countryside, the people, and the customs. He felt very much at home in this land that was being called Trinacria for the first time.

"Trinacria," mused his agent, Giuseppe. "Where did that come from, anyway?"

It was a term that had been coined recently, referring to the three capes of Sicily, on northeast, northwest, and south, and had become part of legend over the centuries. In the contest between the kings, each who claimed to rule all the provinces from Apulia in the east to Trapani in the west, Trinacria had come to refer to the island itself, the western portion of what was being called the Kingdom of Sicily.

"It's an ancient name," Frederick explained as he jostled forward in the saddle of the hefty mare that he was astride. "The name refers to the three points of the island and is now used to carve out a piece of the empire that I intend to claim at Caltabellotta."

"Do you mean the Kingdom of Sicily, altogether?" Panguin asked.

"Of course."

"But, sire, few treaties are made where one side gets everything."

Frederick bounced in the saddle in rhythm with his horse's steps but said nothing.

———

Frederick timed his arrival at the castle perfectly. He had fewer kilometers to travel than Charles, but he intended to arrive last, forcing his opponent in this affair to wait for him and his entourage to enter the city. And he chose to arrive on horseback, sitting high in the saddle and towering over the people of the city, rather than sitting on a cushion in a ribbon-bedecked carriage, all the better to portray a victorious conqueror.

Caltabellotta was a strange place to choose for the signing. It had its ancient origins, as did much of southern Sicily, and the weathered pattern of the winding streets were witness to the events and wars that had been waged in this part of the island. And yet, the city itself had little history of its own – or contributed little history to the island's millennia – so why meet here?

Panguin and Giuseppe had been in contact for several months through emissaries, and the Frenchman, Panguin, had originally floated the idea of Caltabellotta.

"It belongs neither to King Charles nor to King Frederick," he claimed erroneously. Caltabellotta was a part of Sicily and, therefore, would certainly belong to one of the claimants. But he intended to communicate an age-old premise of Medieval times: A city that had not been fought over in preceding decades or centuries would be the most peaceful place to bring the warring parties together for settlement.

He also knew that Frederick would already be in Sicily so choosing a place like Palermo would have given the Spanish rival the upper hand. If his king would have to travel, he wanted the Spanish king to have to travel. His last reason for choosing Caltabellotta was that he had been informed, incorrectly, that mountains stood between Palermo and the choice of cities. Panguin wanted Frederick's journey to be at least somewhat tiring to offset the effect it would have on his own king, but he had been misinformed. A western curve around the mountains would ease Frederick's path, keep it on level ground, and only add a day to the trip.

Just as he had planned, Frederick entered through the gate of the city to cheers from the local population. Any applause that may have attended the arrival of Charles had long since died down, and now Frederick was the hero.

He dismounted from his horse and handed the reins to a livery boy, then scanned the perimeter of the square looking for signs of the French delegation. He could see the carriage that Charles rode, and he assumed that the king's horses were stabled where his would be.

"Giuseppe, where do we lodge?" he asked.

"Casa d'Elymi, sire." It was a large building that loomed over the Piazza del Conte, the largest structure in the center of the city, and just steps from the Castello del'Ormi where the peace of Caltabellotta would be negotiated.

"And where is the grand prince of France?" he asked Guiseppe. It was common for rival kings to refer to their counterparts as princes rather than kings.

"King Charles resides in the Villa Bastiana," he replied, pointing to a structure opposite the Casa d'Elymi. It was then the middle of the day and the sun was high in the sky. Giuseppe knew Caltabellotta better than his French counterpart, who was probably as misinformed on the urban streets as he was about the Monti Sicani. Giuseppe knew that his king's residence stood on the east side of the Piazza del Conte, and Charles's residence was on the west. So, he also knew that Frederick's Casa d'Elymi towered over the Villa Bastiana and would cast its shadow on the lesser structure for the entire morning.

They repaired to their lodgings without planning to meet with Charles for the remainder of the day. Visiting kings didn't come calling; they would only meet on the following day to begin discussions, and they would do so by entering the Castello del'Ormi separately.

———

At the appointed hour, Charles and Frederick met in the piazza in front of the Castello del'Ormi. Smiles and greetings were exchanged, but the King of Spain left no doubt that he was seriously focused on the matter of the day. Meanwhile, Charles seemed to consider the whole business a necessary, but uncomfortable ordeal. He knew the outlines of the discussions already held between his dukes and those of Frederick, and he had read what Panguin had to say about the division of land. So, nodding to his adversary in the leather waistcoat, Charles turned toward the iron gate at the portal to the castle and walked through it into the cool rooms inside.

Frederick was in fact more focused than Charles. He intended to take all of Sicily if it wasn't granted to him, and he had cautioned Giuseppe not to yield too soon, or too much. He nodded back at Charles and followed him up the stone steps into the castle.

In a windowless room in the heart of the castle, a long wooden table had been arranged with maps, documents, and lighted candles. There were only two chairs, one on each side, for the kings. Charles stepped lightly toward his and, lifting his coattails, plopped down onto the cushion. Frederick watched in amusement at his French counterpart's affectations, but chose to stand beside his chair, all the better to lean over the table and command a greater presence by his height.

Noticing that Frederick would not be sitting down, Charles stood quickly, his motion seeming a bit awkward, more of a defensive move than anything else.

The absence of natural light in this interior room made it necessary to bring in more candles, which the pages did, hauling long-stemmed candelabras for the floor surrounding the table and shorter, multi-stemmed instruments to be placed on the table near the maps.

Panguin and Giuseppe began the discussion, pointing out the rough outlines of the agreement made thus far. Each of the kings demanded some land, so it would either be divided up in some way or fought over. The agents had worked for weeks to formulate a thesis for dividing the land, using approximate land area, ancestral claims, proximity to the sea, productivity of the environment, and levels of cooperation from the city officials and the citizens.

"Of course, all of Trinacria is too much for one kingdom," began Panguin, but Giuseppe interrupted him.

"And, of course, all the land south of Rome is too much for one kingdom."

They talked about taking half for each king, then reverted to gross land area or measured coastline. Panguin raised the matter of successful taxation, going back as far as the Roman Empire, to argue that Trinacria was more abundant than the southern provinces of the peninsula. Giuseppe parlayed that by reminding his counterpart that trade with the Italian provinces of Calabria, Lucania, and Apulia allowed transportation over land, and trade with Trinacria always required sea travel.

The debate continued like this for hours, but it was a carefully staged debate. Both men had practiced their thrusts and counter-thrusts and knew before coming to Caltabellotta what the other side would fight for, and what they would reject. After a long dialogue between the agents, they fell silent and retreated to chairs on the periphery of the room. They had opened the conversation, infused it with ideas already vetted, and it was time that they waited for their sovereigns to argue it out.

"This is just barely enough," said Charles, pointing to Apulia and eastern Trinacria.

"But you draw your finger across most of southern Italy, and then across the mid-section of the island far to the west of center," countered Frederick. "How about this?" he asked, pushing Charles's north-south line on the island farther toward the east so that he, Frederick, could also take Agrigento and Gela. Then he drew his finger across the lower part of the peninsula, incorporating all three provinces without uttering a word, silently claiming Calabria, Lucania, and Apulia in one swipe.

The gesture was not lost on Charles, who only chuckled at the audacious move.

"I will take those," he said to Frederick, using his open hand to sweep across the entire lower peninsula, "and..." he added, but Frederick cut him off.

"Yes, and I will take this," sweeping his hand across the island of Trinacria, from Trapani in the west to Catania in the east, from Messina in the north to Mazara del Vallo in the south.

The conversation continued much in this form for another hour, although the division just hinted at by both men – Charles in Italy and

Frederick in Trinacria – seemed to be taking hold. Each kingdom had something to lose, but each would gain a land with promise and without conflict.

By that time, servant girls had arrived bearing cups of wine for the agents and their kings. Charles and Frederick continued to argue but the result was winding its way toward the division of land that Panguin and Guiseppe had planned, and orchestrated.

The Peace of Caltabellotta was signed that day, August 31, 1302, and established a new Kingdom of Trinacria under Frederick, now Frederick II as he assumed the throne, and the Kingdom of Sicily which existed only on the peninsula itself and included none of the island formerly known by that name. It was ruled by Charles II. It ended twenty years of war between the Spanish and French royal houses and transferred full control of the island to Spanish interests.

1347 C.E.

MESSINA

THE HULL OF THE SHIP MADE A RESOUNDING THUD AS IT VEERED into the dock. A rogue wave shook it from contact, but the ship rocked back again, sending vibrations through the timbers and a jolt down the spine of a man below deck. He was isolated from his fellow seamen, the brown spots on his face signaling to all to stay clear of him.

The second thump of the hull also shook the cargo that shared space with the lonely man. The bales of cotton from North Africa and the spices from the Levant shook and, with the motion, ejected a swarm of black rats that had smuggled away on the Genoese ship plying the eastern Mediterranean in search of marketable goods. The rats skittered across the lower deck, hopping over small obstacles and circling the shaft of the mainmast that was planted in its oaken collar in the darkened space in the cargo hold.

Maserato Imbolati stood upon his captain's deck above, calling out for the sailors to tie up the boat, as they tossed lines to the dockhands and pulled the lumbering ship tightly into berth. He was the descendant of Genoese sailors and – thanks to his fertile wife – the scion of another generation of them. It was his duty to ship and receive cargo from Iberia to Tunisia to Egypt, using waystations like this one on the eastern shore of Trinacria to refill his food supplies.

But it was not only his duty; life on the sea was also his passion. Despite the warmth and love he felt for Regina, the wife he left behind in Genoa, Imbolati was never as satisfied as when his legs were absorbing the rhythmic rocking of the waves on the sea. And never so energized as when he lay beside his other wife in Cairo. That city had been his last landfall, and he recalled Olabisi's slumbering smile when he rose from her bed to embark on another journey.

It was in Cairo that he took on his biggest freight, highly marketable goods coveted by the northern Europeans near Genoa where he was heading. But it was also in Cairo in the year 1347 that he took on his other passengers, the horde of black rats hidden in the bales of cotton which carried the fleas infected with the Black Plague. He would deliver both the goods and the rats, depositing some at ports along the way like this one in Messina and introducing Trinacria to the most virulent disease to have been visited on Europe since the Biblical era of Moses.

Imbolati walked down the gangplank to the docks below while his men continuing securing the ship.

"We've got a full hold," he told the agent on the shore. "But only a little to trade here."

The agent, a local man who had worked the docks since his tenth birthday, was simply named Berio. Known to all who visited this harbor, he seldom left the water's edge, living out his thus-far forty years in a wood-planked shack perched on the edge of one of the docks. It was said that his father had gone to sea and never returned, and that his mother had thrown herself under the waves in grief. But Berio would not confirm these stories; he just turned silently away when asked.

"What do you have?" he asked Imbolati.

"Some spices, some fine African wood. But most is already bought and paid for, in Genoa," he said. "But also, we have a sick man in the hold. We would like to put him down here, so that he can get some fresh air and a doctor."

Berio thought the "offer" of fresh air was an odd one, since the breath on the seas was about as clear as it could be. But his status did not allow him to question Imbolati. Instead, he decided to consult the harbor master, Stario d'Esta, and take his advice on the matter.

"Sì, *maestro*," he replied to Imbolati, "I will request permission from Signor d'Esta." He knew that the harbor master would wave him away, granting the visiting captain's wish only because he didn't want to be bothered with such decisions. But at least Berio would let someone else make the decision about a sick man being released among the people of Messina.

Disease was a constant companion for the people of Europe, and Trinacria was not immune from its troubles. Deaths among the young kept the average lifespan not much longer than the reproductive years and were caused not only by the spread of disease itself but also by the insufficient medical knowledge of the time. Berio was an uneducated man, at least in the formal sense, but he knew that each sick person who entered his city brought with him the possibility of a deadly illness that could take his life and more than a handful of people around him.

Berio excused himself and left the captain on the docks to supervise the settling of the ship. As he had said, there would not be much to trade, and nothing would be removed from the ship until a contract had been signed. But he noticed some rats scurrying down the ropes that tied his ship to the dock. It was the latest of many invasions of the island, but Berio had no idea of the scurge of this particular invasion.

In advance of word from d'Esta, however, the sick man was led to the deck by a sailor who stood ten paces back – and told to leave the ship. He had been in the sunless hold for two days and his complexion had faded and his cough increased. Imbolati could now see the freckling of brown spots that covered the man's face and exposed hands, and he watched as the stricken man hobbled down the gangway onto the dock where workers knew enough to stand back to let him pass.

The man's path didn't bring him close to the captain, so Imbolati stood still and watched him go, then turned to watch as the man cut a path into the streets of Messina. Just then, a filthy rat scuttled across Imbolati's boot and he reflexively kicked from the knee to send the vermin into the sea.

An hour later, Berio found Imbolati sitting at a table outside a café near the dock.

"Sire, Stario d'Esta, the harbor master, has ruled that the man can come ashore," he began, "but he must be sent directly to the hospital there," he added, pointing to a rude hut near the harbor, "before entering the city."

"Thank you," Imbolati replied, sipping his wine, "I will tell him that." The captain decided not to tell this insignificant dockhand that he had already released the man to the city and that he was long gone.

1392 C.E.

PALAZZO CHIARAMONTE, PALERMO

From the journal of Matilda Ludovica d'Stefano:

"Oggi è 15 Luglio, nel'anno 1392. Sono seduto con la mia signora, Costanza Chiaramonte nel prigione di Palazzo Chiaramonte, qui, in Palermo."

"Today is the 15th of July, in the year 1392. I sit with my lady, Costanza Chiaramonte in the prison of the Palazzo Chiaramonte, here, in Palermo.

"The honorable lady Chiaramonte is being held prisoner by the barons who control Sicily and she is not allowed to communicate with anyone. She is also not allowed to write anything down, so I have secretly brought paper, a stylus, and ink so that I can write this for her."

"It must be in your hand," she told me. "You are not forbidden, but if the writing is seen to be mine, I will be executed along with my brother."

"My lady's brother, Andrea, was taken last month by the Aragonese of Martin I. He had been kept here, also, imprisoned along with the other members of the Chiaramonte family, and he was taken to the square just outside of this palazzo and beheaded. My lady looked out from the window of this room and saw what was happening. Signor Chiaramonte did not scream or fight with his captors, but submitted his head to the block, where a powerful man swung an axe down on his neck.

"*My lady flinched as her brother's head leapt from the wooden slab, and again as it thudded to the ground. But other than that reaction, she did not cry. Instead, she retreated to the chair that she always sits in – and sometimes sleeps in – waiting for the decision on her fate.*

"*She asked that I write down the history of her family, here in this journal, and that is the assignment that I will complete for her. I know much of the Chiaramontes, even at just my age of thirteen, because I have been with my lady since I was only six years old.*

"*Costanza Chiaramonte was married to Ladislaw of Aragon when she was twelve and I was ten. By then, her father, Manfredi III, had brought me to the castle to be his daughter's companion, and I have lived at court with her and her brother, Andrea, and the rest of the family for the last seven years. She treated me like a sister, or at least a cousin, but I never pretended to be. There were times when she had to ignore me, to take on the role of Sicilian royalty, and she couldn't be seen as too friendly with a servant. But when we were alone, we would play together and, when she was married, we would talk quietly at night about her husband, Ladislaw, and the many families who surrounded the thrones of Sicily, Aragon, Naples, and others.*

"*The story of the Chiaramontes began about one hundred years ago, when Manfred I came here from France. It is said that their name may have been de Clermont, but it was changed to Chiaramonte when Manfred set his sights on this island. He was a powerful man and built his riches along with his castles. The Chiaramonte family became known as one of the wealthiest in the world, and they invested their money in building even more castles all over the country, on the coast and in the interior. With fame came power, and with power came more money, and with more money the Chiaramontes could realize their dream of ruling the island of Sicily.*

"*Through succeeding generations, they built castles in Palma di Montechiaro and Naro near the sea and not far from Licata. Then there was a castle in Modica in southeastern Sicily which was celebrated by the sons and grandsons of Manfred as generations of counts of Modica. They even crossed the water and built a castle on the island of Malta to the south.*

"By the time Manfred III took control of the family's fortune, he ruled Trapani, Agrigento, Licata, and Messina. The Chiaramontes had succeeded in Manfred I's dream: They ruled the island. They were so strong that it was only natural that they should contest with the King of Naples. The challenge went well and Manfred III might have taken control of not only the kingdom of Sicily but also the Kingdom of Naples, but he died last year before the conquest was completed and his son, Andrea – my lady's brother – took the throne.

"He was not as strong or as wise as his father and his father's father. The battle with Naples was ill-conceived but the Chiaramontes might have survived under Manfred III. Under Andrea's hand, it faltered. He had sided with the French Angevins for support so the other barons of Sicily rose up against him, supporting Martin I of Aragon in a siege of Palermo.

"Martin's wife was the honorable Maria of Sicily and, as the one most people thought deserved to take the throne of Sicily, she was the choice of the barons. Martin chose to use Maria's connections and support, and he believed the rude lies that he made up about the Chiaramonte family would swing the popular attention toward his side.

"The Aragonese threw the entire weight of their massive navy on Palermo, quickly dispatched the soldiers guarding the harbor, then mounted a charge against the city itself. One night two months ago, they laid siege on the Palazzo Chiaramonte itself, and we were left captive inside this place from that moment on, fearful of going outside the walls and being taken hostage by the Aragonese.

"Some of the servants slipped out in the darkness. They told me that they hoped to find solace and forgiveness among the armed soldiers outside. Because their escape was managed at night, I didn't see what might have happened. I have no information on their fate.

"Other servants remained but lived in fear. Andrea and Costanza maintained their roles as royal family in the palazzo, but there was an obvious loss of pride and confidence as the weeks wore on.

"One day, the officers of Martin's army ordered the soldiers to storm the palazzo. By then most of the servants were gone and the soldiers who had protected the Count had been left outside to guard it. They were probably *imprisoned or killed, but they were not here to protect us against the onslaught of the Aragonese and the forces of the three powerful barons who sought the crown that Andrea wore. We were quickly overtaken.*

"I was granted clemency and allowed to remain to tend to my lady. Our captors respected anyone who wore the crown and they wanted Costanza taken care of, hence my continued service, at least until they decided how to dispose of her. Her brother was also treated with care, but he was locked in his room and denied all requests to roam about the castle.

"One morning, they came for him. I walked to the window with my lady and we listened as the charges against him were read out. A man in flowing robes of scarlet and black held aloft a parchment decree and spoke in a loud voice for all to see. The crowd that had gathered in the square was mostly the soldiers of the opposing army; most of the Palermitani were too afraid to attend.

"'It is the judgment of the King of Naples, the Count of Modica,' he declared, and by saying so had already informed us that Andrea had been replaced as Count, 'that this man has committed offenses against the crown and usurped powers that were not his to take.'"

"It was a longer decree, but tears welled up in my eyes, and my ears began to buzz in fright, so I didn't hear much more. After the words ended, the man in robes lowered the parchment and nodded to the big man dressed only in a black tunic. The executioner stepped toward my Lord, who was already forced into a kneeling position next to the block. The executioner swung his axe back and forth as if he was testing its weight and his muscles, as another man, smaller in stature but obviously proud of his role in this murder, leaned over Andrea and bent him from the waist to put his head on the block.

"Andrea's face was pushed down onto the wooden surface but, almost in a reflexive movement to soften his position, he turned his chin to the side, resting his right cheek on the block. He knew his fate had come but his life of style and comfort still commanded his actions as he sought a more commodious position.

"Andrea lay still, his face pointed toward the window that we occupied, and his eyes looked up in the direction of his sister. I saw it too; his visage* *was stone cold. At that moment, a face that had always been so full of lightness and cheer, showed no emotion at all. His eyes even seemed to be hollow and empty, black dots in a fleshy surface of face and nostrils devoid of feeling, hope, or future.*

"The executioner raised the axe, swung it once behind him to get the feel of the weapon, then swung it forward before arcing it back and above his head in the grip of both hands and brought it down with force on Andrea's neck.

"Costanza's back shivered as the blood spurted from her brother's neck and shivered again when the head bounded forward and thudded onto the ground. There was no basket to receive it as would be usual for a beheading – another insult to the man the barons hated – so the impassive face with empty eyes bounced once and then settled in the dirt beside the executioner's feet.

"My lady took many days to sleep, sitting in her chair at night but with eyes open. I woke occasionally to see that she had not fallen under sleep's power. I sat with her often, holding her hand and hoping to comfort her, but she remained distraught.

"After some weeks, Costanza seemed to gather herself and then she ate and slept with some success.

"Two days ago, the door to our room opened suddenly and the same man in the scarlet and black robes entered. He told Costanza to stand to receive her sentence. I could see that her face went white in terror, but she obeyed his command. Once she was on her feet, the man raised a parchment that looked frighteningly like the one that had sent her brother to the gallows.

"'It is the judgment of His Holiness the Pope that what was termed a marriage between Costanza, daughter of the criminal Manfred III, and Ladislaw of Aragon was an abomination. He took Costanza as consort and she expected that to constitute a marriage. According to the proclamation of His Holiness, this relationship is removed, ended, and annulled, as if it had never happened.'"

"My lady's shoulders slumped, but it seemed odd to me. I would expect her to be devastated that she had been used in this way, to be taken

advantage of by Ladislaw and the barons, but she seemed to be relieved. She was no longer married – although she had given herself to that man – but she would live. Perhaps, after witnessing her brother's execution, she felt fortunate.

"Today, we have been given our instructions. We are to leave this place, the Palazzo Chiaramonte – which I have been told will be renamed Palazzo Steri – and to find our way to Messina and thence to Rome. I will follow my lady, and we will find out what the gods have for us."

AUGUST 2018

CAFÉ AMADEO

THE BARISTA SLUMPED DOWN IN THE CHAIR ACROSS FROM ME. VITO wasn't there so I suppose that I was a captive audience.

"*Bon giornu*," he said with a smile. His sleeves were rolled up casually to the elbow, top two buttons on his shirt left open. His thick black hair tossled in a curly mess that any woman would swoon over. And his eyes, sparkling with youth and energy, held me in a tight embrace. After two beats, he leaned back as if he was resting in a lounge chair, one arm over the back of the wooden slat on the chair, the other spread lazily across the table.

"Vito. He is unmatched," he began.

"How do you mean?" I knew that the old guy was one of a kind, but it seemed like the barista had more to say.

"Vito. He has many years, and he remembers so much."

"Is that good, or bad?" I asked, prying for information about whether Vito has lived a hard or happy life. The barista shrugged his shoulders.

"*Lo stessu*," he replied – "it's the same." It was the kind of laconic response I knew was part of the mysterious Sicilian psyche. But then he smiled again.

"Sicily, and Mazara del Vallo, would not be the same without Vito."

"How so?"

"He reminds us of who we are, even when we forget. He tells the stories of the ancient people, but it sounds just like me, or you, or..." then pointing to the people seated in the café – "or them. Vito's telling of the history of Sicily is as if he lived it, from one century to the next, as if he is the story."

I was about to reply, but then Vito himself walked through the door. I was still focused on the barista's very clear description of my mentor, and then looked over at Vito. For a brief moment, time slowed down enough for me to see him more clearly. He didn't shuffle, although the weight of many years had clearly taken its toll on his body. He did walk bent over, and I knew that his was not a young man's back. But his eyes still sparkled, they weren't clouded by the cataracts of old age, even though they had seen war and pestilence, health, happiness, and death.

It wasn't until Vito slipped into the chair next to me and tapped my forearm that I realized how time had slowed and the sounds of the café had disappeared. With the tap of his finger, everything came back to order, the motion in the room returned to regular pace and the clink-clink of cups and saucers returned as I, too, returned to the present. The barista had already excused himself and was banging on the espresso machine's handled basket to shake loose the old grounds and prepare it for a new charge.

"Inquisition," Vito said.

I took a deep breath, not to prepare myself as much as a sign of re-entry into the present.

"The Spanish Inquisition was very difficult for my country. It began in the early Fifteenth Century and involved the usual chain of trial-torture-confession-execution that the practice did in other European countries. By the time it took hold, the Arabs in Sicily had been expelled, but there were still small pockets of Jews here, living peacefully and minding their own business, but their lives were a constant challenge to the power assumed by the Inquisitor General, Tomás de Torquemada.

"Have you heard of the word *neofiti*?"

I shook my head.

"Jews were persecuted throughout the centuries, particularly so during the Spanish Inquisition," Vito continued, while I thought about the plight of the Jewish people throughout history.

"In many places, the Jews who were forcibly converted to Christianity were called *anusim*, but in Sicily and most of southern Italy the term was *neofiti*."

"I'm not sure I understand how that works," I interjected. "You can baptize someone but how do you 'forcibly' convert their beliefs?"

Vito smiled wanly.

"Sì," he responded. "This is exactly the challenge that the Inquisitor General used when he needed to. The Spanish government, through its religious arm of the Office of the Inquisition, imposed a new set of rules on the people of Sicily. At first, it seemed a bit tolerant; those who wanted to leave could, and they should if they wanted to avoid persecution. But many Jews decided not to leave what had become their homeland, so they agreed to convert to Christianity."

"In what way?"

"Just as you said. They agreed to be baptized, but they didn't accept the new religion in their hearts. Many of the *neofiti* adopted styles of dress that conformed to this new religion, cut their hair consistent with what was expected, and abandoned accessories such as the prayer shawl so that they wouldn't stand out. Many also attended services in the Christian churches, but they also continued to practice Jewish traditions and religious ceremonies in private."

"That sounds like it would have put them at risk."

Vito nodded solemnly.

"It did, just as the early Christians in Rome risked their lives and livelihood by secretly practicing their religion in the underground meeting places. The *neofiti* were often called out under suspicion, and they would be brought before the Inquisitor. Torture was the regimen for questioning, and many broke under the painful process, either confessing that they were still practicing Jews or even making up things that weren't true, just to end their imprisonment. And they were frequently executed for the things confessed.

"At times, Jews or others in Sicily were brought before the Inquisitor not because of their own practices but because the Spanish elite who ruled the country at that time coveted something that belonged to the alleged criminal."

"Like what?" The thought stirred fears in me.

"Usually houses or land that the Inquisitor or his aides wanted for themselves." After a pause, Vito continued. "But there were other things that they coveted...sometimes the wives of the men taken to prison, sometimes their riches, and sometimes their children. It was an ugly time."

"The Spanish Inquisition was a blight on all of Europe," I offered as a way of suggesting that Sicily wasn't the specific target.

"Sì, this is true," Vito replied quietly, "many people suffered at the hands of religious fanatics. But the core of the Inquisition was not religion."

This surprised me, so I asked for clarification.

"As with many fanatical movements to crack down on small groups within a population, the Spaniards who supported the Inquisition had other motives, and used the divine purpose of God as the justification for pursuing those other motives."

"You mean like confiscation of property?"

"That, and more. Often the seeds for such a movement begin with the preachings of an extremist – think Rasputin or Savonarola – whose speeches whip up popular anger and develop momentum. Then other people who see how they can satisfy their own selfish interests ally themselves with these self-proclaimed seers. The union of the two – the religious fanatic and the power hungry selfish parasites – catalyze the movement and push it beyond reason."

"I like the word catalyze," I said, though regretted that I interrupted Vito. "It seems like the two elements combine to create a synergy that neither could accomplish on their own."

"*Esattumentu*," he commented. "And each gets what they want, in the beginning. The fanatic who thinks he's inspired by God gets more civilian power behind him, and the greedy types who align with him and attach to his message get the weight of divine inspiration to justify their terrible actions. But the synergy between the two creates an explosive blend. They both believe their goals are the most important and over time they begin to fight between themselves for primacy in the movement."

"How long did the Spanish Inquisition last?"

"Too long," but then Vito laughed. "Well, all such periods last too long, but the Inquisition lasted for centuries. Much too long."

He paused as if pulling some distant memory from his recollections.

"Do you remember the *mikveh* in Ortygia?"

"Yes, I do. The sacred baths. What of it?"

"It was very important to the Jews in that city, and so were *mikvehs* and temples around Sicily. To disguise their apostasy..."

"Do you mean their abandonment of Judaism?" I asked, but Vito laughed in a merry way.

"No. The Christians would have considered Jewish practices to be apostasy, but the Jews still had to hide that from the authorities. Anyway, to hide their prayers and practices – their apostasy from Christian dogma, if you will – the Jews allowed the temples and *mikvehs* to be forgotten, sometimes even allowing them to be buried or hidden within new walls."

"And how does this apply to the *mikveh* in Ortygia?"

"By the Fifteenth Century, a new structure had been built on that site, a Christian church that hid the fact that a Jewish *mikveh* lie beneath."

"Is it still there?"

"Sì, it is. In Via Alagona. And it's been found and excavated. You should go see it when you go to Ortygia." Another gentle nudge from my mentor to get out and see the island.

"Do you remember the *kanats* in Palermo?" he asked.

"The underground irrigation system built by the Arabs, right? You called it one of the greatest engineering feats in European history."

"Or the world," he added with pride, but then he chuckled. "Another *mikveh* that went undetected until recent discovery is in Palermo, and it's fed by the natural springs brought to it by the Arabs' water supply."

Vito paused to appreciate this irony.

"I think that's perfect," he said into his cup of espresso, hardly hiding the smile on his lips.

1492 C.E. – 1713 C.E.

SPANISH

AUGUST 2018

CAFÉ AMADEO

"Spanish," Vito said, when I entered through the door of Café Amadeo the next morning.

It was very humid outside and the faint air conditioning inside the building left a film of condensation on the windows. No American would say the place was "air conditioned" but compared to the Sicilian way of life, this was positively chilly.

"Sì, Spanish," I echoed.

"Fourteen Ninety-Two was a very important year," he continued. "For centuries, the Spanish empire was growing stronger but it wasn't until that year that the rulers, Ferdinand II of Aragon and Isabella I of Castille, captured the Emirate of Granada. By so doing, the expelled the Muslims from their country – from most of Western Europe – and ended about eight centuries of rule by Islam."

"Funny, I thought you were going to say that 1492 was important because the Spanish crown funded Christopher Columbus' expeditions to North America."

"Sì, sì," he replied with a dismissive wave of his hand. "That happened too, but it was not as important. At least at the time. And, by the way, Colombo didn't sail to America…"

"I know, he sailed to China but ran aground in the islands off North America before getting there." My wording was purposely twisted to inject irony into it.

"In any case, the king and queen of Spain had recently merged their kingdoms – of Aragon and Castille – making them more powerful in union than separately."

"What does that have to do with Sicily?" I asked.

"Remember that this was at the height of the Inquisition, and 1492 was the year that the Inquisition forced non-Christians to convert throughout Spain and Sicily. Muslims, Jews, whoever. So, this particular year marks a dividing line in the history of the Mediterranean.

"It signaled that Spain was to become the first true world power, and Colombo's expeditions in search of spices and riches only added to the mystique.

"But for us, in Sicily, there was very little engagement by the Spanish, and few if any visits by royalty from the mainland. This resulted in much distrust by the Sicilian people and their Spanish royal family. Once again, my country was being governed by outsiders from afar, and we were only existing to send them money, grain, and goods. Instead of having our own king right here in Palermo, or Trapani, or Siracusa, all we got were declarations and laws from some distant capital in Europe, and more taxes to fill their treasury. Our land was governed by viceroys, not unlike the former provincial governors but – in the new format – now they were outsiders appointed by the king."

I had noted Vito's frequent use of the words 'my country' or 'our country' and mused about how it connected him so vitally to the land. But he also frequently said 'now' when describing a past era, as if he was also vitally connected to that time. Or perhaps still living in it as if it was the present.

"This distance between the rulers and the people might have contributed to another force at play in Sicily – a population explosion."

I laughed but had to ask, "What's the connection?" I thought about the baby booms that often follow wars, when the soldiers would return home to 'hungry' wives and immediately set about making babies.

"Peace," Vito replied. "You see, a long period of peace contributes to a sense of well-being, when fears for the future give way to hope. Consciously or unconsciously, this is an incentive for couples to have children.

"Besides, the absence of war also means that the death rate goes down, leaving more people to count and more people to procreate."

A gray cast suddenly spread across Vito's face and his smile drooped.

"There is another side to the Spanish time. It was a good side, but the light that shone upon us then also illuminated how poorly we had been treated before, and how poorly we have been treated since."

"Wait," I pleaded. "Most of what you have described of Spanish rule was disappointing, certainly not uplifting. Foreign kings, high taxes, outsiders for viceroys. Why do you sound like you miss that time?"

"I don't, really. But since that time, when Spain reigned in our country, we have been under the rule of Savoy, the Austrians, the Bourbons, the Hapsburgs, the Fascists. In recent times, we have been overrun by the Germans, the British and Americans, and the Mafia.

"Long ago, Sicily was the land of Greek philosophers, the educated wise men from Islam, explorers from Scandinavia, and the rulers of Swabia. Not all was good, but we felt like Sicily was evolving into one of the world's great empires. And if you measure it by its merchant fleets, the produce from the land, and the booming economy of places like Messina, Siracusa, Palermo, and Agrigento, we were a great empire.

"This is what the rulers from Spain were after. But when it was given to Vittorio Amadeo II of Savoy, it was like the clock was turned back on Sicily, returning this rising culture to the time when the island was just a resource to be plundered."

1535 C.E.

CASTILE, PALERMO, AND MESSINA

LUTHER WAS PAINFULLY AWARE OF THE POLITICS OF THE situation.

His lordship, King Charles of Spain and Italy and, as the Holy Roman Emperor, was the one person who reigned over an empire that now sprawled across most of Europe and the Mediterranean. And the king thought kindly of Bishop Bernardus. He liked his advice – particularly on matters of politics – he enjoyed the bishop's jovial behavior, and he laughed heartily at the man's ribald jokes.

But Queen Isabella was not as tolerant of the cleric. She took particular umbrage at his unspeakable behavior with women – including ladies of the queen's own court. She only expressed her concerns in private with her husband the king, but her cold treatment of the bishop left no doubt of how she felt about him.

And, so, Luther, as Charles' agent and principal advisor at court, had to manage the difficult days of Bishop Bernardus's upcoming visit to the royal residence in Castile. The formal events might have been the most dangerous venues but, in actuality, Luther thought these scripted occasions to be the easiest to handle. The queen would always be seated on the king's left and Bernardus, as the most prominent visiting dignitary, would be the ruler's right. At least that guaranteed that the queen and bishop would always be separated by the king himself.

Luther smiled at the thought. It was exactly the same arrangement in the ancient Persian game of *shatranj* that had become so popular in Europe. In that game, officers of the court were moved about the squares of a board with king and queen dominating, but with bishops and knights to assist them. All were surrounded by minor subjects – or pawns. In *shatranj*, the king always stood between the queen and bishop. Facing his own challenge of household politics, Luther suddenly realized why it was so.

So the formal events might take care of themselves. The informal events would prove to be more delicate for Luther. Slow walks down the arched walkway of the royal house or in its gardens could mean chance encounters between the bishop and the queen, unsolicited questions from the cleric in the middle of the day might catch the king in the company of his wife. Even the times when Charles climbed the steps to the battlement above the castle walls might end in a chance encounter with Bernardus. If the queen was in the company of her husband – which she was often so that she could monitor her husband's attraction to young girls – Isabella would not be able to avoid contact with Bernardus.

The afternoon before they embarked to Palermo was one such occasion. The bishop had suggested a court hearing with the king and indicated that he would like to hear from Charles' military leaders. It was a bit presumptuous, thought Luther, that this man of the cloth would want to be briefed by the king's officers, but he knew that Charles would comply and that it would be left to him as the agent to go along.

Charles had fought many battles over the years, attacks by outsiders to snip portions of his empire off and attacks by those within his domain who challenged the king's supremacy. He ruled over a kingdom that surpassed anything in the history of the world, so there would always be dissenters on the edges conspiring to take a piece of the territory. There were continuing wars with the princes of Germania and the barons of Italy. The Ottoman Empire threatened his rule as often did the series of popes who wanted to set limits on the expansion of his empire and prevent Charles from ruling even the Papal States.

The military that Charles amassed to fight wars on all these fronts was a miracle of innovation and invention. Supported by a large treasury built upon the resources of the territories he controlled, Charles had encouraged development in the tools of war. Lances were improved and pikes distributed to entire battalions. Horses were now commonplace and units of cavalry accompanied every military encounter.

The cannon had become a standard feature of combat over the preceding century, made possible by the invention of black powder. First discovered by the Chinese, this fiery substance was, at first, unstable and given to sudden unintended explosions, but when mixed with a bit of sulphur, the combination of charcoal and potassium nitrate was easier to handle. Black powder could be used to send large stones or rounded metal balls long distances, as long as the forged barrel of the iron cannon itself didn't explode.

Machinists in the town of Pistoia, in Italy, took the invention a bit further. With precise measurements and a careful miniaturization of materials, they invented a small device that looked and operated like a cannon but could be held in the hand. Without the wheels and carriage that would absorb the kick of the cannon, the man holding their new *pistola* would have to maintain a firm grip on the instrument, so they forged a twisted or ribbed handle at the rear of the weapon so that the soldier's fingers could be wrapped around the tool and held tight.

A captain in Charles's employ had returned from a campaign in Italy with one of these instruments.

"It is from Pistoia, sire," he said, presenting the *pistola* to the sovereign with a bow.

Charles looked at the weapon with a curiosity borne of his interest in science, but still could not connect the metallic thing in his hand to the very large cannon.

"It can fire a ball of metal, just like a cannon, but smaller," said the captain.

The soldier was impressed with the new weapon and he could tell that the king was too. Neither man gave much thought to the fact that the unstable trajectory of the ball would require close-in combat; but the soldier still knew that it was better to fire a weapon at an enemy than have to engage him in hand-to-hand combat.

Luther was present for that exhibition and at the demonstration that took place that same afternoon. Charles seldom showed excitement when in the company of his subjects, but the *pistola* robbed him of his usual reserve.

"It is magnificent," he said after viewing the damage the ball did to the piece of leather hung up for the demonstration. "Can we get these for my soldiers?"

It seemed a quaint question from the man who was the Holy Roman Emperor, but he was still in thrall of the discovery.

"Quite certainly," Luther responded, without waiting for the captain's assent. And so it was done. The *pistola* became a common instrument of war in Charles's battles against encroachment of his domain. The first to be equipped were the *tercie* – that is, the squadrons of pikemen – and swordsmen, plus these new soldiers called *pistolese* – who could enter battle with long guns and pistols that would spit fire and fling metal balls at the enemy.

And it was on the afternoon before heading to Palermo to inspect the *Tercio de Sicilia* that Bernardus wanted to hear Charles's plans for battle on that island.

The theatre, or so the room was called in the palace where Charles entertained a large number of people, was set for the king and queen, the bishop, assorted military experts and court assistants, and others who might be called upon to describe the plan for Sicily. It was a warm afternoon with only a little wind, so Luther hoped the uncomfortable circumstances would keep the meeting short. He wanted to limit the time that Bernardus could interject his thoughts into the campaign. Unlike Charles, Luther didn't think much of the man of the cloth and he knew that Isabella would frequently interrupt the proceedings if Bernardus insisted on waxing philosophical.

For about an hour, various persons presented their information about Sicily, the history of the people there, the nature of Palermo, and the expulsion of the Muslims not so distant as to have been forgotten. After a description of the campaigns conducted in Spain, Italy, and elsewhere, the military portion of the briefing was reaching its conclusion.

"The *Tercio de Sicilia* is positioned in certain posts around the island," said Candido d'Andrea, Charles's military strategist. "The people of the island have not been a problem, sire..."

"It's too bad we don't have such peaceful situations in the rest of the empire," muttered Bernardus. His presumptuous use of the royal 'we' irritated Isabella, and she shifted her hips on the marble throne as a subtle show of protest.

"The people of Sicily have been quiet," repeated d'Andrea, "and we have not had to use your military to calm them. This is a tribute to your leadership, your highness."

Charles rubbed his chin with the back of his hand and considered Bernardus's comment.

"If we can have peace in Sicily, what are we doing there that we are not doing elsewhere?" he asked.

Andrea paused to consider the best way to phrase his answer. He wanted to credit Charles with the successful atmosphere in Sicily, but he had reached his own conclusion a long time ago. He knew that the tribes on that island had been invaded and subjugated for so long by so many different nations that they had given up their resistance.

"It could be, sire," he began hesitantly, still trying to frame his reply, "that appealing to their nature and the kindness of your rule has made all the difference."

Luther was no more fooled by this answer than was Charles, whose twisted grin revealed his own doubts.

"So, we shall go to Sicily and see for ourselves, their nature and the kindness of my rule," Charles concluded. "Yes?"

Everyone in attendance bowed at the king's rhetorical question.

The flotilla bearing the royal party disembarked from Iberia toward Sicily. It would sail first to Trapani to inspect the *tercio* there but, more importantly, its landing at this port farther west and south of Palermo would allow the proper news of King Charles's arrival to reach Palermo, so that arrangements could be made in advance of his approach to the city.

It was mid-summer and the heat was oppressive.

"You will be the guest of Guglielmo Aiutamicristo, sire," said Luther. "while you are in Palermo. He is the baron of Misilmeri and Calatafini."

"But why not stay in the royal palace in the city?" Charles asked.

"The Steri Palace is very beautiful, my lordship," replied Luther, setting a cadence for his words that would draw the king's attention. He knew that Charles had never been to Sicily. "But Signor Aiutamicristo's family is very wealthy, and they have spent liberally on their own palazzo. The Palermitani now think of the Palazzo Aiutamicristo as more beautiful than anything in their city."

"More beautiful than my own palace?" asked the king, showing a combination of annoyance and embarrassment.

"Sire," Luther continued, "the Palazzo Steri was built by the Chiaramonte family," tossing out the name of a discredited family of ancient times. "But the Aiutamicristos are loyal subjects and have contributed freely to your war efforts."

Luther knew that little needed to be said. Charles and Isabella – and unfortunately also Bernardus – would remain there while in Palermo. He, Luther, would stay at the Aiutamicristo residence also, with some soldiers for security, but the rest of the travelers would be housed in the city.

When they arrived in Palermo two days later, a slender boy of about thirteen led the small team of stableboys who would take the reins of the royal party. He was Antonio, the son of the farrier who tended the horses at the Palazzo Aiutamicristo. He bowed his head when the king descended from the carriage, and bowed even further when the queen followed, to avoid making any eye contact with even the hem of her dress. But he had already seen the harness and braided ropes that controlled the horses when the party was first approaching. He smiled at the colorful *shaffron* that covered the horses' jowls and nostrils; the red, blue, and yellow *crinet* that covered the neck; and the polished leather *crupper* that bound the saddle to the belly of the animal.

He also noticed the shiny silver buttons and brass buckles that adorned the carriage, and the shiny silver tubing that covered all the exposed edges of the wagon.

'It is an amazing vehicle,' Antonio thought to himself, and he was unable to control the impulse to look up at it again. Fortunately, it was only Luther descending from the carriage, and the agent was tolerant enough not to chide the stableboy about gazing at the royal carriage. Luther just stepped down and walked past Antonio.

But Bernardus was just descending from his carriage at the same time and he was too haughty to miss an opportunity to upbraid the youth. With a snap of the short leather strap he carried that caught Antonio on his bare forearm, Bernardus also snapped.

"Don't look at me, you little bastard," he said curtly. "Lower your eyes."

The gesture of bowing was owed to the king and queen and not the bishop, but the whip still got Antonio to comply.

"It is the most beautiful thing I have ever seen," he told Nicolà later that evening. The girl, about as old as Antonio, had come to live with Antonio and his father at the age of ten, when her parents died from a suspicious illness. Antonio and Nicolà had begun as young playmates but there were only two beds in the little house, so they shared the one left vacant by Antonio's father. In a very short time, their physical contact at night overwhelmed their notion of a simple friendship.

"Tell me about it," Nicolà said, with an excitement that equaled Antonio's. He described the horses' trappings and the design of the carriage in great detail. He lingered over the artistic expressions that made the king's vehicle so different from anything they had seen or used in Palermo. Then he described the height and strength of the animals.

"They could win a war with riders," he exclaimed, although on that point Nicolà had to wonder how that would work.

"I would like to work for the king and to care for those magnificent animals," he said.

Antonio's father was sitting in the corner of the room but at this, he smiled. He, too, had loved horses since his childhood and had dreamed of caring for the best. When the Baron Aiutamicristo saw how the farrier had nursed a mare back to health, he hired him to run his stable. Now, thought the man, he had what he had dreamed of, and he knew how his son felt at that moment.

———

Three weeks later, Charles called his barons and other officers of the court to a Parliament in Palermo. Peace reigned in Sicily, as d'Andrea had advised him, and bringing this lower rank of officials to a meeting would be a sign to all that peace and justice could thrive together.

Throughout the centuries of outside rule, there had been few from Aragon or Spain who had bothered to visit the land. So festivities were in order to celebrate his visit as well as the conclave of barons and notables. It was mid-September by the time all arrived, so the intense heat of the Mediterranean summer had faded, allowing parades and marches by the *tercio* to begin while the sun still shone.

For days at a time, sessions of legal experts and political seers were interrupted only by the bell signaling meals, but long and filling meals they were. Charles intended for all to follow his decisions of law, so Luther advised him to feed the barons well and save the most contentious matters for the evening when wine had been used to soften any objections they might have.

The parliament went as Luther had planned, which meant that Charles was successful in portraying himself as a wise and strong ruler; Isabella was successful at proving to the Sicilians that she was an appropriate spouse for their sovereign, and Luther was successful in keeping Bishop Bernardus on the fringes of the debates.

The king decided to leave Palermo and visit some other regions of this land. The visit had taught him much about the people and the land, although the stories that reached him were told mostly by the barons who kept the common people under their thumb. Charles remarked to Luther on one afternoon that it was good that he had come to Sicily.

"We will travel across the island and depart from Messina," Charles suggested. Luther knew that this meant he would be sending the ships ahead around the northern coast of Sicily so that Charles and his retinue could travel over land.

"Yes, sire," he replied with a bow. It was autumn and the weather would be more appealing, thought Luther, and Bernardus was too lazy to travel by land so he would sail with the others.

MARCH 1669 C.E.

CATANIA

THE HISSING STEAM HUNG IN THE AIR OVER ETNA FOR DAYS, BUT the people of Catania had seen it before. The great mountain belched sulphurous odors time and time again, sometimes accompanied by the roaring of explosions within, and the Catanians had come to terms with it. The volcanic soil that survived the ancient eruptions was so fertile that the plains around Catania, Mascalucia, Misterbianco, Trecastagni, Paterno, and other villages that lay south of the volcano were home to sprawling hectares of farmland. No one alive in the town had known the kind of destructive eruptions that were talked about in folk tales, so why leave?

Even the tremors of the earth that had been persistent but subtle were slowing down.

One night, the hissing and the clouds of steam and smoke suddenly went quiet. Everyone assumed that the great mountain had finally gone back to sleep. For several hours everyone in the area slept without fear. Catania was at rest, as were the other villages on the southern slopes of Etna.

Then a rumble could be heard and felt. People throughout Catania woke to the noise and fled to the edges of the city where a great wall had been built by their ancestors. Such barricades were common protection against enemies in medieval times, although every Catanian had heard the stories about how this wall was meant to stop a very specific enemy: the lava that poured from the volcano during its worst times. The wall on the northern periphery of their city was thicker than the one on the south precisely because it faced the mountain, but most of the villagers thought the barricade was erected as their answer to the folklore of the god of the mountain. It all seemed like a child's tale.

When they ran from their homes on that night they could see bright orange, yellow, and red flames thrown high in the sky while black clouds burst and curled from the gap at the top of the mountain. Flames, thunder, and smoke combined to send a collective shiver through everyone in the area; they knew this eruption was one of those the elders talked about.

More thunder, red flames, smoke, and sulphur filled the sky and huge blocks of stone hurled upward from the mouth of the volcano. Brilliant, luminous rivers of fiery lava began to pour down the southern slope of the mountain and set fire to anything in its path. The sickly, muckish lava burned bright on its front edge and left a smoking, blackened hulk on its tail as the melted rock cooled into pipes and tunnels that carried the hot liquid straight toward Catania.

Diego de Pappalardo was one of those people standing on the tower abutment on the north edge of Catania, as people around him screamed about the true anger of the gods.

"It is the end of the world!" cried the man standing next to him, but Pappalardo wasn't so fatalistic. As he watched each hot river create its own tunnel of cooled lava on top and molten lava in the pipeline, he had an idea.

'If the red broth of the gods can make its own tunnel,' he thought, 'why can't we make tunnels for the broth to go another direction?'

He jumped down from the wall and ran to the crowd of people clustered in the middle of the piazza. They were arguing about whether to remain in the city – "They built the wall to protect us," someone shouted to no one in particular – or to rush out of the southern gate to safety.

"That won't work, that can't work," said another. You can't outrun the gods!"

"The gods don't care about us," said a woman in the crowd. Many standing next to her stepped gingerly away as if they were guarding against a bolt from the gods for her blasphemy.

"But we can outrun the lava," said another man.

"I have an idea that will save us and save our city," said Pappalardo.

No one had been thinking of saving the city, just themselves, so the idea sounded like a useless fantasy.

"Listen to me," Pappalardo continued. "We can go to the mountain and move the lava away from us."

"*Sei pazzu*," came a retort from the crowd – "You're crazy!"

"Look at the mountain," Pappalardo said, pointing up the slopes of Etna that were visible from their position in the town. "The broth comes down the mountain, cools, and hardens."

"And more of that fire comes out the end!" answered the woman.

"But if we teach it to go here," Pappalardo said, drawing his finger to the west, "or here," then signaling the east, "the lava will go down the mountain away from Catania."

"And how do you intend to do that, ask the gods to reshape their mountain?"

"No," he said simply, "we will reshape it."

Doubters argued but Pappalardo was now getting the attention of some of the younger, braver men in the crowd. They talked about how to accomplish his plan, what tools they would need to do it, and how they should approach the mountain. After some discussion, the clique of believers dispersed to their homes to collect shovels, picks, and other tools that they could use to dig channels to change the course of the lava flowing toward Catania.

The lava flowed for days as the Catanian team made its way up the slope. Pappalardo was in the lead but he depended on Giorgio, his cousin, to hang back in the crowd of about fifty men and talk to them as they ascended the slopes of Etna. Pappalardo's job was to find the best spot to attack the cooled lava pipeline; Giorgio's was to continue to encourage the men and keep them from abandoning the cause.

With each hour of walking toward the volcano, the intensity of the heat increased not only in the air itself but also the heat that penetrated their thin leather footwear. They carried leather bags with water but that soon was gone, both through evaporation and their consumption, and yet the heat – and fear – continued to increase.

Finally, Pappalardo chose a spot to begin their experiment. The men gathered around him for instructions, but he first made them turn around and face Catania.

"That is our city. That is where our families live, and where we have lived throughout our lives. We must save Catania."

That reminder served to stiffen their resolve and Giorgio smiled at Pappalardo for his insight.

The team was gathered at the western edge of a bulbous pipeline that still emitted steam and smoke but was otherwise grayish black and crusty looking. Pappalardo held his pike horizontally at waist height and jabbed it into the lowest edge of this pipe. With a hollow 'thunk,' the pike bounced back. So Pappalardo raised the tool a bit higher and tried again. The sharpened point of the pike jabbed and stuck in the side of the lava wall but didn't make much of an impression.

Giorgio stood next to Pappalardo and tried the same thing with his pike but held it above his shoulders and jabbed downward onto the roof of the pipe. The tool punctured the crown of the crusty tunnel and a cloud of smoke and gas spurted out. The sudden reflex of the lava made the men jump back, but they realized that the level of the flow inside the pipe was a bit below the top of the pipe, so they knew they could work on the top of the curve of cooled lava first.

The men lined up and began stabbing and jabbing at the blackish wall with their pikes, shovels, and long rods, creating a crumbling mess of heated rock and dust at their feet. They were frequently assaulted by fiery debris as it fell from the wall of lava onto their feet and the leather coverings soon were singed and blackened from the contact. But the men persisted.

After creating a long, jagged horizontal rift in the tunnel at about chest height, the team paused to consider what to do next. This is where Pappalardo's plan came into play.

He had chosen a portion of the lava tunnel not based on the shape of the tunnel itself, but on the slope of the ground on which it stood. He called the men to a halt, then pointed to the swale in the ground at his feet.

"This natural channel," he said, pointing to the long, irregular trench that ran from where they stood to a point down the western slope of the mountain, "this will carry the lava in this direction, away from Catania."

While he directed the effort, the men returned to their task of chopping through the wall of the lava pipeline at a position exactly matching the swale on which they stood. This was a more dangerous task than cutting through the roof of the tube that contained the lava. Now, if the wall suddenly burst, the men would be trapped in the flow of scalding lava and certainly be burned alive.

Pappalardo dared to climb on top of the tunnel itself, gingerly testing his footfalls to be sure he didn't fall through. From this position he could supervise the work, pointing to faults in the lava wall that the men should exploit but be prepared to retreat from.

Giorgio stood below ready to drag a man to safety if a sudden breach threatened him. By now, the men could sense a victory and so they forgot about tired muscles, singed hair, and shallow breathing.

After a couple hours of carefully supervised work, one man's pike shattered the wall below the surface of the flowing lava, and the hot brew poured forth over the edge of the breach. The heat and power of the lava took over the work the men had done and widened and deepened the opening for them. Red-hot lava and gas escaped through the gap and began running down the swale that Pappalardo had identified at the very start of the operation.

A cheer went up from the tired men just as another team from Catania was arriving. Seeing the success of the first explorers, this relief team quickly set to work on another breach where Pappalardo directed them, a breach that had both thin walls in the lava tube and a naturally cut swale in the mountain side.

The Catanians efforts continued for several days in this manner and they successfully diverted the western-most edge of a large lava field away from the main stream. They knew they could not divert the entire flow from the mountain toward Catania, but they were counting on those ancient walls to hold back what escaped their diversionary tactics.

Another few days of work passed as teams of Catanians took turns on the mountain. One morning, while clouds still obscured the sun and gas and heat still filled the air, a new team of men came from another slope. They were from Paterno, a small village below Etna, but to the west of Catania. They were led by Fantine, a muscular man with a ferociously angry look on his face, and his wife, Mona, the first woman to dare to climb the volcano.

"*Diavolu!*" he shouted at the Catanians. "You are burning our city!"

The effort by Pappalardo and his men was successful in protecting Catania, but they had sent the lava down the mountain toward a less-protected Paterno, and in the ensuing days the burning river had reached their outskirts of the village and destroyed not only their farms but was now threatening their homes and workshops.

"You are burning our city!" went the cry once more. Pappalardo could see that the Paternians had come to the mountain with their pikes and axes, but these weapons would be used against him and his men before they were directed at the lava.

A battle broke out on the hellish slopes of Etna that day, each party fiercely defending their city. The Catanians were already exhausted from days of torturous work, and the Paternians were driven by hate at the Catanians for their actions. In hand-to-hand combat over one hundred men – and even Mona herself – fought astride the lava pipes. Behind them, the still brilliant reddish-orange fire belching from the mountain made the scene appear to be something out of hell itself. Pikes struck heads and pierced legs, bones were broken and screams were heard. They continued fighting until all nearly collapsed from fatigue; and the lava still continued to flow.

The Paternians came to the mountain with greater reserves of strength and beat the Catanians back down the mountain. When they were gone, Fantine led his men to reverse the course of lava toward Catania. Over several days of work, they were successful in cutting off more flow, having accepted the river of heat that already had made it to their village.

And the Catanians had managed to steer enough of the lava away from their town so that it survived initially. Despite their efforts, the great wall of Catania was breached in time as Etna continued to spew its molten brew for weeks, and thousands of villagers perished.

It took many weeks but, in time, Etna slowed her horrible explosions and returned to slumber. The people of Catania and Paterno repaired their homes and workshops and swore that they would never again attack the mountain.

AUGUST 2018

CAFÉ AMADEO

"The centuries of rule by the Spanish could be looked upon as the most peaceful in our long history," Vito said over a bottle of Nero d'Avola that evening.

"Peaceful?" I asked, "or uneventful?"

Vito smiled. Perhaps I had hit just the right note.

"Both, I suppose. There were fewer wars. Although the kings who ruled during that period took resources from my country – men, grain, money from taxes – to fight their wars, few were waged on our shores. I guess that's a plus. And, yes, the Spanish period was relatively uneventful."

"Despite the occasional eruption at Etna," I added.

"Even the Spaniards couldn't prevent that," he offered. "You know, that thing that happened in 1669," and he paused to laugh. "The king outlawed it after that experience."

"Outlawed eruptions?" I said but I couldn't contain my own laughter.

"No," he said with a guffaw. "What the Catanians did. They tried to interfere with nature and, in doing so, endangered Paterno. The king proclaimed that such action was an affront to nature, and to his rule.

The proclamation was respected by law and remained on the books for a very long time..."

"Wait," I interjected. "You mean the Italian people made it a crime to divert lava from destroying their town?"

Vito waved a finger at me in reproach.

"Not the Italian people. The Sicilians," he said, and I was instantly embarrassed at missing the distinction.

"And, yes, the Sicilians made it a crime," he continued with a wide grin.

"So, what about now? Is that still a law?"

"Oh, I don't know," Vito said. "It might still be on the books, but I think the authorities would overlook it if you invented some way to stanch the flow of molten lava toward your house or something."

"Okay, so let's go back to the Spanish rule," I offered to get us back on track.

"Among the changes they brought about was a concentration of wealth in the baronial class and an impoverishment of the peasant class," Vito began.

"I thought that was well underway for centuries," I said.

"Surely, but the Spanish kings allowed the barons more latitude in how they managed the affairs of Sicily, and the barons managed things so that they could take more from the land. I think you call that the 'hollowing out of the middle class' in America. More people fell into poverty, lost their land, and moved to the already over-crowded cities while wealth was concentrated in a shrinking upper class. To avoid uprisings, though, the kings continued the trend toward rule-by-law rather than rule-by-monarchical-whim. More laws meant that well-argued cases could be asserted and achieve some fair treatment for the people.

"There was some structure to labor laws by the early-Fourteen Hundreds and farmers, serfs, and shepherds would at times be heard in court arguing for their rights. Kings and parliaments that had codified rights and privileges often found themselves stuck with precedent. For example, in 1446 A.D., the baron of Calatabiano prohibited local shepherds from pasturing their sheep on public lands. The shepherds took the case to court and the judge ordered the baron to rescind his prohibition and allow the grazing."

"I've been listening intently for weeks," I said, "and most of the history of Sicily has seemed to be one struggle after another. Now it seems, during the Spanish reign, that things began to settle down. Is that a fair assessment?"

"It's fair. Not that life in medieval times was easy, but compared to what came before, yes, I would say that things had begun to settle down."

"That's also the longest period of any one occupation?"

Vito smiled and peered at me.

"You say 'occupation,'" he responded. "Do you consider that to be the proper word for our history?"

"Well," I stuttered a bit, fearing that I had offended him. "It seems to me that when country after country, king after king, lay claim to the island, steal its resources and force the people into poverty from taxes...that sounds a lot like occupation." Maybe my careful response seemed a bit defensive. I couldn't tell.

"Yes, I suppose you're right," he replied. And I relaxed, knowing that I hadn't offended him, but not when I pondered the plight of the Sicilian people over the centuries and millennia.

"Art and architecture changed slowly in Sicily," Vito continued, "more slowly than on the continent. Do you remember when I said a while back that our isolation protected us from some of the things in Europe, but also pre-ordained that Sicily would evolve culturally more slowly too?"

I nodded.

"Well, the Renaissance essentially passed us by. We had our artists and philosophers, but they were the exception. We did not enjoy the bounty of brilliance that inhabited Pisa, Firenze, Milano, and elsewhere. And distant as we were from other influences, architecture evolved here in its own unique way. The Chiaramonte family developed a style all their own, called Chiaramonte Gothic, but otherwise our styles remained strongly influenced by the Arab ornamentation and design that came to the island hundreds of years before.

"The one thing that seemed to be much like the mainland was education. In the Middle Ages, the abbeys were the locus for education, so the masses were instructed in religion and the arts, at times in mathematics and language, but it was influenced by the religious orders who dominated the region. The Benedictines and Dominicans were the first and lasted the longest, but then the Jesuits came to the island.

"Another phenomenon: The Arabs and Jews all believed strongly in general literacy. It is the foundation of their religions. And, yet, the Christian church was not as interested in pursuing this. I don't know whether they feared an educated public..."

"Like the white slaveholders in America feared an educated slave class?" I interjected.

"Perhaps. But it could also be that the Church just didn't value formal learning for the masses. Education, like anything else, requires funding and Rome was leading the way toward great art and abundant treasuries. Teaching peasants to read and write didn't contribute anything to that.

"Then came the treaty of Utrecht in 1713," Vito continued. "It may just be the most important event in European politics and culture in the early Eighteenth Century."

"In what way? How did it affect Sicily?"

"It divided the chips of Europe – the countries and provinces – among the ruling families at the time. Sicily got the House of Savoy and Victor Amadeus II."

1713 C.E. – 1718 C.E.

SAVOY

1713 C.E.

PALERMO

Victor Amadeus II, Duke of Savoy, was already middle-aged when the wars that would determine the future of his family's reign were being fought.

The First Partition Treaty of 1698 had fallen apart with the death in 1691 of Prince Joseph Ferdinand, heir to the Spanish throne. France, Spain, and the Dutch Republic had divided up much of Western Europe like pieces of a pie, but the treaty also specified that Prince Joseph Ferdinand of Bavaria would become heir to the Spanish throne. He was six years old at the time and his death at age seven threw the contract back into dispute.

War in the Spanish kingdom complicated things, made worse by the death of Charles II in Spain in the year 1700, especially since he died childless. Philip – the grandson of France's King Louis XIV – was proclaimed king of Spain which led to more wars involving France and Spain over sovereignty. The Treaty of Utrecht in 1713 seemed to solve the matter. In concert with other treaties, it granted Spain, England, France, Portugal, Savoy, and the Dutch Republic certain territories and rights in ruling a partitioned Europe.

The treaty also made Victor Amadeus II the King of Sicily. He was more interested in maintaining his hold on Piedmont in northern Italy, but he was persuaded to accept the arrangement to maintain a balance of power in the Mediterranean. Victor Amadeus was devising plans to trade the island for other regions that he preferred, including keeping his interests in northern Italy, but the Treaty specifically forbade him from exchanging Sicily for something else.

It was clear that Victor Amadeus was unimpressed with the Sicilian territory being added to his empire. It served the interests of England and other Mediterranean allies, but he looked on it as a compromise for what he wanted: hegemony in western Europe.

———

The British fleet rose up from the horizon north of the shores of Palermo. The colorful sails and flags that fluttered from the masts of the many ships were impressive in their display, and the Palermitani who first noticed the approaching armada called out to their fellows throughout the city.

News of the arrival of the new king and queen, Victor Amadeus and Marie d'Orleans, had reached Sicily days before. The viceroy of the city, the newly named Count Annibale Maffei, was prepared for the royal party and had arranged for celebrations and parades in the streets to honor them. Secretly, he and his agent, Vicente Lora, suspected that the visiting monarch would quickly grow tired of Palermo and its affairs and soon retreat to their palaces in the north. Others had done so for years; why should Victor Amadeus be any different?

Lora had survived the transition from the previous viceroy, Carlo Filippo Antonio Spinola, to his new regent, Maffei, and he was confident that he understood the workings of foreign governors better than anyone present in Palermo at that time. He would advise Maffei in managing Victor Amadeus, but he – Lora – would also be vigilant to protect his interests. It was this attention to detail and the variety of agendas that had helped him stay through previous transitions, and he planned to survive the next one.

Some hours later, the ships docked in the Palermo harbor which had been decorated for the occasion. Colorful flags depicting the regions of the island flapped in the breeze, the dock had been scrubbed in preparation and was oiled to bring out the shine in the planks. Maffei and his retinue stood at the end of the pier smiling broadly at the arriving visitors. The count swept his gaze from the bow of the boat to the stern, scanning the deck to get a glimpse of the new king and queen, but saw no one who appeared regal enough to fill those shoes. A look of disappointment came over him until Lora nudged him and pointed to the captain's cabin in the aft section of the deck.

The sun was fully overhead as three people emerged from the cabin. The black and purple robes with golden brocade worn by the king and queen shone brilliantly in the daylight. The captain of the ship was a step behind, all three appearing on the deck at just the moment when the crowd on the dock had grown to its largest size.

Sailors lowered a gangway from the ship and Maffei and his party stepped toward it to greet the king. It was too soon, according to protocol, which Lora knew well. He reached out to put his hand on Count Maffei's elbow and gently restrain him. The agent knew that the king would not be the first one down the gangway – in fact, there would be many deckhands descending to tighten the lines that bound the ship to the shore and prepare the area for the king. Lora didn't want the count to be caught up in that gaggle on the docks.

When these preparations were successfully carried out and the king and queen appeared at the ready, Lora once more reached out to Maffei and offered a subtle push in the direction of the gangway. This was the time to receive Victor Amadeus and Marie.

Maffei waved his right arm in front of himself and that action alone cleared the path for him. The count was the only local royalty, and the people knew to accord him the privileges of his rank, even when faced with a true flesh-and-blood king. Lora was at the count's shoulder to ensure that the peasants and dockhands gawking at the visitors were brushed out of the way.

When Count Annibale Maffei reached the bottom of the gangway and looked up, King Victor Amadeus looked down and smiled. The king raised his hand as if to salute or give a benediction, but then turned toward his queen and offered it to her. Marie rested her hand lightly on the king's silk tunic, on the white fabric that extended below the cuff of the purple-and-gold-embroidered cloak. They stepped down the wooden planks of the gangway in unison, the king shortening his stride to permit the queen to remain at his side. As if in slow motion, their movement down to the dock seemed like its own very private parade with a silent and admiring crowd awaiting them below.

Victor Amadeus approached Maffei, over whom he towered, and lifted his ringed hand to be kissed by the count. Maffei obliged in a halting way. He knew that such an observance was necessary for visiting royalty, but the count had been the ruling party on the island of Sicily until that moment, and he didn't like taking a position of subservience that he had long viewed as appropriate for lesser people.

"This is Lora, your lordship, my trusted advisor," Maffei said, turning to indicate his agent.

"It is a great and glorious moment to be in your presence, your lordship," said Lora in a tone that almost conveyed insouciance. He had enjoyed living in the reflected glory of the past viceroy and now Count Maffei, and he didn't take easily to being outshined among the people he had often lorded over.

The crowd pressed close to the royal couple and the count and his retinue. The were respectful murmurs in the crowd.

"Have you ever seen a king?" whispered Antonio.

"*No*," Gaia replied.

"Has there ever been a king?" he asked.

"*Sì*."

"A king of Sicily?"

"*No*," came the curt reply. "Why are you asking these questions?" Gaia blurted out, a bit louder than she intended.

Antonio just shrugged his shoulders.

"Sicily has a king now," he said, "but we didn't before. What does it mean?"

It was Gaia's turn to shrug.

———

Later in the evening at the Palazzo Steri, Count Maffei entertained King Victor Amadeus and his queen in splendor. They feasted on roast duck and quail, were served *frutta di mare* – small anchovy fish, sardines, and baby octopus fried in scented oil – wild pig *arrosto*, *trippa ripiene* – cow's intestines stuffed with ground sausage, chopped onion, millet, and herbs – and more wine than they should consume. Dancers in traditional costumes of Trinacria performed and a poet sang the praises of the king in Greek.

The king smiled throughout the poet's performance but kindly asked for a translation of what the man said, since he spoke Spanish and Latin, "but not the Greek."

Lora jumped in since his count was also a bit weak on Greek.

"He sang about how the people of Spain and France have brought tenderness and art to the poor island of Sicily, how the country and its citizens now have a bountiful future and hope for their children."

Lora didn't say that the poet ended up warning that poor management of the island would cast it back into the 'rings of hell,' thinking that this prophecy was best left out of the night's conversation.

The king was heard to mutter – too loudly – that since Sicily now had such bounty, the crown would require its fair share in exchange for protection.

Lora caught the leer from the poet out of the corner of his eye and prayed that the king did not notice the same response.

The wine flowed and women in Sicilian costume took the place of the men, dancing for the king's pleasure. Count Maffei was particularly interested in one, especially since his wife had retired for the evening, claiming a '*mal del stomaco*.' The dancer's beads jangled and sparkled, and Maffei stared in a trance-like state, brought on by the wine but enhanced by the woman's smiling eyes.

Late in the night, the king and queen retired. Count Maffei had managed to stay awake and remain the host, but Lora was the one orchestrating the evening's activities by that time.

––––––

"I have no idea what to do with these people," the king told Marie when they were alone. Although many royal couples kept separate sleeping quarters – made necessary by the amorous assignations of both king and queen – Victor Amadeus and Marie slept together.

"What do you want to do?" she asked, slipping beneath the ample feather coverlets on the high bed.

"I want Piedmont, but the treaty says I can't have it. Or at least I can't trade this for that."

"Why do you care so much about Piedmont?" Marie asked.

"It's closer to home and I understand Europe. Not this far-off land in the middle of the ocean. And look at this 'castle,' as they call it. It was built by Arabs..."

"No, it was built by Normans. They told me," she said to her husband.

"Well, well, whatever. But the Arabs built a lot of this city. This Palermo," was his response, with an unmistakable hint of disgust in his voice.

"The Arabs built a lot of your kingdom, my lordship," Marie answered in rebuke. "Don't you remember how you ran them off? And they ruled your land for centuries before you."

Victor Amadeus often lost arguments with his wife and he didn't want to spoil his record. So he huffed and crawled into bed with her, closed his eyes and went to sleep almost immediately. The wine had done its job.

––––––

"I have it." the king said, almost before Marie's eyes were open in the morning.

"What?" she replied, still groggy.

"Sardinia," he said.

"What do you want with Sardinia?" Marie said, sitting up in bed.

"They said that I couldn't trade Sicily for other European crowns. But if I trade it for the crown of Sardinia, and then use that as my base, I can build an army to take most of Europe."

"Is Sicily worth that?"

"What do you mean? I don't want to be king of Sicily."

"I mean is Sicily worth the trade? Can you get Sardinia for this island?"

Victor Amadeus had to consider the possibilities. He concluded that he needed to improve the island, build its defenses, impose systems of government to crush the rising tide of corruption, re-invigorate agriculture, increase its treasury, and portray Sicily as a military base without peer, and then he would trade it for Sardinia. Paying for all these improvements would be simple: tax the people on the island.

Over the next several weeks, he met with Maffei – with Lora always by his side – to discuss 'what I can do for the Kingdom of Sicily' as he put it. Victor Amadeus was intent on promoting the idea that Sicily was his first concern; after all, they had made him king and ruler of the island. And although he had other motives, improvement of the country would also benefit the Sicilians.

As with most Eighteenth Century countries, defense was the first and paramount concern. Victor Amadeus knew a bit about the history of the region, including the fact that the monarchs in Naples often vied for control of Sicily. The Hapsburg family that currently controlled Naples would always be seen as a threat, so they must be dealt with. Fortunately, his agent and counselor, Alosio d'Elmonte, had anticipated this and encouraged the king to bring many ships and soldiers to Sicily with his entourage. English ships were considered among the best in the world and, although Victor Amadeus was from Spain, the English had argued for his installation as the King of Sicily, so he was prepared to showcase the English vessels as examples of fine craftsmanship for the Sicilian artisans to copy.

The soldiers would be used to assert authority until the local *polizia* could be re-established and funded. Victor Amadeus sent word back to his agents at home to bring funds to buy land back from some of the nobles and redistribute it among the fiefs, and to rebuild roads and bridges across the country. He hired architects to recommend improvements in irrigation and urban development, and he studied the crops and farming sectors of his new realm with vigor.

The king also toured the island to talk to his subjects. When he did so, he abandoned the trappings of royalty and circulated among the common people in sturdy clothing and boots as if he was about to engage in the farming and building that he was encouraging in others.

One error Victor Amadeus made that prevented him from capturing the Sicilians' hearts: He employed many Spanish and French barons in positions of great power. Over the previous centuries of foreign rule, the people of the island had grown accustomed to ruling themselves and only showing obeisance to absent rulers on ceremonial occasions and when they were paying taxes. The very presence of Victor Amadeus, and his active participation in all things on the island, rubbed many of the previously powerful indigenous leaders that wrong way, and having to answer to additional outside forces who had come to the island seem to make the problem even worse.

Victor Amadeus pursued his improvements with vigor, but he only remained on the island for a year, then turned over the economic and governmental systems to his non-Sicilian friends. In his wake, the fundamental educational, farming, and industrial programs flourished, but he was not there to witness it.

AUGUST 2018

CAFÉ AMADEO

"Sardinia," Vito said as I slid into the chair beside him.

"He got what he wanted," I added. I followed up our conversation of the previous day with research in the library. The period of rule under Savoy was very short, only a handful of years really – unless one counts the decades and maybe even centuries that members of the Savoy dynasty worked behind the scenes in all matters Sicilian.

"Si, he got Sardinia."

"It sounds like Victor Amadeus did a lot for the country, though."

Vito shrugged his shoulders.

"He raised taxes, too, and put his friends in charge of large enterprises. Perhaps the most insulting to the Sicilians was when the king abandoned local financial policies and institutions and installed systems that he had relied on in Europe. He brought Gian Giacomo Fontana, his financial minister in Piedmont, to serve as the budget director and tax advisor in Sicily. Together, they introduced new taxes, including some short-term special taxes on exports, and some – what do you say today, consumption? yes, that's it – consumption taxes that imposed additional burdens on Sicilians in addition to the land-use taxes."

"I'm almost afraid to ask," I said hesitantly, "but were these taxes necessary to get Sicily back up on its feet? If so, wouldn't they be justified?"

Vito shrugged again.

"That can be asserted, but not proven. It was probably an accounting trick. Victor Amadeus and Fontana wanted to showcase Sicily at its finest in art, architecture, farming, and military might, but also show how the island's treasury was growing, a multi-pronged approach certain to attract outside interest.

"He installed thousands of Piedmontese soldiers as the military on the island. That might have been important to re-establish order, but to the Sicilians it meant just one more invasion by a foreign power. He expanded the naval fleet which had the twin purposes of appearing to be a mighty empire while also improving the ability to actually protect this kingdom in the Mediterranean Sea.

"By 1714, the king believed that he had put Sicily right, so he departed the island and left Annibale Maffei in charge. The count – now retitled the Viceroy of Sicily – had Victor Amadeus's army and navy at his disposal, he inherited the land and law reforms, and could count on a regular investment in the treasury due to the new taxes that had been promulgated."

"So, did Maffei have it easy? Especially with the king out of the way?"

Vito shook his head.

"Not really. Maffei had to contend with Savoyard barons installed by the king, an unruly populace, and constant threats from overseas. Victor Amadeus had to contend with the corruption that grew out of hundreds of years of mismanagement and foreign control. Maffei had it no easier. Meanwhile, the European royalty continued to conspire against Sicily," Vito said with a laugh.

"*Perche*?" he asked rhetorically. "Why? What did we do?" and he laughed again.

"While Savoy and Victor Amadeus reigned over Sicily," he continued, "the European pot of intrigue was boiling. First, newly installed Queen

Elisabeth of Spain – King Philip's second wife – decided that Sardinia belonged to her. Excuse me..." Vito remarked with a smirk, "...to Spain! But she took it very personally, so she launched the Spanish fleet against that island."

"Wait," I pleaded, jotting notes. "Do you mean that the queen of Spain launched an invasion of Sardinia, not the king?"

"He was a...let's say...a very tolerant man."

"You mean she ran over him."

"*Sì*," Vito replied with a grin, "I like that American phrase. She 'ran over him.' Elisabeth was of stronger stuff than her husband. So, she made most of the momentous decisions for the Spanish throne from their marriage in 1714 until her husband passed in 1746. Of particular interest is her conduct of foreign affairs in that period.

"*Allora* – anyway – she launched the campaign against Sardinia in 1717 and soon captured the island. Her confidence grew with the victory, so she launched another invasion in 1718, this time against Sicily."

"And how did that go?" I ventured.

"The ships and soldiers weren't from Piedmont, so the people of Palermo who first spotted the invasion thought it came to liberate them from Victor Amadeus, and they welcomed them. But their welcome did not last long. Charles VI..." he said.

"Charles, the Holy Roman Emperor Charles?" I asked.

"*Sì*," he replied, as I tried to keep order in my notes. "That one. Anyway, he never really liked Spain holding Sicily, so he hired the British navy – he didn't have one of his own – to retake the island. There was a British captain, named George Byng, renowned for his past accomplishments on the high seas. Charles VI sent him to chase the Spanish fleet from Sicily and destroy them, capturing the island for the empire. Byng began his campaign against the Spanish fleet off the coast of Italy, near Naples, then chased them through the Straits of Messina, sinking some ships and setting others ablaze, until the final battle took place off the coast of Sicily, a town called Passero at the far southeastern corner of Sicily.

There, Byng finished off the Spaniards and took captive whatever vessels could still float."

"Did that return Sicily to France?"

"Somewhat. But Britain also, since Charles had made use of his treaty between France, Austria, and Britain to carry out this naval attack." Then Vito laughed. "Unfortunately, no war was actually declared, so Spain was apoplectic about the attacks on their island – Sicily – and their navy. The warring parties engaged in years-long battles across the island, burning farms, razing cities, torching monuments and temples, and generally terrorizing the Sicilian population who stood aghast at the destruction raining down on them by outside forces. 'We are once again someone else's battleground' said a man from Palermo at the time.

"At one point, in a place called Francavilla, the Spanish appeared ready to celebrate a significant victory. They attacked the Austrian forces and would have won, except that the British navy waited offshore throughout the engagement and stood positioned to resupply the Austrian contingent. In time, they wore down the Spanish who had no such supply lines.

"At last, Spain quit the campaign, its troops leaving destruction and death as their signature."

"What happened to Victor Amadeus?" I asked. "Wasn't he somehow related to all this?"

"Well, of course. He was on the side of Spain. But ironically, he got what he had wanted from the start. In surrendering Sicily to the Bourbon dynasty, he took Sardinia as a consolation prize."

"That must have made his wife very happy," I joked. "What about the Hapsburgs?" I asked, picking up a theme that I read in the library. The Austrian empire run by the Hapsburg family seem to be all over Europe, and they had a significant presence in Sicily from 1713 to the 1730s.

"They were very important on the continent," Vito confided, "but other than briefly being given Sicily to rule, their presence wasn't very important in my country."

"Explain?" I pleaded.

"*D'accordo,*" he said – 'okay.' "The Hapsburgs...h-a-p-s-b-u-r-g, but some people spell it h-a-b-s-b-u-r-g...honestly, I don't know how you spell it," he segued. It was one of the few times that Vito was at a loss for the right historical fact.

"The Hapsburgs were mainly from Spain," Vito began, then he chuckled. "That sounds like 'enry 'iggins." He was referring to Henry Higgins, the central character in "My Fair Lady" whose instructions in elocution for the uneducated Eliza Doolittle included repetitive phrasings of "The rain in Spain falls mainly on the plain." I shook my head in delight, wondering whatever it could be that Vito didn't know.

"No, excuse me," he said, "the Hapsburg empire came to acquire Spain, but it was based in Austria and Germania, but included Spain among its possessions. In fact, the Hapsburg family may have been the first international world power."

"Hold on," I begged for patience. "Earlier, you said that Spain had become the first true world superpower."

"*Sì,* I did. But consider the difference. Spain was a world power because of its military might and its exploratory map. The kings and queens of Spain fostered global exploration and capitalized on it. But in the Eighteenth Century, Europe was still 'the world' – he said this with air quotes – and the Hapsburgs controlled Europe."

"So, North America didn't matter?"

"Of course, it had long since mattered. After discovery and settlement, North America was a territory to be fought over. But in the old sense. There was no United States at the time, and even Britain's interest in it wavered over the decades. But let's get back to the Hapsburgs, since you asked.

"The Hapsburgs hailed from Austria but also showed an uncanny ability to land the throne of the Holy Roman Empire."

"What do you mean?" I asked.

"That family held the throne for almost half a millennium, from 1438 until 1806. Plus, they spawned kings in multiple countries around

Europe, like Hungary, Croatia, Germany, Ireland, Portugal...even Mexico!

"But Sicily seemed like nothing more than another crown. Charles VI, Holy Roman Emperor from 1711 until 1740, added Sicily to his résumé, but he didn't care about the island. His interest and involvement were only from afar."

"So as Charles VI went, so went the Hapsburg empire in Sicily," I offered, somewhat as comment and somewhat as question.

"*Certu*," Vito replied – 'certainly.'

"Is there anything to be learned from the time that the Hapsburgs controlled Sicily?" I asked.

Vito stared up at the ceiling and rubbed the stubble on his chin. He eyes wandered back and forth gazing at the intricately frescoed ceiling panels.

"Not really," was the only answer he could offer, then he chuckled.

We sat in silence for a moment, sipping the next round of espressos brought by the barista, each consumed by our thoughts.

"Just a minute," I said suddenly as a thought dawned on me. "Has Sicily ever been governed by someone from the island itself? A true Sicilian?"

Vito shrugged and took one last draft of the espresso.

"*Si*, I suppose you could say that we were. We've had barons and viceroys and mayors born here; don't forget Constance..."

"And lots of kings, queens, regents, and others not from here," I added to complete his thought.

"What about the Bourbon kings?" he asked.

I hadn't gotten there yet, hadn't had time to read about the Bourbon dynasty...really, hadn't found time to keep up with Vito yet.

"What about them?" I asked.

"Cadets," he replied.

Okay, cadets, I thought.

"I'll bite. What are cadets?"

"They are the secondary and, in some cases, the tertiary lines of royal families, the second, third, or following sons and daughters denied the crown because the rites of primogeniture guaranteed the inheritance to their eldest brother. In this case, cadets of the Bourbon dynasty included Charles, son of Philip V of Spain and Elizabeth Farnese."

I quickly raised my left hand while scribbling notes with my right.

"Yes, but, wait..." I pleaded. I knew I had come across something in my research about Charles. And he wasn't a cadet. I was willing to challenge Vito with this.

"Charles was the eldest son of Philip and Elizabeth."

"Sì," Vito agreed, but then smiled in a 'gotcha' way. "But Elizabeth Farnese was Philip's second wife.

My shoulders sagged.

"Maria Louisa of Savoy had already given Philip sons, in the name of Louis I, another Philip, Ferdinand VI..."

"Okay, okay," I pleaded with a hand up to stop him. "I got it. Philip and Maria had lots of kids."

But Vito had a twinkle in his eye.

"Well, that was about it," letting me down easily. "Maria died early at age twenty-five."

"So, back to cadets," I suggested.

"*Esattumentu*," Vito said excitedly. "Let's talk about Charles. But first, we need to talk about the complexities of the houses of Bourbon and Hapsburg. They ruled most of Europe for a very long time. In fact, descendants of the houses still occupy thrones and seats of power across the continent."

"And they intermarried," I suggested. It wasn't a claim based on historical fact, more of a resignation to the histories of the royal houses of Europe.

"*Esattumentu, ancora*," he replied – "Exactly, again. But try to figure it out."

Vito then reeled off a long – and I mean very long – list of children, grand-children, husbands and wives who intermarried, produced kings, queens, duke, duchesses, and other royalty. All from these two houses and spread all across Europe.

"They held thrones of royal positions in Spain, Naples, Sicily, England, Germany, Hungary, Croatia..."

"Wait," I interrupted him. "The two families didn't jointly hold these thrones."

"No, not exactly. But wherever the Bourbons weren't, the Hapsburgs were."

"What does this have to do with Charles, and Sicily?"

"Or, for that matter," he suggested, leaning forward in his chair, "The rest of Sicilian history. But before we get there, let's clarify something. Do you know what the Kingdom of the Two Sicilies was?"

"Yes, it was the combination of the island of Sicily and the Mezzogiorno, the southern half of the Italian peninsula."

"And why was it called the Two Sicilies?" Vito pressed.

"Because the land areas were separate. There was an island, and what's called the mainland. Two Sicilies." I hoped that my answer was right but had a sinking feeling that it was not complete.

"Not exactly," Vito said, confirming my fear.

"Originally, the Kingdom of Sicily – singular – included both of these parts. It was this way because the King of Sicily who ruled mostly from Naples claimed as his territory the entire island and all land from Naples to the south on the mainland. In 1282, the War of the Sicilian Vespers tore the two apart, leaving Angevin King Charles of

Anjou with the peninsular part and giving the island nation to Frederick III."

"This is the part where the island was renamed Trinacria, right?" I offered.

"Sì, for some people, but that name was used interchangeably with Sicily. And this only added intrigue to the history of the 'two Sicilies.'

"Remember, Charles of Anjou – who had always considered himself the King of Sicily, although he ruled from Naples – was now deprived of the island. He didn't like that new fact so he continued to call himself the King of Sicily, as did his descendants for over one hundred fifty years. Meanwhile, Frederick and his brood actually were kings on the island..."

"So they had to call themselves something else?" I asked, "like King of Trinacria?"

"That was partly true, but Frederick came from proud stuff. So he called himself the King of Sicily."

"I suppose that would drive cartographers crazy," I laughed.

"Well, such as they were in those days," Vito smiled. "About 1442, King Alfonso of Aragon reunited the two parts and called his realm the Kingdom of Naples and Sicily. But, as things happened in those days, the kingdoms continued to evolve, switch hands, and divide. Alfonso's death resulted in his brother taking the island, and his son taking Naples.

"Back and forth it went for another few hundred years until 1816 when Ferdinand III of Sicily – also called Ferdinand IV of Naples – inherited the kingdom. At this point, his unified realm became known as the Kingdom of the Two Sicilies and remained in the hands of the Bourbon family until the Risorgimento in 1860."

"We got here by me asking whether Sicily had ever been ruled by a true Sicilian," I queried.

"Yes, we did," responded Vito, "but not yet."

From his terse comment, I hoped that 'not yet' meant by 1816, not by today.

1734 C.E. – 1816 C.E.

BOURBONS

1799 C.E.

NAPLES AND PALERMO

In late 1798, Ferdinand joined British forces to attack Rome and take it from the French occupiers. Timing was critical; his wife, Maria Carolina of Austria, reminded the king that Napoleon was occupied in Egypt and, therefore, Rome would be vulnerable. He enlisted the support of British Vice Admiral Horatio Nelson who brought a massive fleet to Naples and they moved on Rome.

Victory appeared to be in the offing, but the French forces recovered and swept Ferdinand's forces from the city, then chased them back to Naples. Even there, Ferdinand didn't feel safe so by January 1799 he fled to Palermo, to be replaced by Francesco Pignatelli Strongoli in Naples. Before long he, too, surrendered to the French and raced to exile in Palermo.

———

"There is a ship on the waters," came the cry from the crow's nest on the dock in Palermo. Such surveillance measures as watch towers were normally not necessary, but with the recent arrival of King Frederick IV and reports of revolution in Naples, he ordered constant monitoring of the seas. He had been defeated in Rome and chased from Naples – of course, these were not the reasons given to the Palermitani for his arrival – and he didn't intend to be caught unawares in his refuge in Palermo.

"Where?" came the question from Italo below the watch. He was the dock captain, usually responsible for cargo and merchant traffic in the port of Palermo, but lately was also assigned the responsibility of monitoring unexpected seagoing vessels and assessing any threats to the harbor.

Pietro swiveled a bit in the nest to face the oncoming ship and threw his right arm out in that direction.

"There, sir," he replied, pointing roughly to the northeast. There was only a speck of black on the surface of the water from Italo's perspective but, from his perch, Pietro could see the vertical black line of the mast and the beginnings of the white sheets of sail.

"About four hours," declared Italo, muttering to himself. He was calculating the wind speed and distance and he concluded that the vessel would reach Palermo just before midday.

"Send a message to the Palazzo Steri," he told Beppo, the eight-year-old boy apprenticed to him. Beppo followed Italo around wherever he went and, this morning, he was right by his side. "Inform the king's soldiers that there is a ship arriving and tell them when we expect it."

Beppo was dressed in a flimsy cotton shirt and leather britches, but Italo always kept the boy in sturdy leather shoes because the youngster's principle duty was running errands and delivering messages.

When Beppo arrived at the palazzo twenty minutes later, he approached the pike-bearing soldier standing in front of the massive oaken door.

"I have a message for Signor Talenti," he said, referring to King Ferdinand's counselor.

"From whom does the message come?" asked the soldier.

"Italo."

The mention of the watch officer's name was enough to open doors. Besides, the soldier knew that Beppo was Italo's apprentice from earlier visits to the palazzo that he was guarding.

The soldier turned on his heel and rapped on the door with his pike. Beppo had noticed on prior visits that the soldiers at the gate used this method rather than raising and lowering the heavy round knockers on the door. The boy was quick to notice why: Anyone can pound with the iron knocker and the guards inside would not know who was at the door. But the sound of the pike was distinctly different and indicated that the soldier himself was summoning someone to the door.

Once inside, Beppo knew exactly where to go, which he did with quick steps up the broad stone stairs to Raphael Talenti's office. There, he stopped and rapped on the threshold with his fist, and then waited. Talenti was older than the boy's grandfather and, although he wielded considerable power in his influence over the king, he was slow on his feet. After a count of twenty – Beppo had adopted his little game of counting the seconds for the gray-haired man to reach the door – the hinges squeaked and the door swung open.

"There is a ship," Beppo said, looking directly ahead at Talenti. The boy was the same height as the little man.

"Where?"

"It arrives from the northeast. Should be in port around midday."

"Who is it?"

"Signor Italo can't tell yet. But it appears to be a single ship."

Talenti could read the meaning behind that. Attack forces came in droves; fleeing ships were often alone. He turned toward the door and swung it shut without acknowledging the boy. Beppo, too, turned and ran back down the steps to the front gate of the palazzo where he had to request permission from someone else to open the door.

———

Francesco Pignatelli Strongoli stood on the deck of the ship while it plied the open waters of the Tyrrhenian Sea. After a quick exit from Naples two days before, he never looked back. He had assumed command of the city after Ferdinand fled, but he was unable to withstand the French forces. So, sensing a slim chance to get out before being imprisoned by the enraged Napoleonic forces, he had commandeered this vessel and its crew and set out for Palermo. He knew that Ferdinand had sailed there and he hoped to convince the king that he, Francesco, had in fact been loyal to him despite claiming the city that the king had been chased from.

In the distance, he could see the island of Sicily. Approaching from the northeast, he first noticed a plume of gray smoke coming from the far eastern point of the island and nodded his head as he quickly determined that this must be smoke from the ever active Mount Etna volcano. Sweeping his eyes to the right, across the central mountainous spine of Sicily and settling on the western promontory, he saw the city of Palermo growing bigger in his field of view.

"You should have something to eat," said the captain's mate standing behind Strongoli. "We will arrive when most of the people are eating, and with the business of docking you may have to wait for the next meal."

Strongoli thought it strange to contemplate eating at this moment. He was still in flight mode and survival meant avoiding a violent end, not minding sustenance. But the idea had merit, so he retired to the mate's cabin beside that of the captain where he fed on wilted greens, crusty bread, and fruit that required him to brush the flies off before biting into. There was wine though, which he preferred to the barrels of water on ship. Water alone wouldn't chase the fears that came with him. Besides, water often made him sick in the stomach; wine never did.

Before finishing the meal, Strongoli could hear voices, first from the deck of the ship and then some more distant. He could tell from inside the cabin that these voices were coming from the dock, and that the process of landing and tying up had begun. He quickly emptied the contents of his wine mug and walked out onto the deck.

Docking was a complex process for large ships, and this was one of them. Many hands were involved in roping, pulling the hull closer to the dock, and lowering the bridge to allow the men to climb down from the ship. Noise attended the actions too, so the entire process of bringing the ship to its slip was a loud, raucous cacophony, one that Strongoli was familiar with but which, on this day, brought some pleasure because he felt solace in reaching Palermo.

He walked down the bridge onto the dock and was greeted by Talenti.

"*Bienvenu*," he said to Strongoli – 'welcome.'

"Thank you," was the reply. "I am…"

"I know who you are. Francesco Strongoli, the king's replacement in Naples."

Strongoli was actually on the king's side in many matters of the past, but he detected some trouble in Talenti's way of describing his role in the former city.

"And you, sir, are Raphael Talenti, the king's closest advisor."

Talenti nodded.

"Yes, and I will advise the king that he has a visitor. Follow me please."

A carriage was brought around for them and Talenti and Strongoli boarded it to ride to Palazzo Steri.

"I will have your belongings sent up," said Italo to Strongoli, who nodded that he heard him.

The two men – one wizened and gray, the other a recent exile from the mainland – didn't talk much on the thirty-minute ride to the palace. Only a few perfunctory comments, but nothing of substance.

"So, Napoleon now has Napoli," said Talenti.

"Well, no, not Napoleon. But his army. He is still in Egypt."

Talenti snorted at this. Only a king owns the city or country. His legions merely stand for it. What Talenti was actually referring to was Strongoli's surrender of the city that his king, Ferdinand, still claimed as his right. Strongoli knew this was the old man's intent, but he decided not to confront it here, in the carriage.

They arrived at the Palazzo Steri and the gate opened wide to permit the carriage to enter the courtyard. There, the two men climbed down onto the cobblestoned piazza, and Talenti turned away from Strongoli toward his own office, and toward the king's living quarters, leaving Strongoli standing alone next to the carriage.

"And where shall I retire?" the visitor asked to Talenti's back.

Talenti only waved a hand in the air, giving no specific instructions. But a young boy approached Strongoli and said he would guide the man to his quarters, on the opposite side of the palazzo's courtyard.

———

It was nearly nightfall on this winter's evening when Strongoli first had an audience with Ferdinand. Unfortunately, it wasn't a private audience as he would have preferred, but he had a seat at the supper table along with ten other people, family members, attendants, and the ever-present Talenti.

Strongoli was escorted into the room and presented to Ferdinand, then seated at the other end of the long table. The meal proceeded and entailed several courses of food, from fish and vegetables to roast pig served with baked apples and candied cranberries. The repast ended with platters of prepared fruits and bowls of nuts that the attendants dutifully cracked for the king. The wine served throughout the meal helped to ease the tense atmosphere and led to conversations that Strongoli had wanted to pursue.

"What is next," he asked the visitor. Ferdinand was expecting the man who had just joined his household to have a plan to retake Naples.

"It is said that the French forces cannot last long in your city, sire."

"Why? Are they not provisioned?"

"No, that is not it. I have heard that they still have business in northern Italy. That they returned to Naples only to chase you away," and

Strongoli quickly regretted his wording. The king would not want the others at the table think that he had been chased away. Even if that was the truth.

Strongoli tried to gather himself.

"The French forces will soon return north, and the city will be left only lightly guarded."

"So, we can plan to retake it," said Ferdinand. It wasn't a question.

The rest of the meal proceeded and everyone returned to their quarters for the night. But over the next two months, King Ferdinand IV of Sicily prepared himself to retake Naples and reunite his kingdom.

———

"Did he?" I asked Vito.

"Sì," he responded. It didn't come until the next year. Ferdinand sent a force to conquer Naples and imprison the French forces who remained there. He did not accompany the fleet, fearing a repeat of his last time in Naples, but when victory was accomplished he returned to the throne of Naples. He remained there for several years but was once again attacked by Napoleon and his army. In time, he was forced to flee Naples once again, retiring to Palermo to resume his position of King of Sicily. But this time he stayed there, an unusual thing for that time."

"Unusual? In what way?" I asked.

"Kings of Sicily had ruled from afar for centuries," Vito said. "Even as late as the reign of Ferdinand II in the early years of the Nineteenth Century, the kings lived in Naples. He was the first king of Sicily to be born on the island. In fact, his birthday – January 12 – was a day of great importance to the Sicilian people. But not until he was thirty-eight years old," said Vito with a broad grin.

1804 C.E.

MAZARA DEL VALLO AND LA GOULETTE, TUNISIA

INDIRITTO HAD WORKED AS A PORTER ON THE DOCKS OF MAZARA del Vallo since he was only seven years old. Now, at thirty-seven, he already felt the effects of decades spent on his feet, using his hands and arms to lift and carry large crates, and relying on the strength of his heart to carry him through every grueling day until the next one began, as usual, before dawn.

He had been born into a poor family. His father, Augusto had produced thirteen children, four by his first wife who died in childbirth along with the fifth child, and nine by his second wife, Marie. None of them had lived well, getting by on the pittance that Augusto made by labor on the docks. But he taught his sons how to work so that they wouldn't starve.

Marie came from Algiers, fleeing that city as a girl of fourteen when she was told by her mother that she was too pretty and that capture by the Barbary pirates meant being sold into slavery. She made her way to Mazara del Vallo on a fishing boat, in search of security and freedom. At first, the language barrier made her keep to herself, hiding among the cargo containers from merchant ships that unloaded their goods on the docks of Mazara. There she met Augusto. At first, she shied away from him as she did from any contact, but he saw her need, and her fear, so he brought her food and promised to provide shelter.

Augusto was recently widowed and had compassion for the waif. He needed a wife; she needed a life. So they married in a small chapel on the outskirts of the port and began producing children. Vittorio was the first and he joined his father in work as soon as he was old enough to hold the tools and grip a rope.

The ports of Europe were like the newsrooms of the world. All reports of activities arrived first there, on the ships bearing cargo, and so dockhands and sailors became the earliest form of international communication. Vittorio was always working near the boats as they arrived from other places, and so he heard stories of wars fought between the various countries, and how the kings and dukes continued to swap territories. He also heard tales of how the British and Americans had come into the wars, fighting the Berbers and their slave ships and even blockading some of the ports of Tunis.

As the stories increased in intensity, Vittorio spent more time at the docks, but reduced his hours of labor so that he could idle his time on the bales and listen to the sailors disembarking from their ships. Some told ribald jokes about their plans for the night in Mazara among the taverns and brothels, but there were also stories of naval battles that raged even as the sailors were spinning their tales on the docks.

Vittorio listened attentively. At thirty-seven he was considered an old man, but he had never traveled, and so stories of what lie beyond the waves washing onto Mazara's shores still intrigued him.

He picked through the conversations he could overhear from twosomes and threesomes leaving the ships, quickly focusing on those that had to do with politics and wars. He heard that the American president, this man called Jefferson, had sent a small flotilla of boats that were taken by the Berbers and had to be reinforced by more boats. He heard about the British naval commanders who still held a grudge against the Americans who had quit their kingdom three decades before. He heard these same British commanders and their crews boast of how they intended to get the so-called 'Americans' back as a British colony.

And Vittorio heard stories of the slave trade that existed between North Africa and his island. Sicilians from as far east as Siracusa and as far west as Trapani were vulnerable to the Barbary pirates who plied the waters and struck without warning. Hundreds of Sicilians could be captured at once, shoved down below decks and delivered to the Arab rulers of the African caliphates as slaves. At times, Vittorio worried about his own safety, and whether he might be taken.

His brother, Becari, who was only sixteen, had begun work at the docks and survived under Vittorio's guidance and support. They worked together and Becari learned from his older brother not only how to greet the ships and be hired to unload their cargo, but also how to bargain for proper wages and avoid trouble with the sailors.

On this particular day, Vittorio and Becari were hired to unload the *Victor*, a British ship that had arrived from the port of London with cotton, wool, and agricultural products on board. Vittorio had to laugh at the cargo. He knew the British Isles had lamb and some cotton fields, but Sicily was still the breadbasket of the Mediterranean. Why would these British be bringing agricultural products and fruit to the island?

He quickly accepted the assignment; pay was in short supply and a man who lived on the edge of the economy didn't ask very many questions. But the report of the cargo still nagged at him. As he and Becari boarded the ship, he noticed other things, too. The vessel rocked more than a loaded ship should rock. And when he looked below decks, he saw that there was a very small load.

There were some bales on the deck that the dockhands were asked to deal with. They were obvious from the shore, and the presence of these bales made the boat seem to be a regular merchant ship. But whenever he was hired before, Vittorio knew that the ship's sailors didn't bring the cotton on deck to help them, and the ship wouldn't sail with soft cargo like that exposed to the weather. These bales should have been below decks.

He grabbed Becari by the forearm just as a dark-skinned man appeared on the gangway. He approached from the dockside, not the boat itself, and he boarded the ship quickly and confidently as if he was one of the crew. Vittorio then saw that he wore a curved sword at his waist which he was now drawing from its scabbard.

Without another thought, Vittorio yanked on his brother's arm and jumped into the water. By the time they surfaced, there was a full-scale battle going on the ship's deck. Vittorio pulled again on Becari's arm and they swam away from the ship, out to sea first, and then made a wide arc around the berth before returning to the docks. In this maneuver, they hoped to swim beyond the circle of pirates that by now had captured the boat and the workers lured onto it.

It almost worked.

As they clambered up the pylons on the fringes of the port, more Berbers met them. The pirates swung clubs – a weapon that Vittorio quickly concluded had taken the place of swords because the pirates intended on capture, not striking a deadly blow – and beat both Vittorio and Becari on their arms and backs. The two Mazarans ducked and fought, pushing the clubs away when they saw them coming, buckling under the blow when they didn't.

Becari slumped to the ground and curled up in a ball while Vittorio – seeing his brother in trouble – raged at the pirates. He was able to throw his attackers off but watched helplessly as his younger brother was dragged unconscious toward the ship. Again and again, Vittorio swiped at his attackers. At one point he wrestled the club away from one of the men and swung it with such force that he cracked the man's head in two. While fighting to free himself from the marauders, Vittorio kept throwing glances at his brother. Becari was being dragged away from him, and at that moment Vittorio realized that there was only one way to save his brother.

He fought like an animal, killing the men who surrounded him and laying eight of them down with fatal blows to their heads and chests. When the circle of pirates was laid out around him, Vittorio stood breathing heavily and sobbing too. His hard breaths were from his fight; his sobs were for his brother who was now out of sight.

But Vittorio knew that the young man would be on the boat, the *Victor*, and he intended to get him back.

The fierce combat on the deck of the slave ship had quieted down as the captors chained the captives below. Vittorio knew the docks and knew where best to hide, so he made himself invisible among the wharf rafts and crates, while he kept a watchful eye on the *Victor* itself.

As darkness fell, he knew that the slave ship might slip from the port, so he carefully approached it along the dock. It was still roped to the harbor, although the gangway had been removed, so Vittorio tiptoed up to one of these lines and tested the knot that bound it to the ship. He knew that later in the evening the tide would go out and pull the ship out a bit, and this would pull the line tight. When that had happened, he could quickly pull himself along the rope from shore to ship and stow away among the slaves.

Vittorio had to be sure not to let the ship leave before the tide went out, so he didn't sleep. And he knew that he would have to slip among the captives below decks without being seen. He had two advantages: The slavers on deck were not looking for someone coming onto the ship so their attention would be directed elsewhere. And when he joined the captives below, he wouldn't be chained as they were, so he would be able to move about once hidden in the darkness of the hold.

The moon was full but that didn't worry Vittorio. He counted on his first advantage to avoid being detected as he boarded the ship by climbing along the rope that had been pulled tight by the tide. And he avoided detection in the night light by quickly sliding through the first open hatch he found amidships. From there, he could wander below and find his brother.

Timing was on Vittorio's side because soon after he decided to jump aboard ship, he heard the commands to pull up lines and push off. By the time he had gained his footing below decks, the boat was rocking out of the port.

At first, he tried finding Becari by sight, but in the darkness everyone looked the same. They were all brown-skinned Sicilians, stolen from their towns in Mazara del Vallo, Gela, and Agrigento to serve the Arab slave trade in Tunisia and east of there. There was so little light to guide him that Vittorio took to whispering Becari's name.

Soon, a response came.

"Here," was a quiet call from the darkness.

Vittorio reached his brother and embraced his head. No other part of the young man's body could be held because it was chained to the planks on which Becari was laid.

"Why are you not shackled?" he asked of Vittorio.

"I escaped," the older brother replied, but there was shame in his voice. How could he escape and let his younger brother be taken?

"I came aboard to take you."

"How is that possible?" Becari asked, jangling his chains lightly to avoid being heard.

"I will find out," was all that Vittorio could promise.

———

After a night and day, they arrived at a bustling port on the northern coast of Africa. Vittorio was able to sneak about the hold and peak out of the portholes, such as they were, but he didn't recognize anything. The voices were strange and spoke in a tongue that he could not decipher, the dockside itself was like nothing he had ever seen – rough, rugged, and primitive – and the buildings that loomed over the dock were made of a dark brown wood and were devoid of the colorful touches that he remembered from the harbor of Mazara del Vallo.

When he heard and felt the ship being tied up to the dock, he slipped down among the captive slaves that were still shackled to their berths. He needed to follow his brother but, when the slaves were taken from the hold and chained together, he didn't know how to keep his freedom and yet be among those led from the ship.

"Trust me," Vittorio whispered to Becari, as he crouched down and stepped quickly from the hold. He decided that the best thing was for him to escape the ship unbound, then follow his brother's movements when the slaves were marched from the hold. With that decision, he slipped onto the deck undetected and lowered himself quietly into the water to swim ashore.

Once on shore, he was able to discern more about the people of this port city. A sign was written in scrolling letters that he couldn't untangle, but he heard passersby talk about La Goulette. Not knowing their language, Vittorio doubted what he had heard, except for the frequent use of La Goulette.

'If this isn't the name of the city,' he thought to himself, 'I will think it is. And I will free my brother from this La Goulette.'

What he didn't know is that the British fleet and the Sicilian people had long despaired of the theft of human souls taking place on the slave ships and had mounted a force to counter it. Great ships and crews were being assembled on the shores of Sicily and they were blessed by the king and bishops in their quest to conquer the Berbers and free the men, women, and children who had been taken into slavery by the men of Tunisia.

The involvement of the navies of Britain and the United States turned the tide. Until that time, the Barbary pirates employed galleys that carried many armed soldiers but few cannon, so they could not stand and fight the heavily armed ships from England and America. British and American ships still suffered occasional losses on the seas, but the trend was against the Berbers. Over time, the Barbary pirates and their slave-trading partners were defeated and driven from the seas.

Vittorio and Becari were caught in a battle waged in these waning years of the Arab slave trade. Because of this, the movement of chained humans took on a different form, more challenging for the freedom fighter, but also more likely to yield results.

Vittorio hid among the people on the dock. It was not an easy task. With the dark skin of a Sicilian dock worker, he fit in, but he couldn't understand the local language and so he avoided conversation at all costs.

After two hours of hiding among the crates and buildings on the dock, Vittorio saw Becari appear in a line of slaves being driven down the gangway of the ship. They lumbered along, unfamiliar with the gait necessary when hooked together in a human chain, and reached the dock huddled together. From there, command of the group was taken over by another man who carried a whip as a warning, but didn't use it.

He led the string of men and two women toward a dilapidated building at the edge of the harbor, and Vittorio followed in the shadows.

When the slaves were boarded up in the building and the door was locked, an armed man was positioned at the door. Vittorio waited until the guard relaxed a bit, and after an hour he saw that the guard had slumped to the ground to assume a more comfortable position, perhaps for sleep.

Vittorio knew that he might have a chance, but only one, and he didn't want to waste it. He had no weapon and decided that the attempt to steal one might fail before he could even attempt an approach to the slave quarters. His plan was to move on the guard without a weapon, but he would wait until the middle of the night so that the man would be in a deep sleep.

That, too, proved a challenge for Vittorio because he had not slept the night before and now he was trying to outlast this man at the door of the building. But his excitement level was higher than that of the guard, and he knew that he could prevail.

Hanging in the shadows of another harbor building, Vittorio continued to check on the guard. He watched as the man's chin sagged, then jerked upward. He repeated this motion several times until his chin went all the way to his chest. Vittorio watched and waited, waiting to be convinced that the guard was asleep.

He looked around the dark corner where he was hiding for something that might be used in his assault. There was a chain and some hooks used by fishermen. He saw a pike that appealed to him as a perfect weapon. But a pike would have to be driven into the man's chest which might still elicit a scream, alerting other people in the area. As attractive as the pike was, Vittorio elected to use the heavy wooden plank about the length of his arm. With it, he could bludgeon the man and probably avoid any noise to alert others.

He lifted it, weighed it in his hand, and swung it once to get the feel. Peeking around the corner of the building, he saw that the guard was in fact asleep. Vittorio's pulse quickened as his body prepared for the fight. As he concentrated on the task at hand, sounds were coming from the harbor. It sounded like a fight, like armed men were in combat with each other.

A fight at the harbor that was involved in slaving sounded good at first, but Vittorio quickly determined that the noise would also wake his sleeping guard. If he waited for the battle at the docks to be decided in his favor, the guard could turn on his captives and kill some. If he plunged ahead and took the guard before he woke, he would be on his own without the assistance of the uprising that he was sure was happening over his shoulder.

Vittorio grunted and gripped the plank more firmly in his right hand.

"Now," he said, concluding that his surprise action against this guard would have a greater chance of success than counting on the success of people over his shoulder that he could not gauge.

Vittorio stealthily approached the guard, raised his club in silence, and then whispered only two words.

"*A dio!*" he said – 'to God.'

And then he brought the blunt instrument in his hands down onto the top of the man's head. The sound shocked him, coming as it did in the relative quiet of the dark night. The man's skull literally split into two halves with a bone-crushing thunk. Otherwise, the guard – taken by surprise – didn't move. He was killed in an instant and most likely didn't know what had happened.

Vittorio stood over the lifeless man for a moment, enduring a bit of shock at what he had done, then shook his head to clear his senses.

He still held the club, now bloodied by the man's brains, and turned toward the door of the building where the slaves were held. He swung his weapon down on the locking mechanism as if he was still swinging it down on the head of the slaver. After three strikes, the lock sprang open and the door flew past him in an arc that nearly clipped his arm. Vittorio stood in the doorway of a darkened room, and he could hear the whimpers of hundreds of humans chained to the walls on every side.

He wanted to find his brother but couldn't resist the pleas of the others that he passed. So he wielded his weapon again to shatter the bonds that held them and, by the dozens, the men and women held captive there tore free of the chains and bolted for the door.

When Vittorio had worked down about one-third of the bunks holding the slaves he looked straight into the brown eyes of Becari, wet from tears but not from fear or sadness. A smile spread across the young man's face and Vittorio smiled back. With a single swing of the club, he smashed the iron anchor that held the chains around Becari's wrists, freeing his brother. For a brief moment, they hugged, and then Vittorio pointed toward the door.

"Go, I will find you. I must free these others."

"No, brother. I will assist you. You have freed me so that I may free the others too," he said, picking up a broad wooden plank that had been crushed and severed from the bunk.

And so it proceeded. Vittorio and Becari worked in parallel lanes swinging their clubs and liberating all the Sicilian slaves taken by the Arabs and Barbary pirates.

1848 C.E. – 1860 C.E.

REVOLUTION

1848 C.E.

PALERMO

January 9, 1848: Printer's workshop on Via Tarragona

IT WAS HOURS BEFORE DAWN, BUT FRANCESCO BAGNASCO AND HIS fellow printers labored by candlelight to complete their task. They moved quickly from the trays of letters, cast in metal and arranged neatly in the rows that Bagnasco had used for many years. But they worked in darkness to avoid discovery, and the master printer was having to teach his apprentice revolutionaries to make them into printing assistants – a doubly difficult job.

"Set the tray," he told Carlo, pointing to the four wooden slats that lay unused on the printing frame.

"Where? How close?" came the confused reply.

"Like this," the printer said, quickly moving his hands over the printing platform. He moved the two pairs of wooden slats into a rough rectangular shape.

"But keep them loose at first," Bagnasco added, as his hands continued to sweep across the platform with practiced excellence.

"Now, the letter frames," he added, picking up seven three-sided metal trays. They were about the length of his forearm, with low sides and exactly wide enough on the cross section to match the butt of the metal letters that he reached for next.

"Now, the letters," Bagnasco said. He looked at Carlo quickly, then demonstrated by grabbing a handful of letters from the box and placing them randomly into the trays.

"That doesn't say anything," Carlo complained, pointing to the mish-mash of letters. "Besides, they're backwards."

For once, Bagnasco laughed.

"It is because you are unfamiliar with reading type backwards."

Carlo thought for a moment, concentrated on the trays of random letters, and spoke slowly.

"GuffauBitorzg," he said, and Bagnasco laughed again.

"Just to demonstrate," he said with a smile, then picked up the tray of letters and dumped them out onto the printer's bench.

"Here is the message," Bagnasco continued, pointing to his hand-lettered manifesto that lay beside their worktable. It was seven lines of words, exactly the number of trays that the printer had swept up for his demonstration. "Take letters from the box and repeat this message on the platform, here," he told Carlo.

Meanwhile Rubio, another man eager to join the fight, worked in the darkened corner near the press itself. He had been instructed to oil the works – "but not the plates!" warned Bagnasco – and he proceeded with his assignment in quiet.

The printer went to another section of his pressroom and gathered up the papers that he would use for printing. Looking up at the ceiling with closed eyes, he silently counted how many posters he wanted to produce that night. Enough to alert the entire city of Palermo, but if too much, the soldiers would simply burn them all.

"Ninety should do." Bagnasco also knew that the posters would be nailed to poles and buildings as well as handed out to willing citizens of the city, and he only had time for one size. He decided to make them all square papers about one-half meter, large enough to be seen from a short distance and small enough to fold and take away in case the king's servants came to call.

He brought the stack of papers to the press that Rubio was preparing and went to see how Carlo was managing with the type. His new apprentice was standing with his hands on his hips, staring down at the typeset metal letters. There were seven trays, as he suggested, but the letters were all wrong. A casual observer would have been simply confused, but Bagnasco was a seasoned printer. He knew the problem right away.

"You have arranged the letters left to right," he said, staring with Carlo at the 'finished' product.

"Sì," he said uncertainly.

"But they must go right to left."

Carlo jerked his head back in non-recognition.

"Perche?"

"When the paper is set upon it, it is the reverse of all that you have set."

"But..." stammered Carlo. "I cannot do that. I barely have enough reading to put it the right way."

Bagnasco took pity on the apprentice and knew that he could make it right faster than teaching this one-night helper. So, he took over. With swift movements of his hands, he rearranged the letters into an order that left Carlo with a confused look on his face. Then Bagnasco quickly lifted the tray and delivered it to the platform that Rubio was preparing. He slipped one of the papers from his stack into the frame that was hinged above the printing press.

Then he took the trays of letters and laid them into the frame on the platform and squeezed the four wooden blocks around the trays and pressed them close together with a guide that he tightened on the table. Pressing the trays left and right then up and down, Bagnasco was satisfied that the seven trays of letters would not shift while printing.

"Give me the bumpers," he said, but neither Carlo nor Rubio understood what he meant. So, Bagnasco ran around to the other side of the printing press and grabbed a dish of shallow ink and two cotton-padded 'bumpers,' hand-held tools that were covered with a wad of cotton on one end. He pressed the two bumpers into the ink, then dabbed the ink on the letter trays, inking them into a black shine.

Without waiting for his assistants, he stepped to the side and took hold of the hinged piece that held the paper waiting to be printed. Swinging it over and onto the letter trays like closing a sandwich, he was careful not to shift or move the paper once it had come into contact with the inked letters. Carefully he slid the sandwich to his right under a heavy wooden plate suspended just inches above his printing sandwich. Once the tray was in place, he pulled a lever that lowered that heavy plate onto his printing surface and, pulling mightily with his arms, he squeezed the plate onto the printing sandwich, and then released it.

After the wooden plate was raised up to its original height, he slid the printing sandwich back out, swung the frame holding the paper off the letter trays, and observed the result. He smiled in appreciation of their work and of the significance of the moment, then resumed the process inking trays and printing more copies of the poster.

What they produced in the overnight hours at their printing press was signed by the Revolutionary Committee, and proclaimed:

'Dawn on January 12th, 1848, will mark the glorious epoch of universal regeneration.'

Bagnasco knew the importance of January 12 – it was the birthday of King Ferdinand whom they intended to celebrate with a revolution.

The manifesto went on to promise that those who met in the piazza on the following day would be given arms to take up against the Bourbon army that suppressed them. It reminded the would-be revolutionaries not to damage property but to use 'their strength and their weapons' to resist the soldiers of Ferdinand and restore sovereignty to the Sicilian people.

———

January 10, 1848: Piazza Alberto Visconze

"That's outrageous!" shouted Luce Adamante. "What right do they have?"

He was asking all the wrong questions, and his next in command tried to tell him that. But Adamante, the king's captain of soldiers in Palermo, wasn't listening. He was the son and grandson of soldiers who had fought for the Bourbon family in Sicily, he was true to his calling and to his king, and he couldn't believe that the rabble from Sicily would dare to confront him, much less the sovereign.

Adamante held one of Bagnasco's posters in his hands and he trembled with rage.

"January 12," he shouted, "and on the king's birthday, no less!"

His eyes darted around the gathering of soldiers, looking for traitors in his midst, but also focused on his primary responsibility – protect the king and his power over this island. Adamante was a native Sicilian but with two – now three – generations of military service to the crown, he felt that his family was destined to protect Ferdinand II and his family against all threats.

"I want all of you," he said, sweeping his arm to include all those uniformed soldiers around him, "to go into the streets today. We are not waiting for January 12. We will stop this murderous rebellion right now."

And, with that, the squads of soldiers went out and roamed the streets looking for men whom they believed had instigated this uprising. Adamante intended to take them all, to leave no rogue standing who might light the fire of rebellion. Selecting out the guilty was not as easy as he thought it might be; the rebels had planned to stage their protest on January 12 and, as of January 10, they were purposely still keeping quiet.

But to offer a show of force and intimidate those who might fight, he picked out eleven men and accused them of insurrection. They were dragged from inns and trattoria, and one from his very home, and sent to the prison cells alongside the Palazzo Steri.

———

January 12, 1848: Fieravecchia neighborhood

He seemed a bit out of place. He was of average height and stocky just like many Sicilian men, but whiskers hugged his cheekbone and curled outward in an elegant display, and his close fitting, brocaded waistcoat made him look more like a leader than a follower.

And that is just what Giuseppe La Masa, the baron of areas lying beyond Palermo, intended when he showed up in the poor neighborhood of Fieravecchia in the early morning hours of January 12. He had been born poor, orphaned, and then adopted into a family of modest means, and he had used his natural intelligence and penchant for hard work to rise up the social ladder of Italian society, wisely insinuating himself into the well-bred upper class to wed a woman of style and position.

Throughout 1847, he had followed the growing disaffection of the people in his homeland of Sicily, and so he returned to the island to lend a hand to the proceedings, perhaps to light a match that would kindle a flame. But whether he was the instigator or the protagonist didn't matter to him. La Masa had become accustomed to standing out and he just assumed that the people of Palermo would welcome him into their protests.

He appeared in the piazza while the air was still cool and the skies were gaining light from the sun rising above the rooftops. There were some citizens of Palermo milling about, including the local people inhabiting this muddle of narrow streets and crowded alleys in a place at the center of Palermo. La Masa walked around the edge of the piazza, warmly greeting strangers as if he was already their elected leader, and he stopped in front of a long wooden table behind which stood a middle-aged woman in simple clothing and sandals.

"*Signore*," she said to stop La Masa from walking by, "*un po dell'acqua per lui?*" – a bit of water for you? She held out a wooden cup filled with the cool, clear liquid and, when La Masa took it from her, she immediately refilled her hands with bits of fruit and spices that she was hawking at the table.

La Masa smiled back at her, gulped down the water, but put his hand up to refuse the other items for purchase. Then he continued on his way, greeting people and striking up idle conversations on small matters. There was no talk of revolution, but he could sense a general unease.

After surveying the crowd, La Masa mounted the low shelf at the base of the fountain in the square and turned to address the crowd.

"You have been ruled by foreigners for centuries, kings who know nothing about you and who know nothing about your lives," he began.

"The king was born here," shouted someone from the fringe.

"*Sì*, this is true, but Frederick is not one of you. He was born in Palermo but lives in Naples." La Masa turned away from the shouted comment so that he could return to his theme.

"You have had true injustice. But now you have seen the pamphlets," he shouted, waving one of Bagnasco's printed posters, "and you have heard the cries of those tormented and deprived by the king and his army."

La Masa was a good speaker and he knew when to pause and let the audience absorb his statements. But he also knew not to let the pause last too long and create a gap that would allow someone else to usurp his podium.

"I have seen, and I have heard, also," he declared solemnly. "And we must rise up against this unfairness."

"It is more than unfairness," shouted someone in the crowd, a man who raised his fist in anger.

"Sì, it is more than unfairness," La Masa intoned. "It is a crime, it is a sin, it is against humanity!"

Shouts of 'aye, aye' came from the assembly, accompanied by jostling in the crowd and angry exchanges of words and gestures. The faces of the men were filling with color, the eyes of the women were growing wide at the increasing fury. And all the while, La Masa smiled at the insurrection that he believed he was the author of.

From the outer edges of the crowd more men joined the crowd, and pikes, pitchforks, and firearms were appearing among the people. Each new person brought two or three weapons, keeping one and handing out the others to equip the crowd. There was a general shape-shifting of the mass of people, as waves pushed toward the perimeter of the piazza. Shops that had dared to open on this morning had their wooden tables taken to create barriers, closing down the intersections and surrounding the piazza with a makeshift barricade against the Bourbon king's army that was fast approaching.

There was a momentary calm as quiet reigned over the square, but the report of single rifle fired from the soldiers into the crowd set off a blaze of gunfire. As the soldiers stormed the barricades from outside, the insurgents on the inside of the barrier fought back with pike and short knives, with muskets, shovels, and whatever tool or weapon they had at their disposal.

The fighting raged for several hours and, by midday, the soldiers had overcome and subdued the protesters. Many were jailed; some were killed. And the neighborhood of Fieravecchia was quarantined by the army so that no new uprisings would be allowed to begin there.

———

January 13, 1848: Protests continue in Fieravecchia

News of the events of January 12 spread around Palermo and even to cities beyond it. Overnight, hundreds – and then thousands – of peasants from the rural areas came to Palermo to join the fight and support their brothers. They cared little for politics; it was the decades of subjugation, high taxes, and arrogant rule by outsiders that had crawled under their skin and left the farmers and other workers angry, dispossessed, and ready to revolt.

The Fieravecchia uprising instigated other groups who cared little about politics or subjugation. They were outlaws and they were attracted to the fray to loot the city and take away whatever they could manage. In addition to the general melée in the city itself, towns outside Palermo were being ransacked. City offices were attacked and their records and files were destroyed; some of the government officials who stood to protect the offices were killed for their efforts. Even farms and woodlands were set afire by the mobs that roamed the countryside without leadership or agenda.

The general outrage burned red hot for several days, causing even the thousands of Bourbon soldiers to step back from the fray and hide in the fortress of Castellamare. It was at the edge of the most riotous areas of Palermo, but close enough that the army could bombard the various neighborhoods that were causing the greatest damage.

———

January 15, 1848: Palermo harbor

In Naples, King Ferdinand had been getting regular reports of the riots in Palermo and beyond, and he dispatched five thousand more troops at the first sign of trouble, on January 12. By the fifteenth of the month, the ships were arriving in the Palermo port and positioning themselves to contain, and then squash the rebellion.

The revolutionaries controlled all essential parts of the city by that time, and it was a standoff between the king's forces in the harbor and the rebels in the city. In the stalemate, messengers were sent back and forth from the Palazzo Steri in rebels' hands to the Bourbon army's ship in the harbor. The leaders of the insurrection demanded reinstatement of the constitution of 1812, which gave more power to local leaders. When Frederick's emissary refused, the rebels dug in.

Next, they demanded complete separation from Naples and control by the king, a demand that drew a derisive scoff from the Bourbon captain of the ship at sea. But while these negotiations were going on, the rebellion was spreading beyond Palermo by word of mouth, and by weapon. Other cities were falling to the rebels and local officials were either switching loyalties from the king to the revolution, or they were being imprisoned and, sometimes, murdered.

Over the next week, most of the areas of western Sicily had succumbed to the revolution. Messina remained a solitary holdout, but the king's forces could do little to expand upon that pocket of resistance to bring the insurrection to heel.

———

January 23, 1848: Naples and Palermo

Still receiving reports from the island, Ferdinand was becoming more disgusted with his army's failure to control the mob, and with the mob's potential to wrest Sicily's entire population and government from his hands. By January 23, sitting in his royal residence in Naples, Ferdinand II of the Two Sicilies granted a constitution to the people of Sicily, a constitution much like the one from 1812 which gave more power to the towns and cities of the island, established a Parliament, and instituted a more representative democracy.

Vincenzo Fardella was elected president of the new Parliament and immediately began preparations to conduct business so as to establish barriers to the king's resumption of control. Ruggiero Settimo was appointed president of the Senate but, in fact, acted as the prime minister of the new government. Together, they declared that Ferdinand II of the Two Sicilies had been deposed.

―――――

February 2, 1848: Palermo

Fardella's quick actions made a difference. By the first week of February, the revolutionary committee that he had formed had applied the constitution of 1812 and began to fill the offices called for in its pages. The Bourbon troops were withdrawing from the city and calm was being restored.

Over a period of about six months, hope grew as Sicilian institutions were brought back to life. Agricultural concerns remained, as did the growing poverty in the cities, but the newly liberated Sicilians believed that their new, localized government would find solutions.

Ferdinand had other ideas. As the government of Fardella and Settimo took the reins of power, the king was plotting a return to Palermo. He waited through the initial phases of the revolutionary uprising and then the establishment of the local government – against the advice of counselors who said that delay could allow the locals to set up firm protocols – but Ferdinand believed that the long-enduring lower classes would soon realize that even their Palermitani insurrection couldn't fix the ingrained problems of Sicilian society.

In September 1848, more of the king's ships were dispatched from Naples. This time, rather than make a frontal assault on the capital of the revolution, Palermo, he chose to send his army to Messina, the city that had remained loyal to him during, and after, the revolution. It was a prescient move. In very little time, the Bourbon troops – using Messina as a base – marched across the island, retaking towns and cities along the way, and seized Palermo with very little struggle. By March 1849, the island was once again in the king's hands.

On March 13, 1849, facing down a new revolt centered around the oath of office for the chamber of deputies, Ferdinand sent his army to break up the Parliament. With that act – without the king even referring to or rescinding the new constitution – he retook control of the island as an absolute monarch.

AUGUST 2018
CAFÉ AMADEO

"*QUARANTOTTO*," VITO SAID. "THAT'S WHAT THE DAY, THE YEAR, the revolution has been known as."

"Forty-eight?"

"*Sì*. Forty-eight. It was a very good year," he added as the barista delivered a new plate of orange slices and cups of espresso. Vito nodded once in appreciation and the black, curly-haired barista retreated with a nod and a smile.

"It began in Sicily, in Palermo," he continued, turning back to me, "but it spread across Europe. There were uprisings in Naples, Rome, Venice, Florence, and Milan, even in a normally quiet place like Lucca and Parma.

"And it spread outside of Italy, to Paris, Warsaw, Budapest, and Vienna. The people of Sicily were tired of being ruled by outsiders and kept under the thumb of a Bourbon king. But the other countries experienced revolutions for their own unique reasons. But let there be no mistake, the world's Revolutionary Year of 1848 began in Sicily!" he proclaimed with gusto.

"There was also a little-known person who flitted around the edge of the rebellion," Vito continued after a sip of espresso. "The rebels' big plan was to present a constitution that would unify all the Italian city-states into a single country. Giuseppe Garibaldi listened to this and formulated his own ideas about how to bring the Italians of Venice, Naples, Rome, and elsewhere together into a single country."

"Garibaldi," I said, "the leader of the Red Shirts?"

"Sì, but not to be confused with the red of the socialist republic that came decades later." Then he laughed that round, belly-shaking laugh. "It turns out that when Garibaldi was ready to surface as a leader of the opposition, he came into a large, unplanned shipment of red shirts. From South America, I believe. And he distributed those among his followers as clothing, a sort of uniform. And this is the only reason his army came to be known as the Red Shirts."

"But let's finish with 1848 first. The riots that broke out across Europe signaled an end to many of the entrenched monarchies of the time. As we talked about earlier, Ferdinand II was forced to institute a new constitution in January of the year, Leopold II in Tuscany followed suit in February. In Piedmont, Charles Albert succumbed to the revolutionary forces in March, as did Charles, Duke of Parma. You know of the French Revolution of 1789, right?"

"Of course," I replied. "The French people rebelled against the monarchy as a recognition – and reflection – of what the American colonists did."

"But did you know there was another French revolution in 1848?"

I didn't, but I didn't want to admit it.

"And Austria? Where the Hapsburgs were overthrown? All this began on a cold, quiet morning in Palermo. Oh," Vito continued with a twinkle in his eye. "and you know what else? The Manifesto of the Communist Party? By Frederick Engels and Karl Marx? It was published in February 1848, in London. What a year," he concluded.

"It sounds like La Masa stirred up the crowd," I said, returning to Sicily. "Was he responsible for the uprising?"

"Ferdinand was responsible," Vito replied, effectively dodging my question. The people were rising against the Bourbon rule – and the outside influences that controlled Sicily before him. La Masa was a stirring orator, to be sure, but he was not the reason for the rebellion in Palermo that morning."

"It wasn't much longer before Garibaldi appeared, right?" I asked.

At this Vito smiled and seemed prepared to move on to the next chapter.

"Sì," he said simply. "He learned lessons from the insurrection of 1848, some good, some bad, but he learned. It's an historic irony that Garibaldi's first true acceptance, the people who first saw the future in his eyes, were the denizens of Fieravecchia, the poor, humble neighborhood in Palermo that twelve years earlier had welcomed La Masa and the other protesters to bring down the Bourbon king."

He paused to sip some espresso and munch on an orange slice. Vito seemed deep in thought and I wanted to accord him that freedom.

"It was called 'The Expedition of the Thousand,'" he said finally. "Garibaldi. The Expedition of the Thousand."

1860 C.E. – 1945 C.E.

RISORGIMENTO

1854 C.E.

RACALMUTO

PIERO D'IMPELLI STOOD AT THE MOUTH OF THE TUNNEL THAT LED down into the sulphur mine. His right foot rested on top of the knee-high boulder that stood at the edge of the opening, and his notebook was balanced on his raised knee. Scribbling quickly with the lead pencil in his hand, the mine manager was keeping count of the cars of sulphur that were pushed out of the mine by the men, and an approximation of how full each car was.

The d'Impelli family had been in the mining business for three generations. His grandfather, Luigi d'Impelli had discovered this mine near Racalmuto while prospecting north of Agrigento. He was only twenty years old at the time and – in the 1780s – Sicily was still experiencing occasional battles between the British and the Bourbon family from France for dominion over the island. Luigi knew that his country had sulphur deposits in many places, a highly useful compound mined since ancient days for metalworking and, later, for production of gunpowder. With a history of conflict on the island, he concluded that gunpowder would always be a marketable commodity, so he laid claim to the site and hired men to help dig for the precious item.

Over the decades, Luigi's sulphur mine made him a wealthy man, and he passed on the successful enterprise to his oldest son, Mario. By the early 1800s, though, when Mario became the mine owner, the British and French families that had taken root in the island were buying up land and buying out the locals Sicilians. Seeing that the d'Impelli mine was still producing large quantities of sulphur, Mario was tricked into selling it on a promise of less work and a steady income. In fact, the deal took the mine and all its profits from Mario and the d'Impelli family and left him to serve as the mine supervisor. That 'steady income' meant a pittance paid to keep Mario in his office in Agrigento and withheld the profits that were promised him.

By the time Piero was old enough to take over for his father, Mario, the mine was no longer a family business. His grandfather Luigi had been the mine owner, his father was reduced to mine supervisor with a desk in a small office, and he – Piero – became just a hired hand, a mine manager who didn't even have an office but had to work in the heat of the day counting cars of sulphur as they were pushed out of the darkened mouth of a cave that seemed to stretch down to the gates of hell.

"Take some water," he called to Adelfio and Roberto, the two men pushing the next car out of the tunnel. Piero had been in the mine himself and knew that the temperature there could soar past forty degrees Celsius, so the men stripped down to little more than a diapered tunic – sometimes less – and their muscular arms were slick from sweat and grim. Piero's instruction was meant to protect the workers and keep the process going, but there was also a note of sympathy in his voice.

"It's a small car," the manager commented, referring to the contents of the load and not the vehicle.

Adelfio shrugged his shoulders, then took another ladle of water from the oak barrel at the entrance.

"*La minieru è stancu,*" he replied – "The mine is tired."

As hard as the work was, neither the manager nor the workers liked to think like that. He meant that the trove of sulphur was declining, something that Piero had noticed over the last two years. At first, he thought he had hired workers who weren't as efficient – the British family who owned the mine thought the same thing – so Piero brought back some of the older men who had worked for his father and asked them to inspect the mine.

Daniele Fabresi was one of them. He had worked for Mario d'Impelli until his arthritic hands refused to grip the axe or pick up the sulphur that was chipped from the wall of the mine. He emerged from the darkness in the light of midday and came to Piero, disappointment obvious in his lowered gaze.

"*È stancu*," he said, offering little more than a sad and bewildered look to make his point.

Piero was pushed by the British owners to continue to work the mine, to extract whatever might be left, but the manager knew that its days were numbered. And when the d'Impelli mine, as it was still known, went dry, the men who had worked in its bowels for decades would have to find another way to support their families. Those who had died in the tunnel were saved the stress of finding new jobs.

So, on that day, as he appraised the yield in the car pushed by Roberto and Adelfio, Piero could see the future before him. He wanted to keep his job, thought maybe he could keep his job, for a few more years. He was still young compared to others in his circle of friends, and perhaps he could find some other work as a manager, maybe in another mine.

Gianni Costante was the next man to emerge from the mine. He was carrying the tools that the men wielded in the darkened interior, collecting the things that kept them employed. He nodded to Piero as he passed by him, then locked the tools up in a shed near the mouth of the cave. There would be an armed watchman there all night to protect the shed, the miners' cars, and the general area of the mine.

"*È finito*," Gianni said – "It is done."

"Time for the family!" he added with a happier tone in his voice.

Gianni's wife, Luisa was expecting another baby, an addition to their so-far small family. There was Matilda, the three-year old daughter, who had recently progressed from walking to running, which kept Matilda constantly chasing the laughing little girl to keep her safe from unexpected encounters. And there was Alessandro, the nine-year-old who was already mimicking his father and saying he wanted to grow up to be a miner.

Gianni smiled at his son's admiring look but whispered to Luisa that he never wanted his son to go into the mine. At the end of each day, as now, Gianni's only interest was in going home to a meal with his wife and children, and a bottle of the good wine that the Sicilians made throughout the land.

He nodded again at Piero as he left the site. The men had known each other for years and although Piero was the manager, everyone knew that his family's status had been successively reduced. As a result, Piero's attitude toward his men had been more cooperative and solicitous. They were all aboard a slowly sinking ship.

"*Ciao,*" said Gianni with a wave. "*Bon sira,*" – "Good evening."

Piero had never married and envied his friend's situation. Gianni could go home and forget about the mine for a while playing with his kids. Piero would go home to an empty house, spending many of his nights still pondering how to reclaim the d'Impelli mine. It was the only trade he had known, and he understood the constant demand for it among the British and French forces that occupied different parts of Sicily, not to mention the forces of Savoy in Piedmont, other European countries, even the Americans.

Exporting sulphur by itself, or after converting to gunpowder, could be a lucrative business, if Piero could only get back control of the d'Impelli mine, or get another one of his own.

In his youth and early adulthood, while his father was still working in his office in Agrigento, Piero was introduced to the map of mines that dotted the island. From the cliffs around Enna to Agrigento, and from Siracusa to Caltanisetta, sulphur mining was common. Where once wheat farming had supplied the export to ancient Rome, to the Arabs and others, now sulphur took over as the prime export from that region.

'I have a nose for this business,' he told himself that evening. 'The British and French who have taken our land do not understand it the way I do. They will only take our land once we have found the sulphur, but once I have my own mine, I will not let it go.'

It was an unspoken rebuke of his grandfather, Luigi, which was not his intention, but Piero thought often about how the d'Impellis had let this great fortune slip away and he didn't want to repeat the mistake.

But how would he find a mine and how would he afford to buy it?

On a similar evening some weeks before, Piero decided that he would spend his days off – few as they were – searching the southeastern part of the island, following rumors he had heard and examining the soils from the areas that he visited. Prospecting for sulphur was a gamble. There was no test that would reveal it; the only way was to dig where you thought it might run and hope for the best.

Sedimentary riverbeds seemed to work in the past. The sulphur would be caught in the layers of soil and could be recovered by digging. Once found, the thread of sulphur could continue into the earth, which would necessitate mining.

Piero studied the geology of the area between Agrigento and Racalmuto, making notes of areas that appeared to have ancient riverbeds. He mapped these carefully on daily journeys by horse and on foot, then returned to his home to compare his notes with the known existence of other mines. He was very clever in screening potential sites and reducing the population of prospects. By cross-referencing and then mapping the path of the underground tunnels that he knew about, Piero was able to raise the probability of finding the right places to dig.

On the evening that he was inspecting the d'Impelli mine and saluting goodbye to the miners who worked for him, Piero went back to his home to conduct a final review of his guesses. He highlighted each spot for digging with a rough circle drawn around them on the map, using the same stubby pencil with which he had counted the cars of sulphur that day. Then he stood up to get a better look at the spatial arrangement of the prospective dig spots.

"They are too far apart," he said. So, he sat back down again and drew a line connecting three spots that were near Racalmuto and on the road going south to Agrigento. Then he drew another line connecting four spots that were northeast of Racalmuto, on the road that led to Enna. He decided to try one grouping at a time.

The next morning, while his men were celebrating their one day off from work, Piero put some shovels and picks into the back of the wagon and hitched up the horse that he had kept healthy and groomed since his late teens. Nero, his name for the animal with the shiny black coat, was a strong workhorse and could easily pull the light wagon behind it.

Starting at sunrise, Piero and Nero bounced along the rutted road toward Agrigento. Two of the spots that interested the mine manager were close together and came up first on Piero's map; the third was a bit farther away so he wouldn't get there if either of the first two bore results.

Piero watched the changing countryside carefully, one that he had traveled many times since his youth, but this time he was studying it more for clues about possible deposits. He consulted his map often, satisfied that Nero would continue to pull them along without Piero having to mind him. The gentle bouncing of the wagon made it hard for Piero to focus on the smallest notations on the map, but his pencil markings combined with the geology alongside the road provided ample clues.

Pulling on the reins, he brought the wagon to a halt. He climbed down, unhitched Nero and tied the horse up to a tree, then brought an armful of hay from the wagon and a dented metal bowl into which he poured water from the large barrel that was also on the wagon. He delivered these to Nero under the tree, then retrieved his tools and set out scraping the earth and examining its makeup.

A long, curved line of rounded stones and fine sand would be a sure sign of an old spring, and some compressed sedimentary deposits existed below standing water, as in lakes. Piero used all of his experience and all of his research to exclude barren sites and focus on a few where digging would commence immediately.

He spent most of the day on those two areas, scraping at the ground and crouching down to lift and smell the earth at his feet. Piero was disappointed when he turned toward home with nothing, but he knew that this would not be an easy task.

When he had made it to his home in Racalmuto, he went to the local trattoria for a light supper and then retired to his house. With one part of his new mining business underway, he switched his attention to the second part: finding buyers for the sulphur that he would inevitably find.

There was a British merchant who came to visit the d'Impelli mine on occasion. The mine was owned by a British family, but this man, this Philip Ambrose, had taken a liking to Piero, and the mine manager had risked telling his new friend about his ambition to open his own mine.

"Do that, and I will buy from you," Ambrose said, clapping Piero on the shoulder.

So, in the darkened quiet of his home, Piero considered how best to approach Ambrose with a real offer. If he found a mine, he could turn to Ambrose and make a deal. But what if he couldn't afford the mine, or to hire the miners? Piero also considered the possibility of getting Ambrose to give him money, to become his partner, and how maybe this might hurry the process along. In any case, Piero knew that his way out of the lost d'Impelli mine and into his own new Braccato mine – named after his mother – was through finding and then selling the sulphur to someone with an endless need for it.

"Maybe there will be war," he mused, but then smiled. There is always war, especially in Sicily.

The next week, after performing his duties as mine manager at d'Impelli, he hitched Nero up to the wagon again and drove farther toward Agrigento than the last time to reach that third spot that he had identified as a potential. And he came back that evening tired and empty-handed.

Another week went by and Piero tried the sample spots going northeast toward Enna. Three appeared together and he kicked the stones and scraped the dirt in dozens of areas within the range of these spots and got nothing. He returned on another weekend and tried again, this time in a cluster that lie just west of the line he had drawn. Although he found some small clumps of ore that contained sulphur crystals, it wasn't enough to continue searching there. Piero was becoming discouraged and almost decided to stay at this spot anyway, since this was the first place that had yielded any hope. But he knew that was illusory.

Three more Sundays spent prospecting for sulphur left him with hlittle hope, but Piero had made up his mind on another tactic. In the intervening weeks, Ambrose had visited twice more and liked to joke with Piero about his ambitions.

"*Shhh,*" the mine manager said, putting his finger to his lips when the other men were around. "Don't let them know what I am doing."

"Oh, of course," Ambrose replied, but smiled. "They already know!"

Piero scoffed at this but didn't pursue it. He did look more closely at the miners like Roberto and Adelfio, though, trying to figure out if they were listening in. He didn't mind what they thought, but he didn't want word to get back to his British employer. And he knew that Ambrose was British and that, alone, could be the way the employer found out. And that would be the end of Piero's job.

When he had tried and discarded the possible mine locations within a day's ride from his home, Piero knew that he would have to travel farther. That would require more time away from the d'Impelli mine, time that he wasn't allotted under his contract. He was supposed to work six days per week, every week. If he went overnight or for a few days, he would not be paid and would probably be fired.

Ambrose listened to Piero describing his plight one afternoon as they sat under the tree sipping grappa from the grapes grown by Piero's uncle. And he offered a suggestion.

"You cannot go, right? How about if I go?"

Piero couldn't figure out what his British friend was suggesting. Ambrose couldn't prospect for sulphur. He knew nothing about it, except perhaps its market price.

"How? What do you mean?" he asked.

"I would go instead of you. I travel all over Sicily and no one expects me to be in one spot all the time, like you," Ambrose said, tapping Piero on the chest.

"But what do you know about prospecting for sulphur?"

"Nothing," the Brit laughed, "but I can learn, can't I?"

Piero was skeptical that a man who had not grown up around the sulphur business could credibly learn the nuance of prospecting for it, but he was willing to consider it.

Over the next three Sundays, the two men rode together in the wagon pulled by Nero, noticeably annoyed to have to pull twice the human weight now. Kicking stones and scraping earth continued while some crystals of sulphur were found. Piero came to respect Ambrose's quick learning, and he enjoyed the company on these day-long trips.

Soon, they agreed that Ambrose could make longer trips and look for possible mining prospects at distances that would take up to a week to visit, while Piero remained closer to Racalmuto and the d'Impelli mine. Piero worried at times that he had taught someone to be his competition, but the Brit was a serious and faithful friend. He reported back over the weeks and months and told Piero where they might begin digging.

One Saturday, Ambrose rode up the d'Impelli mine on his horse with a look of smug satisfaction.

"I've found it," he said simply.

Piero and Ambrose retired to the shade of the tree and studied the map for the place where the Brit said he was sure would work. The mine manager was impressed, both with Ambrose's find but also with his own knack for pinpointing such a promising area.

Ambrose had also researched the ownership of that area before returning to Racalmuto, and he found that a farmer who was old and feeble owned the land. No one had considered sulphur mining, so the farm remained mostly untouched.

Now it was time for Piero to make a big decision. He had no family to leave behind, but if he went with Ambrose to this place he had never seen, he would be quitting his job and never be able to get it back.

But he made up his mind before the afternoon even turned to dusk. Owning his own mine had been Piero's dream for years, and this was the best prospect he had found so far.

"We will go," he said with excitement, and he and Ambrose shook hands.

The following day, instead of reporting to the mine at dawn as he had done for so long, Piero hitched Nero to his wagon, piled some supplies in the back, and joined Ambrose who was already on horseback for the trip west toward the mine that the two men would work.

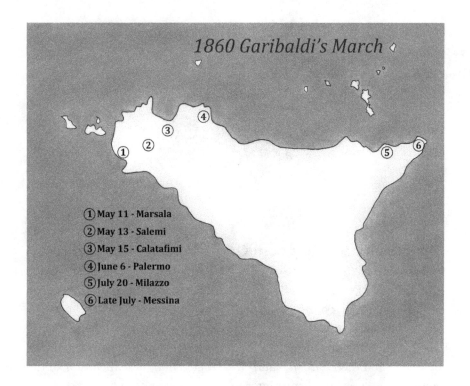

1860 Garibaldi's March

① May 11 - Marsala
② May 13 - Salemi
③ May 15 - Calatafimi
④ June 6 - Palermo
⑤ July 20 - Milazzo
⑥ Late July - Messina

1860 C.E.

MAY 11, MARSALA

THE SHIPS FROM GENOA WITH GIUSEPPE GARIBALDI IN COMMAND approached the island of Sicily on May 11, 1860. There were French and British frigates in the harbor at Marsala, and Garibaldi had been ordered to avoid contact with the French. He wasn't very good at following orders, believing that his instincts were best, but he also knew that the heavily armed French vessels could attack and sink his ships, the *Piemonte* and the *Lombardo* and, with that action, his expedition would come to a sudden and dispiriting end.

Divided between his two boats he had approximately one thousand men ready for battle. Garibaldi knew that 'ready' might be a stretch. His army, what had already become known as *I Mille* – The Thousand – was composed of more lawyers, merchants, and accountants than soldiers. But they had heart and they were following the impeccable leadership of Garibaldi. He had faith.

Still, he tarried in the waters to the north of Marsala until he saw the French frigates embark on a surveillance tour of the surrounding seas. Their departure gave him an opening and he took it. He brought the *Piemonte* and the *Lombardo* into port alongside the British ships, assuming rightly that the French would not attack with heavy cannon and risk hitting a British vessel. Garibaldi also counted on the long association of the Sicilian sulphur trade with the kingdom of Great Britain. Like any warring nation, the British needed ample supplies of the basic ingredient for gunpowder and they had bought Sicilian sulphur for decades. The admiral of the British fleet in the Marsalese harbor that day didn't want to risk that relationship, so he ordered his men to stand down when Garibaldi's ships approached.

The delay for the French to reach the harbor and engage in close-in fighting allowed Garibaldi the time he needed to land and bring his forces onto the island to fight. The French ultimately sank one of his ships and captured the other, but *I Mille* was by then on land.

_____

MAY 13, SALEMI

The success of Garibaldi's daring invasion of Sicily was proclaimed throughout the island. With the long dissatisfaction with Bourbon rule and the uprisings in various cities, Sicily seemed ripe for a serious revolution.

The landing in Marsala could hardly be called a victory, since the main purpose of *I Mille* was to land and escape the clutches of the French army. And by quickly departing the western region around Marsala, Garibaldi dampened the French resolve to pursue him.

By May 13, his little army had grown to over four thousand and reached the town of Salemi in full force. The citizens there welcomed *I Mille* and turned the city over to Garibaldi. The Sicilian dominoes were falling so easily that it prompted Garibaldi to proclaim himself dictator of the island on May 14, although he did so swearing fealty to Vittorio Emmanuele, whom he expected to crown as king of a united Italy before this enterprise was over.

_____

MAY 15, CALATAFIMI

The march of *I Mille* continued and, by May 15, they had captured Calatafimi. Unlike the escape from Marsala and the victory over Salemi, though, Calatafimi posed a greater challenge.

The Bourbon forces had massed on a hill called Pianto Romano and used their numbers and their position above the marching army of Garibaldi to their advantage. Despite the favored position, though, the Bourbons failed to overcome *I Mille* and, despite what history books would describe as a near draw at the end, the reputation of Garibaldi and his men soared.

———

JUNE 6, PALERMO

Garibaldi continued the quest and decided that the Sicilian capital would be next. He brought his now-larger force to Palermo near the end of May and surrounded the city. Once again, *I Mille* faced fierce opposition, but this time the citizens that Garibaldi sought to liberate rose to his defense and helped to bring down the French forces that occupied the city.

The struggle, unfortunately, destroyed much of the historic city. Faced with certain defeat, the Bourbon army surrendered when the arriving British fleet spoke up in favor of Giuseppe Garibaldi and his revolution. They had wanted to protect their access to sulphur and, in the end, sustained a rebel army that would move on to capture the entire Italian peninsula.

———

JULY 20, MILAZZO

But first, Garibaldi had to march is army across the island to the eastern shore and capture the recalcitrant cities there, including Milazzo – the ancient port city of Mylae on the northeastern tip of the island – and Messina – the fortified city that had resisted revolutions throughout the decades.

Once conquered, the people of Milazzo joined with Garibaldi and marched on Messina, where the city was put under siege and ultimately conquered later in the month of July. In two short months, the 'dictator of Sicily' had captured the hearts, the capital, and the major cities of the island and proclaimed that string of successes as the beginning of the unification of Italy.

AUGUST 2018

TRATTORIA BETTINA

"*I MILLE*," VITO SAID AS I WOVE THROUGH THE CROWD TOWARD HIM that evening.

"*Sì*, The Thousand," I translated. It was the historical nickname for the small band of followers attracted to Giuseppe Garibaldi in the leadup to the revolution in 1860. The actual count varies from seven hundred to nearly eleven hundred, but *I Mille* has become the folklore captured in history books.

"Before Garibaldi arrived, there had been protests in Palermo and Messina in April," Vito continued, "but the Bourbon king of Two Sicilies, Francis II, was able to put them down quickly. Then Garibaldi entered the picture and things began to change."

"How so? I read he was from Nice. What was he doing in Sicily?"

"That makes an interesting story, an historical 'what if?' so to speak," Vito said with a chuckle.

"He wasn't French," he continued, "but then again neither was Nice. It was originally known as Nizza when it belonged to Piemonte, but it was lost to France in the Treaty of Turin. So, technically, that made Garibaldi a French subject. He didn't like it and he had a reputation as a firebrand who would very likely have taken up swords against the Bourbon lords who now owned his birthplace.

"Camillo Benso, the Count of Cavour, was the Prime Minister of Piedmont-Sardinia then, aligned with Vittorio Emmanuele II of Piedmont. Cavour was worried that Garibaldi would attack the French in Nice to regain his fatherland, which would drag Cavour and Piedmont into a long, drawn-out battle."

Vito swatted away a fly and then looked around at the noisy collection of drinkers crowding the bar.

"Let's go for a walk," he suggested.

We stood from the table and wormed our way to the edge of the terrazza before I realized that we hadn't paid a bill. Just another thing about Vito, I thought with a smile. 'I wonder if anyone charges him.'

Once on the sidewalk, Vito slipped his hand through the crook of my elbow and continued talking as we walked. I could tell that he was using my balance for his own benefit, much as I had seen him do with his students when I encountered him on the street.

"Cavour talked to Garibaldi and convinced him that the real battle, the battle that might lead to unification of Italy – Garibaldi's primary interest – would begin in Sicily. 'Look at Messina and Palermo,' he said. In that way, the count convinced the ambitious young man to turn his attention to our country."

"When, and how did it begin?"

"He sailed from Quarto, a place near Genoa, with two ships – the *Piemonte* and the *Lombardo*. They neared Sicily on the west side and launched their invasion of the island from there. Seeing that there were French ships from the Bourbon king in Marsala's harbor, he chose to wait them out on the island of Favignana."

"Wait," I pleaded, holding up my left hand while flipping through pages with my right.

"That's...wait, that's where Fansu is."

He laughed a bit.

"Close," Vito laughed, "but not quite. The ancient records suggest that Favignana might have been called Fave. Fansu was among the island group though and might have been one of the drops of land in the sea where the early Sicanians lived."

It seemed ironic to me that Garibaldi would be pushing off from the same island to invade Sicily that tribes of proto-Sicanians had used to migrate to the island ten or eleven thousand years before.

"Back to Garibaldi," he said. "The French and British both had interests in Sicily, and that's not just their empire interests. The island had been over-farmed by the Nineteenth Century but other resources were found that were worth more."

"Like sulphur," I said.

"Exactly. Sulphur. It had lots of uses, but the one that brought the French and British merchants to the area was sulphur's role in the production of gunpowder. I think Sicily mined and sold more sulphur during that period of time than any other country, making the little island in the Middle Sea much sought after."

"As if it hadn't been sought after for millennia already," I added.

Vito shrugged.

"So, the sulphur market was expensive and lucrative, and the British wanted to protect their sources on the island. Garibaldi suspected this and lay in the shallows off Favignana until the French frigates went out on patrol. Then he sailed quickly for Marsala.

"Out of respect for their commercial relationship, Rodney Mundy, Admiral of the Crown on the British ships in port at Marsala, chose to look the other way when the *Piemonte* and the *Lombardo* slipped into the harbor beside his fleet. Once docked, Garibaldi's vessels were safe from an overt assault by the French, at least from afar. The time it took for the French to return to port allowed *I Mille* to slip onto the shores of Sicily and begin their campaign."

"So, I know that Garibaldi waged a successful war across the island, capturing many cities and having the local populace quickly surrender and turn into allies of his cause. Was Cavour right? Was this really the principal chapter in the Risorgimento?"

"At first, it seemed so," Vito returned to his narrative. "After conquering Sicily and promising land reform and limited government – remember those points, Luca – he captured Messina and launched his raid on the mainland from there. Taking over Calabria and then marching north, Giuseppe Garibaldi was hailed by all as the savior. Or, as he preferred to be called, Dictator of Sicily.

"Garibaldi reached Rome, which was being squeezed between two forces, I Mille from the south and Cavour from the north, and once that was won, he relinquished his rule to Vittorio Emmanuele who was crowned the first king of a united Italy. Garibaldi served in the government of the new kingdom but he was more of a soldier than a politician."

We walked around the piazza, Vito's hand on my elbow, and people young and old waved to him. He stood more erect during this *passeggiata*, and I sensed that he felt he should stand tall – well, at least as tall as he could at his diminutive size – when he was in effect parading around Mazara del Vallo.

"The Risorgimento would have happened with or without Garibaldi, so he is not quite the hero that people like to think. He was there, and it was time, but he had to be tricked into doing it the right way. As for Sicily, we don't have that many fond memories of him. In defeating the Bourbons and driving them from Sicily, *I Mille* destroyed lots of things, including farms and farmhouses. And the land redistribution that Garibaldi promised never really worked out. Making promises is easy; keeping them is hard."

"Does he deserve all the streets, buildings, and squares named after him?"

Vito thought for a moment and then nodded his head once or twice.

"Streets and squares have to have names, right?

365

———

"*Latifundia*," said Vito as he sat gently into the seat at Café Amadeo on the following morning.

He looked a little tired, as if the evening before and our slow walk around the piazza was still affecting him. But then he smiled as if he understood my look and had to reassure me. The barista had already served my espresso but magically had a small cup for Vito as soon as he sat down. Espresso is best made at the moment, so I wondered how the man always knew the exact moment when Vito would appear. It wasn't the same time every day, but the elderly gentleman's arrival always seemed to be anticipated. Was someone calling the café when they saw the little man walk by?

"*Latifundia*. You mean farms, right?" I asked.

"It was a system, actually," Vito began as he settled into the conversation. "Men who had served the king were often rewarded with large tracts of land. In the case of Sicily, they applied techniques familiar to feudalism and turned these sprawling farms into smaller parcels where local families would work them and give portions of the resulting crop, or mine, or craft to the lord or baron. The Risorgimento had promised to change that, and Garibaldi himself had said that the sharecropping system would be abolished. The peasants and dirt farmers of Sicily – and not incidentally most of southern Italy since it was traditionally a part of the Two Sicilies – bought into Garibaldi's promise and hoped to get freedom from serfdom and receive their own parcels of land.

"But it didn't work out that way. It's not that promises weren't kept; it's just that the government established after the unification of Italy – mostly governed by the north and the interests of Piedmont – wasn't very receptive to the needs of the people of my country. Industrialization, mechanization, and the buildup of a strong export market all focused on the goals of the northerners, and the Sicilians were just an afterthought. At best, we were just the laborers who supported the agenda of the north; at worst, we were the farmers, laborers and miners who were treated as the lowest rung of a very long ladder of power."

"That couldn't have gone over well," I surmised. "After centuries of being held down and subjugated to the Bourbons or Savoy, or whomever, Sicilians must have felt that it was their time for independence."

"Exactly," said Vito. "Not long after the unification, in 1866, the Palermitani rebelled against the power structure again. But, by then, the government of Vittorio Emmanuele II was strong enough to resist, and they squashed the revolt in mid-stride."

"Was it even-handed and final?" I asked. But then I wondered what he meant by the structure.

"Yes, and no," Vito replied. "The battle commenced with the city under bombardment from the Italian navy. Then soldiers landed and, commanded by Raffaele Cadorna, arrested many of the rioters and executed others."

"Was that it?"

"The forces of Vittorio Emmanuele owned the island and, in this show of force, they reminded the Sicilians that they intended to keep it. There was a smattering of attacks against the standing army, but few were organized enough to accomplish anything. The end result was that these mini-revolts gave the Italian army an excuse to imprison and execute insurgents, in the thousands.

"If you apply twenty-twenty hindsight, you might conclude that the unification of Italy, which was driven by Nineteenth Century ideals of industrialization and internationalism, was not adaptable to my country. We were an agrarian society with some strong markets, for example for wheat, sulphur, and other products, but the north was thinking of mechanization and large-scale factories. That wasn't what Sicily was all about. So, throughout the period of progress following unification, the north ignored the south, and the south – including Sicily – fell farther behind the progress being made by the rest of the country."

"What happened?" I asked. Although I already knew the answer.

"Major emigration. From the Two Sicilies, literally," he said. "Southern Italians left their hometowns in search of better conditions in Argentina, Brazil, and the United States. Sicilians – the other of the Two Sicilies – followed them. In the late-Nineteenth and early-Twentieth centuries, whole towns in southern Italy and Sicily were abandoned as the citizens sought opportunity elsewhere."

MAY 30, 1894

PALERMO

THE JUDGES SITTING ON THE DAIS FANNED THEMSELVES IN THE heat of an early summer. Large windows were open to the air and, as the time was midday, the sun shone slightly in only through the south-facing windows and heated the air throughout the old courthouse building.

There were four men sitting in the prisoners' cage in the courtroom. They were a mixture of young and middle-aged, all from diverse parts of Sicily, all accused of insurrection against the crown. They had been rounded up by the *polizia* and brought to Palermo where they were kept in jail for four months already. Their pleas had been heard and the evidence presented a month earlier, and now they stood impatiently waiting for the sitting judge to issue his pronouncement.

These men – Giuseppe de Felice Giuffrida from Catania, Rosario Garibaldi Bosco from Palermo, Nicola Barbato from Piana dei Greci, and Bernardino Verro from Corleone – were among the founders of a movement to win workers' rights and safer conditions. From farmers whose profits were cut by taxes to sulphur miners who worked in hazardous conditions, the working class in Sicily needed a staunch ally, one who would fight the government and reduce the burden on the workers. The movement was named *Fasci Siciliani,* taking the Roman word *fasci* meaning 'bundle' – indicating that while one man could be broken, a bundle, or *fasci*, could resist.

Their movement combined peaceful protest with some instances of violent action, all addressing working conditions across the island. But the government of Prime Minister Francesco Crispi decided that the *Fasci* had a more pernicious agenda, that they had allied themselves with factions that would separate the island of Sicily from the unified country of Italy. That accusation was the primary charge being weighed by the judicial panel on this very hot day in Palermo, a charge that could land these men in prison for many years.

"We say to our friends outside," Barbato declared when given an opportunity to present a defense, "do not ask for pardon, do not ask for amnesty. Socialist civilization should not begin with an act of cowardice. Martyrs are more useful to the holy cause than any propaganda. Condemn us!"

He sat down to icy stares from his compatriots. They supported his socialist agenda, but they were trying to avoid prison sentences, and Barbato's outburst would surely infuriate the judges. Giuffrida fiddled with his tie while Verro stared at the ceiling as if looking for inspiration. Bosco simply looked down at his feet.

———

The sulphur mines had employed men for decades in terrible conditions, intense heat, stale air, and darkened tunnels that made the bravest miner tremble in fear. Young children were also brought to work in the mines because they could squeeze into tight spaces to dig out the handfuls of sulphur that remained after the easy pickings had been removed by the men.

In the fields, Sicilian farmers struggled to produce enough to pay off their taxes, suffering under increasing export taxes and other impositions of the government. The favors promised during the Risorgimento had never materialized, and the decade leading up 1890 had seen a precipitous drop off in agricultural productivity. Wine, oil, and sulphur had buoyed the Sicilian economy since ancient times, but tariffs from abroad and international competition from emerging markets in the United States and northern Europe threatened to turn the Sicilian economic engine completely off.

As exportation of resources declined, exportation of the Sicilians themselves increased. The poverty of a nation long held in bondage, coupled with dropping productivity and the Italian government's favoritism shown to the industrial north drove many Sicilian peasants to leave and settle in Brazil, Argentina, North America and elsewhere. Many would come and go in a repetitive cycle of emigration, trying to earn higher salaries abroad and bringing their collected wages home to the island to support families that remained behind. But cycles of travel out of and back into Sicily often ended up with the immigrants settling for life outside their home island in the Middle Sea.

The *Fasci Siciliani* – also called *Fasci dei Lavoratori* – couldn't hope to solve these gargantuan problems, but their aim was to make life for the Sicilians who remained on the island better, safer, and more profitable. Their demands were straightforward: land reform, a more balanced relationship between worker and employer, and a less onerous tax structure, at least one that rewarded the peasants in the South as it did the industrialists in the North. The revolutions that had swept through the Americas and Europe – and kindled a fire in Sicily in 1848 – weren't lost on the *Fasci Siciliani* either. They insisted on freedoms enjoyed in many countries, including freedom of speech and worship, and the freedom to assemble and to strike against unfair practices.

In just a few years, the agenda preached by leaders like Giuffrida, Bosco, Barbato, and Verro caught on across the island. The *contadini* – peasants, farm workers, and miners – seldom participated in organized protest. That was a thing for city dwellers and the intelligentsia. But the weakening economy combined with the spread of newspapers and literacy fed a growing discontent and drew the *contadini* into the struggle.

By 1893, every major city on Sicily had a chapter of *Fasci Siciliani* and many of the smaller towns and villages did also. The ranks of membership swelled to about two hundred thousand and their demands were repeated frequently in published broadsides, while their activities were eagerly reported in the newspapers. The government of Prime Minister Giovanni Giolitti could hardly miss the threat to his government, although he preferred to let civil unrest work itself out. Growing impatient with the persistent murmur of dissent, he ordered the arrest of thousands of members of the *Fasci* across the island, bringing these four ring leaders to the courtroom to Palermo.

Giuffrida took a hard line on the government crackdown. He recognized that in the current state of anarchy, with protests, strikes, and violent actions on both sides, the island of Sicily was ripe for revolution. At a general meeting of the leaders of the Fasci Siciliani in January 1894, he called for a broad revolution to topple the power structure and install a more sympathetic government. But the other leaders, including Barbato, Verro, and Bosco – socialists all – preferred a more orderly, if also lengthier – strategy to remedy the working conditions and general imbalance in Sicily.

———

"Stand," the sergeant of the court ordered, calling the men in the cage to attention. The four prisoners were all proud men and they all stood promptly. They embodied the resolute words of their partner, Barbato, even if they didn't loudly affirm them. The four had worked tirelessly in the ranks of the socialists, risen to positions of power including mayor of their towns and leadership roles in the committees. They knew that the government would find them guilty and, most likely, hand down lengthy sentences.

"Giuseppe de Felice Giuffrida. You are guilty of the crime of sedition against the government of Italy and for multiple crimes of inciting the peaceful population of Sicily to riot against the government. You have encouraged violence and show no repentance for your crimes. This court finds you guilty and sentences you to eighteen years in prison."

There was a gasp from the audience in the courtroom. Although there were several members of the local government in attendance, most of the spectators were peasants and local merchants sympathetic to the things that Giuffrida stood for. They also had participated in many of the riots for which the gray-haired gentleman in suit and bowtie had been hauled before this tribunal.

"You should show deference to this court," the judge continued, "and deference to our king. When you demonstrate remorse for your actions and when you repair your attitude toward the welfare of this country, you may receive some charity. Sit down."

Giuffrida sat as calmly as he had stood. The observers in the courtroom could not tell whether he had anticipated this sentence; his face was too inscrutable. But he sat with his back erect and, despite the weather and his heavy woolen suit, this hero of the people never seemed to break a sweat.

"Rosario Garibaldi Bosco. You are guilty of the crime of sedition against the government of Italy. This court is aware of your attempt to flee the country on the steamship *Bagnara* on the night of your arrest. This court takes this as a sign that you recognize your guilt and that you were fleeing justice."

Bosco stood beside his fellows and did not flinch or show any emotion.

"This court finds you guilty and sentences you to twelve years in prison. You should show deference to this court," the judge continued, "and deference to our king. When you demonstrate remorse for your actions and when you repair your attitude toward the welfare of this country, you may receive some charity. Sit down."

Bosco sat just a few feet away from Giuffrida but the men did not look at each other.

The judge proceeded to call upon each of the remaining two men, Verro and Barbato, and handed down the same sentences, twelve years each. But he reserved special words for Barbato.

"You have not asked for mercy; instead, you have asked this court to sentence you. So it is. And may God preserve you from rotting in jail."

The four men were led from the courtroom and replaced with others to be tried and sentenced that day. The Prime Minister had intended to break up the *Fasci Siciliani* with the arrests and stiff sentences, but riots and strikes swept the island in reaction to the brutality of the police and the harshness of the treatment of the prisoners.

AUGUST 2018

CAFÉ AMADEO

"I think the American phrase is 'all hell broke loose,'" said Vito chuckling.

We had arrived at the door of Café Amadeo at precisely the same moment and I held the door open as my friend limped across the threshold. He seemed to linger a millisecond more on each step, measuring his gait and watching the floor for obstructions. It was the unconscious behavior of a man worried about his balance, so I held back another second or two before following him, so as not to step too closely to his own stride.

The barista brought two coffees to our table as we slumped down onto the chairs. Then he swiftly spun around and grasped two plates that he had already arranged on the counter behind him. One had orange slices and the other was piled with *cantucci*, Vito's favorite morning snack. He set the plates lightly on the table with a smile, then retreated to his station to let us talk.

"Do you mean after the guilty verdicts?" I asked.

"Sì," he replied. "The peasants and miners had come to believe that help was on the way. They believed in the *Fasci Siciliani* message, and they believed that the toughness of their resolve would deliver the workers from their seemingly permanent state of bondage.

"Then the government arrested these men, shot many others, and imprisoned as many as they could bring false charges against."

"But, according to Barbato, these weren't false charges. The *Fasci Siciliano* had, in fact, waged a battle against the system, against the government. Most political historians would call that an insurrection."

Vito nodded and sipped his espresso. His eyelids drooped, but his eyes still shone with the fire I recalled from our first meeting.

"An insurrection, you say," he repeated my words. "But wasn't an insurrection called for?"

"I suppose, but you wouldn't expect the government to quietly acquiesce, would you?"

Vito smiled at that.

"No, of course not. But it was not for nothing that they fought the powers in Rome. There was this guy, Antonio di Rudini. He's...well, let me begin again.

"Crispi called for a crackdown on the *Fasci*, and the arrests. He even ordered the sentences of the accused. But he fell from grace soon afterward. Maybe it was because of the constant, low volume of protests that continued throughout Sicily. Maybe it was because his own government was growing to distrust his decisions. Maybe the people of Italy just didn't like him, but he was soon replaced by di Rudini as Prime Minister.

"Di Rudini had long held softer positions regarding the working class and peasants. He thought many of the pronouncements of the *Fasci* were correct, that the low wages, high taxes, and generally poor working conditions were wrong. So, when he took the position as Prime Minister in 1896, he pardoned Giuffrida and his pals because he said that the sentences were too harsh, and because the crackdown on the *Fasci Siciliani* was nothing more than brutal repression. And, perhaps more importantly for Sicily, he adopted many reforms, including safer working conditions, higher pay, abolishment of child labor, disability and old age pensions, and more.

"Wow," I said in amazement. "That seems like a remarkable turnaround."

"It was. But while all this happening, and before much of it had come to pass, many Sicilians decided to vote with their feet."

"You mean move."

"Right. The Great Migration had already begun. Famine, earthquakes, crop failures, economic dislocation had all contributed to millions of Europeans moving to other continents, principally North and South America. The United States alone took in so many that the American government feared they were being overrun by migrants. They reacted to the influx by setting limits on immigration. The Chinese Exclusion Act was the American paradigm, although that happened earlier. The U.S. government set quotas on immigrants coming from Europe. With southern Italy – the Mezzogiorno – and Sicily so hard hit, and considering the people of these areas were already living on the edge, most of the Italians trying to get into the United States came from the south.

"There was an interesting result, here, too. Americans in your time, Luca, they think of red wine, pizza, and pasta with red sauce as true Italian food, and black hair and dark skin as the Italians themselves. Well, that's because the Great Migration was led by southern Italians and Sicilians, exactly the kind of people to bring that look and that food to America."

I had to laugh a bit. This mistaken stereotype wasn't still common among my generation of Americans; we had been introduced to the fine food and wine of Italy and studied the culture and art of the northern part of the country. But Vito was right about my parents' generation.

"But there was also a much more intriguing outgrowth of the *Fasci Siciliani*. The Fascists common in the days of Benito Mussolini were right-wing authoritarian types with a nationalist agenda, while the *Fasci Siciliani* were Socialists. So, remember, between 1895 and about 1920, the word *Fasci* referred to Socialist reforms in labor and government.

After that time, Mussolini co-opted the name – he seemed to like the optics of a 'bundle' being stronger than a single reed – and created his hardline nationalist party that would stop the Socialist movement and centralize power in his government.

"Well, actually, in him."

1922 C.E. – 1943 C.E.

FASCISTS

APRIL 1929

PALERMO

"DON'T TOUCH THAT," CLAUDIA SAID, ADMONISHING HER LITTLE daughter to stand back from the grimy toilet in the corner of the cell. 'What's the use,' Claudia thought. 'It's a filthy place in a filthy city in a filthy country.' She sometimes hated her husband Paolo for the protests he insisted upon.

Paolo Infante had railed against the government of Benito Mussolini for years, but never as loudly as now when his puppet prefect, Cesari Mori, had taken absolute control of the city. Known for unmerciful treatment, Mori would imprison the protesters if he could capture them, or imprison the man's family if he could not. In this case, Paolo had eluded capture and so his wife and daughter were now in Mori's filthy jail cell.

The prefect of Palermo was remade into the mold of his benefactor Mussolini, a rigid man with little conscience who brooked no compromise and wielded his power like an iron hammer, a practice that earned him the sobriquet of *Prefetto di Ferro* – the Iron Prefect. In elevating Mori from the lesser post of prefect of Trapani to the same position at the more powerful city of Palermo, Mussolini had declared quite boldly:

. . .

"Your Excellency has carte blanche; the authority of the State must absolutely, I repeat absolutely, be re-established in Sicily. If the laws still in force hinder you, this will be no problem, as we will draw up new laws."

It might have been called martial law but that concept was too limited to fully describe what Mori wrought on Palermo and Sicily generally. He laid siege to any town that opposed him, summarily executed dissidents – taking particular pleasure in pursuing Socialists – and reinterpreting the laws to support his agenda.

Claudia and Francesca Infante were caught up in Mori's purge of protest across the island. When Paolo received word of his family's detention, he was in hiding in the Peloritan Mountains in eastern Sicily. The news threw him into a fit of anger and it was hours before his comrades could get him to calm down and act rationally.

"What would you have me do?" he shouted at Lorenzo. "Leave them to die?"

"They will not die and, yes, you should rescue them. But you cannot do that until you consider the right action."

"The right action would be to cut Mori's throat," Paolo spat out.

"And that would be nearly impossible with the hundred armed soldiers that always surround him. Let's think."

Throughout the night they two men and others in their gang considered the next steps against Fascism in general and Mori in particular. All grand actions, to be sure, but Paolo remained focused on some very specific actions to save his wife and daughter.

———

Both Mori and Mussolini held a grudge against the Mafia. The criminal organization had operated outside the control of the official government in Sicily for decades, replacing the government in most places and reassuring the Sicilian people that it, the Mafia, was the one to protect them and their freedoms. It was a conflicted relationship.

On this island, where outside rule had been the norm and every Sicilian had suffered from unfair pressure from the government, the Mafia was seen as a protector. However, at the same time, the Mafia exerted its own pressure, requiring *pizzu*, or payment in bribes, to ensure that this protection was maintained. Sometimes, when protection was refused, suspicious attacks on the business in question suddenly occurred without warning. These attacks reinforced the need for protection and guaranteed that the Mafia's next offer would be accepted.

Mussolini was offended by a lot of things going on in Sicily, but the Mafia particularly grated on him. For Mori, the feeling was much more intimate and immediate. The Mafia's activities on the island reduced Mori's control, challenged his authority, and diminished the benefits that he believed he could reap as the prefect. Following the meaning behind the words of Mussolini – *Il Duce* – Mori intended to abolish the Mafia.

At the same time, he had to confront the Socialists like Infante and his band hiding in the mountains. When it was convenient, Mori lumped the Mafia and the Socialists together, publicizing the acts of either when the news would be counted on to outrage the Palermitani. Or dividing the two when lecturing one or the other, driving a wedge between them. When he had Claudia Infante arrested, he charged her with cooperating with the Mafia. Mori smiled at this. He knew that Paolo Infante would be outraged at the accusation that his wife was involved with the Mafia, but the man would also be humiliated at the thought that his wife was in the company of other men. Mori's very personal taunt would tear Paolo apart mentally, and that was his plan. Imprisoning the man's ten-year-old daughter was just icing on the cake.

Mori had learned his ruthless tactics from the man who had put him in power. Mussolini had formed the party of Italian Fascists some years before. Through manipulation and coercion, he had risen to the position of Prime Minister of Italy by 1922 and he was slowly transforming the political machinery in the country to support his nationalist agenda.

Wielding the levers of power, Mussolini forced compliance through extra-judicial means, threatening his opponents or outright jailing them until they complied with his interpretation of the laws.

Mori was ready to do things the same way. After all, it was Mussolini who had put him in power in Sicily and, if he played it right, Mori could expect further advancement in the *Partito Nazionale Fascista* – the Italian Fascist Party – that now controlled the process of government throughout the kingdom, effectively overpowering even King Vittorio Emmanuele.

By selectively imprisoning Sicilians he thought were a challenge to his rule, Mori could terrorize the rest of *le pecore* – the sheep – as he called the people of the island. He expected them to collapse in the presence of power as he surmised they had always done whenever faced with a powerful and aggressive threat. But Mori had too little experience with the Sicilians to understand them. He grew up in central Italy but had a brief stint in Trapani before returning to the mainland and living in Florence. After World War I he was sent back to Sicily to deal with the scourge of criminality there, although his career included a brief tenure as prefect of Bologna where he was insulated from the affairs and culture of the island in the Middle Sea.

Through his travels, Mori developed a level of cynicism about Fascism itself. He held few beliefs tethered to a system of morality but viewed the criminal behavior of the Mafia as paramount and thought that the Fascist movement was inadequate to arrest the progress of that organization. His view was that the Mafia achieved its success by appearing invincible and that, to defeat them, the people had to be shown that the Mafia itself could be intimidated. If he could portray the weakness of the Mafia in this way, the people would be more likely to recognize the official government, Fascist or otherwise.

———

"It is time," Paolo pronounced. "I will go to Palermo tomorrow and I will free my family and kill Mori."

"This can't happen," said Lorenzo, trying to soothe his friend without inciting greater anger. "Mori is in Mazara del Vallo now, rounding up more criminals."

"What do you mean 'more criminals?'" Despite his intention to avoid inciting Paolo, Lorenzo's words had been poorly chosen.

"Not more, as in your family. 'More' as in all the others that he has arrested."

Paolo harrumphed at this. He was still angry and agitated, and his mind was preoccupied with visions of his wife and little daughter in a dirty cell in Mori's Palermo.

"I will go with you," Lorenzo said.

Paolo was too wise to refuse; he knew that his mission would require careful thought and help from others. He knew people in Palermo, but as soon as he appeared in the city, news of his arrival might reach the authorities so that he, and his family, would be at risk immediately.

"*Grazie*," was all he said, and clapped Lorenzo on the shoulder.

When the two men saddled horses in the early hours of the next day, two sympathetic friends joined them. The four rode off in the mist of the morning westward toward Palermo.

———

The streets of Palermo were quiet in the early hours of the morning when Paolo led his small squad down a darkened street toward the jailhouse on the main square. He stopped at the end of the narrow avenue and peered around the corner. There were some shopkeepers sweeping the sidewalks and rolling up the exterior shutters that protected their shops in the night. And there were some dock workers trudging through the piazza toward the shipyard, carrying leather pouches filled with the usual worker's lunch: bread, sausage, and wine.

Lorenzo had tried to convince Paolo on the evening before, spent in the outskirts of Palermo, that they should make a plea for freedom directly to the authorities. But his suggestion was quickly rejected.

"They want me. This is why they took my family. If I plead for their freedom, I am doomed," he reasoned.

"But if what you want first and foremost is their freedom," Lorenzo challenged, "then you will sacrifice yourself."

Paolo had to nod in agreement with this reasoning, but he also knew that his service in the Socialist cause for workers' rights would be extinguished. If taken prisoner by the Fascists who now ruled Sicily, he would be executed before nightfall.

"I can free them and remain free myself," he told his friend.

"But then they will be on the run with you," Lorenzo countered. "Is that freedom?"

"I will send them away so they can be safe, and free. I will remain here to fight."

Lorenzo didn't have to remind Paolo that this plan would make his family another type of captive and leave them in constant fear for him.

So, on this morning in the clear, crisp air of Palermo, Paolo intended to free his wife and daughter and somehow escape with them.

Their plan was to hire a young child to deliver breakfast to the police officer inside the jailhouse. There would only be one officer on duty at this hour. This would momentarily distract him and Paolo and the other three men would slip in and suppress any resistance from him. With that done, Paolo could open the cells and release all imprisoned there.

He offered a few coins to a boy about his daughter's age who was outside a café helping his father, the proprietor. But the father of the boy rejected the offer, angrily refusing and saying that such a thing would put the boy and himself in danger.

When two school children walked through the piazza, Paolo was ready to try again but didn't want to approach two youngsters for fear that one would report the offer. Paolo and Lorenzo returned to the shadow of the side street where their fellows remained. After a few minutes, a teenage girl came down the cobblestoned street with a basket over her arm. It was filled with fresh loaves of bread still steaming from the oven.

"Who are those for?" Paolo asked her.

"The café," she replied. "I sell our bread to them each day, in return from fruit and coffee."

Quickly, Paolo stepped into the situation. He walked with the girl to the café and bartered for the goods in exchange for bread. But instead of selling her entire basket of baked goods, Paolo held two loaves back, and added the fruit to the basket. He gripped a large mug of coffee and gave to the girl.

"Take this bread and fruit and coffee to the man in the jailhouse," he said, then he slipped several lire notes into the pocket of her apron.

"This is for you," he said. "Just deliver the food and coffee and leave with your empty basket."

The girl agreed and walked off across the square toward the building. She pushed open the heavy wooden door open and stepped inside. Paolo leaned around the corner and watched as the door swung closed behind the girl. After another moment or two, the door opened again and just as the girl was stepping across the threshold, Paolo and the other men slipped in through the opening.

It was easy to overcome the guard inside but Paolo had miscalculated. Instead of a single officer, there were two. While Lorenzo was tying up the first one still chewing on a hunk of bread, a second officer appeared from the back. Paolo quickly pulled a knife from his belt and held it up to the man's throat.

"You will not interfere," he whispered, pressing the blade to the man's skin. The officer shook his head 'no.'

"Do you have family?" Paolo asked, once more applying light pressure to the blade.

"*Si*," came the reply through tightly pressed lips.

"Then go home to them and say nothing of this," Paolo instructed. "You were not here yet."

One officer was bound and the other escaped the building on a dash back to his home. Paolo and Lorenzo quickly found the keys to open all of the cells, finding Claudia and Francesca locked into one near the back. The entire operation took little more than five minutes and Paolo, his family, and his comrades were back out and headed for the edges of Palermo to make their escape.

1939 C.E. – 1945 C.E.

WORLD WAR II

OCTOBER 1942

MAZARA DEL VALLO

"Move them," Colonel Werner said waving his hand at the crowd, and his assistant did as he was told, pushing young and old Sicilians alike out of the way of his commanding officer. Werner and Lieutenant von Stöhl were walking through the Piazza Santa Caterina in the shadow of the Cattedrale dello Santissimo Salvatore and the senior officer didn't like too much contact with these people.

Manfrit Werner, an officer in the forward detachment of the German occupation had arrived in Mazara to sign up local men to serve under him in the North African campaign. The Third Reich already had a large force of German soldiers in the Atlas Mountains in Tunisia but, for their plans to succeed, they wanted more men, preferably only lightly armed men who would stand and fight to survive, but whose actual role was to stall the Allied forces before dying on the battlefield. Werner and other Nazi officers operating in the south coastal cities of Sicily were organizing Sicilian volunteers into such a supplementary battalion.

Werner's instructions were to sign as many men as possible to short-term orders and ship them to Africa. He and Klaus von Stöhl, the lieutenant by his side, had no idea how these Sicilians would be used by Field Marshall Rommel, and they didn't care. The Nazis needed more meat to throw at the Allies machine and that was what they would do.

The threat to Sicily was real and the young men of Mazara, Gela, Agrigento, Siracusa, and other cities on the southern coast of the island felt the threat more keenly than other people on Sicily. If the forces of Great Britain and America pushed their campaign off from North Africa, they would invade Sicily first on their way to the continent. Once again, the island would be used as a battleground between opposing armies and – once again – the people who lived there would die in someone else's war.

Young men who had worked the farms and come to the cities for jobs were easy marks for the German enlistment campaign. Sicily was already poor and the economy had not recovered from the decades of financial failure, and this new global war made things even worse, especially on those who already had no expertise or advanced skills. There were no jobs in the cities so the influx from the rural areas just brought more impoverished families to crowd the cities and risk the already limited resources.

Werner and von Stöhl had set up an office on the edge of Piazza Santa Caterina and another one in the Piazzetta Bagno beside the ancient Arab Kasbah that still flourished with markets. Each of the offices was not much more than a single room on the first floor of an apartment building, but it gave Werner and von Stöhl places to which they could bring likely volunteers and explain the benefits of signing a six-month or one-year offer.

The lieutenant thought very little of the recruits. "*Stupidu*," he said too often to be discrete, having heard the word a farmer used for his goat. 'They can all be killed, for all I care,' he thought to himself, and he complained openly to Werner.

"These goatherds can hardly serve as soldiers under Herr Rommel."

"They aren't soldiers," Werner explained patiently, "they're a line of defense for our good German boys. These Sicilians will absorb the bullets first while our young men survive to charge the enemy. Besides, Rommel needs a large force to push ahead and it doesn't matter if most of them die. Just so long as the bodies are Sicilian."

Werner shared some of von Stöhl's disrespect for the Sicilians but he had fought alongside Italians in the north and had more respect for them than his lieutenant did. These were men – although a lesser order of men, he thought – and they would fight to live. That fact was enough to put rifles in their hands and let them stand between the German soldiers and the enemy.

He also knew that these new recruits would not be paid once they were in the field. So, to attract them, he had to promise that their families would receive financial support back here in Mazara, the same promise that was being made by Werner's colleagues in Gela and Agrigento to families of men recruited there. To be convincing, however, there had to be money for the men upfront, money they could give their wives before they shipped off to war.

Checks drawn on a bank were worthless. In the uncertain times of war, bank failures were common and with the devaluation of the lira, cash was the only thing that would be accepted. Werner had chosen the office near the Kasbah specifically because it had once been a bank and there was an unused safe in the corner for him to stow the bags of Italian lire and German marks that he had brought to Mazara for his recruitment campaign.

He had little success at first and only a handful of men visited the office, so he and von Stöhl got in the habit of trolling the squares of the city. He greeted the people with a smile, one that he had practiced before and which came across as only slightly feigned. But he didn't like the smell of the crowd, so he brushed quickly through when the crush of people was too much.

It was just this way on this particular afternoon in Mazara. Despite the late season, the sun was high and the temperature was above normal, and Werner didn't like being so close to these people.

Werner and von Stöhl reached their other office in Piazza Santa Caterina and unlocked the door. There were young men milling around on the street but they did not line up in front of the German post right away. Werner noticed this and so he made a big show of being there, leaning on the open door to the office and smoking a long cigar, blowing smoke rings outward so that they hung in the air just beyond him.

Von Stöhl was also putting on an act, but within the office. He didn't like talking directly to the Sicilians, so he remained seated at the desk visible inside the window, shuffling papers and appearing to be quite busy with the work of the Third Reich.

"*È bellu*," Werner would mutter to no one in particular, "*è bel giornu*" – 'it's a beautiful day.' Although it seemed a vapid comment, Werner felt he had to smile and seem particularly happy, starkly above the general mood of the Mazarans passing by who appeared tired and concerned about their fate in this war. Werner's show of confidence and joy attracted the attention of passersby, and muttered remarks could be heard among the women who saw him.

Young men were also drawn in by the act, wondering why this German could stand among them, seemingly happy and obviously successful, when they wondered if they could afford a meager dinner or loaf of bread before nightfall. So, some inquired of the German's business there and, being informed that he was recruiting "strong men to fight the enemy," they decided to listen to what he had to say.

"They will take your women and your homes," Werner said in a well-rehearsed speech. "The Führer and your *Il Duce* are determined not to let them treat you this way. Herr Hitler has ordered battalions of his own soldiers into North Africa to fight the Americans and British, to defeat them there, and not to let them come to your island. But we cannot do this alone. We cannot defend your entire country without the help of the Italians who want to keep their own land free."

Werner made one slip in this speech, referring to the Italians rather than the Sicilians, but the local men listening to him let it pass. They didn't consider themselves Italian, but they knew that their fate and the fate of Sicily would be tied to preservation of the lands of Italy itself, so they factored that into what Werner was saying.

"For the glory of the Third Reich and the survival of the Italian people, we will fight together to stop the invasion of the Americans!"

This rousing declaration of purpose was always successful in getting a few men to sign up. As the weeks passed, the trickle of men increased to a steady flow, each young man coming to the Germans' office having heard stories of other volunteers getting an envelope of money for their wives to buy food, and each deciding that the Americans and British must be stopped before they landed on the beach at Mazara.

Not all men were so easily taken in. In the piazza outside Werner's office near the Kasbah there were cafés that drew small crowds each evening. In the crowds were some of the Socialists who had been members of the *Fasci Siciliani* and who saw through the empty promises of this new German incursion onto their island. There were educated men and women who resisted the thin veneer of Nazi propaganda and who recognized the colonel and his lieutenant as functionaries sent only to recruit fodder for the enemy's cannon.

And then there were those who occupied middle ground, not the poor and dispossessed and yet not the elitist intelligentsia who scoffed at every promise made by the Nazi representatives sent to Mazara.

A young man sat at the café and listened to the debates that went on around him. He heard the hopeful promises made by recent recruits to their wives, spending precious money on a last evening at the bar before shipping out to Africa, and he listened to the impassioned pleas of the dissenters who warned that nothing the Germans said was true.

He was Vito Trovato. He had just completed his second year at *L'Universitá di Palermo*, enough education to prepare him to teach literature if he chose, even enough to contrive a way to escape his home in Mazara aboard ship to the United States. He didn't fall for the promises of Werner but he also didn't agree with the dissidents who fought everything the Germans said. Trovato wanted to remain in Mazara and fight for his city – against whatever enemy it faced – and he decided that his role in this war was to make sure his city and his culture survived. If the Germans could win and give Mazarans their freedom, he would fight for them. But if after a while it appeared that the Allies would treat his ancient city with more respect and deliverance, he would side with them.

It was in this frame of mind that young Vito Trovato entered through the door of Werner's office near the Kasbah one Sunday afternoon. He wanted to interview the colonel – a turn of the table on the proud German officer – and he wanted to see if Werner could convince him that service to *Il Duce* and the Führer made more sense than siding with the Allies.

"Why would we fight the Americans?" he asked when he sat in the chair next to Werner's desk. An audible scoff could be heard from von Stöhl, and Trovato turned to appraise the man who would show him such disrespect.

"The Americans want to take your country. Is that what you want?" Werner replied patiently.

"Well," began Trovato, looking down at his hands as if for inspiration. "Many people have taken our country over the centuries. How about..."

"But do you want another?" insisted Werner.

Trovato paused, but then resumed his comment.

"How about the Germans? Isn't the Third Reich taking our country?"

At this, von Stöhl jumped to his feet. He didn't intend to have a stupid Sicilian challenge the destiny of the Reich. But Werner only smiled.

"No," he said, tapping his fingers on the desk, and motioning with his hand for von Stöhl to sit down. "We do not want your country. Yes, of course, it is here between Africa and Italy and, yes, we have to fight over it to keep you safe. But we, the Germans, we do not want to keep your country."

Werner shrugged his shoulders and then looked directly at Trovato.

"We only need it to keep the Allies from marching north. You do not want that; we do not want that. But we must fight together to keep them off your land."

Trovato did not easily fall for that reasoning, but he had to admit silently that he wanted to keep the battle off his island. If the war could be fought in Tunisia, perhaps it would spare Sicily the pain of open warfare.

"It can't be that easy," he said.

"What?" blurted von Stöhl, interrupting the conversation and earning a scowl of disapproval from the colonel.

"You will fight to keep Mazara safe..." Trovato continued.

"All of Sicily," Werner interrupted.

"Sì, all of Sicily," Trovato conceded. "And then you will leave?"

Werner demurred for a moment, a pause too long for Trovato, but then he regained his composure.

"The Third Reich has no interest in Italy," the colonel continued. "*Il Duce* rules the country and we are satisfied that he will assist us in fixing all the things that are wrong with the world."

Werner was tiring of the conversation and wanted to get to the part about enlistment.

"So, are you willing to be a part of saving your country?"

Trovato smiled back at him but didn't reply right away.

"I can see that you are an educated man," Werner said. "We need someone like you who could show the men how to fight."

"I know nothing about fighting," Trovato replied.

"But you know much about leadership," Werner continued. "We need a smart man like you who would lead the men and explain to them what the Allies will do when they get to Sicily. How they will take your farms and your women." Pausing for effect, he added, "and take your little girls."

Trovato didn't like any of this, but he especially didn't like the thought of being overrun by yet another country, another in a long line of cultures that had subjugated Sicily. And he knew that pushing the battle off the shores of his island might help keep the bloodshed and destruction farther from his homeland.

So, he signed up with Werner to be a volunteer in the Sicilian battalion to fight the Allies. He knew that he would be immediately sent to the front in North Africa, but he wanted to keep his silent promise to the people of Mazara and wage the war away from their shores.

AUGUST 2018

CAFÉ AMADEO

"Mazara," Vito said in his inimitable one-word style. We had both arrived at the Café Amadeo at the same moment; I held the door for my friend and we walked to the table at the corner of the room. The barista appeared with our *due espressi,* one plate of *cantucci,* and another of orange slices. It all seemed so familiar and so permanent, although I knew – as did Vito – that my time to depart had arrived. I was due to board a train for Catania that very afternoon, to spend the night there and to train to Rome on the following day. We had talked about my departure before, particularly when I first thought I would have to go in July but stayed longer, reluctant to leave Vito and Mazara del Vallo.

What went unsaid throughout our many days together was my original plan to tour the island and see life as it is in Sicily. Still, I felt like I had toured Sicily vertically through history – rather than horizontally through geography. I believed that destiny would bring me back; Vito didn't look so sure. He would be here, in Café Amadeo, as always. Right?

But life goes on. I realized that as the calendar turned to the middle of August, I would have to leave Sicily and return to America. I hoped that I would carry with me all the experiences and memories of this place, all the stories told by my mentor, and all the late night thoughts that I collected in the files of my memory about the people of Sicily – those who came here as immigrants and those who came here as invaders.

"Mazara," he repeated as he sipped from the tiny cup of espresso.

I had never been to this city before landing here six weeks ago, but I felt as though I had become a citizen of Mazara del Vallo by my deep dive into its history. I sipped at the coffee cup, sneaking glances over its rim at Vito and wondering how I would have discovered Sicily without him as my guide. How did I find him?

Or, rather, how did he find me?

Six weeks. It seemed like more than a lifetime. I made my trip to this island to research the history of my parents and grandparents, back at least to the 1890s, and found myself drawn inextricably into the past. The deep past.

Vito had been my guide, my mentor, and my friend. My path through Sicilian history had been far more than I had anticipated at the outset, but I felt – this morning – as if anything less would have been a disappointment.

"Mazara," he said again. "Do you know that it was spelled differently before the war."

"Huh?"

"Mazara. I don't know why," he continued, and I immediately wondered how there was anything that Vito hadn't figured out – "I don't know why, but the spelling of the city changed from Mazzara del Vallo, with two 'z's', to Mazara after the war."

I couldn't help but read into that, just as Enna had changed from Henna over the centuries, and Agrigento had carried so many different names, not to mention Balharm-Palermo, Nassina-Naxos, Drepanon-Trapani, and so on. But the changed spelling of his own town seemed especially important to Vito, even if just a single 'z.'

The barista returned with another round and stood by the table longer than usual. It was as if he suspected the change in atmosphere, my impending departure, and the end of the cycle of history.

"The people of Mazara del Vallo," began the barista, "we have survived most of the invasions, from the ancient people to the Germans, and then the Americans." At that, he shrugged his shoulders as if the constant flux of foreigners was nothing new.

"Can I get some *biscotti al limone*, or chocolate rolls for you?" he asked.

I had to smile. The barista knew that I was leaving, and he had never offered anything but the Sicilian standard breakfast – hard rolls, orange slices, occasionally pastries, and the usual *cantucci* – but he seemed to recognize that this morning would be different.

"Sì," I said with a smile, raising my espresso cup in salute.

Vito remained silent, but then excused himself to attend to the men's room.

———

By the time Vito had returned, the barista had delivered not only the biscotti and chocolate rolls, but another round of espresso. Signaling to his partner behind the bar to take over the counter service, the barista also brought a third cup to the table and sat with us.

"Luca," Vito addressed me, waving his hand toward the barista, "this is Roberto."

I couldn't help but smile. This broad-shouldered man with the rolled-up sleeves, the thick, tossled hair, and the ever-present smile, was already my friend and companion. But his name had never come up in conversation. He was the 'barista,' a title eminently appropriate and thoroughly complete.

I reached across the table to shake his hand.

"He was my student," Vito continued, "what do you say...*way back...*" and he chuckled at the thought.

"Not so way back. It was ten years ago," commented Roberto.

"He was a good student..." Vito said, but I interrupted him.

"Okay, so I know you taught Italian literature, but from the people in Mazara I've also heard that your lessons were spiked with tales of Sicilian history." Then I paused. "Or was it history classes spiked with Italian literature?"

Roberto smiled broadly and laid his hand gently on Vito's shoulder.

"*Sì,*" was the barista's reply, obscuring the two subjects just enough to convince me that they were inseparable. Throwing back the last of the espresso and slipping a *cantuccio* off the plate, Roberto returned to his station.

"You know that Benito Mussolini rose to power about the same time that Adolph Hitler did," Vito said, stepping easily back into the lesson of the day. "In the period between the two great wars."

I nodded.

"*Il Duce* took over the Italian government in 1922, rather soon declaring himself Prime Minister, but before long he dropped the pretense of democracy and became the dictator of the Italian states. *Herr Führer* tried to take the German government by coup in 1923 but failed. Mussolini drifted from socialism to nationalism, and Hitler moved from membership in a workers' party to dictator of Germany."

"What does this have to do with Sicily?" I asked.

"Everything has to do with Sicily," Vito replied with a smile.

"Mussolini felt that the Mafia was an impediment to him gaining full power over the island, so he appointed local officials to crack down on them."

"Officials like Cesari Mori."

"*Esattumentu,*" Vito answered. "But the Sicilians were opposed to being governed from afar; they had had too much of that for centuries already. So, Mori's attempts to squash the Mafia actually led to their rise on the island. Still, the Mafia isn't the real story."

"Go on."

"If Mussolini had stayed out of Sicilian politics, the people here might have just overlooked his tyranny. They never quite identified with Italian politics and government anyway, but the distance from the mainland offered them some isolation, enough that they could ignore the dictates of Rome when it suited them to do so. But Mussolini couldn't keep out, and his interference brought renewed anger into the relationship between Sicily and mainland Italy. The Mafia saw an opportunity and sided with the anti-fascists in Sicily against Mussolini's meddling, which gave them roots in Sicilian society that they might otherwise have been denied.

"And with Italy fighting on the side of the Germans, a nation already historically at odds with Sicily, Mussolini's government had even more trouble on the island. Squeezed between the northern nations like Germany, France, England, and others, and the African Campaign of the Axis, first, and then later the Allies, Sicily became the middle of the chessboard again. Neither of the sides waging this war in the southern theater seemed to care much about the people whose farms, homes, and cities were used as staging grounds for the battles. Sicilians hunkered down and tried to survive the war being fought over their land. Some of them joined the forces of one side or the other, and some fled to America.

"First, Pantelleria to the south was bombed by the Allies to soften it up for the march north to Sicily. Then after the Allies landed here, the bombing of Palermo, Gela, Messina, and Siracusa began. The Americans came to liberate Sicily and, in the process, Italy surrendered and lent support to the Allies who had, by September 1943, gained control of the mainland."

Vito went silent for a moment, and I could see that his eyes were focused on something far, far away. I didn't want to let any opportunity slip when I might learn more before departing. But I also knew the importance of giving him some time of quiet.

"I was there," he said. "I was there when the Nazis fought the Allies in North Africa. And I was here, on Sicily, retreating from battle alongside the Germans. When the Allies came ashore at Gela and Agrigento. It wasn't long before the Americans swept toward the west, toward my city of Mazara del Vallo. And while I had volunteered to join the Germans and keep the Americans out of my city, I was caught up in the German withdrawal going east on the island instead, toward Messina...away from Mazara."

Vito fell quiet again, his head drooping slightly, eyelids drawing halfway closed.

"I enlisted to fight for my city, Mazara, and I ended up running from the Allies and away from my city. We backed up to the strait at Messina but were still being pursued by the Allies."

Another pause.

"We Sicilians had fought for thousands of years to keep the foreigners off our island, to fight for our own freedom while others enslaved us. I was one of those Sicilians who fought, but we lost. Once again.

"I woke up one morning just before the German troop carriers began filling to take the soldiers across the strait to Reggio di Calabria on the mainland, and I decided that it was time for me to go home. I was a Mazaran, not a soldier of the Third Reich. And I wanted to go home."

Vito's heartfelt plea to return home nearly brought tears to my eyes. I had become more of a Sicilian in these two months, but I was still an American. And in that moment, I suddenly became terribly homesick.

"The war drew to a close and everyone left Sicily. The Germans were defeated and the Americans and British didn't care about us anymore. Maybe we should be thankful that no one was interested in our country for once.

"Over the last seventy years, there have been no wars fought on our island, no invasions from foreign powers. Immigration...oh, yes, lots of immigrants have come to my country since the time of bloodshed and strife in Africa and the Middle East.

"Once more, we are a way station on the journey to somewhere else.

"But these immigrants, while they tax our social systems and provoke problems for the local authorities to deal with, they are not an armed invader intent on setting up a puppet government, ruling from another continent, and taking all the resources that the Sicilians should, by right, claim as their own."

Vito paused for a sip of espresso, his lips drawn into a tight line. Then he looked up at the geometric designs on the ceiling, designs imprinted on Sicilian culture by the Arabs over a thousand years ago. His gaze dropped slightly but alighted on the nude statue of the wine god Dionysus, a gift from the Greeks more than a millennium earlier. From there, I followed his eyes to the other end of the bar where we saw Bacchus, the Romans' god of wine implanted in the Sicilian culture and psyche around the time of Christ.

"One of my students asked me long ago if I was full Sicilian. I said 'yes.'"

I smiled at the thought, but let Vito continue.

"Then I asked her if she was, and she said 'yes' also. So, I began reciting the list of invaders who have come to our country and then I asked her the age-old question: 'Is it possible that invading armies never got off their horses?' Fortunately, this was a college-level class so I would be forgiven the naughty nature of my question."

"What did she say?"

"Luca, it was a rhetorical question!" he replied, almost as a reprimand. But I really wanted to know how the conversation proceeded, not what this particular student said. So, I clarified my question and asked again.

"The intrinsic beauty of being Sicilian," my mentor replied, "is the fact that none of us are pure Sicilian, and yet all of us are Sicilian. The Americans call their country the melting pot while the world frets over the infusion of outsiders that are labeled as migrants. But Sicily is the truest melting pot of the world, certainly of Western Civilization.

"We inherited bloodlines from the Middle East and the Americas, from Scandinavia in the north and from Africa in the south. We were first settled by aborigines of unknown origin, who were supplanted by Iberians, then Elymi from Anatolia, and later the Siculi who traveled down the leg of Italy to join the rest. Every great dynasty of this hemisphere – the Phoenicians, Greeks, Carthaginians, Romans, Arabs,

British, French, Spanish – have at one time or another claimed Sicily as a province.

"So are we pure Sicilian?" Vito asked.

I paused to let him answer his own question, assuming this was another rhetorical question, but Vito surprised me.

"Yes, we are pure Sicilian."

My look of confusion – accented by an expectant smile – made Vito cheer up from his historical reverie.

"It is one of the great ironies of culture that to be pure Sicilian, you have to be a mutt."

For a moment, Vito slipped into himself once again. Roberto saw the change and stepped toward the table with a glass of water and another espresso for each of us.

I had a moment to look at Vito full on. His gray hair, deep wrinkle lines cutting across his cheeks, and the bend of his arthritic fingers. His mouth was slack for a moment and it seemed that the eternal flame of joy that burned within him had gone out, until I looked at his eyes. Even without a smile etched across his face, the sparkle of his eyes easily showed Vito to be a man of great energy and great happiness.

As Roberto the barista had once told me, ""Sicily, and Mazara del Vallo, would not be the same without Vito. He reminds us of who we are, even when we forget. He tells the stories of the ancient people, but it sounds just like me, or you, or..." pointing to the people seated in the café – "or them. Vito's telling of the history of Sicily is as if he lived it, from one century to the next. As if he is the story."

EPILOGUE

"*IL SIGNOR VITO TROVATO È MORTO IERI MATTINA. LUI HA novantotto anni...*"

"Signor Vito Trovato died yesterday morning. He was ninety-eight years old," read the announcement. It had come to me in the mail, in a small envelope on which my name and address were neatly lettered.

"Signor Trovato was born in 1920 to parents who remain unidentified. He was adopted as an infant by Michele Innocenza and Maria Grazie Innocenza. Signor Trovato's surname – a common name for orphans meaning literally 'found' – was given to him by the adoption agency and it remained the same after his adoption. He lived his entire life in Mazara del Vallo and is best known for his keen understanding of the history of the Mediterranean region generally, and the island of Sicily specifically.

"He will be sadly missed by the many thousands of students who have sat in his classroom and listened to his unique blend of Sicilian literature, folklore, and history. Signor Trovato leaves behind no living relatives, never having married. His will had only one clause, that his library be given to a woman named Mia Cristina. A celebration of his life will be held on..."

I stopped reading as the tears welled up in my eyes and my chest heaved in great sobs. The date and time of the celebration had already passed, so I had missed it. It was too late to pay my respects; too late for me to see my beloved friend one more time.

I knew from the weeks we spent together in the summer of 2018 that Vito was the most important person I had ever known. His life was lived as many others are lived, from birth through childhood, working life, and old age. But he was a Sicilian treasure. And he had taught me to appreciate the treasure that Sicily itself was, his "country."

I put the newspaper clipping down on the table and rested my hand on the back of the chair to steady myself. When I closed my eyes, I could see Vito's smiling face, the thick gray hair, and the way he tapped his fingers on the table to make a point. His eyes blazed with life and good cheer. As if in a silent movie, I could see his lips moving while he gestured with his hand. No words were heard, but his eyes roamed across what I remembered of the Café Amadeo, taking in the artifacts of the myriad cultures that had claimed his land, artifacts that had left their mark on his country.

Vito should have lived forever, I thought. But, then again, maybe he does.

In our many hours of conversation, Vito frequently referred to the places that I had yet to see around the island of Sicily. Perhaps I should use my notes as a map to begin that process.

That tour of the island will help me complete this book, a tribute to my mentor, Vito, and the only way I know how to capture for all time the stories that he spent so much time describing for me.

ANCIENT PLACE NAMES AND APPROXIMATE ERA WHEN THEY FIRST APPEARED

(NOTE: FICTIONAL NAMES APPEAR IN ITALICS)

Ancient Place Names and Approximate Era When They First Appeared

(**Note**: *Fictional names appear in Italics*)

Far Ancient Times	Ancient Times	c. 1500 BCE	c. 1000 BCE	c. 500 BCE	c. Year 0	c. 500 CE	c. 1000 CE	c. 1500 CE	Current
	Ankara	*Akra*				Agyrium		San Filippo d'Argirò	Aggira
				Acragas	Agrigentum		Girgenti		Agrigento
					Hippo Regius				Annaba
	Letopolis	Khem							Ausim (Egypt)
			Entella						Belice
		Euteso		Euesperides					Benghazi (Libya)
					Brundisium				Brindisi
			Gadir						Cadiz (Spain)
		Italoi			Bruttium				Calabria
									Calatafimi-Segesta
				Triocalla		Qal'at a fīmī			Caltabellotta
				Capeva					Capua
	Caselto	*Casegno*							Castellaro Vecchio
							Castello de Hauteville		Castello Aragonese
				Katane					Catania
				Cephaloedium			Gafludi		Cefalù
			Centuripa	Kentoripa				Centorbi	Centuripe
	Kaptara	*Keftiu*							Crete
						Adrianople			Edirne (Turkey)
			Henna	Hennaion		Henna	Kasr Janni	Castrogiovanni	Enna
			Eryx				Cebel Hamid	Monte San Giuliano	Erice
	Ahalla		Inessa	Aetna					Etna
Fave									Favignana
								Île Julia (in 1831)	Ferdinanda
	Sypho	*Sintelia*		Gela			Terranova		Gela
		Knossos							Heraklion (Crete)
		Troy							Hissarlik (Turkey)
					Ietas				Iaitas
				Byzantium		Constantinople			Istanbul
			Oenotria						Italia

				Shalem	Yerushalayim		Jerusalem
Fansu	Lefansu	Lentinoi					Lentini
	Bevira	Phorbantia		Algusa			Levanzo
			Phintius				Licata
						Lemusa	Linosa (island)
Tirsa			Maleth	Melita			Malta
	Maia						Marettimo
		Lilybaeum			Mars-al-Allah		Marsala
Masra		Massalia					Marseille
	Mazar				Mazara[1]		Mazara del Vallo
			Melite	Meltie	al Madinah		Mdina (Malta)
	The Great Sea	Syrian Sea	Mare Nostrum		Bahr-i Sefid		Mediterranean Sea
		Zancle	Messana				Messina
	Myla	Mylae					Milazzo
				Miniu			Mineo
	Mylia						Misrata (Libya)
	Elyma	Hyblaean Mountains					Monti Iblei
	Motya				San Pantaleo		Motya (Mozzia to Sicilians)
							Naxos
	Nassina						Nebrodi Mountains
	Netumo		Netum				Noto
Mamta	Zis	Panormus			Bal'harm		Palermo
	Euonymos	Hycesia					Panarea (island)
	Puntea	Cossyra			Bint al-Riyâh		Pantelleria
	Picta						Peloritans Mtns
						Piana dei Greci	Piana degli Albanesi
						Piazza	Piazza Armerina
			Rhegium		Rivâh		Reggio Calabria
		Halyciae			Alicia		Salemi
		Didyme			Salâm		Salina (island)
	Precipio					San Filadelfio	San Fratello
	Akrotiri / Thera						Santorini (island)
	Rivesa	Thermae			as-Saqqah / Syac		Sciacca
	Egesta						Segesta
		Selinus					Selinunte
Ganta	Sikania / Dian / Gania	Trinacrium					Sicily
	Syrakosai / Stentinello	Siracusa			Siracusae		Siracusa

[1] "del Vallo" added in 19th century

	K.fra	Pillars of Hercules		Cathago		Bilad al-Sham	
							Soluto
		Pillars of Hercules					Strait of Gibraltar
		Strongulē					Stromboli
						Bilad al-Sham	Syria
					Tingis		Tangiers (Morocco)
		Tauro	Tauromenium				Taormina
		Taranto	Tarantum				Taranto
		Himera	Thermae				Termini Imerese
Adda		Heracleion					Thonis (Egypt)
Pani	Drepanon	Drepanum					Trapani
		Oea	Regio Syrtica		Regio Tripolitana		Tripoli (Libya)
		Qart-ḥadašt		Cathago	Carthage		Tunis (Tunisia)
					Ifriqiya		Tunisia
			Tyndaris				Tyndari
Wallee			Osteodos				Ustica
Vera			Therassia				Vulcano

LIST OF CHARACTERS

(NOTE: FICTIONAL NAMES APPEAR IN ITALICS)

71 B.C.E., Siracusa

Gaius Verres – male, Roman governor of Siracusa (actual)
Marcus Tullius Cicero – male, Roman statesman and orator (actual)
Fenestra – female, Siracusan farmer
Livaius – male, Siracusan farmer, Lilia's husband
Lilia – female, farmer, Livaius's wife
Pilio – male, Siracusan citizen
Antipias Quadras – male, Roman captain
Timeus – male, Siracusan protester

36 B.C.E., Tyrhennian Sea

Sextus Pompei – male, Roman general (actual)
Octavian – male, Julius Caesar's heir and first Emperor of the Roman Empire (actual)
Mantius – male, Greek slave aboard a ship of republican Sextus Pompei
Samson – male, slave from Africa

59 C.E., Siracusa

Balfornus – male, captain of Paul's ship from Corinth to Siracusa
Saul/Paul – disciple of Jesus (actual)
Taritius – Roman soldier

350 C.E., Casale

Nomitius – male, foreman for construction of the Villa Casale
Cantone – male, transport chief for construction materials
Proculus Populonius – governor of Sicily (actual)
Daphne – dark-skinned female slave, Nomitius's woman
Europa – light-skinned female Greek slave
Dintare – male, bricklayer
Linaeus – male, artisan in charge of the mosaics for the villa

536 C.E., Siracusae

Clio – female, Theodes' wife
Theodes – male, Clio's husband
Belisarius – male, Byzantine commander (actual)
Salidus – male, Calic' Bellu (tavern) owner
Hermedes – female, daughter of Clio and Theodes
Calentus – male, son of Clio and Theodes

655 C.E. – Ortygia

Anatole – male, Jewish laborer
Azriel – male, Jewish stonecutter, Dina's husband
Dina – female, Azriel's wife
Rebecca – female, Dina's unmarried sister
Tzadok – male, rabbi
Elisa – female
Yosef – male, rabbi
Shemule – worker at mikveh

674 C.E. – Cathedral of Siracusa

Zosimo – Catholic bishop (actual)
Penarius – male, assistant to Zosimo, Julia's husband
Julia – female, Penarius's wife
Martha – sometime prostitute, Zosimo's consort
Ottimo – apprentice builder, Penarius's assistant
Acctual – foreman of the slaves, a slave himself

827 C.E. – Mazara

Mu'awiyah – second caliph of the Umayyad dynasty (actual)
Yazid ibn Abi Sufyan – brother of Mu'awiyah (actual)
Uqba ibn Nafi – Muslim commander who conquered the Maghreb (actual)
Euphemius – Byzantine general in Sicily (actual)
Constantine – Byzantine general in Sicily (actual)
Homoniza – a nun, Euphemius's love interest (actual)
Ziyadat Allah I – Muslim emir, ruling from Syria, assigned Asad ibn al-Furat to go to Sicily (actual)
Asad ibn al-Furat – Muslim philosopher, headed up Muslim invasion of Sicily (actual)
Muhammad ibn Abu'l-Jawari – successor to Asad ibn al-Furat (actual)
Zubayr ibn Gawth – successor to Muhammad ibn Abu'l-Jawari (actual)
Sister Anita – mother superior at convent where Homoniza lived
Galal – officer in Asad's army

829 C.E. – Enna

Galal – captain of Muslim forces
Euphemius – Byzantine general (actual)
Santoro – emissary from Enna
Zubayr ibn Gawth – successor to Mohammad

859 C.E. – Henna

Ludovico Parmentum – captain of Byzantine guard

LIST OF CHARACTERS

Attilio Vergine – strategos (general) of Byzantine army
Abu'l-Aghlab al-Abbas ibn al-Fadl, Muslim commander (actual)
Philippus – tourmarch, leader of the Byzantine infantry at Henna
Diryas – male, Rashidun (an elite Muslim infantryman)
Naaqid – middle level commander in Muslim army
Inamur – male, Rashidun, an elite Muslim infantryman
Aqsa – female, accompanying the Muslim army
Ibrar ibn Afsad – commander of the Muslim assault on Henna
Traestum – Byzantine soldier
Sterios – Byzantine soldier
Venatos – male Ennaean, farmer
Eshaal – female Ennaean, farmer

878 C.E. – Siracusa

Michael III – Byzantine Emperor (actual)
Eudokia Dekapolitissa – Michael III's wife (actual)
Eudokia Ingerina – Michael III's mistress (actual)
Leo – son of Eudokia Ingerina (and possibly of Michael III) (actual)
Basil I – Byzantine Emperor, successor to Michael III (actual)
Ja'far ibn Muhammad – Muslim commander (actual)
Abu Ishaq – son of Ja'far, succeeded him in command of Muslim forces (actual)
Italo – gardener in Siracusa
Romano – assistant to Jafad

954 C.E. – Bal'harm

Saabih – male, Muslim architect
Nudair – male, Muslim architect
Aqsa – female, Saabih's wife
Sawrat – male, tunneler for qanāt system
Imtiazud - male, tunneler for qanāt system
Mahira – female, Imtiazud's wife
Isha – female, Sawrat's wife

1061 C.E. – Reggio

Robert Guiscard (de Hauteville) – Count of Apulia and
Calabria (actual)
Albert Prater – military assistant to Robert Guiscard
Roger I (de Hauteville) – Count of Sicily, younger brother of
Robert Guiscard (actual)
Henry – captain of the guard for Robert Guiscard
Ayyub ibn Tamim – emir of eastern Sicily, son of the Emir of
Ifriqiya (actual)
*Ahmed ibn Agha – officer in charge of Muslim garrison in
Messina*

1146 C.E. – Palermo

Roger II – first King of Sicily (actual)
Hanislaw – Roger's captain of the guard
Peter – Roger's banker
Pope Eugene III – ordered the Second Crusade (actual)
*Pater Michael – priest who served at Roger's chapel, came from
Cefalù*

1204 C.E. – Siracusa

Alammano da Costa – merchant seaman and owner of
Carroccia, from Genoa (actual)
Gaspardo – captain of the Carroccia
Ferdinando Renata – Pisan governor of Siracusa
Abulafe – wife of Ferdinando Renata
Don Filippe – banker for Renata
Telio del Stanno – captain of the Pisan force in Siracusa

1239 C.E. – Palermo and Mazara del Vallo

Palermo

Frederick II – Holy Roman Emperor, King of Sicily (also the
King of Germany (1212-1220) and

King of Jerusalem, (1225-1228) but not at the time of this chapter (actual)
Isabella – wife of Frederick II, Holy Roman Empress, Queen of Sicily (actual)
Mateo d'Amato – counselor to King Frederick
Baron Sirico Laurentiis of Mazara
Baron Dante Cremia of Agrigento
Baron Adolfo Triponte of Gela
Verelli – Captain of the Palermitan army

Mazara del Vallo

Principe DeLoro – military commander; second in command behind Baron Sirico Laurentiis
Gino Stefano – advisor to DeLoro
Kaabir – Muslim man

1282 C.E. – Palermo

Charles I – French king of Sicily (actual)
Alaimo da Lentini – captain at arms in Messina (actual)
Peter – King of Aragon and Valencia (also known as Peter III of Aragon and the King of Sicily (1282-1285) (actual)
Franken – burgher from Palermo (actual)
Roger of Lauria – Italian admiral and commander of Peter's navy (actual)
Guillem Galceran de Cartellà – Catalan commander working for Peter (actual)

1302 C.E. – Caltabellotta

Charles II of Anjou – king of Anjou (actual)
Panguin – agent to Charles II
Frederick III – king of Trinacria (actual)
Giuseppe – agent to Frederick III

1347 C.E. – Messina

Maserato Imbolati – captain of ship
Regina – Imbolati's wife in Genoa
Olabisi – Imbolati's wife in Cairo
Berio – dockhand in Messina
Stario d'Esta – harbor master in Messina

1392 C.E. – Palermo, Palazzo Chiaramonte

Matilda Ludovica d'Stefano – companion of Costanza
Chiaramonte
Costanza Chiaramonte – sister of Andrea Chiaramonte, wife of
Ladislas of Aragon, daughter of Manfred III (actual)
Andrea Chiaramonte – 8th Count of Modica, brother of
Costanza Chiaramonte, son of Manfred III (actual)

1535 C.E. – Palermo

King Charles V, Holy Roman Emperor, King of Italy, and other
titles (actual)
Isabella of Portugal – King Charles V's wife (actual)
Luther – agent and counselor to King Charles
Bishop Bernardus – Roman Catholic bishop visiting Charles V
from Corsica and traveling with him to Palermo
Candido d'Andrea – Charles V's military strategist in Castile
Guglielmo Aiutamicristo – grandson of the Baron Guglielmo
Auitamicristo (heir to the Palazzo (actual)
Antonio – stable boy at Palazzo Aiutamicristo
Nicolà – Antonio's girlfriend

1669 C.E. – Catania

Diego de Pappalardo – citizen of Catania who formed the team
to divert the lava flow at Mt. Etna in 1669 (actual)
Giorgio – citizen of Catania
Fantine – citizen of Paterno
Mona – Fantine's wife
Angelo – citizen of Paterno

1713 C.E. – Seville and Palermo

Victor Amadeus II (a.k.a., Vittorio Amadeo II) – King of Sardinia, King of Sicily, Duke of Savoy (actual)
Anne Marie d'Orleans – wife of Victor Amadeus and Queen of Sardinia, Queen of Sicily, and Duchess of Savoy (actual)
Alosio d'Elmonte – agent and counselor to Victor Amadeus
Annibale Maffei – Count of Sicily under Victor Amadeus (actual)
Vicente Lora – agent for the viceroy of Palermo, then for Count Maffei
Antonio – male peasant waiting at the docks for King and Queen
Gaia – female peasant waiting at the docks for King and Queen

1799 C.E. – Naples and Palermo

King Ferdinand IV of Sicily (actual)
Italo – watch officer at port of Palermo
Pietro – crow's nest watch in port of Palermo
Beppo – eight-year-old apprentice to Italo
Raphael Talenti – counselor to King Ferdinand IV
Francesco Pignatelli Strongoli – briefly the regent of Naples (actual)

1804 C.E. – Mazara del Vallo and La Goulette

Augusto – dockworker in Mazara del Vallo, Marie's husband
Marie – Augusto's second wife, from Algiers
Vittorio – dockworker in Mazara del Vallo, son of Augusto and Marie
Becari – dockworker, younger brother of Vittorio

1848 C.E. – Palermo

Franceso Bagnasco – author and printer of the pamphlet issued by the Revolutionary Committee (actual)
Carlo – Bagnasco's assistant

Rubio Stella – Bagnasco's assistant
Luce Adamante – captain of King's forces in Palermo
Ruggero Settimo (actual)
Vincenzo Fardella (actual)
Ferdinand II of the Two Sicilies (actual)
Giuseppe La Masa – baron, leader of the January 12, 1848, uprising in Fieravecchia (actual)

1854 C.E. – Racalmuto

Piero d'Impelli – mine manager
Adelfio – miner
Roberto – miner
Daniele Fabresi – old miner brought back to inspect it
Gianni Costante – miner
Luisa Costante – Gianni's wife
Alessandro – Gianni and Luisa's nine-year-old son
Matilda – Gianni and Luisa's three-year-old daughter
Philip Ambrose – British merchant

1860 C.E. – Risorgimento

Giuseppe Garibaldi (actual)
Francesco Crispi – close political ally of Garibaldi (actual)

1894 C. E. – Palermo

Giuseppe de Felice Giuffrida – a member of the Fasci Siciliani from Catania
Rosario Garibaldi Bosco – a member of the Fasci Siciliani from Palermo
Nicola Barbato – a member of the Fasci Siciliani from Piana dei Greci
Bernardino Verro – a member of the Fasci Siciliani from Corleone

1929 C.E. – Palermo

Paolo Infante – socialist activist in Trapani
Claudia Infante – wife of Paolo Infante
Francesca – ten-year-old daughter of Paolo and Claudia Infante
Cesare Mori – Prefect of Palermo appointed by Mussolini
(actual)
Lorenzo – friend and comrade in hiding with Paolo

1942 C.E. – Mazara del Vallo

Manfrit Werner – German colonel
Klaus von Stöhl – German lieutenant
Vito Trovato

VOCABULARY

THE FOLLOWING TERMS AND WORDS HAVE BEEN USED THROUGHOUT THE BOOK AND ARE LISTED HERE FOR THE READERS' BENEFIT.

(Note: Fictional words appear in Italics)

Word	Translation
ager publicus	public land
allaghia	6th century Byzantine cavalry
allu	garlic
almogavars	lightly clothed but armed soldiers from Iberia who fought for Peter of Aragon
alod	in feudalism, an allowance for land owners to keep their land if owned before the feudal system was imposed
anusim	anyone forcibly converted to Christianity; see neofiti
As-Salamu Alaykum	Arabic for "I will be with you"
Pbacu	abacus
Bagno Ebraico	Hebrew Bath; Roman and Siracusan name for the Great Mikveh of Siracuse
baldric	a leather strap bound around the chest and shoulders; used to carry weaponry, especially to sheathe a sword
bandon (pl. banda)	6th century Byzantine army detachment; approximately 150 men
bireme	two-decked ship, each deck with its own set of oarsmen
bon sira	good evening
boviu	cow
brit	beer
bucellarii	armed soldiers in a private army
Calic' Bellu	name of tavern in Siracusae, 535 C.E. (translates to "Cup of War")
cameriere	waiter
cantucci	little biscuits, like biscotti
cassata	cake
cataphract	armed and armored man on horseback; also the armored horse itself
catepano	referred to person in charge in a Byzantine army, "the one placed at the top"
cheeka (see gira)	Masrian word for spring onion
ciciri	chickpeas
coniglio	rabbit
contadini	peasants, farm workers, and miners
corvus	wooden bridge hinged to a ship that could swing out and couple with another vessel to allow boarding
cubit	Roman unit of measurement, equal to one and one-half feet
denarius (pl. denari)	Roman unit of money
dhimmi	Jew or Christian in a Muslim society
dolmen	primitive stone constructions, usually a simply arrangement of two or more vertical members spanned by one horizontal member above
dulcis in fundo	dessert made of honey, nuts, milk, and flour
Elymi (a.k.a., Elymians)	tribe from Anatolia to migrate to Sicily
Fasci dei Lavoratori	see Fasci Siciliani

Fasci Siciliani	protest movement in 1890s in Sicily, arguing for workers' rights; a.k.a., Fasci dei Lavoratori
feudi	parcels of land distributed by the king in a feudal society
gebbiu	cistern, from Arab word *giebja*
ghulam	soldier slave
gira (see cheeka)	Addian word for spring onion
hecatontarch	Byzantine leader of the cavalry
hijab	Muslim dress for women, covering all but the face
Hoplites	citizen-soldiers of Ancient Greece
infama	lowest class of Romans, just above slaves; also used to refer to prostitutes
In shā'a llāh	As Allah wills it
isolani	islanders
jizya	a tax on all non-Muslims (see zakat)
kanat	Arab irrigation system of tunnels under Palermo
kasbah	marketplace, from the Arab word
keyla	olive tree
kottabos	a drinking game in which the celebrants would fling the remnants of wine from their goblets at a disk trying to dislodge it from its perch
koursorses	Byzantine cavalry
lateen-rig	a triangular sail set on a single mast
latifundia	systems of farms
lazzaroni	poorest class of people in 18th century Naples
lochagiai	6th century Byzantine infantry
Magreb	region of North Africa
mal del stomaco	stomach ache
mangonel	a type of traction trebuchet
Mare Nostrum	Roman name for the Mediterranean Sea
mattanza	circling a school of fish with boats, then closing the circle until the fish could be clubbed and brought aboard
minieru	mine (Italians would say miniera)
moirai	6th century Byzantine division of soldiers
Naxians	people from Naxos
neofiti	the word in Sicily for the anusim, or Jews converted to Christianity
Notinesi	people from Noto
oecist	Greek term for someone who founds a city or settlement
oinos	wine, word used by the Greeks by 750 B.C.E.
pazzu	crazy, wild (Italians would say pazzo)
pecore	sheep
pistola, pistole (pl.) (sometimes pistolese)	pistol, pistols
pistolese	soldier with a pistol
pizzu	bribe (Italians would say pizzo)
pomolo	lentils
poncho	*Posidonia oceanica*, Mediterranean marine plant, also known as Neptune Grass
Potnia	Elymian goddess of love and fertility; same as Phoenicians' Astarte and Roman Aprhodite (and Venus Erycina)
pugio	small dagger worn by Roman soldiers

qadi	judge in an Islamic Shari'a court
qanāt	water management system employed in Bal'harm (Palermo)
rashidun	elite Muslim soldier in Middle Ages
rishta	noodle-like pasta introduced to Sicily by Muslims
seah	a unit of volume used by Jews, roughly equivalent to 15 liters
seeio	hello
shatranj	early Persian name for the game of chess; the name persisted into the era when it was introduced to Europe in the 13th century
Sicanians (a.k.a., Sicans)	first tribe to settle in Sicily
Sicels (a.k.a. Siculi)	tribe from mainland Italy to migrate to Sicily
sida	obsidian (before 3950 B.C.E.)
sidia	obsidian (after 3950 B.C.E.)
skutatoi	6th century Byzantine archers
strategos	general (or commander) in the Byzantine army
sūrah	chapters of the Quran
Svevi	Swabians
tartrae	truffles
tercio, tercie	Spanish infantry
Tercio de Sicilia	Charles V's infantry in Sicily
tevilah	Hebrew word for full immersion, as in a mikveh
tina	wine
toma / tomae	olive / olives
tourmarch	Byzantine leader of an infantry
trichiagon	tarragon
trireme	three-decked ship, each deck with its own set of oarsmen
tumarch	leader of infantry in the Byzantine army
tyropatinum	tyropita, sweet soft cheese with honey and raw eggs
wāli	Muslim governor
yero	bitter vetch
zagara	blossom, from Arab word zahra
zakat	a tax required under Islamic law to aid the needy; in some areas like the Maghreb, the zakat is supplemented by the jizya (see)
zibbibbu	raisins, from Arab word zbib

ACKNOWLEDGMENTS

A writer's world is inhabited by many beings. Some are imaginary, like the muse whispering in our ears – both distracting and inspirational in equal measure. Some are the spirits who come back to us from distant memories, or the phantoms who materialize from the shadow of our fears. Some are the real, flesh-and-blood people who come and go in our lives, and who stay and persevere throughout the insanity of the creative processs. The sane and encouraging influence in mine was that of my wife, Linda. The literal "push-in-the-back" came from my good friend Don Oldenburg, who after I had been researching this for several years admonished me that "sooner or later, you have to start writing." And the drive to complete the work came from the memory of my father and the encouraging presence of my daughter, both Sicilians connected by me.

Although *The Sicily Chronicles* is a work of historical fiction, the story it tells would not have been possible without the research and insights of numerous historians, sociologists, archeologists, anthropologists, and other writers. From their works I have been able to construct a plausible, sensible, and detailed chronology of Sicily, from ancient times to the present day.

Great thanks and respect are due to hundreds of diverse sources, but the following references are among the most influential in the research I have conducted over the years.

Abulafia, David, *The Great Sea: A Human History of the Mediterranean*, Oxford University Press (Oxford, 2011)

Attenborough, Richard, *The First Eden*, Little, Brown (1987)

Benjamin, Sandra, *Sicily: Three Thousand Years of Human History*, Steerforth (New Hampshire, 2006)

Booms, Dirk, and Higgs, Peter, *Sicily: Culture and Conquest*, The British Museum (2016)

Brownworth, Lars, *Lost to the West: The Forgotten Byzantine Empire That Rescued Western Civilization*, Broadway Books (New York, 2009)

Cline, Eric H., *1177 B.C.: The Year Civilization Collapsed*, Princeton University Press (Princeton, 2014)

Cook, Michael, *A Brief History of the Human Race*, W.W. Norton (New York, 2003)

Crowley, Roger, *Empires of the Sea: The Siege of Malta, the Battle of Lepanto, and the Contest for the Center of the World*, Random House (New York, 2009)

Cunliffe, Barry, *Europe Between the Oceans: 9000 BC to 1000 AD*, Yale University Press (2011)

de Souza, Philip (ed.), *The Ancient World at War*, Thames & Hudson (London, 2008)

Dickson, D. Bruce, *The Dawn of Belief: Religion in the Upper Paleolithic of Southwestern Europe*, University of Arizona Press (1990)

Farrell, Joseph, *Sicily: A Cultural History*, Interlink Pub Group (Massachusetts, 2014)

Keahey, John, *Seeking Sicily: A Cultural Journey Through Myth and Reality in the Heart of the Mediterranean*, St. Martin's Press (New York, 2011

Lacey, Robert and Danziger, Danny, *The Year 1000: What Life was Like at the Turn of the First Millennium*, Little, Brown, and Company (Boston, 1999)

Linder, Douglas O., "Famous Trials: Gaius Verres Trial (70 B.C.), http://www.famous-trials.com/gaius-verres

Mendola, Louis, *The Peoples of Sicily: A Multicultural Legacy*, Trinacria Editions (2014)

Mendola, Louis and Alio, Jacqueline, *Norman-Arab-Byzantine Palermo, Monreale & Cefalù*, Trinacria Editions (New York, 2017)

Miles, Richard, *Carthage Must be Destroyed: The Rise and Fall of an Ancient Civilization*, Penguin (London, 2010)

Mitchener, James A., *The Source*, Dial Press Trade Paperback (reprint, 2002)

Nesto, Bill, and di Savino, Frances, *The World of Sicilian Wine*, University of California Press (Berkeley, 2013)

Norwich, John Julius, *Sicily: An Island at the Crossroads of History*, Random House (2015)

Piccolo, Salvatore, *Ancient Stones: The Prehistoric Dolmens of Sicily*, Brazen Head (London, 2013)

Privitera, Joseph F., *Sicily: An Illustrated History*, Hippocrene Books (New York, 2002)

Robb, John, *The Early Mediterranean Village: Agency, Material Culture, and Social Change Neolithic Italy*, Cambridge University Press (2007)

Runciman, Steven, *The Sicilian Vespers: A History of the Mediterranean World in the Later Thirteenth Century*, Cambridge University Press (1958)

Sammartino, Peter, and Roberts, William, *Sicily: An Informal History*, Cornwall Books (1992)

Simeti, Mary Taylor, *On Persephone's Island: A Sicilian Journal*, Vintage (New York, 1995)

Simeti, Mary Taylor, *Pomp and Sustenance: Twenty-Five Centuries of Sicilian Food*, Henry Holt (New York, 1991)

Toussaint-Samat, Maguelonne, *History of Food*, Blackwell Publishers (1992)

White, Randall, *Dark Caves, Bright Visions: Life in Ice Age Europe*, W.W. Norton (New York, 1986)

Useful websites:

www.bestofsicily.com

www.sicilybella.com

http://www.wondersofsicily.com/

http://www.italythisway.com/

www.timesofsicily.com

Dear reader,

We hope you enjoyed reading *Crossroads of the Mediterranean*. Please take a moment to leave a review, even if it's a short one. Your opinion is important to us.

Discover more books by Dick Rosano at https://www.nextchapter.pub/authors/author-dick-rosano

Want to know when one of our books is free or discounted? Join the newsletter at http://eepurl.com/bqqB3H

Best regards,

Dick Rosano and the Next Chapter Team

You might also like:
A Death in Tuscany by Dick Rosano

To read the first chapter for free, please head to:
https://www.nextchapter.pub/books/a-death-in-tuscany

ABOUT THE AUTHOR

Dick Rosano's columns have appeared for many years in *The Washington Post* and other national publications. His series of novels set in Italy capture the beauty of the country, the flavors of the cuisine, and the history and traditions of the people. He has traveled the world but Italy is his ancestral home and the insights he lends to his books bring the characters to life, the cities and countryside into focus, and the culture into high relief.

Whether it's the political drama of *The Vienna Connection*, the workings of a family winery in *A Death in Tuscany*, the azure sky and Mediterranean vistas in *A Love Lost in Positano*, the intrigue in *Hunting Truffles*, or the bitter conflict of Nazi occupation in *The Secret Altamura*, Rosano puts the life and times of Italy into your hands.

OTHER BOOKS BY DICK ROSANO

Islands of Fire: Sicily Chronicles, Part I – An historical novel of the island at the center of Western Civilization from the arrival of its first inhabitants tens of thousands of years ago to the time of Julius Caesar.

A Death in Tuscany – A young man mourns the suspicious death of his grandfather while preparing to take the reins of his family's winery in Tuscany.

The Secret of Altamura: Nazi Crimes, Italian Treasure – Secrets hidden from the Nazis in 1943 are still sought by an art collector in modern days. But evil stalks all those who try to reveal it.

The Vienna Connection: Hidden stories connect the American establishment to suspicious activity in Vienna, Austria, and Darren Priest is called back from retirement to unravel them.

Hunting Truffles – The slain bodies of truffle hunters show up, but the truffle harvest itself has been stolen.

Wine Heritage: The Story of Italian American Vintners – Centuries of Italian immigration to America laid the groundwork for the American wine revolution of the 20th century.

OTHER BOOKS BY D.P. ROSANO

A Love Lost in Positano – A war-weary State Department translator falls for a woman under the blue skies of the Mediterranean, then she disappears.

Vivaldi's Girls – The young red-haired prodigy could make women swoon with the sweeping grandeur of his violin performances – even more so after he traded in his priest's robes for the dashing attire of a rich and notorious celebrity.

To Rome, With Love – Some memories are never forgotten. As Tamara discovers the charms of Rome in the arms of her first love the sights, food, and wine sweep her away.